WRONG QUESTION
Right Answer

ALSO BY ELLE CASEY

ROMANCE

By Degrees

Rebel Wheels (3-book series)

Just One Night (romantic serial)

Just One Week

Love in New York (3-book series)

Shine Not Burn (2-book series)

Bourbon Street Boys (3-book series)

Desperate Measures

ROMANTIC SUSPENSE

All the Glory

Don't Make Me Beautiful

Wrecked (2-book series)

PARANORMAL

Duality (2-book series)

Pocket Full of Sunshine (short story & screenplay)

CONTEMPORARY URBAN FANTASY

War of the Fae (10-book series)

Ten Things You Should Know About Dragons
(short story in The Dragon Chronicles)

My Vampire Summer

Aces High

DYSTOPIAN

Apocalypse (4-book series)

WRONG QUESTION
Right Answer

ELLE CASEY

Montlake
Romance

Text copyright © 2016 Elle Casey

Published by Montlake Romance Publishing, Seattle
www.apub.com

Amazon, the Amazon logo, and Lake Union Publishing are trademarks of Amazon.com, Inc., or its affiliates.

ISBN-13: 9781503938205
ISBN-10: 1503938204

Cover design by Lisa Horton

Printed in the United States of America

For my husband, Craig.
Any time one of the male characters in my books is sexy, funny, kind,
or loving, readers get a little glimpse of the man I married.

CHAPTER ONE

I'm the first one to show up at the pub. I order myself a Long Island iced tea and find a spot at the end of the bar where I won't be bothered. I didn't come here to hook up, and that should be obvious to anyone looking at me; I have my long, dark, straight hair up in a messy bun with a steel pin holding it in place—a pin that could be used to puncture a lung if necessary—tight jeans, a white tank top with a well-worn denim jacket over it, and my high-heeled, black leather work boots, zipped up to the knee. I'm off the clock, but I can kick ass and take names in between sucking down my cocktails if the need arises. I never go out unprepared.

The rest of the team is supposed to be here soon, and if I'd known they were going to be late, I would've delayed coming. I hate being in bars alone. Guys hit on me, and when I turn them down, they get offended and piss me off. It's better if I avoid losing my shit. I don't have the best temper in the world, and I'm woman enough to admit it.

The door opens and a big guy comes through. I perk up, thinking it's my boss, but when I realize it's not, I go back to nursing my drink. Checking my black Suunto military watch—a gift from the team—I frown. They're ten minutes behind schedule. *Assholes*. Like

I've got nothing better to do than hang around here and wait for them to show. After hissing out an annoyed breath, I take another long pull from my drink, glaring at the door over my highball glass. I swear I can hear the seconds ticking away inside my brain.

I sense someone coming up next to me and look over. It's a guy in a button-down shirt, his hair gelled and styled to appear as if he hadn't spent thirty minutes getting it just right. He's got an expensive Citizen watch on his wrist, a leather belt that matches his loafers, and not a scruffy beard or scar in sight. I try really hard not to sneer. He is *so* not my type. I call him Skip in my mind.

"Hey. I haven't seen you around here before." Skip gestures at me with his beer bottle and smiles. His teeth could star in a Colgate commercial.

"Really? That's funny, since I've been coming here for over ten years." I take another sip of my drink, hoping my rude and completely unenthusiastic delivery will be enough to send him away. I've played this game enough times to know how it should work. Smart guys walk away to flirt another day; dumb ones leave with scars. But it's not my fault. I send off all the right signals: Cold-hearted bitch here. Do not approach.

I used to let guys pick me up in bars when my ex, Charlie, and I would go through periods of being on the outs, but I don't do it now that he's gone. And if I were going to start doing that again, it wouldn't be tonight. I'm not in the mood. This was supposed to be me meeting my team here so we could celebrate our latest victory and the bonus that came along with it, not me fending off guys who decided to take a walk on the wild side for a change. Hopefully Skip knows how to play the game too and he'll beat it before things get awkward.

"Really? So, you're a local girl. Cool. Love your accent, by the way."

Or not.

"It's cute and sexy." He winks.

Okay, so he definitely doesn't know how the game is played. Maybe it's because he rarely gets turned down. He has that vibe to him: confidence in spades, a cluelessness often suffered by the wealthy and attractive males in the area. Unfortunately, their complete lack of self-awareness is fully supported by many of the women here who'd just as soon flash their tits to earn a necklace as anything else.

I say nothing. I just stare at him as I take another sip of my drink. *Can he not feel the icicles I'm launching into his soft body with my cold glare?*

"I guess I should've figured from the accent you were New Orleans born and raised."

I shrug lightly. "Maybe." I have nothing to say to this guy, but I can't just stare at him and watch him squirm. I do have some mercy in me. A very, very little smidge of it. Time served and two years' probation will do that to a girl.

"You here with someone?" Skip looks around the room.

"I will be."

His eyes light up.

I realize my mistake as soon as I see his reaction; I've given him hope. I put my drink down on the bar and shake my head. "I'm waiting for somebody else."

He loses a bit of his smile. "Oh yeah, sure. Someone else. He must be late." My new friend makes a big show of checking his watch, thinking he's being cute but inadvertently letting a little of the asshole side of his nature show.

A ghost of a smile comes to my lips. Now I'll finally see the real man behind the mask. Skip was all sweet and polite when he thought he was going to get some, but his manners are fading fast. Just like every other guy in the world—my teammates excepted, of course—he puts on a show to get what he wants, and then the true

3

person appears from behind the veil later to wreak havoc, after his prey is hooked good and solid. At least now I have something to entertain me until my friends arrive. *No mercy for assholes.*

"What's the matter?" I ask. "Does it piss you off that I'm waiting for someone else?"

The muscles in his jaw tense before he answers. "No. It doesn't piss me off."

"Your body language says otherwise." I smile even bigger, taking a sip from my drink. I'm more than half done with this generous cocktail, and already looking forward to the next. I lift my finger at the bartender to get his attention. He nods, knowing exactly what I'm saying. He's already filling another glass with ice for me. *Yeah, buddy. Bring on that vodka-tequila-rum-gin-and-triple-sec buzzzz . . .*

Skip's body is as stiff as a board. "It wouldn't bother me if what you were saying were true."

I look at him sideways. "Are you calling me a liar?"

He shakes his head. "Women like you are all the same." He takes a big swig of his beer, like he's Mister Cool now, when Mister Playing-With-Fire is who he really is.

I turn on my stool partway and lift my chin at him with a quick jerk of my head. "You know me after walking up to me in a bar and talking to me for all of ten seconds, is that it?"

He shakes his head, refusing to look at me now. "You came in here looking for attention tonight, but when somebody finally gives it to you, you act like a bitch. Like you're too good."

I lose a little bit of my good humor. I might have a slight issue with being called the b-word, and that could be because a man I thought I loved liked to use that as my nickname when he was in a certain mood.

I get partway off the stool, letting my left foot drop to the floor. "Tell me you didn't just call me a bitch. Tell me you didn't come into *my* bar while I'm trying to relax after work and call me a bitch just because I turned you down."

He looks at me, surprised. "You own this bar?"

"No, *Skip*, I don't own this bar, but I might as well." *Been coming here since I was fifteen.* "Why don't you just get the hell out of here before you really piss me off?" My other foot drops to the floor. Adrenaline trickles into my veins as my brain quickly assesses the situation and what might happen. I have to be prepared for anything. I spread my legs and get ready to rumble.

He laughs, but there's no humor to it. "It's a free country. I can drink a beer wherever I want . . ." He pauses before delivering his last word. ". . . Bitch."

My first impulse is to punch him in the side of the head, but that'll get me kicked out of here and then I'll miss the celebration with the team. Danny, the bartender and owner, is a friend, but he draws the line up pretty short. So instead, I lift my leg, put my stilettoed boot heel against the guy's hip, and shove as hard as I can while hanging onto the edge of the bar.

Skip wasn't expecting the contact or the force, so he loses his balance easily and goes flying, taking his drink with him. Tripping over his own feet, he lands on his side on the ground, his beer bottle smashing into the floorboards. Beer sprays everywhere, dousing the legs of the person sitting at the nearest table.

The recipient of the spray, an old, bearded guy wearing motorcycle leathers, stands up in a hurry, sending his chair backward. He glares down at the one responsible for covering his pants in beer. "Hey, man! What's your fucking problem?"

"It wasn't me!" Skip yells, pointing in my direction. His voice is up a full octave. "It was her!"

The old guy looks at me, and I smile, giving him the girliest shrug I know how to make. "He just fell over. Tripped on his fancy shoes, maybe. I think he's had too much to drink." I frown real pretty.

Skip struggles to his feet as the bartender moves down toward us. Danny places my new drink next to my old one. "What's going on over here?" He looks at me. "Toni? Are we going to have a problem tonight?"

I shake my head. "No problem here, Danny. That guy just took a dive." I point at Skip, my eyes open wide to help me look more innocent.

Skip is standing now, so angry he's shaking. "She *kicked* me! She knocked me over! All I was doing was talking!"

I stand away from the bar a pace, showing off my diminutive stature, my current 5'3" height made possible only by my substantial heels. "Yeah, right. *I* knocked *you* over." The guy has at least a foot and ninety pounds on me.

After hearing me, people sitting nearby look at both of us and do the math, shaking their heads at Skip. *Shame on him, blaming a tiny girl for his own stupidity.* Only Danny glares at me. He knows me better.

"What were you drinking?" Danny asks Skip, sounding tired. "The next one's on me. Just take it down to the other end of the bar." He gestures to a spot as far away from me as the man can get and not be out the door. Mister Matching-Belt-and-Shoes glares at me and looks like he wants to say something, but he just hisses out a breath and walks away, shaking his head. I was kind of hoping he was going to use that b-word again, but no such luck. I guess he's not as stupid as he looks.

I smile to myself as I get back on my stool and pick up my drink to finish it off. In my experience this little drama will either ensure me an evening of uninterrupted drinking pleasure because I've scared off all the other guys in the bar, or it'll guarantee a line of 'em will be trying to pick me up after, convinced that I'm just looking for a more attractive catch, which of course means them. I wait the few seconds it takes for things to settle down and start in on my second drink with gusto.

The door to the bar opens, and this time the man walking over the threshold is my boss, Ozzie. And he's brought his girlfriend, my teammate May, with him.

I breathe a sigh of relief. I'm fine with violence and sticking up for myself when necessary, but I'd much rather just have a drink and talk to the people closest to me about a job well done. And it's not that I need someone to have my back, but I prefer it. Sometimes when I go it alone, I get a little too hot-headed and then crazy comes for a visit. I'm trying to avoid inviting crazy in for the rest of my life if I can help it. I already narrowly escaped, nearly killing myself with it once. I push away the ache in my chest when it tries to intrude. I'm not going there right now; tonight is supposed to be about celebrating, not regretting.

I wait for them to see me and jut out my chin in recognition as May waves. She's always way too enthusiastic. Her constant cheer is something I've almost gotten used to after six months of working with her, but it hasn't been easy. Sometimes I just want to put her into a headlock and squeeze that absurdly overdone happiness out onto the floor. I smile when I imagine her as a giant tube of glittery toothpaste that needs emptying.

Ozzie is more low-key, letting me know with a vague nod that he sees me sitting at the bar. Just behind the couple come my brother Thibault and my teammate Lucky. I've known Lucky practically my whole life, so it's tempting to say he's like a brother, but I can't do that. When we were kids, we got stupid and kissed once, so I could never see him like I do Thibault.

Lucky and I never repeated that mistake, but that doesn't stop me from thinking about it from time to time. Now is one of those moments. He looks especially good in that black leather jacket, with his hair all messed up and hanging in his face. When he broods like I think he's doing now, I can't stop thinking about what might be bothering him. I've always been drawn to the darker side of things.

May interrupts my wandering memories by grabbing me in a hug. "You're early! Oh, and you smell good! Like cherries."

I shrug inside her embrace and finish off my drink over her encircling arm, picking out and crunching down on the cherry that had been floating in the ice. Danny always gives me extra; he said once he was hoping they'd sweeten me up eventually.

"I had to get my tea on," I say. "Couldn't wait for you guys all night."

When May finally releases me, Ozzie gives me a fist bump and my brother reaches over to pinch my cheek.

"Uh-oh. She's drinking Long Island iced teas," Thibault says.

I jab him with the toe of my boot. "Shut up."

Ozzie takes a credit card out of his wallet and taps it on the bartop. "Drinks are on me tonight. Got a nice bonus." He lifts a hand to signal Danny, who gives him a nod in response. Ozzie is well known here, just like the rest of the team. Whenever we finish a case, this is where we celebrate. It's where we've been coming since all of us were way too young to drink. They have several pool tables in the back and pretty decent music. The crowd is mixed, locals and tourists, Skip being of the latter crowd. He's trying to pretend he doesn't see us down here.

Ha, asshole. Told you I was meeting someone.

"Hey," Lucky says, taking the stool next to mine and glancing over at me before scoping out the liquor bottles lined up behind the bar. He's squinting, but I know he's got eagle-eye vision.

"Hey, yourself." I look away. There's something going on with him. Usually he's full of smiles and comments that put people at ease, but tonight he seems single-minded, maybe even depressed. But I'm not interested in figuring out the puzzle that is Lucky; not tonight, anyway. There are at least two more teas waiting for me and a celebration I plan to fully enjoy, especially now that it's Ozzie's credit card picking up the tab. If something's really going on with Lucky, he'll act weird tomorrow too, and I'll ask him what's up then. Delving into it now when I'm getting my drink on could get complicated.

I'm not known for my self-restraint when under the influence, and I am definitely going under tonight. It's been a long time since I've really let my hair down. Almost five years, actually. The anniversary of the last night I wasn't thinking clearly is approaching, bringing with it a lot of really messed-up memories. I could stand to forget a few of them tonight.

I raise my glass to my friends. "To he who falls first!" I finish off my second cocktail with a heavy dose of slurping through the straw. *Time to get this party started, yo.*

CHAPTER TWO

I'm three cocktails in when I realize it's just Lucky and me at the bar. I look around the room, squinting. "Where'd those assholes go?"

Lucky doesn't look at me when he answers. "They're in the back room playing pool." He's hunched over a beer, his shoulders up around his ears, his leather jacket still on. He's staring at the label on his bottle like he's trying to memorize it.

In the back room? "They left without asking me to play?"

"They did ask you, but after you told them to fuck off, they left."

I spin around and jab him with my elbow. "I did not."

"Yes, you did." He turns and looks at me. "Your memory is crap when you're drinking."

I glare at him. "You looking for trouble?"

The edge of his mouth quirks up in a sad half-smile. "Maybe."

I shove him away from me, knowing he's just playing and not seriously flirting with me. Lucky is the king of charm, the hottest guy God ever created, and he knows it. He's not a heartbreaker, generally speaking, but he knows how to play. I hate that all these cocktails have made my heart go on the fritz, made me think for a second that he's actually into me. I have to take a deep breath to calm myself down. The damn memory of that kiss in junior high keeps trying to take over my head, and the sober me knows that I'd be no good for Lucky.

"What's up with you, anyway?" he asks, leaning into me a little. "You're all fired up for some reason."

He straightens and takes a swig of his beer, never taking his eyes off me. It sends a shock of desire through me like lightning, striking me right in the pants. I'm in no mood for it or his careless games. Maybe he's forgotten that the anniversary of the worst day of my life will be here in a few days, but I haven't.

"I gotta go make a phone call." I grab my purse off the bar and slide down from my stool. I need to go find a quiet alcove where I can hear myself talk. The place is packed now and my ears are ringing from the noise.

Lucky turns around on his stool, suddenly very interested in my plans. "Who're you drunk-dialing?"

"What business is it of yours?" I pause, standing in front of him, as I search through my bag for my phone.

He shrugs, his hands hanging between legs that are bent up, his feet on the stool's support rungs. "All your friends are here. Who could you possibly want to call if not one of us?"

His question pisses me off. I know what he thinks, and he might be right, but it doesn't matter. It's none of his business what I do with my private life. *So what if I want to call the brother of the man I killed?*

I glare at him, my phone dangling from my hand. "You think you guys are my only friends?"

His smile is lazy this time, dulled from the beer. "I know we are. You're too mean to have other friends."

"Apparently I'm not mean enough, since you think you can say that shit to my face." I drop my purse and reach up to slap him, but he grabs my wrist and holds it inches from the cheek I was about to turn flaming red. His lazy smile hasn't budged.

"Let go of me," I grind out, my arm rigid.

He overpowers me and lowers my hand to my side before releasing it. "Don't start something you can't finish, Toni."

I don't know exactly what he means by that, but it makes me want to squirm in my boots. "Oh, shut up." I snag my purse from the floor and walk away with quick strides.

How dare he. How dare he suggest I don't have friends, tell me what I should or shouldn't do, stop me from slapping him when he deserves to be slapped. I want to do a one-eighty and march right back over there to give him a lesson good and proper, but I don't because he's too sharp for me right now. He needs to drink another few beers before I'll be able to get one over on him.

I make my way to the back of the bar, where there's an alcove hosting an old payphone that doesn't work anymore. Aside from a bathroom stall, this is the quietest place in the whole joint. As I scroll through my contacts, my tea-addled brain is assuring me that this is a great idea. I'm going to call Rowdy and apologize for shooting his brother five times in the chest. I grit my teeth hard to keep the emotions that want to take over in check, and my chin trembles with the effort.

Maybe if I can get one person in that family to forgive me, I could work on forgiving myself. It's a long shot, but at this moment, with my head spinning right round like a record, baby, it seems like an awesome idea.

I press the button that will dial up his number, put the phone to my ear, and wait for the call to connect. But suddenly it's just my fingers there at my ear and my phone is gone. It takes me a couple seconds to figure out what's happening.

I turn around and find Lucky there, holding my cell phone in his hand and smiling at me. He looks at the screen as he presses the red button to disconnect the call. "Rowdy LeGrande." His playful smile turns into a frown as he glares at me. "You're calling Rowdy? Are you completely insane, or what?"

My nostrils flare as I grit my teeth. Lucky is so going to pay for that. I hold out my hand. "Give me my phone right now. I'm not kidding."

He shakes his head. "Nope. Can't do that."

I take a step toward him but he raises the phone above his head. He's over six feet tall, so even with my heels, I don't stand a chance unless I bring him to his knees, which is very tempting right now.

"Ah, ah, ahhh . . . keep your distance, girly."

"If you don't give me my phone in the next five seconds . . ."

He lifts his brows. "What? You'll shoot me?"

There is no conscious thought that passes through my mind before I launch my attack. I throw myself at him, screaming my war cry and going right for the eyes.

Unfortunately, he sees me coming and throws my phone so he can capture both of my wrists using only one hand. With the other he pulls me against him.

We both fall backward as one. When his spine hits the wall behind him and he smacks his head on the wood paneling, he hisses out a grunt of pain, but he doesn't let go.

Our faces are only inches apart. I want to claw him, scratch his eyes out and make him bleed for saying what he said, but I can't do any of it. He has me in a viselike grip, and I'm too drunk to tap into my real power. The room is spinning and his face is so, so close. I can smell the beer on his breath. It should be disgusting, but it's not. My heart feels like it's going to explode, I'm so angry and confused. I have never known him to play so dirty before.

"I'm sorry. I shouldn't have said that." His voice is gruff, maybe with regret, but I don't care. He crossed the line, big time.

"Goddamn right, you shouldn't have." I struggle against him, trying to get away, but he's twice as strong as I am. I bring my knee up, hoping to catch him in the balls, but he senses that coming and turns sideways, taking the hit in his thigh. The strike was hard enough to leave a bruise, but he doesn't loosen his hold on me.

"I'm just trying to help you . . ." he says through a hiss of pain, ". . . try to stop you from making a big mistake."

"I don't need your help, asshole." I thrust our interlocked arms up at his face, but he stops my attempted punch an inch before it makes contact. I change my mind about his breath; it is gross. *Budweiser. Ick.*

"Looks like you do need my help. You were about to call Rowdy, the guy who masterminded the plan to kidnap your co-worker but got away without any jail time because he agreed to mental health counseling . . . the guy who still wants to beat your ass or worse. Come on, Toni, you know better."

I don't know why his words hurt me so much, but they do. I hate that I'm weak, that I seek the acceptance of the people I work with. It shouldn't matter to me what they think. I choose my own way, I live my own life, and I don't answer to anyone. *So why do I care what he says?*

"Shut up, Lucky. You don't know me."

His expression softens, though his grip doesn't. "I know you better than you think I do."

I snort and then sneer at him. "Please. You think because you kissed me in junior high you know me?"

Too late I realize I've shown him my hand. I should probably just forget about the whole damn thing like he has. It was ten years ago, after all. *A lifetime.* It doesn't seem that long, though. Probably because, even after all this time, my heart hasn't learned to leave the memory alone. Like it or not, that moment with Lucky has carried me through some really hard times. I've often dreamed of what could have happened with us and with me if I'd followed through on that emotion with him instead of running to Charlie.

He shakes his head. "I'm not talking about that kiss." Then he smiles, looking really proud of himself. "But I'm happy to know that you're still thinking about it." He tilts his head. "How long has it been? Ten years? Fifteen?"

I'm livid. Not only is he thinking he can tell me what to do with my life, but he's mocking me, too. "Who gives a shit?" I go completely still and fix him with a stare. "Let me go, and I'll give you thirty seconds to get away before I come after you. Consider it an early birthday gift."

"I've got a better idea." He stares down at me, not at all intimidated by my threat.

I'd like to lock eyes with him, but I've had too much alcohol. The room is spinning, so I have to look away. "Oh yeah? What's your idea?"

His finger goes under my chin and he uses it to turn my head toward his. I look up into his face, unable to resist as he moves in closer. "Let's try this again," he says.

And before I know it, his lips are touching mine and we're kissing.

CHAPTER THREE

The insanity of that kiss lasts only about three seconds before I go ape-shit crazy, punching Lucky in the chest and yelling at the top of my lungs. If I had a weapon, I'd use it on him. *How dare he! How dare he take my heart and play with it like it's a toy!*

Lucky releases his hold on me instantly and jumps back, putting space between us so he can better control the situation. I recognize the move from our training. He holds out his hands in a gesture that might be designed to calm me down.

People are looking over at us, wondering what's up, but this is the kind of place where unwelcome kisses are a nightly event, so no one moves. They're back to their beers and cocktails in no time, and I'm left with Lucky in the alcove, my heart going way too fast for comfort.

"What are you doing?" I growl at him, wiping the back of my hand across my mouth. My lips are tingling. It feels like he's still there touching me, his tongue licking mine, so I swipe with my hand again. I feel like spitting, I'm so mad.

Lucky looks confused. "I'm sorry. I don't know . . ."

I look out of the alcove, praying no one on our team saw him do that. There's no sign of anyone there, though. They're probably still playing pool. Without me. My heart feels like it's cracking in three different places.

I grab my purse off the floor and throw it over my shoulder, bending a second time to scoop my phone up. *Great. Screen's cracked.* I have to get the hell out of here before I do something worse than I already have. I shove past Lucky on my way to the front door.

Unfortunately, he's right behind me. "Where're you going? You can't drive. You've had too much to drink."

My breath is labored, and I don't understand why. I run fifty miles a week. I could drop my bag and do a marathon in heels right now if I wanted to, but for some reason I can't get enough oxygen into my system. Then I realize the problem; I'm suffocating because he's so close.

"Leave me alone. You don't need to worry about what I'm doing." I have a whole lot to add onto that sentence, like *I'm not your girl-friend,* or *Who do you think you are? Or Why are you suddenly interested in me now when you let me go so easily ten years ago?* But that would open up the door for him to say things I'm not sure I want to hear. He doesn't like me, and I don't like him. Not in that way. Not anymore. That kiss was a mistake, and we both know it. Both of them were.

I don't shout at him. I don't say any of the things that would dredge up memories from ten years ago that need to stay gone, even though it might be satisfying to get those words out of my head and out into the world; instead, I search the street, hoping beyond hope that there'll be a car out there that can take me home.

I fully expect to see nothing, because my luck is complete shit, and yet there, just down the street, is a taxi with its green light on. God himself is looking out for me tonight. *Thank you, Father, Son, and Holy Ghost.* I break into a jog. When I get to the passenger side of the car and lean down, I'm out of breath. "You available to take me home?"

The cabbie, reading a newspaper under his car's dome light, looks up at me, in no hurry to answer. His drawl is slow and heavy. "Are you with Bourbon Street Boys?"

Not expecting to hear that, I stare at him with my eyebrows scrunched up for a few seconds. I could have sworn he said . . .

He continues in his rumbling voice. "I was hired to bring home people from the Bourbon Street Boys team. My fare's already paid for the employees. If you're on the team, I can bring you home."

"Yeah, yeah, I'm on the team." I put my hand on the door, holding my breath as I wait for his acceptance.

"Show me your ID proving who you are or call yourself another cab." He looks like he's about to pick up his newspaper again, so I wave my hand in his window.

"No problem. I have ID. My name is Toni." I don't waste any more time, fearing Lucky's going to get it into his head to come after me. I open the back door and slide in, flashing the cabbie one of my business cards so he can see I am who I say I am.

There's a hint of cigarette smoke clinging to the interior of the vehicle, and the upholstery has seen better days, but I feel like my knight in shining armor has arrived just in time to save me from myself. I turn around and see through the rear window that Lucky is walking over, heading to the passenger window where I was just standing.

I grab the side of the front seat and use it to pull myself forward. "Let's go. I'll give you directions on the way. Head north." I point out the front window to encourage him to hurry.

The driver turns to look at me as he points out his side window. "That guy with you?" Lucky is leaning down, his flawless face suddenly in full view.

Dammit! Now he knows I was trying to escape him. I throw myself back against the seat and hiss out a long breath. "No. That guy is most definitely *not* with me."

Lucky acts like he didn't hear, but I know damn well he did.

"Hey. Can I share this cab with you?" He smiles at me, making me want to both punch him in the face and kiss him again.

I shake my head vigorously. "No. Get your own." I can't look at him. That face breaks my heart. *How dare he kiss me like that!*

"Is he with the team?" the cabbie asks.

Lucky and I answer at the same time.

"No!" I exclaim.

"Yes!" he affirms.

The cabbie shakes his head. "Y'all need to figure out your stories. I got a job to do and I don't earn my pay 'til I start doin' it."

Lucky leans into the cab, fixing the cabbie with a stare. "You were hired to bring home the Bourbon Street Boys team members, and we're both on the team. And she's as drunk as a bicycle, so I'm just going to make sure she gets home okay before you drop me off."

Before I can say anything, the cabbie is looking at me in his rearview mirror and nodding at Lucky. The front door opens and Lucky gets in, slamming it shut behind him. He didn't even have to show ID, the bastard. *Bastard cab driver, too. Sexist pigs.*

I glare at the two assholes in the front seat, trying to decide what to do. I really want to get out of here and find myself another ride, but I've got way too many alcoholic teas in my stomach, and I don't feel so hot. I need to get home and into bed. I'm going to mix myself up a very special cocktail before I pass out, though. It's Thibault's guaranteed no-hangover mix. I have a feeling I'm going to need a double dose.

"We good?" the driver asks, looking at me in his mirror.

I look out the side window. "Whatever." Lucky better not think he's coming into my house. I'll break his frigging nose if he does. I'm trying like hell to do the right thing here, but I can only be so strong mentally before I have to let my fists take over and do the talking.

CHAPTER FOUR

The cab pulls up to the front of my house, and I get out. I don't bother tipping, because I know Ozzie took care of that too. This is one of those perks we get with the job; when we celebrate, he makes sure we get home okay. Usually, it's him driving us in his truck, but I guess he had other plans with his girlfriend tonight.

I try not to be bitter about that. May's a nice enough person, but my life was a lot easier when she wasn't around. I had a lot more of Ozzie's attention and focus and someone I could talk to when I had stuff on my mind. I don't have the hots for him; he's too much like an older brother for me to feel that way about him. But he's kind of the center of my universe as my boss, because my job means everything to me. It rescued me from a really dark place, and it keeps me busy enough that I don't think about my past all that often, and that's a really good thing. I have an army of skeletons in my closet, and they're each ten feet tall and always banging to get out.

A second door slams behind me and I speed up my front walk, knowing what that sound means.

"Wait!" Lucky is coming from behind at a good clip.

"No!" I'm practically running by the time I get to my front door. I'm scrabbling in my bag, looking for my keys, when I hear the taxi drive away. I look up to confirm that it's leaving the curb and find Lucky halfway to my front door. *Dammit! Where are those frigging keys?* I need a smaller purse.

I don't even look at him as I speak. "You'd better just keep on walking around the side, Lucky." My brother lives in a cottage behind the main house and Lucky can hang out there. He knows where the key is. We inherited the entire property from our parents, but Thibault let me have the larger dwelling. I didn't protest much, because I like having a lot of space around me. And maybe someday when I'm fifty years old I might get married and have a bunch of dogs or something. No kids, though, thanks.

Kids and I don't really get along. They make me uncomfortable. I never know what to say to them or do when they're standing there just staring at me like they do. Jenny's son Sammy is probably the only child I've ever felt comfortable around, and that's maybe because he acts like a strange man in a little body. He's more a character than a kid. Dev's son isn't so bad either, but I don't see him much. Sammy, however, has almost become a regular fixture at the warehouse. His mother comes by to drop files off or pick them up and often has him in tow. I see him at least three times a week, and he always shakes my hand and calls me Miss Toni. Kid cracks me up.

Lucky's voice forces my head back into the game. "I'm just making sure you're okay." Sand crunches between his feet and the concrete as he approaches. He's smart enough to stop ten feet away.

"If you come any closer, I'm going to send your nuts up into your throat."

Lucky shakes his head like he's disappointed in me. "Why the hostility, babe? All I did was give you a kiss. There wasn't even any tongue involved."

I narrow my eyes to try to get a better look at him. He thinks he's being funny, egging me on. This is so not like him. "Babe? Since when do you call me babe? Who are you, stranger, and what have you done with Lucky?"

It's been a really long time since I've seen him act like this. Normally he's subdued and keeps mostly to himself, but tonight he's not only stealing kisses, he's playing guardian angel and teasing, too, but only after moping at the bar looking like he wanted to drown his sorrows in alcohol. It must be the beer messing with his head. Or maybe it's an aftereffect of working with Jenny.

May's sister Jenny joined the team a few months back, and she and Lucky work together a lot. I think he was bored before she joined, but now he and Jenny have their own little team that's kind of separate from the bigger one. These days, he comes to work earlier and stays later, and I'd be willing to bet she's been psychoanalyzing him every other second she's been with him. She's the kind of person who likes to crawl into people's heads and figure out what makes them tick. That's why I'm very happy we don't work together on projects. I like the things in my head kept private where they can't scare anyone off.

I get how being on a team with her could make Lucky more open, more free with his words and his actions. Being a part of something special has changed my life, too. Lucky and Jenny hunker over their computers, whispering and laughing about the stuff they find there. It's all a big mystery to me how they could enjoy what they do. Computers and I don't get along very well. I prefer to be out in the field doing surveillance work. I try not to be jealous about the idea of Jenny getting so much of Lucky's time. The fact that she's head over heels in love with and loyal to our partner Dev makes it easier. I probably shouldn't be getting jealous of anyone where Lucky is concerned, but I haven't figured out how to stop my heart from doing what it wants.

"What do you mean? It's me. Lucky. The guy you kissed in junior high." He gives me what he thinks is a sly smile and winks.

The light on my porch is illuminating his teeth, making them glow. He reminds me for a second of Skip from the bar, but then that image disappears. There's no comparison. Lucky is . . . Lucky. There's nobody like him.

I should probably stay pissed at him, but he's so freaking adorable I can't help forgiving him for pushing himself into my life tonight. Truth be told, it's probably not a good idea that I be left to my own devices, what with the anniversary of my biggest sin so close, looming over my head. I hiss out a breath and shake my head, turning so he won't see me smile back. "You're never going to let me live that down, are you?"

"Why would I? It was the best day of my life."

My ears start to burn at his words and my heart beats faster. *Is he serious or is he messing with me?* It's weird how this physical reaction I'm having is very similar to the one I experience when I think I'm about to get caught by one of the bad guys we're surveilling; talk about an adrenaline pump. *Must be the teas.* I shake my head to get it out of the clouds. No way could Lucky be serious. I would've known if he'd had feelings for me all this time.

I finally find my keys in the bottom of my bag and insert the right one into the lock. "Whatever." I know he's just saying this crap to be a good guy. Lucky is pretty brilliant; not much gets past him. Over the years he's always been there, watching over my shoulder. Whenever he sees me getting hot under the collar, he steps in and says something stupid that manages to cool me off a little.

Before, I thought his little rescues were my imagination, but now I'm thinking that looking out for me has been his design all along. *But why? Why would he do that?* If he were into me, I'd know it, but he never gave me that impression. He's always just been there in the background of my life. I don't blame him for feeling sorry for me after all the mistakes I've made. I step in whenever I see someone doing something that could bring the team down, too.

I get the door open and step inside, holding the edge of it as I turn around to face him. "I'm fine now. You can go on about your business. Feel free to let yourself into Thibault's place." Everyone on the team knows where the hidden key is along with the code to the alarm.

I step the rest of the way into my house and begin to shut the door as I tap in the code that will deactivate my alarm system. Lucky comes forward to stand two steps away from the threshold. On any other day I would just slam the door shut in his face without another word and go straight to bed; but this is not just any other date on the calendar.

The anniversary of the day that changed my life forever is upon me, mere days away. I can feel it like a heavy cloak over my shoulders, hot and uncomfortable, something I wish I could take off, but can't. The closer it gets, the more I feel like I have to struggle to breathe. Every year I nearly suffocate on the memory of killing my ex-boyfriend, Charlie. It may be the reason why I had three too many Long Island iced teas tonight. I hate being alone when Charlie is haunting me so strongly.

"Let me in." He takes another step forward.

So tempting . . . I shake my head. "No, I'm going to bed. Alone. Go away." My grip on the door tightens. I should just shut it. I should just walk away.

He takes another step, his foot rocking on my threshold. "I want to come in, though. I want to talk to you." He sounds serious, which gives me pause.

I cock a hip and rest the length of my arm to my elbow on the edge of the door. "Talk about what?"

Lucky doesn't open up very often, but I know I'm not the only one dealing with a bad anniversary; his sister died almost two years ago. I frown as I try to remember the exact date, but then I have to blink a few times trying to make the alcohol-induced dizziness go away. I want to be able to look into his eyes when he tells me what-ever it is he wants to talk to me about. It'll calm me down and give me the patience to hear him out.

There's something about Lucky—I don't know how to explain it; he's *steadiness* to me. He's this presence, almost like a mystical thing—a guardian angel who I know would be there if I really needed him to be, no matter what the cost and no matter where I am. Thing is, though, I don't like being weak. I hate depending on anybody for anything. So I've never called on this guardian angel before, and tonight is not going to be the day I start. I wait for him to answer my question, but at the same time I'm almost certain this will end with me shutting the door in his face.

"I don't want to talk about it out here. I need to come inside." He shoves his hands into his pockets and looks down at the ground.

My curiosity is piqued. This is the first time all night, the first time in a really long time, that I've seen Lucky appear unsure of himself.

"Is it about Sunny?" Lucky has this goldfish he really cares about. To anyone else it might sound crazy, but I get it. Kind of. It belonged to his sister Maribelle. Maybe he wants to reminisce about her. Jenny told everybody on the team that Lucky needs to talk about his sister's death to help him work through his grief over her suicide, which means I'm going to feel guilty as hell if I shut the door on him now.

I step back and pull the door open wider. "Come on in. I'm going to go mix up a batch of Thibault's hangover special."

Lucky walks inside and shuts the door behind him. "Before you do that, just wait one second. I need to do something."

I pause in the hallway that leads to my kitchen, confused. He walks toward me, but I don't flinch. I don't move a muscle. The spinning that was threatening to overwhelm me disappears in an instant as he gets close enough for me to touch.

I look up at him, at the fire smoldering in his eyes, and ask the question dancing around in my brain. "What are you doing?" I don't know for sure what his answer will be, but that doesn't stop my pulse from pounding like a war drum.

"Something I've been thinking about doing for a really long time. I decided I needed to stop thinking about it and just do it."

"Why?" I'm stalling, trying to figure out his angle.

"A friend recently told me I should do something each day I'd regret not doing in the future, so here I am." He keeps walking, which forces me to go backward. He's crowding me, taking my personal space, making my heart race as my mind tries to make sense of what he's doing. I was prepared to listen with a compassionate ear, to be gentle when I normally can't be that person. What he's doing now is throwing me for a loop. It doesn't compute.

"I don't . . . I don't understand . . ." I run into the wall. There's no more going backward for me, but Lucky is still coming.

He stops mere inches away and looks down at my eyes. "Toni, I'm going to kiss you again. Please don't knee me in the nuts or punch me in the face."

I bite the insides of my cheeks, trying not to smile. He looks so desperate, so serious. And this time he's smart enough to warn me about what he's going to do before he does it. I'm so busy trying to calculate whether I should say yes or no, I miss out on the fact that he's already coming for me.

He places his hands on either side of my face and leans down, his eyes closing.

Should I duck under his arm and run? Should I knee him in the nads, even though he asked me not to? Should I close my eyes and just wait and see what happens? *Too many teas, not enough time.* Something whispers in the back of my head, another part of me, not as addled by the liquor as my conscious mind. *No, it* whispers, desperate to get me out of here. *Don't do it! You'll destroy him! He'll destroy you! Nothing good can come of this!* Unfortunately, I'm really good at ignoring great advice.

Lucky's lips touch mine, gently at first, but things heat up pretty quickly. For a few moments, I imagine that I'm going to force myself not to respond, let him run the show so he'll see that I'm not interested in playing these games with him; but something in me catches fire and I lose all control in a matter of seconds. That little, rational voice inside my head is getting fainter and fainter. *Sorry, brain, wrong answer.* My answer to his request to kiss me is not *no.* It's a resounding *yes, yes, yes!*

He presses me into the wall, his hands moving down from the sides of my face to my shoulders. I grab at his waist and squeeze his shirt, twisting it and hanging on like my life depends on it. He tastes like pure recklessness and smells like Lucky, a potent combination. I want to feel more of him on me, work out this antsy emotion threatening to swallow me whole.

He moans, sending my blood pressure spiking. My fingers go up to tangle in his hair and pull him closer. One of his hands is on my breast, squeezing. I'm hot. So turned on. It's been too long since I've let a man touch me.

I don't even know who I am right now, what my life is all about, what I plan to do with my future. All that matters is this moment, these few seconds that Lucky and I are stealing from the world, from reality. He's been in my life for as long as I can remember, always there, always in the background, always smiling, always being a way better man than I deserve. Being with him can't be right, but I'm doing this anyway. *Hell yeah, I am.* I'll deal with the consequences later.

His tongue is hot, his lips full and soft. I have tingles running all over my body from his hands roaming everywhere they shouldn't. My nipples are hard and my panties are wet.

He grabs me around the back while he's still kissing me and pulls me away from the wall.

"Where're we going?" His teeth scrape my lip and I dive in for more. I can't get enough of him tonight.

"Just kiss me," he says, guiding us through the house, crashing into furniture and knocking things over on the way. We end up in the living room and collapse onto the sofa together. The weight of his body pushes into me and I can feel his rock-hard length pressing into the soft spot between my legs. I'm on fire. I can't think straight. The only thing going through my mind right now is how bad I want him inside me.

Screw the consequences. Screw the awkward moments that are bound to follow tomorrow and years after. One kiss from junior high lasted ten years; how long is this one going to last? *Screw it.* I convince myself it won't last at all. Or not for long. We're adults. We'll get over this in a couple days, and life will go back to normal. I need him. *Now.*

"I've wanted you like this for so long," he mumbles against my mouth.

I don't like that he's trying to complicate things. This can be just about sex for me. I can do this and so can he. "Shut up," I growl, yanking his shirt out of his jeans. "Just take your clothes off and get inside me."

He pauses, breathing heavily into my neck. "Are you sure?"

I glare at him, furious he's asking me this question now. As if he gave me the option. "Go to hell, Lucky."

His smile, so close, so beautiful, goes sinister. "That's what I like about you, Toni. No nonsense."

I'm secretly thrilled, but I'm not going to tell him that. "I'm not going to tell you to take your damn clothes off twice."

Suddenly, he's scrambling. His jacket goes flying, along with the shirt. I take a moment to admire his chiseled chest and rounded shoulders. Then his hand is on my shirt, yanking it up over my head. It's not pretty or graceful in the least, but we're both naked in under a minute and then he's sliding into me.

I let out a long moan as his full length slips in achingly slow. I'm so wet, so ready for him. I cannot believe this is happening. The boy I've been crushing on since I was flat-chested is sliding in and out of me, sweating on me, moaning above me. I will allow myself to enjoy this moment for now. There will be plenty of time for regret later.

I reach around to his back and hang on for dear life, scoring his skin with my blunt nails as shivers of pleasure move out from my center.

He hisses in response to the pain and rams into me. "I'm fucking you, Toni."

I bite my lower lip and grip onto him, tensing myself up to meet him and pull him into me more deeply. "No, you're not. I'm fucking *you*."

His laugh is deep, more like a growl, and he picks up the pace. Our bodies slam into each other, sweat making us slippery. I meet him thrust for thrust, pound for pound. We're both breathing heavier as the sensations build between us. I can tell he's just as affected as I am, the way he's trembling all over.

"I can't hold off much longer," he groans.

We should both be dulled by the amount of alcohol we've had, but I'm right there with him. "Don't wait on me." I'm panting like a dog, so close to falling over the edge. It's been too long for me, and I've thought about Lucky for so many years. This is way better than I ever imagined it could be.

I start to feel something dangerously close to happiness, but I fear that emotion; it usually means pain is just around the corner. I push the thoughts away and focus on his thickness filling me, drawing me closer and closer to the edge. Lucky somehow knows exactly what I need and gives it to me without a word.

His arm goes under my waist and he lifts me up, pounding into me faster and faster. I'm yelling now, unable to stop the emotions from bombarding me, zinging out from every corner of my mind and my heart. I've never had sex like this before, and I'll probably never have sex like this again because this will be a one-time event. And now it's nearing the end, the bittersweet moment we've both been waiting for that I'm probably going to regret for the rest of my life.

"I'm coming!" he yells. His entire body is tensed up, hard as a rock. Sweat is rolling off him.

Hearing his words, feeling his body pulsing above me, is all I need.

"I'm coming too!"

We orgasm together and it feels like some kind of miracle has just happened in my living room. At the same moment, we both explode inside, clinging to one another lest we float off into the universe untethered, never to return. I imagine fireworks in my brain. Fireworks inside me. I'm pulsing with need and spent ecstasy. Lucky's body does the same. And then, as all the heat and fire and intense emotion fade out, he collapses on top of me, smothering me in two hundred pounds of what-the-hell-did-we-just-do.

I can feel his heart beating against mine, the hard thump-thump-thump waking me up to reality. But I'm too tired and spent to do anything about it. I'll hate myself tomorrow. Right now, I'm just going to enjoy the afterglow.

Lucky levers himself up and looks down at me, but he doesn't say anything.

The glow fades fast under his scrutiny and I start to feel uncomfortable. "Why are you looking at me like that?"

His expression is one I know well. *Regret.* He's still not saying anything.

A push on his chest with all my strength forces him to roll over enough that he slips out of me and falls onto the floor.

There's a big thump and a crash as he knocks things off my coffee table. "Ow," comes his voice from the floor.

I stand up and quickly gather my bits of clothing from various places. I'm on my feet walking away by the time he's sitting up.

"Where're you going?" He sounds confused, which makes no sense. I'm doing what needs to be done, and he should be thanking me for it.

I take the stairs two at a time. "Away!" I yell, eager to put as much distance between us as I possibly can. I cannot believe I just had sex with Lucky. *What in the hell is wrong with me? Have I not punished myself enough? Do I need to destroy him, too?*

His voice follows me up the stairs. "Can I join you?"

I pause just outside my bedroom door before answering. Even though it's tempting to continue this train wreck, I know I can't. My life is already screwed up enough, and I don't need to take Lucky down with me. "No!" I slam my bedroom door behind me and lock it, pausing a moment to rest my trembling hand over my racing heart before continuing on to the shower.

CHAPTER FIVE

I'm lying in my bed staring up at the ceiling when my phone buzzes a second time. The first buzz woke me. I turn my head and look at the nightstand where it's resting. The screen is lit up, indicating there's a message waiting.

How did it get there? I don't remember bringing my phone up to my room. And now that I think about it, I don't remember bringing myself up here. There's a vague sense that something's off in my life but I can't quite put my finger on what it is.

I let my mind wander, attempting to put together the little clues that are trying to filter into my sleep-fogged brain. My stomach churns, reminding me that I had way too much to drink last night. *Where was I? Oh yeah, I was at the pub.* I was there with the team and they were late. I kicked some guy's ass and almost got him busted up. *Why don't I remember the team being there?*

A vision of Lucky's face flashes across my mind. My heart nearly stops when I remember what we did in the alcove by the old phone booth. *Oh, shit! Not again!* I force my hands to stay next to me on the mattress. They want to touch my lips that are now tingling with the memory. Other parts of me begin to grow warm.

I'm remembering more: A cab ride. *Lucky followed me home. Came inside.* I clutch at my shirt over my chest, the pain under my ribs abrupt and sharp. *Oh, God! I slept with him!* I turn my head and look at my phone again. *Is that him calling me?* I'm both freaked out and hopeful, a sad mix of emotion.

My pillow feels damp next to my cheek. I reach up and touch my head, finding my hair wet. *Did I take a shower? With Lucky? No, not with Lucky.* I remember the shower, and he definitely wasn't in it with me. But holy shit, I remember other things now. Lots of things. Feelings . . . sensations . . . hope . . . fear . . . his heavy body on mine. Heat builds between my legs.

The back of my hand rests on my hot forehead. I can't believe I did that with him! What's wrong with me? Do I want to completely destroy my life? Haven't I done a really great job of that already?

I roll over, hissing out my anger. *Dammit.* As if my life weren't complicated enough. I get to my feet and sway a little, the alcohol still working its black magic. I rub my stomach. *Damn. I need to get something in there. Thibault's magic no-hangover mix, for one.* I walk over to the other side of my bed and pick up the phone, almost fearing I'm going to see Lucky's name there.

I'm both relieved and disappointed to find a text from Thibault waiting for me.

T-BO: *Have you seen Lucky?*

His message makes no sense to me. *Have I seen Lucky?* I smile bitterly. *Yeah, I have. Hanging over my face.* The memories are coming back way too fast and way too furious: the sweat dripping off him right before it landed on me, the feel of him inside me, the fire he set in my heart. It's all too clear now, almost like he's still here with me. I shake my head, forcing the memories to go away as I tap out a response on my phone.

Me: *Not since last night.*

That's an honest enough answer.

T-BO: *He's missing.*

I frown at my phone. It's 9:30 in the morning. Today is Saturday and there were no plans for us to go to work this weekend. How could Lucky possibly be missing?

Me: *Shut up Thibault. Ur drunk. Go back to bed.*
T-BO: *I'm coming over.*
Me: *I just got up. Give me 10.*
T-BO: *I'm coming over now.*

When my brother gets his head stuck on something, there's no changing it. I stumble around my room grabbing my dirty jeans and a pair of short boots with small heels, pulling them all on in record time. I throw on a ratty T-shirt and am running a brush through my hair just as the front door opens and then slams shut downstairs.

"You up there?" Thibault shouts.

"I'll be down in a sec. Start a pot of coffee!" It's too late for Thibault's no-hangover mix to have any effect; I should have drunk some last night. I'm just going to have to take the pain of my headache and bad choices like a woman. I'd take them like a man, but then I'd have to whine all day, and I don't like whining.

I slide a toothbrush and some paste around my mouth a few times before abandoning my efforts at looking halfway decent to go downstairs and meet my brother in the kitchen. He's seen me look way worse than this.

I find Thibault standing over an empty pot he's just starting to brew. I walk over and pull two mugs out of the cabinet to his right. I can't face him. *What if he knows?*

"You haven't seen Lucky?" Thibault asks.

"I told you, I saw him last night. Just like you." My pulse is racing again. I hate lying to my brother, but I hate even more the idea that I was so weak last night. I shouldn't have let Lucky in. He played me like a fiddle just so he could get some. *Asshole.* I'm definitely kicking him in the nuts when I see him again. He'd better not tell anyone what we did.

"Did you know he was at my place last night?" Thibault asks.

I shake my head. I don't trust my voice to sound honest.

"He left me a note. Said he was gonna be out of touch for a little while. What the hell does he mean by that?"

"I have no idea."

I'm panicking. *Did he leave because of me?* Of course he did. Why else would he disappear? I hate that I was so coldhearted last night. I should've let him stay. He could've slept on my couch, at least. I'm so messed up right now. I want to punch him *and* hug him at the same time. *Maybe he's more messed up about his sister than we realized.*

Thibault turns around and leans his lower back against the counter. "Why was he over here?"

"How am I supposed to know?" I busy myself with gathering sugar and cream that neither of us ever uses. I'm angry now. Angry that I'm being forced to lie to Thibault.

"Why are you so touchy? It's just a question."

I shrug. "I'm worried about him, just like you are. Is that a crime?"

Thibault stares at me for a few long seconds. I ignore him, walking over to the pantry to find something to eat. I'm not really hungry now, though; more than anything, I'm avoiding his penetrating stare. I swear, sometimes he sees right through me.

"Did he share a cab back here with you?"

I answer from inside the pantry. "Maybe. I don't remember much of last night, actually. I had too many teas."

Thibault grunts his response. The coffee starts to percolate and the smell filters through the kitchen. I pretend to be very busy hunting up breakfast when what I'm really doing is avoiding facing the music. *He knows. I know he does.*

"I hope he can be back for work on Monday. We really need him on the next case."

"Oh yeah?" I stick my head out of the pantry. "What's going on?"

"Ozzie got a call late last night from Captain Tremaine. They're having a problem up in the Sixth Ward again."

I grab a random box of cereal and come out. "What are we going to do?"

"We don't have all the details yet, but it sounds like one of the groups over there is getting a little more sophisticated. Using a lot of social media for their transactions and linking in through private chat groups. They want Lucky and Jenny in on this one, but they also need us to do some old-school surveillance."

I nod. "Cool." This is exactly what I need to get my mind off Lucky. Work. Danger. Adrenaline. *Yeah, buddy.*

I get out two bowls and pour the cereal, grabbing spoons out of the drawer on my way back to the table.

"You sure you don't remember Lucky coming over here?" Thibault is staring at me again.

I can't meet his eyes. I set the bowls down on the breakfast table with a bang and drop into my seat. I jab at the sugar-frosted flakes with my spoon. "I already told you, no. Quit asking me. Jesus, I feel like I'm in an interrogation right now." I look up at him and glare. "Did I do something wrong?"

He shrugs. "You got really drunk. You weren't there when Ozzie got the call, so you couldn't be part of the meeting."

I throw my free hand up. "As far as I knew, we were there to celebrate, not work. And when I celebrate, I drink tea. End of story." I take a big bite of my cereal, crunching it and letting an errant drop of milk fall from my lips to the bowl.

"Maybe next time you should drink just one and stop there."

I talk with my mouth full. "Maybe next time you should mind your own damn business." I throw my spoon down, get up, and leave the kitchen, afraid I'm going to blow up at him more than I already have. Thibault is used to it, but normally I have a good reason to go off, so it's cool. Right now, though, I don't exactly know what's fueling my anger. Am I embarrassed? Ashamed? Worried? I can't make any sense of it. I hate it when I don't even know my own mind.

I go upstairs to my room, shutting and locking the door behind me. Grabbing my phone off the table, I send out a quick text.

Me: *Where are you? What's going on?*

I wasn't going to talk to Lucky. I had planned to let this thing fade into the background for us and move on with my life like nothing ever happened, but his disappearance changes things. If he left some strange, mysterious note for Thibault after leaving my house, I have a responsibility to look into that. No one on the team is allowed to go off the range. We watch out for each other. It's dangerous being out in the weeds without backup.

I wait for an answer that doesn't come. It pisses me off. We had sex less than twelve hours ago. He owes me a response at least.

Me: *Listen, asshole. You need to answer me.*

My hands are shaking. I don't know if it's from anger, worry, or something else.

I try one more time.

Me: *If you don't answer me I'm going to tell everybody what you did.*

The answer comes quicker than I expect.

Lucky: *What WE did, you mean.*

I can't stop the smile that comes over my face. I am such a sucker for a bad boy. Lucky's no bad boy, but he sure knows how to act like one sometimes.

Me: *I was drunk.*
Lucky: *So was I.*

His reaction makes me more than a little sad. *Damn it all.*

Me: *Where are you?*
Lucky: *Don't worry about it.*

I want to throw my phone across the room, but I don't; the screen's already cracked and almost falling off the damn thing. I send another small message.

Me: *Tell me.*

Nothing comes, and I'm not going to beg. If he wants to be a jerk and make everybody worry about him, fine. I know he's alive. He'll come back when he's done with whatever it is he's doing. He's probably nursing his wounds. I know I will be for a while. I put the phone back on my side table and go downstairs.

"He's fine."

Thibault fixes me with a stare from across the room where he's waiting on the coffee to finish. "Lucky? You talked to him?"

"Yes. Like I said, he's fine. He's just going to lie low for a little while." I sit down at my spot, pick up my spoon. "I don't know why." No way can I tell my brother what Lucky and I did or how I was able to get in touch with him so quickly.

"Why's he answering your text and not mine? Or did you call him?"

I dive into my bowl of cereal, talking around the limp flakes. "I texted him. But he's not going to text me back anymore. Just leave him be." I stare into my bowl.

Thibault walks over and sets a hot mug of coffee down in front of me. Taking the chair across from mine, he digs into his cereal as well. I think we're going to eat in companionable silence, but he destroys that idea with one question.

"Something happen between you guys last night?"

I drop my spoon with a clang into the dish and glare at him. "Could you mind your own fucking business, please?"

Thibault smiles at me, sly fox that he is. "Something happened. Don't try to deny it." He narrows his eyes. "But what could it be to get you so riled up? Hmmm . . ." He pokes at his flakes with his spoon, never taking his eyes off me. He takes a bite and chews real slowly.

I get up from the table, swiping my bowl and spoon off it and walking over quickly to dump them in the sink. "I'm done here. See yourself out."

"You think that's a good idea?" Thibault's words follow me down the hallway.

"Not talking about this with you!"

"I just don't want to see you get hurt!"

Too late. I run up the stairs, determined to put this behind me, my heart aching in my chest. *God, please take care of Lucky. I'm not there to watch his back, and I don't want him to get hurt.*

CHAPTER SIX

The weekend goes by way too slowly. When Monday finally arrives, I end up at work an hour early. It's 8:00, but I'm not alone. Dev and Jenny are in the workout area getting an early start on the day too. She's several months into her fitness program with Dev, the man in charge of our training, and it's really paying off.

When she first arrived she looked like a typical computer geek—someone who sits at a desk all day munching on chips. But now she's a lean, mean, case-cracking machine. Mostly. Dev has been trying to teach her how to use a singlestick, but she's resisting. Unlike her sister May, Jenny is a pure pacifist. I can hear her whining from across the warehouse.

"But I work at the computer. I'm never going to need to hit anybody with a stick."

"Probably not," Dev says, "but that doesn't mean you shouldn't be prepared. Just because you're cute doesn't mean you get to be an exception to the rule."

She giggles and I roll my eyes. The two of them are so ga-ga over each other it's stupid. I'm not jealous, though. Their love works, even though the deck is stacked against them. Between them they have four kids and two disabilities, a mother who took off after one of the kids was born, and an ex-husband who isn't a shining example of fatherhood to the other three. They'd never admit it, but I think they like coming to the warehouse; it's less work than being at home with that loud, crazy crew.

"Hey, Toni," Dev says, emerging from the shadows. "How was your weekend?"

"Fine," I lie. No way would I ever tell him how long and empty it seemed and how I second-guessed myself every five minutes. Regret is already eating away at my soul.

Dev and I are friends, and I consider him practically an adopted brother, but he's never been somebody I've shared my feelings with. Nobody is, really, except maybe Ozzie. He pretty much sponsored me when I got out of prison, and he managed my life for me when I couldn't. He's the only one in the world who knows how I feel about anything, and we haven't talked much since May entered the picture. Even my brother is kept an arm's length away. Thankfully, Thibault didn't say another word to me about Lucky over the weekend, or I don't know what I would have done to him. It might have helped that I avoided him like the plague.

I don't like anyone in my business. Charlie—my ex-boyfriend—once told me it was because I fear that once people get a really good look at what I have inside, they'll run for the hills. Whatever. I'm okay with being only half there, so long as I can be there at all.

"I hear you and Lucky disappeared Friday night," Dev says.

Jenny comes out of the workout area and stands next to Dev, looking up at him. "Really?" she asks. "Why am I just hearing about this now?" She looks at me and smiles, wiggling her eyebrows suggestively. "What happened?"

I frown at both of them. "Nothing happened." My voice comes out sharper than I mean for it to. It makes me sound guilty, and we all know it. I try to soften my tone. "Nothing happened at all. I don't really know what he did. I got piss-drunk and took a cab home." I lift my chin at them, moving for a re-direct of the conversation. "What'd you guys do? I didn't see you there."

"We couldn't make it," Jenny says.

"Yeah," Dev adds, "the kids had a sleepover planned, and we had to pop popcorn and supervise."

The two lovebirds smile at each other.

I force a smile to be polite. "A sleepover? Sounds like fun." *Not.*

Jenny is no dummy; if I keep talking, she's going to figure out that something's up, so I walk toward the stairs. Jenny's one of those girls who's always in matchmaker mode, and the last thing I need is to be matched with a guy who tangles me up inside the way Lucky is doing right now. When I finally do settle down with someone, he'll be boring. He won't get me riled up; he'll calm me down.

"I'm just going to head on up," I say casually. "I have some papers to organize." My messenger bag is over my shoulder, but there's really nothing inside it other than a legal pad, a pen, and a switchblade.

"We'll be up in a couple minutes," Dev says. "I just need to whip her butt with a few more sets."

Jenny snorts. "You can try." I look back to see her lifting her upper arm to flex her biceps. A tiny lump pops up, standing out against her lean arm.

Dev leans over and squeezes it between his first finger and thumb. His hands are huge in comparison to her petite frame. "Nice," he says. "All my hard work is finally paying off."

"*Your* hard work?" She shakes her head and walks toward the gym equipment. "Come on. I need to school you some more."

He chuckles, falling in behind her. He smacks her on the ass and she fake-screams, running away.

I open the door to the upstairs and walk in, glad to be alone again. Their games make my heart ache. Maybe it's the super-potent happiness that hurts.

In the past six months, I've seen two of my brothers-in-arms fall in love with girls who I never would have suspected they'd even like. But what do I know about love? I've only ever let myself totally fall for one person, and I ended up killing that guy. I'm checking out of the love game forever. I don't want to kill anybody else, and men who break my heart sure do tempt me.

I walk through the room filled with Dev's toys—mostly swords—to get to our kitchen and meeting area. Taking my seat at the table, I drop my bag next to me.

There are no new texts on the screen of my cell phone. A little piece of me was hoping there'd be something there from Lucky. My fingers hover over the keyboard. *Should I? Just one little message?*

I throw my broken phone down on the table, hissing out a sigh of annoyance. It's like I'm in junior high all over again. We didn't have cell phones back then, but if we had, I probably would've done stupid shit with mine. I probably would've texted a guy who didn't deserve to hear from me.

My mind wanders. I think about junior high on that day Lucky kissed me. It was at a school dance that he and my brother had teased me into attending. I told them dances weren't my thing, but they didn't care. I think they were hoping they'd catch me on the dance floor, but there's no way in hell that would've happened.

Lucky caught me trying to sneak out. He begged me to come back and dance with him, but I refused. That's when he grabbed me and kissed me. I didn't resist for a second or two. Maybe I should have, but I'd been staring into that beautiful face for too many years to put up a fight.

He went from being my brother's best friend and a quasi-member of the family to being my lifelong crush in that moment. I knew it was a mistake, but the heart wants what it wants. Our neighborhood family was really close, all of us hanging out near Bourbon Street, getting into trouble. We were a group of kids

45

who did everything together, good or bad. None of us had much of a moral compass back then. Ozzie's influence came later. Even though I was only fifteen years old, I knew something between Lucky and me would've messed everything up for the whole group of us. I pushed him away that night and ran. I don't even remember how I got home after the dance; I may have hitched a ride, knowing me. But that kiss burned my lips for years after.

I resist the urge to reach up and touch my mouth. I swear I can still feel his touch from Friday night.

It was the decision I made the night of that dance ten years ago—to stay away from Lucky and preserve our family unit—that drove me into Charlie's arms. I told myself I needed to find a boyfriend so I could get my mind off Lucky and let him know that I wasn't available, and Charlie was just there: the quintessential bad boy, with his motorcycle and his leather jacket, smoking a pack of filterless Camels a day. He'd noticed me before, offered me a smoke, a ride on his bike. I'd ignored him up until then, but I stopped after Lucky's kiss.

I dove right in, committing myself fully to letting him wreck my life. At the time, I thought he was perfect for me, of course. I didn't see what was right there in front of my face: alcoholic, abusive father who was in and out of jail; a temper he couldn't control; a chip on his shoulder so big there wasn't room for much else in his life.

We were together for a lot of years, but it was never a happy pairing. Bouts of tormented passion alternated with periods punctuated by drunken arguments and drag-out fights; the relationship was physical on many levels. For a long time, I was able to hide the bruises from the guys. I played sports, so I could easily blame the other team. But one day Thibault caught Charlie shaking me hard, making my head snap back and forth, and he got suspicious.

After that, they all kept a closer eye on me, and it was only a matter of time before they busted him hurting me. That was my senior year; Charlie had been out of school for a while. I should've ended the relationship then. Hell, I should've ended it long before then, but I was addicted. I was addicted to Charlie, I was addicted to the adrenaline, and I was addicted to the pain. Suffice it to say, I was in a very low place.

I don't blame Lucky for any of it. He never would've wanted that stuff for me, and he'd offered up affection that would never have brought me pain. I just couldn't take it. My adopted street family was too important to me, even before we started working as the Bourbon Street Boys team.

I should've left after the first time Charlie got rough with me, I know that now. But back then, I was too rebellious to do the right thing. I made excuses for him. My brother tried to warn me off him, but I wasn't going to let anyone tell me what to do or how to do it.

I guess I'm still a lot like that, but I want to believe that I can look in my rearview mirror from time to time and see the mistakes I've made so I can avoid making them a second time. That's why I don't date and why I don't let guys pick me up in bars. It's better that I just stay away from guys I don't know, since I can't trust myself to pick one who's good for me.

Unfortunately, I didn't learn my lesson the easy way. I haven't done anything the easy way. I stayed with Charlie until it got really bad, and I ended up in the hospital. Then when I finally tried to get away, it was too late; Charlie was just as addicted to our sick relationship as I was.

He came after me one night after I'd moved out, five years ago, and I did the only thing I thought I could do to end it. When he broke down my door and came at me, I shot him.

Five times. Right in the heart.

Normally when someone busts into your house bent on doing harm, you can shoot him to stop him, all legal and proper. But

I didn't just shoot Charlie to stop him; I shot him to punish him for all the things he'd done, and for all the things I had done to myself.

There was no jury in my case. My lawyer thought it would be better for just a judge to hear the evidence. Something about me not being a very sympathetic witness or whatever, plus Charlie's family was pretty well-known in the area, a bunch of street hoods with connections to bigger criminal syndicates, and not many people wanted to get on their bad side. An untainted jury would have been hard to put together, in other words.

Judge Culpepper was a graying man in his late sixties, old-school Louisiana bred, born, and raised. He probably had a couple good ole boys as sons. He didn't really care that Charlie was twice my size or that I had a history of bruises and broken bones documented by the local hospital. He saw those four extra shots for what they were: revenge.

And so I went down for manslaughter. I guess he used up a little bit of that self-defense my lawyer argued about to lower the charge from murder. Lucky for me, I wasn't in prison for long before I was out on probation.

It all went down five years ago today. The anniversary of Charlie's death has arrived once more, and I'm damn glad it's falling on a Monday. I need to drown out the noise in my head with an avalanche of work.

The door opens from the other part of the room and Ozzie walks through, exiting his private quarters. His dog Sahara is on his heels, and just behind Sahara is tiny Felix. He's some kind of Chihuahua mutt that May owns. The mutt doesn't pay me any attention, always focused on his big, hairy girlfriend who's ten times his size but just as in love with him as he is with her. Even dogs are better at relationships than I am.

"Morning," Ozzie says.

I nod. "Morning. How was your weekend?"

"Good." He walks over to take his seat at the head of the table. "You have breakfast yet?"

"Cereal."

"Breakfast of champions."

"Yup."

The door Ozzie just entered through bursts open and May comes rushing into the room. As soon as she sees me, her face lights up.

"Toni! I'm so glad you're here. You get to be the second one after Jenny to hear my good news." She stops near the end of the table and claps her hands a few times before holding them out at me. "Look. Look, look, look!"

I stare at her hands, but all I see are manicured fingernails that are longer than they should be. She's scratched me more than once during our hand-to-hand combat practice sessions.

"What am I looking at?"

She shakes her hands and thrusts them out farther. "Look! Look at my finger!"

My eyes bulge out a little when I finally catch on to what's got her so excited. I suppose I knew this was coming, but to actually see it is another thing than just imagining it. "You have a new ring."

She claps her hands and jumps up and down, squealing. "Can you believe it?" She goes to Ozzie and hugs him from behind, putting him in a loving headlock. "He asked me to marry him last night, the big lug."

Oh well. His funeral. "Congratulations."

May levels her gaze at me. "I want you to know that this will not change *anything* between you and Ozzie or between you and me."

I scowl at her, not quite getting what she's saying, but pretty sure I'm not going to like it. "What?"

Ozzie turns his head and looks up at May. "Would you mind getting me another cup of coffee, babe?"

She pats him on the head like he's a Chihuahua. "Okay, babe. Coming right up." She switches her attention over to me. "Do you want one too?"

I still feel lost. Maybe caffeine will help. "Sure."

When she's in the kitchen making noise, I lower my voice so we can speak semi-privately. "What was she talking about?"

Ozzie shakes his head and whispers back, "She's worried you'll be jealous. Just play along with it."

I hiss out my annoyance. I've never had a thing for Ozzie and never will. She's welcome to him; he's way too bossy for my liking, plus he's too big. He'd never hurt a woman in anger, but I tend to bring out the worst in people. I wouldn't want to see the worst of Ozzie.

"Whatever," I say. "I hope you'll be happy."

"I already am." He means it. Ozzie doesn't do anything half measure. When he puts his mind to something, it's as good as done. Six months ago he put his mind to loving May, as silly as she can be sometimes, so now it's over. Ozzie is off the market forever.

Before May gets back with the coffee, the outer door opens and everyone but Lucky walks through. The meeting will now commence minus the one member I actually wanted to see today. I hate having to admit that to myself. Great sex will be the death of me yet.

CHAPTER SEVEN

O kay, so we've got a new case we need to get started on right away." Ozzie dives in, our morning coffee still steaming in mugs in front of us. "The city's got trouble in the Sixth Ward again. Some of you already heard about this Friday night at the pub, but I got more detail over the weekend from Captain Tremaine. You all remember David Doucet and the crew he ran with?" He pauses as we nod, placing his hand on May's shoulder as her face goes a little white.

How could we forget David Doucet? The hardcore criminal ended up in May's house looking to blow a hole in her after she witnessed him taking shots at Ozzie. Luckily, Dev's training set her up to at least react when things get hot. From what I heard, her self-defense wasn't elegant, but she got the job done.

Dev couldn't have been prouder, but I was just plain relieved. She's a pretty damn good photographer, and I already knew then how much Ozzie cared about her. If something worse had happened to her, it would have torn our whole team apart. Ozzie's as tough as they come, but May can turn him to mush with a single look. It's embarrassing, and I'd tell him so, but he'd probably double my workouts and send me dumpster diving for evidence over it.

I'm glad she's continued her training and gotten better than she first was, because she could be a real soft spot for all of us. She and her sister both. Neither of them was born to the life the rest of us were. Hardening them up, both their muscles and their minds, has been Dev's job since they walked in the door, but we all help out with sparring sessions and pair-work when we can. I don't envy Dev the task he has. It can't be easy. They look like a couple of marshmallows, the way they dress and carry themselves. Before, they were Jet-Puft . . . Now they're the stale store-brand: a little tougher, but still too sweet and soft in the middle.

Ozzie cuts into my thoughts. "Looks like a rival gang is coming into town, and the streets are getting hot. There've been a couple of drive-bys, which wouldn't normally be something we'd get involved in, but the attacks look a lot more coordinated than normal. There are more victims coming from more accurate strikes."

"Isn't that kind of a good thing?" Jenny asks. She looks at everyone sitting around the table. "I mean, they're all drug dealers and gang bangers and stuff, right? Don't we save taxpayer money by letting them kill themselves? Street justice or whatever?"

Thibault shakes his head. "No. These are drive-bys at quinceañeras, baptisms, birthdays, barbecues, and other family events. We've got moms and grandmas taking the heat with these. It's getting real ugly."

Jenny's face falls. "Oh. Now I feel bad. Grandmas?"

May reaches over and pats her sister's hand. "Don't worry, big sis. I got you."

I hold in a laugh. Whenever May tries to sound street, it makes me think of a Muppet dressed as a gangster. Jenny rolls her eyes and then bugs them out at me. She gets it. She's under no illusions about who she is and what she's capable of. I respect her for that.

Dev drapes his arm over the back of Jenny's chair, silently and probably unknowingly giving her his full support. I rub my hand over my chest, trying to ease the ache that appears there. Jealousy has never been a part of my repertoire before, but damn, it's hitting me hard right now. *Why does everybody else get to be happy?* I know the answer to that question, which only pisses me off more. *Charlie.* I need a do-over for my life. Karma is such a bitch.

Then I think about Lucky. He's not happy either. That's probably why he's not here. Could it be that I made him more miserable than he already was? *Great. Awesome. Just what I needed.* I shove thoughts of him aside and focus all my attention on Ozzie so I don't start crying like a damn baby.

"For this job, we need to get into some Twitter accounts and possibly some Facebook accounts, too." Ozzie looks over at Jenny. "Is that something you can do?"

She nods. "Of course. Not a problem." Whenever Ozzie or anyone talks to Jenny about her work, her personality totally changes. She turns from a marshmallow into a tiger. I like seeing that in her. It gives me hope that she won't completely fall apart if we're ever in a tight spot together.

"Are you going to need Lucky's help?" Thibault asks.

Jenny looks around. "Where is Lucky? He didn't answer the text I sent earlier this morning."

I don't say anything, hoping Thibault will explain it off in a way that doesn't get her too interested. She's already way too curious about what happened between us Friday night.

As usual, my bad luck holds. Before Thibault can speak, May pipes up. "Something happened with him this weekend. And Toni." She looks at me, her eyes sparkling.

I scowl at her, seriously itching to throw my mug and all its contents across the table. "Nothing happened."

Thibault speaks up, cutting into what May was going to say next. "All we need to know right now is if Lucky has to be involved in the mission. That's it."

Jenny looks from me to Thibault and then to May, her expression telling me she's confused, but she finally settles on our second-in-command, answering his question. "I don't need Lucky to do what Ozzie mentioned. If all you want is to get into accounts and monitor them, I can handle that on my own."

Thibault nods. "Great. That's what I wanted to hear." He looks to Ozzie. "What else do we need?"

"Surveillance on three different targets, but we don't know yet where any of it should be set up. First, we'll take a look at the accounts, then we'll try to figure out the exact locations from that."

"What do you need me to do?" I ask. I have to be kept busy. All this free time is giving me too much room to think, too much space for my mind to wander in.

"Toni, you're with May. Hop in the van and drive around the general Mid-City and Treme areas, see what you can see, scope it out. Take some shots."

"You think we'll need the Parrot?" I really hope he says yes to that. I like flying the drone, even though I suck at it. May has been giving me lessons, being some kind of weird-ass savant with the thing herself. I couldn't believe it the day she flew the thing right up to the top of a pole, as if she'd been doing it all her life and not for the first time ever. It would have pissed me off if it hadn't been so impressive. She's only gotten better since.

"I don't think so," Ozzie says. "Not right away. You can bring it, but I don't think you'll need it until later. It's going to take Jenny some time to get what she needs, I would guess."

Ozzie looks at Thibault. "I need you on the horn with the detective in charge of the case. He might be able to give you some information that can help." He pauses and looks down at his notes. "Although, from what I'm hearing, they're pretty much clueless at this point. Unfortunately, it seems like time is running out. They're hearing chatter that something big is about to go down, so the chief wants us to put a rush on this."

Jenny speaks up. "Why are we being asked to help?" She pauses and looks at the team. "Is it okay for me to ask that question? It's just that it helps me to know all the details, even the ones that might seem insignificant. They sometimes lend meaning to messages, especially ones that might have some code-words dropped in."

Ozzie looks uncomfortable. "All I can say right now, because I haven't been given all the information, is that the chief suspects that somebody inside the department is helping these guys out. Making it easy for them to make clean getaways and hide their presence."

May's eyes widen. "A mole?" She looks up at Ozzie. "How come you didn't tell me that part before?"

"I just got the information. Of course it goes without saying that we're not going to talk about this outside the team. We don't know how far or how deep this connection to the gangs goes, so keep it cool. Don't assume anything. I don't want you to ignore things you're seeing because you think you know the whole story."

Everyone around the table nods, their expressions serious and their senses on alert. I'm proud to be one of the team, especially on days like today. The fact that the New Orleans Police Department puts its trust in us is impressive, especially considering the fact that most of us were frequent visitors to their overnight jail when we were young.

Back then, we were always looking for trouble. It was Ozzie's stint in the military that made everything right for us. When he got out, he was like a runaway freight train the way he ran us down without stopping. He told us how it was going to be and how we were going to work together, act like upstanding citizens and get our shit straight. We weren't getting anywhere fast. The world was kicking our asses on a regular basis, and Ozzie was offering a steady paycheck. Since we were all pretty much lost souls wandering around looking for trouble, it seemed like a good idea.

He'd saved all his money while he served, so he had a big chunk to get his security business started. It wasn't long before the job started paying for itself, and our reputation got around. Our *new* reputation, that is—the one that we are a group of people who can get the job done no matter what, a team who comes in like darkness itself, hidden, undetectable, invisible . . . gathering information and feeding it to the cops so they can use it for whatever they need. We can do simple things like getting evidence that can be used to convince a judge to sign off on a search warrant, all the way on up to the most complicated stuff, like gathering evidence that'll be used in a murder trial.

Just last month we helped put away a guy for twenty-five years. He won't ever smell freedom again, since he's already in his seventies—a lifetime of crime, stopped finally with the aid of the Bourbon Street Boys. We got a letter of appreciation from the chief and a five-thousand-dollar bonus, paid out of the cache of drug money that came in from the bust. Having been inside the system and out of it, I can easily say I much prefer working with the good guys.

Ozzie hands May a folder. "Here are a few maps with some areas highlighted that Thibault and I think might be good to take a look at, get some shots of. Familiarize yourselves with the neighborhoods. You can head over there now, as soon as you're done with your coffee." Ozzie switches his focus to the group. "The rest of you, stick around, and we can discuss our next moves and do the follow-up on cases we're closing out."

I stand, bringing my coffee mug over to the sink. May's shoulder to shoulder with me in no time.

"I love working with you, Toni. Maybe when we're out there driving around, we can talk about wedding plans together. I'd really like to get your input."

And I thought Lucky being gone was the worst thing going on in my life. "Maybe. But we might be too busy." Maybe the stars and planets will align and a drug dealer will make a run at the van.

I can only hope.

CHAPTER EIGHT

W e're not two minutes into our drive before May starts in on me. "So, what happened with Lucky on Friday?"

I try to act like I'm too focused on the road to answer her question, but does that stop her? No. Of course it doesn't.

"You guys were both there and then you weren't. We just played one game of pool. Why didn't you come back there with us?"

"I was busy."

"Busy? Busy doing what?"

"Drowning my sorrows." I regret the words as soon as they leave my mouth.

"Sorrows? Are you sad?"

I shake my head. "No. I'm happy. My life is grand."

I can sense May frowning at me in my peripheral vision.

"I can't tell if you're being sarcastic or not." She pauses a few seconds. "Do you want to talk about it?"

I look over at her. "You do realize who you're talking to, right?"

She smiles. "Yes, but that doesn't mean I don't have hope. When are you going to open up to me, Toni? I'm impossible to resist forever, you know."

The strongest man I know has found that to be true, so she might be right, but I'm in no mood for it right now, and I can't imagine ever being there. "Not in this lifetime."

"Do you think Lucky's okay?" She's trying another tack, but I can't ignore the worry her words cause me.

"Why wouldn't he be?"

She shrugs. "I don't know. He has issues. And I don't think Sunny is doing so well."

My grip on the wheel tightens. I can't believe I'm suddenly worried about a stupid fish. "What's wrong with it?"

"You mean with *him*. Watch your pronouns, girl. Sunny is a *boy*, he's not an *it*."

"Whatever." I roll my eyes. I'll never get the fish thing.

"Jenny and I had a long talk about Lucky and his relationship with Sunny. We figured out some pretty interesting things."

I have a short laugh at that. "With no effort or input from Lucky, I suppose." I can just see the two of them, psychoanalyzing everyone on the team, assuming a bunch of crap that isn't there, making everything seem way more interesting than it actually is.

May sounds very satisfied with herself when she responds. "Actually, I'll have you know that Lucky and Jenny have shared a lot of information with each other. They've become pretty good friends."

I hate that this makes me jealous. They work together all the time. It would be totally natural for them to talk when they spend so many hours on the job with no one else around. Besides, the relationship between Jenny and Dev is totally solid. She'd never cheat on him.

You'd think with all this rational thought going for me, I'd be fine with the little story May is telling me, but I'm not. I'm ready to cry like a big, fat baby. I must be totally PMS-ing. My attempt at calculating my next period's arrival date is drowned out by May's musings.

"Lucky told Jenny that he really misses his sister, and Sunny is like his only connection to her now. I hate to think what's going to happen to Lucky when Sunny dies. I don't think he's going to handle it well."

"Lucky's strong. He'll be fine."

She shakes her head. "Just because someone is strong, it doesn't mean that they handle loss well. And it doesn't mean they won't fall apart when bad things happen."

I pull up to a stop sign, annoyed at May and the stupid shit she's talking about. I shake my head but say nothing.

"Don't you agree? Or do you think that a strong person has to be tough a hundred percent of the time?"

I tap my thumbs on the steering wheel, not sure I even want to answer. All it will do is encourage her, and May doesn't need any encouragement to run her mouth at sixty miles an hour.

"What's the matter? Cat got your tongue?"

I shake my head. "Nope. Just not in the mood to chitchat."

May shrugs. "That's okay. I can chitchat enough for the both of us."

The light turns green and I take off, right along with May's mouth.

"Did you know that Lucky takes his fish to the vet? Could you imagine? Him sitting there in the waiting room surrounded by cats and dogs and his bowl with the goldfish in it?"

"I doubt he brings the fish over in a bowl."

"Huh. You might be right about that. Too splashy. What do you think he uses? A Ziploc?"

"Who cares? It's just a fish."

"Uh-oh. You'd better be careful."

I look over at her because she sounds genuinely concerned. "Be careful about what?"

"Be careful about blowing off things that are really important to somebody you care about."

Now I'm genuinely angry, but I don't think it's May causing this emotion to well up in me. There's a tingle of truth coming through with her words that I can't deny. It's just that I'm not good with the stuff she's talking about.

Despite my misgivings, I take May's bait. "I don't see what the big deal is about a goldfish, even if it was his sister's. It's not like it's warm-blooded. It's not like you could cuddle up in bed with it or take it for a walk."

May sighs. "I agree with you; dogs are much more interesting pets from my point of view, but it's not my point of view or yours that matters, is it?"

She's definitely waiting for me to answer, and at this point, if I keep avoiding her, she's going to figure out that this whole conversation bothers me and then there will be no rest for the wicked, a.k.a. *me*.

I shrug. "I don't know. I guess."

"If you really love somebody, you have to look at the things that are important to them through *their* eyes. You can't look at it through your own. You can't put your own judgments or your own history on it. You just have to accept it. If Lucky says goldfish are awesome, goldfish are awesome. Period."

"What if the thing they love is bad for them?"

"You think a goldfish is bad for Lucky?"

I shake my head, memories of Charlie haunting my brain as usual. "No. The goldfish is fine, but you said that if somebody I love really likes something, I should just accept it and be good with it. What if it's not a goldfish? What if it's something bad?"

"That doesn't count. When a friend is doing something that's bad for them, that could really hurt them, you have to step in. You have to be a good friend. If you don't, then you're not really much of a friend at all, are you?"

I wonder if May realizes just how much each one of her state-ments is affecting me. It's like she's punching me in the gut with every sentence. Am I Lucky's friend? Am I doing the right thing by him? I wish I knew the answers to those questions. He deserves to have good people in his life, people who look out for him. People who think his fish is awesome even when it isn't.

"You should call him." May nods, absolutely convinced that her advice is golden.

I, however, do not share that feeling. "No way. He doesn't want to hear from me."

"I don't believe that."

There's a weird tone in her voice, so I pull over to the side of the road and look at her. "Why do you say that?" My heart is beating way too fast.

She smiles, looking very sneaky in the process. "I told you . . . Jenny and I have talked about this a lot, and she's with Lucky all the time, so . . ." She shrugs, way too satisfied with herself.

My eyes narrow at her sly expression. If you've ever seen a sly expression on a marshmallow, you'd know why I'm suddenly dis-tressed. "What did you do?"

She holds up her hands. "I didn't do anything. It's possible that Jenny may have made some inquiries or suggestions on your behalf, but I'm completely innocent."

I'm shaking my head as I move the van forward into the flow of traffic. "You have got to be kidding me." Equal measures of panic and exasperation fight to express themselves. I grit my teeth to keep both emotions at bay. My jaw starts to ache. *Jenny the matchmaker strikes again.*

May finally stops talking, which only gives my mind the space to go crazy. Paranoia fills me. What did Jenny say to Lucky? Is that why he was messing around with me at the bar? Does he think I'm into him?

I have twenty questions to ask May and her silly sister, but if I do that, it'll just give them more fuel for their fire. Their matchmaker radar will start blaring and both of them will put all of their sticky, gooey, marshmallowy efforts into getting Lucky and me together. Lucky probably already figured out what they were doing and now he's lying low, waiting for me to lose interest. *God, how awful.*

I say nothing about this fresh hell that's just become the focus of my ire. I grind my teeth and squeeze the steering wheel as we pull into the Mid-City area, off Tulane Ave.

"You'd better go get your stuff," I say to my partner in measured tones. "We're getting close."

"Okay. Cool." May leaves the front seat and climbs into the back of the van. The banging around tells me she's getting out her photography equipment.

"Am I just doing stills, or are we going to shoot some video, too?" she asks.

"Better be prepared for both." Ozzie's and Thibault's instructions were pretty vague. I'm not sure what they expect us to come up with just driving around these neighborhoods, but my plan is to get the lay of the land, so I know the escape routes and the places where the different street thugs hang out during the day.

It's always the case when the weather is decent, which it happens to be right now, that groups of guys hang around outside chatting. Curbside is where deals get done in the Sixth Ward. We never see the big players out here, of course, but the little guys always lead us to the big ones eventually.

May joins me in the front seat. She sits down and buckles up. Seconds later, her attention is on something else. "Look! Hookers." She lifts her camera and shoots off a few frames. When she's done, she takes a look in her viewfinder and smiles. "She's actually really pretty. Did you see her legs? Gorgeous. I wish I had legs like that." She sighs.

I snort. "You'd need a set of testicles to have those legs."

May looks at me, confused. "What?"

"She's a tranny. She's got testicles tucked up underneath that miniskirt. You don't get legs like that if you're born with parts like ours."

"Oh." May looks into the viewfinder again, zooming in. "I don't see any bulges. Are you sure?"

"They tuck that shit up in there so far it practically disappears."

"Seriously?" She frowns. "I'm asking Ozzie about this. I'm not sure I believe you. I think you're messing with me."

I laugh, enjoying her naivety. "Whatever. Ask him."

"Don't think I've forgotten about our earlier conversation." May's voice has gone a little sinister.

"What're you talking about?"

"You know what I'm talking about. Lucky. I really think you should talk to him. Open up a little. Let him see your softer side."

"I don't have a softer side."

"Sure you do. Everyone does. I know that you killed someone, but that doesn't mean you're a criminal. I mean, you *used* to be a criminal, but you're not anymore. It's not like it means you're a horrible, awful person who can never be happy again."

The van jerks to a squealing stop as I slam on the brakes. A horn honks loudly behind us, but I ignore it. I look over at her, shooting bullets at her with my eyes. "Are you *kidding* me?"

She squirms a little in her seat. "Too far? Oops. I'm sorry. I've been meaning to talk to you about it for a really long time, and I've been trying to think of the best way to work my way up to it, but I guess it just spilled out ahead of schedule."

"I don't get where you think it's any of your damn business." I seriously want to slap her right now, or worse, but I'm not ready to deal with the aftereffects that would come from Ozzie if I indulged.

He wouldn't understand. He thinks her inane chatter and complete lack of personal boundaries are cute.

"I don't mean you any harm, Toni. I respect you, and I like you a lot. I've got your back, no matter what. The only reason I would ever say anything to you about something so private and personal is because I care about you." She sounds like she's about to cry. "It's the anniversary today, right?"

I get the van moving again, not sure I trust myself to respond and not be vicious. As far as I can tell, she's the only one who remembers that horrible fact about my life, and it makes me want to rage against the world. *Why hasn't anyone else said anything? Why May?* My anger is like a poison, leaking into my veins from somewhere dark, a deep hole inside me that is pure blackness. I served my time and I learned my lesson, but that didn't get rid of the fury that sometimes threatens to take over. May is very wrong about me. I am a horrible, awful person.

"I know you're mad, so I'll stop talking about it, but I just want you to know that you're important to me and you're really important to Ozzie, and if you want to talk about what's going on in your life or what's happening with you or with your love life or whatever, we are both here for you. We only want what's best for you and will make you happy."

I speak through nearly gritted teeth. "Good to know." And just like that, my day is completely and utterly ruined. Not that it wasn't already shit, but this just puts a cherry on top of it. Not only is the one guy who I really care about blowing me off after having awesome sex with me, but the man who practically saved my life is talking about me behind my back with his Jet-Puft marshmallow girlfriend, who still has no business being on the team as far as I'm concerned.

CHAPTER NINE

I want to forget the whole conversation that happened between May and me, but it's impossible. Snippets float along currents in my mind, still haunting me as I pull up to the warehouse. When I stop the van in the spot where Jenny was accosted by Charlie's brother Rowdy, my stomach churns. *Ugh.* When will this shitstorm end?

After spending four hours cruising the neighborhoods marked out on the maps we were given, we now have enough intel to sift through over the next couple days. Hopefully, Thibault got some information from the detective in charge of the case so we can get started with placing our surveillance. I definitely need something to occupy my time and mind.

Flashes of Lucky's face and the expression he's been wearing lately carry new meaning for me. Has he been asking for help this whole time, and I've been ignoring it? Too focused on myself to recognize someone else's pain? I feel selfish and self-absorbed.

The crazy thing is, I think I could actually be better at managing someone else's pain than my own. Maybe getting a little more involved in Lucky's life might not be the worst idea in the world. It doesn't have to be about sex or a relationship; it could be about our friendship, something that's been there for as long as I can remember.

A tiny piece of my heart is telling me that it's possible May and Jenny are right. Maybe I should call Lucky, push him a little harder. Whenever someone offers to help me, I always say no, just like Lucky does. The only one who's ever gotten through my defenses is Ozzie, and only because he pushed through. Like a steamroller, he drove right over me, giving me no choice but to let him in. I thank God for that; otherwise I'd probably be dead by now. He saved me.

The question is, does Lucky need saving? And am I the right person for the job? Or am I just saying all this to convince myself because I want to sleep with him again? I can't trust myself to do the right thing. I'm horrible with men, and not just regular old horrible. I'm the worst. My relationships end in murder.

But Lucky deserves at least an attempt; that much I know. If I'm wrong, I'll look like an ass for a few days, max. I can handle that. And if I'm right, and Lucky does need someone, maybe I can save him like I got saved. That would help my karmic balance, right? Take a life, save a life?

I feel energized as these thoughts come to their logical conclusion: I need to call Lucky. I need to make him listen to me. Maybe I'll even go over to his place, take a look at his goldfish, and tell him how pretty it is. Or handsome. *How does he even know it's a boy? Do goldfish have penises?* I picture myself standing in front of the tank. "That's a nice goldfish you've got there, Lucky. He's so . . . gold."

Whatever. I'll figure it out when I get there. I press the button that will open the warehouse door and wait the few seconds it takes for it to open wide enough to admit the van.

"So, what are we going to do now?" May asks.

67

"Go upload your photos and trash the bad ones. I'll write down my thoughts about what we saw in a report for the team."

"Sounds good."

I wait until May has gone off to her cubicle before pressing the speed dial for Lucky. He's number seven on my phone, obviously. *Lucky seven*, I think to myself as I wait for the call to connect.

His voicemail picks up, and I disconnect. Then I dial again. He thinks he can turn me over to voicemail? *Uh, no.* He can definitely kiss my ass on that.

My next call goes to voicemail too. This time I don't hang up. "Lucky, it's me," I say into the recording. "Answer your phone."

I disconnect and then hold down the seven key again. This time the call goes directly to voicemail without a single ring. I bang my closed fist on the doorframe of the van, trying to decide what to do next.

"Hey, you!"

I look up and see Thibault standing at the top of the stairs. "What's up?" I ask, trying to sound casual and not like I'm all tied up in knots.

"You got a minute?"

"Maybe two." I don't like the tone I hear coming from Thibault. It's got that older-brother-lecture timbre to it.

"Stay there. I'm coming down."

There's a small piece of me that wants to turn around and run out the warehouse door, which is ridiculous because I'm a grown woman and I could take my brother down if I really wanted to.

"Come on." He gestures for me to follow him over to the exercise equipment. He takes a seat on the bench press, and I grab a spot on another machine nearby.

"What's up?" I ask.

His voice is soft and there's a hint of compassion there, which immediately pisses me off. It's like there's some kind of conspiracy to get under my skin by giving me advice today. I steel myself for the onslaught of good intentions.

"What happened with you and Lucky on Friday?"

I stand, deciding it's better to take off rather than get into a wrestling match with a guy who's got fifty pounds on me. I'm not quite mad enough to overcome that. I need a really dark, righteous anger to pull that off.

"Just sit down," he says, gesturing with his hand for me to take a seat, like he's annoyed with my completely normal, emotional reaction. "I'm not busting your balls. I really need to know. There's something going on."

I do as he says, my suspicions not completely gone, but my curiosity engaged. "What?"

"First, tell me what happened."

"Nothing happened."

"Don't lie to me. I know Lucky was at the house and that he went home with you."

I hiss out my annoyance, hoping he'll take the hint, but he doesn't. Of course. He stares at me, fully expecting me to spill my guts.

"He didn't go home with me, okay? I got in the cab and he jumped in without my permission. Then he said he had to talk to me about something, so he came inside for a little bit."

"What did he say after he came inside?"

I'm caught in a trap I laid for myself. *Awesome.*

"Nothing. Much."

Thibault leans in, resting his forearms at his knees. "I need you to be honest, Toni. I'm not here to judge."

I stand, too antsy and pissed to remain seated. I feel vulnerable and attacked. "Judge? Judge what? It's my life, and I live it how I want. I served my time, okay? I don't need a parole officer anymore." I finished that nonsense six months ago, thank you very much.

Thibault drops his head, shaking it and sighing.

"What?" I'm pissed at him for acting like I'm the asshole.

He looks up at me, his expression almost tortured. "Why does everything have to be so difficult with you?"

My heart feels like it's cracking again. I'm a burden; I know I am. I always have been. "Difficult? Fuck you."

Thibault stands all of a sudden and gets in my face. "Fuck me? No, fuck *you*, Toni. I asked you to talk to me, as your brother, as the guy who nearly lost his mind when you got taken to jail, and you can't come down off that high horse of yours for a single fucking second to show me a little respect and to show a little compassion for a friend!"

My mouth hangs open but nothing comes out. I had no idea that my brother was so disappointed in me. He's never said a word before. It's like a pit has opened up in the middle of my heart and it's sucking the beating muscle right into it. Pretty soon, I'm not going to have any heart left.

He turns away and runs his fingers through his hair. "Shit. Sorry. That came out all wrong."

I walk backward, needing to put space between us. "No, man. It came out just right. I get it." I have to leave. I can't stand here and tell him I'm sorry that I am who I am. That I fucked up. That I don't deserve to be here. He already knows all that, apparently. And I definitely don't want him to apologize for how he feels. That's not fair to him. I'd feel exactly the same way if it were me in his shoes.

"Where're you going?" he asks as I walk quickly across the floor.

"I've gotta go do something. See you later." I can barely get the words out, my throat is so damn sore from holding back tears. I'm not going to let them fall, though. This is life. These are the breaks. I just need to suck it up.

I hop into my car and reverse out of the warehouse as fast as I can without laying rubber on the floor, because Ozzie hates that.

I'm down the road a mile or two before the dam breaks. By the time I get home, the front of my shirt is soggy and my face looks like shit in the rearview mirror.

I don't even realize I'm not alone until I'm halfway up my front walk. It's then that I see a shadow on my front porch. As I draw closer, I realize it's Lucky sitting on my porch swing, and he's holding a clear glass bowl in his lap.

CHAPTER TEN

I go slowly up my front walkway, trying to gauge Lucky's mood as I quickly wipe remnants of smeared makeup from my face. His head is down, and he's staring into his goldfish bowl. He could be asleep, he's sitting so still.

I clear my throat as I approach the porch, but he doesn't lift his head.

"Hey, Lucky. What's going on?" I walk up the three steps and angle myself toward the porch swing.

He looks up. His face is completely expressionless. "I don't know why I'm here."

I gesture at his pet. "Looks like you brought somebody over for a visit." May's advice comes back to me, especially that part about seeing things through Lucky's eyes and not my own. It's not a little puppy he's got in his hands; it's a cold-blooded piece of bait for a dinner-sized fish from what I can see. But to him, it's everything. So, I guess for today Sunny the goldfish will be my everything too. I can fake it for a friend.

"He's not doing so good," Lucky says.

"Why don't you guys come inside? I'll make you some coffee. Or we can have a beer."

"Beer sounds good." Lucky stands, careful not to splash any water out of the bowl. He does such a good job of it, I imagine he's probably had a lot of practice. An inane vision of him taking his fish for a daily walk pops into my mind.

I push the image aside, knowing it will unfairly influence how I see him right now. He needs a space that's judgment free, where he can just be his fish-freaky self and not worry about what someone might be thinking. I can step into his shoes and see this fish like he does. *I think.*

I open the door wide so he can walk through with his fish and not bump into anything. I lock up behind him, all too aware of the fact that there are people out there who would love to find me at home and come at me with an unpleasant surprise. Charlie had several brothers and cousins, and every last one of them harbors a mean streak a mile wide. Aside from Rowdy getting stupid with Jenny a few months back, they've put off messing with me for over two years, but that doesn't mean they're not out there biding their time. Most of them are smart enough to know that the more distance there is between Charlie's death and any accident that might befall me, the less chance there is that they'll be looked at as suspects. Rowdy jumped the gun on that program, though I'm not surprised; even Charlie used to joke that his little brother was one pork chop short of a mixed grill.

"Where do you want me?" he asks, standing in my front hallway, looking lost and ridiculous. He's got that leather jacket on again, the one I love so much, but near his waist in both hands is the fishbowl. And he's right; Sunny doesn't look so good. The fish is sharing time between floating and swimming weakly in circles.

"Go into the living room. You can put Sunny on the table and we can watch him from the couch. I'll be right there."

I keep it cool, walking at a regular pace into the kitchen, even though I feel like running. *What if Sunny floats before I get back? Will*

Lucky leave? I don't want him to go. I want him to stay. The thought makes me nervous as hell.

I don't know what he really wants to drink, even though he said a beer. I start a pot of coffee, thinking it might be good to stay sober for this, but grab two beers from the fridge too. Holding them in one hand, I reach up and grab a bag of chips and some pretzels from a bowl on the counter before joining him in the other room.

I sit down next to Lucky, busying myself with the refreshments. He's in a trance staring at his fish. I'm not sure he even notices I'm back.

I nudge him, handing him a beer. "I made coffee too if you want."

He takes the beer from me, twists the cap off, and swallows half of it in three big gulps, never taking his eyes off his cold-blooded friend.

I shrug. "Beer it is, then." I sip at mine, knowing that two drunk people in this house would be a really bad idea. We already made that mistake, and I don't want to make it again.

"I took him to the vet," Lucky says. "They said there's nothing they can do. He's just old."

"That sucks. How old is he, anyway?" I want to open the bag of pretzels, but I feel like that would be insensitive right now.

"He's six. The Internet says they can live for thirty years, but my vet says in his experience they only live a year or two. So I guess six is pretty good."

"Yeah, that's great, especially when you're kicking it old school." I smile and point my beer bottle at the bowl.

"Old school?"

I immediately feel like an asshole. I didn't mean to, but I pretty much just told him that he's killing his fish by keeping it in a little bowl.

My smile falters and turns into something more like a grimace. "I just meant . . . you know, at the dentist, he's got that big old rig with all the different fish in it and bubbles going and that little treasure chest and skeleton in the bottom . . ." I take another slug of my beer and go ahead and open the bag of pretzels, figuring if I stuff my mouth full of food, maybe I'll be unable to stick my foot in there anymore.

"This is just what I use to transport him around in. Normally he's in a bigger tank alone. I never wanted him to get sick or hurt. Other fish could be bullies and hurt him or make him sad."

I nod, as if this makes all the sense in the world. "I gotcha." Should I be worried about Lucky's mental health? He's talking about this fish like it's a kid going to grade school or something.

The room falls completely silent, except for the sounds of me eating. Normally, I don't notice myself chewing, but it's like I have a microphone up to my mouth. Every crunch of pretzel I make is like the beginnings of an earthquake. I take another swig of my beer to try to dampen the noise.

"I could use another." Lucky puts his empty bottle on the table gently, his eyes never leaving the fish bowl.

I stare at the empty bottle. On a good day, I would happily get any of my teammates drunk as a skunk, but tonight I'd better not. If there were ever a night for sobriety, this is it. I fear what might come out of my mouth if my lips were loosened by alcohol.

"I've got something better. I'll be right back."

I go into the kitchen and dump the rest of my beer into the sink. Pulling out two mugs from the cabinet, I fill them both with black coffee. I'm pretty sure we're going to need to be sober for what's coming next.

Back in the living room, I find Lucky tapping on the glass. His fish isn't swimming anymore. I move across the floor quickly, setting the coffee mugs down on the table. I sit really close to him and lean in. "Is he okay?"

Lucky doesn't say anything. He just keeps tapping on the glass.

I take his finger and hold it away from the bowl, enveloping it in both of my hands.

"What are you doing?" he asks, looking at me.

"Shush." I point at the bowl with our hands to get his focus off me. "Let him be. Give him some peace and quiet."

"What?"

I turn my head to look at Lucky. His face is so close, I can literally see lines of pain etched into his skin. He looks twenty years older today than he did on Friday.

I try to put into words what I'm thinking as I hold his hand in mine. "In my last moments, I wouldn't want somebody banging a drum next to my head. I'd want peace and quiet. Serenity. Life is chaotic enough. We deserve something soft in the end."

It's not what I gave Charlie, and that tortures me every day. It probably will for the rest of my life. He went out in a hail of bullets, surrounded by feelings of hatred and anger, revenge and darkness. I don't want that for the silly fish, because he's Lucky's fish.

Lucky puts his other hand on top of mine and nods. He looks over at the fish again, but not before I see a tear fall. "You're right. Respect. Sunny deserves that."

"We all do. Fish or people."

The fish gives a couple more flutters of his fins, and then it's all over. He goes belly up, and a few seconds later the water stops moving.

I don't know what to do, and I don't know the right thing to say, so I just sit quietly, trying to empty my brain of any thoughts. We stay there, holding hands, until the sun goes down and the temperature drops. When my automatic light timer—set to go off at 6:30 p.m.—flicks on the living room lamp, we're still on the couch.

The sudden light coming on seems to bring Lucky out of the trance he was in. He sits back, letting our hands slide apart, his leather jacket making a squeaking sound as it rubs against itself.

I turn around to look at him, speaking in a hushed tone. "What can I get for you?"

He shakes his head, staring off into space. "Nothing."

I stand. "I'm going to make us some dinner."

"I'm not hungry."

"I don't care. You're going to eat anyway."

I feel bad leaving him in the room with Sunny floating there in front of him, but maybe he needs some time alone with the last link he had to his sister.

I'm way sadder than I expected to be over this. It's just a fish. But when I see Lucky sitting there on the couch all by himself, tears falling down his cheeks in the dim light, I realize Sunny was never *just* a fish. Just like Charlie was never *just* a problem. We all look at things in our lives and give them labels because that's how other people see them, but that doesn't mean it's who or what they really are to us.

Charlie wasn't just a boyfriend; Charlie was my darkness. He represented the anger that has been inside me since I was a very young girl, growing up in an abusive and neglectful household. He brought out the worst in me, but he's not to blame; I let him be that person in my life. I let him control me and use me up when I was at my weakest.

Lucky's always had what seems like a really great life, on the outside. He's a smiling fool and has been since the day I met him downtown, standing in an empty lot where an old building had been knocked down months before. He was there using a BB gun to blow holes into junk, and Thibault and I were anxious to give it a try. Until the day Lucky showed up, nobody we knew under the age of fifteen had one of those. We were both eleven at the time.

I never knew much about what went on at his house, since Lucky preferred to be at ours or out on the streets hanging around, but I always got the feeling that it wasn't great. He never invited us over, and, being kids, we never questioned it. It impressed me that despite the situation, whatever it was, he was always happy. Or at least he appeared to be happy. But maybe I was wrong. Maybe he's just as miserable inside as I've been.

I go through the motions of making dinner for two. It's not much, just spaghetti with defrosted meatballs, but it'll do. I'm not much of a cook, which is why I love eating at Ozzie's place. It doesn't matter that I'm the defrost queen tonight, though; I'm sure neither Lucky nor I will taste much of this meal.

A sound behind me makes me jump. I spin around, my wooden sauce spoon in my hand. I still picture Charlie coming at me whenever someone sneaks up on me. Ozzie says it's post-traumatic stress disorder, but I've always been a little high-strung.

Lucky is standing there, his hands in his pockets. "Sorry. Didn't mean to startle you."

I go back to stirring the sauce, making sure it doesn't burn. It came out of a jar, so I just need to heat it through. "No big deal. I'm just finishing up here." I snag a noodle out of the boiling pot with a fork and pinch it. *Perfect.* After turning off all the burners, I reach up into the cabinet next to me and pull out two plates. "Grab yourself a drink."

"I'm not really hungry."

"Doesn't matter. You can watch me eat." I'm not hungry either, but I'm going to force myself to eat this food. It's better than trying to find the right words. I have no idea what I'm supposed to be saying right now so I settle on recruiting him into service. "Grab the forks and spoons out of the drawer, would you?"

Lucky has been in my kitchen enough times to know where I keep everything. I hear banging around and know he's following my orders as I dish out the pasta and then cover it with sauce and two meatballs each. If he doesn't finish his, I'll bring it to work and give it to Sahara and Felix. Then I'll die laughing inside when they both get horrible gas and make May leave the room with her nose pinched.

"What do you want to drink?" he asks me dully.

"Whatever you're having."

The fridge opens and the clang of bottles tells me we're both having more alcohol. I hope that's not a mistake.

I bring the bowls of pasta over to the kitchen table and sit down across from Lucky. There's only room enough for four people sitting in close quarters, so it's intimate. I'm glad there are no candles on the table, or he'd probably think I'm trying to turn this into a date or something. I sit down, staring at my bowl and the steam coming up from the sauce.

Here's where I normally say grace, but it seems like there's something a little extra special in order. I chew the side of my cheek trying to decide what to do. I don't want to upset Lucky by bringing up Sunny, but the little guy in that bowl deserves a mention.

"Do you mind if I say a prayer?" Lucky asks.

I fold my hands over my bowl, resting my elbows on the table, relieved we're on the same page. I tip my head down, putting it on top of my knuckles. "Go ahead."

Lucky lets out a long sigh before he begins. "Dear Lord . . . thank you for this delicious food that I don't think I can eat but it smells really darn good. And thank you for my beautiful friend Toni, who's patient with me when I know patience isn't exactly her strong suit, especially on a day like today when memories of her past are probably kicking her ass. Thank you for Sunny and thank you for my sister. And I'm sorry I'm flipping out and letting you down. Help me to be stronger tomorrow."

"Amen." My heart is in my throat. He remembered what this day means for me. He didn't forget like Ozzie did. And I feel so terrible for him, but I don't know what to do. I lower my hands and look up at him. He's still resting his forehead against his clasped fingers, and his shoulders are shaking.

I have never seen Lucky fall apart like this, ever. I've never seen anyone on our team fall apart like this. Hell, I've never seen anyone outside the movies fall apart like this. It feels like my world is caving in on me.

I do the first thing that comes to mind as a solution. What do I do when shit is falling apart? Whatever I can to try and hold it together. Abandoning my seat, I go over to Lucky and get down on my knees next to his chair, wrapping my arms around his waist. "I'm sorry. I'm sorry, Lucky. This sucks. This really sucks. Please don't be sad." I squeeze him hard.

His arm drops down and wraps around my back. He holds me firmly too, so I grip even harder. We cling to each other in my little dining area, Lucky sniffing and shaking, and before long, I'm crying, too.

I wish I had thought to put music on earlier so he wouldn't hear me now. I feel cold and callous because I mocked his fish before. I'm not doing it now, but I still feel bad about what I said to May and what I thought in my head about Sunny. I should've known what it meant to him. I should've asked more questions. I should've been more involved in his life.

It's been too easy, blaming everything on Charlie and the messed-up place I was in as his girlfriend, but Charlie's been gone for five years, and I've been out of prison for two. I was released just before Lucky's sister died, but even while imprisoned I could have kept in better contact with him, asked more questions, told Thibault to intervene when I sensed something was off.

It's been two years since Lucky lost her, but I get how something like that can stay with you and feel fresh even years later. I just accepted Lucky as this person who seemed okay on the outside, and never bothered to find out that he was tortured on the inside. He must have felt so let down by me. It literally hurts me to realize that about us. And it makes me see that I need to try harder to be a good friend to him, listen to him, talk to him, find out how he's really feeling.

"She was too young," Lucky says through his sobs. "Why did she do it?"

"You're right. Maribelle was too young. But I think she did it because she couldn't think of any other way."

"Any other way to do what?" His sobbing stops for a moment.

"Any other way to escape. The pain. She just wanted to get away from it. She was a teenager. She was really sensitive. Everything hit her twice as hard as it hit everyone else. I didn't know her that well, since she was so much younger than us, but I do remember that. She cried a lot. I remember how she bawled when she read about those animals being euthanized at the shelter. She went nuts over that, remember? She was only seven or eight at the time."

"Yes, I remember." He looks up, his face ravaged by tears.

I wipe one of his cheeks with the backs of my fingers. "She had a tender heart. She was born with it."

"It didn't help having the parents we did." He looks at the ground, his jaw muscle twitching.

"None of us had a safe haven to go home to. That's why we spent so much time shooting your gun in that empty lot." My heart twists in my chest. Lucky helped save me. I wonder if he knows this. I don't want to say it, though; he'll think I'm crazy.

"But she was too little to hang with us," he says, oblivious to my internal melodrama.

81

"Yeah. And guns weren't her thing."

He gives a sad laugh. "She was a pacifist from the word go. She hated my BB gun. She was always suspicious that I was using it to shoot birds."

I frown at the idea. Lucky's always been an animal lover, just like his sister. "You would never have done that."

He shrugs. "You and I knew that, but she was suspicious of everyone. She had a hard time trusting people, even me."

"Why do you think that is?" Maybe I'm asking more than I should, but I'm hoping this is the way to get him to a conclusion he can live with about his sister. He blames himself, but he shouldn't. He didn't have anything to do with her death.

"I don't know. Our parents were assholes. I wasn't there."

I shake my head. "I don't accept that. You were there with her a lot. You dragged Maribelle around in a stroller, for God's sake."

He smiles sadly. "It was easier when she was younger. When she got older, we grew really far apart. It's like I didn't even know her anymore."

"When she got older, she started reading the news and seeing the outside world. I think it was too painful for her. She saw too many bad people, too many animals being hurt, too many kids being abused. She fixated on that stuff. It's like she couldn't see the happy things because the sad things took up all her head space."

"Why, though? What made her do that instead of focusing on the good?"

I shrug. "I don't know. Some people are just drawn to that darkness, and they can't let it go." I don't tell Lucky the whole truth: that I get where his sister was when she decided to take her own life, and that if it hadn't been for the team and Ozzie, I might have considered a way out like she had. The difference between her and me is that I was open to getting help, and I had a very strong connection to the guys on the team. She never had much of a connection with anyone; she always lived in her own little world. Even her relationship with Lucky seemed like it was only on the surface.

Lucky slowly lets his arm drop away from me, so I release him too. He rubs his swollen eyes. "I just don't get it," he mumbles. "Why was she in so much pain? Why didn't she reach out?"

I shrug. "I don't know. There's no way for us to know. Just life, probably. Sometimes shit happens, and you fall apart over it. Not everybody can be strong a hundred percent of the time." May's voice is like my conscience now. *Goddamn.*

Lucky bangs his fist on the table, making the cutlery jump. "But I should've been there for her! I'm her brother, for chrissake!"

"Exactly." I use the most soothing tone I have in me. "You're her brother. You're not her parent, you're not her guardian angel, and you're not God. The stuff she went through, the way she tortured herself over the world's problems, was not something you could've solved for her. You couldn't have changed who your sister was, and that was the only solution to her problems. She was who she was, that's it. Just like you are who you are and I'm me. We all have our own demons, but hers overwhelmed her. We're fortunate; we manage to keep them at bay . . . most of the time."

He shakes his head, staring off into the distance. "I don't believe that. I don't believe I couldn't have helped her fight those demons."

"I know you don't. You need therapy."

A smile haunts his lips for a second before it disappears. "That's funny."

I give him a half smile. "What's funny?"

"You telling me I need therapy."

I shrug, not disagreeing over the irony. "Yeah, well, I've got experience in being seriously fucked up. What can I say?"

Lucky reaches down and caresses the side of my face, finally looking into my eyes. "Come on, don't say that. You're perfect exactly the way you are. I wish you would stop being so mean to yourself."

I put my hand over his for a few seconds before pushing it away. It feels strange to have him being so gentle and touchy-feely with me. Not that I hate it or anything, but it's weird when he's never been like that with me before.

"Don't try to butter me up," I say, trying for a more light-hearted mood. "There's only one piece of tiramisu in my fridge and it's mine."

His smile is like a huge laser beam of sunshine hitting me right in the eyeball. He leans down until he's just an inch away from me, our noses almost touching. "Trust me . . . if I want that tiramisu, you're going to give it to me."

I cock a brow up. "I'll wrestle you for it."

"Done." And then his lips are on mine and we're on the kitchen floor, rolling around and tearing each other's clothes off.

CHAPTER ELEVEN

Chair and table legs that get in our way are shoved aside. Shirts are pulled out of waistbands in seconds so our hands are free to explore.

Our passion is different this time, not born of a simple school-girl crush and a few too many beers and teas, but one of two adults who find themselves drowning in myriad emotions that shouldn't coexist: Sadness. Rage. Hope. Longing. Loss. Lust. It's all there.

It surges through me like an electric current, and I can't understand why it's not killing me but instead driving me forward. This is Lucky, the boy I've grown up with and treated as a brother for more years than I care to remember. I should be shoving him away and shouting at him, reminding him what a horrible mistake this is, how it'll ruin everything for the team and destroy our friendship; but I don't do any of those things. I welcome the darkness that's sure to come from this mistake. It's way more familiar to me than the light he's pretending we can share together. I'll deal with the night-mares tomorrow.

"You are so beautiful," he growls in my ear before biting my neck. The weight of his entire body presses mine into the floor.

I reach up and grab his hair with both hands to get him away from my sensitive skin. "Shut up. You don't know what you're talking about." I tilt his head and go right for his neck so I can bite him back.

I'm surprised into stillness when he stops everything, placing his hands on both sides of my face and staring down at me from two inches away. "Toni, don't tell me to shut up. You *are* beautiful. I've always thought that about you."

I search his eyes, trying to figure out what he's getting at. What could possibly be the point of showering me with compliments right now? He knows I'm going to sleep with him. I'm lost for words.

He lets out a long sigh. "Maybe we shouldn't do this." He puts his hands on the floor on either side of my head to hold himself above me in a pseudo-pushup.

I give him a wry smile. "Of course we shouldn't. It was a mistake the first time, and it'll be an even bigger mistake the second."

Slowly, he grins at me, the devil in him coming back to play. "I'm pretty good at making mistakes. In fact, I'm better at making mistakes than I am at doing the right thing."

I urge him down to me by pulling on his upper arms. "Me too."

And then we're kissing again. It's just as hot, only this time it doesn't feel quite as desperate. Now we know. We both know what we're getting into and what this means. It's a mistake, but we're going to have some fun, anyway. Maybe this thing—whatever it is—will help us forget the other stuff in our lives that's causing us pain. Even a short respite is better than none at all.

Lucky pauses again.

"What is it this time?" I ask, sighing exaggeratedly. He's acting like a virgin, the way he keeps hesitating.

He rolls over and pulls his wallet out of his back pocket. "At least let me put a condom on this time. Just to be doubly safe."

It takes a few seconds for his comment to sink in. While he's busy pulling the birth control out of his wallet and unwrapping it, my mind is going haywire. I'm not even sure I heard him right.

"What did you just say?"

He sits up and pulls his jacket and shirt off his upper body in one movement. "You heard me. We need to be doubly careful."

He's undoing his belt now, completely oblivious to my panic.

"But you said you need to put a condom on *this time*. What the hell did you say *that* for?"

His belt is unbuckled and so is the top button of his pants. He hesitates and looks down at me from his kneeling position. "I meant what I said. Last time we forgot, but we should never forget again. If this is going to be a regular thing, we have to be careful. That's all. It's no big deal."

I shove him away from me and get to my feet, my whole body shaking. My voice goes up an octave. "Lucky!"

He's clearly confused. "What?"

"Are you telling me that we didn't use any birth control the other night?!"

Lucky's mouth drops open, but nothing comes out. The only thing I hear is the sound of the condom wrapper hitting the ground when it falls out of his loosened fingers.

I back away, shaking my head. "No. That's not right. We used a condom, I know we did."

He slowly sits down on his butt, bending his knees up to rest his elbows on them. The unused condom dangles in his right hand between his first two fingers. "Sorry, babe. I think we both got caught up in the moment. We didn't use one." He shrugs. "I figured you were on the pill, so I wasn't so worried about it."

My hands go up to my head and my fingers sink into my hair, grabbing some by the roots and pulling as I try to wake myself up from this nightmare. I'm staring at his impossibly handsome face that right now I want to smash with my fist. *How could he have been so careless? How could I have been so stupid?*

Lucky gives me what I used to consider an adorable look. "I guess I was wrong about that?"

I slide my hands down onto my face and scrub it a few times. When I speak, it's through my fingers. "Yes, you were wrong about that. I don't take the pill or anything else."

I hear Lucky get to his feet. I sense when he's close. "Why not?" he asks, finally sounding worried.

I move my hands so I can see him. "Because that shit makes me crazy. I don't do so well when doctors mess with my hormones."

He nods, coming off as very serious. "I can imagine that."

I shove him out of my way as I leave the kitchen. "You need to go."

As I walk past the entrance to the living room, the fishbowl catches my eye, forcing me to stop, forcing me to remember why Lucky is even here in the first place. He didn't come to sleep with me; he came because he was suffering and he didn't know where else to go. And nothing has changed in that respect. He still lost something special today that was a reminder of his sister's death—a tragedy he hasn't been able to move on from yet.

I grab a handful of hair and squeeze again, wishing I could cry and fall apart right here on the hallway floor. But I know I can't. I don't have that luxury of letting myself go nuts, imagining all the ways a child would completely ruin my life, because my friend needs me and that's more important than what *might* be happening in my life. I turn around and shout to him from the hallway. "Never mind. You can stay. I just have to go online for a little bit."

I go into my home office and log on to my computer, praying I'll find an answer to my dilemma. Maybe there's a chart I can consult that'll tell me if I was fertile on Friday or whatever.

I don't know why I'm bothering, though. If it weren't for bad luck, I wouldn't have any luck at all, and I'm not going to assume that just because I slept with a guy named Lucky that I'm suddenly going to become fortunate myself. My ovaries were probably busy throwing out ten big, fat, fertile eggs on Friday night. I can just picture those slutty little eggs, too . . . *Here, spermy, spermy, spermy . . .*

Lucky comes up behind me as I'm scanning ovulation charts. I click on an advertisement for a morning-after pill in my hurry to hide what I'm doing. *Oh well. What's another Commandment broken?*

"Toni, don't." Lucky puts his hands on my shoulders and gently squeezes.

I brush him away angrily. "Don't tell me what to do."

He gets a chair and brings it over, sitting down next to me. "You don't need to panic. The chances of you being . . . whatever . . . are very slim. Let's just ride it out." He reaches up and strokes my upper arm.

My finger freezes in the process of clicking the mouse. I turn to look at him, trying not to let the anguish I'm feeling show in my eyes. I hate how weak and scared I'm acting right now. "You can't be serious. Our entire lives would be destroyed if I got pregnant. Kids hate me, and I don't like them either. I'd be a terrible mother. I'd ruin the kid's life!" I can't get the image of a neglected, lonely little girl out of my head. She looks a lot like Lucky's sister.

"No you wouldn't. That's ridiculous." He glances at the ad on my computer screen and then looks at me, sadder than I've ever seen him. Even sadder than when Sunny went belly up. "So, what are you going to do? Start a spontaneous abortion? Is that really what you want?"

I can't handle it. I can't handle his words or his face or the meaning behind everything. I stand up and scream. "I can't, Lucky! I can't! I can't *do* this!"

The idea of ending another life has me seeing red. I know I'm not being rational, that murdering Charlie by putting five bullets in his chest is not the same thing as taking a morning-after pill, but I can't seem to stop the flood of emotion that surges through me. *Charlie, Charlie, Charlie . . . I murdered a man I was supposed to love. I'm a murderer forever and that will never change.*

I grab the nearest thing and throw it, trying to calm the emotion taking over every inch of me. It smashes against the wall on the other side of the room. Unfortunately, it was one of my late grandmother's antique vases, but I don't let that stop me. The emotions are still there, still eating me alive.

A box of books is next. I tip it over, sending the contents spilling all over the floor. The pillows on the settee call to me after I've trampled the pages. I wish I could shred the material and stuffing into a thousand tiny little pieces, but I lack the strength. Instead, I hurl the cushions against pictures on the walls, knocking them all down. They each fall with a crash of broken glass.

I'm crying as I pause to yell at the ceiling. "Why?! Is this part of my punishment, God? Is this what I get? A lifetime of repenting? A lifetime of ruining someone else's life too?" I see a mirror on the wall throwing my ugly image back at me and go after it with both hands out.

Right before I get there, as I'm reaching to rip it off the wall, steel bands close around me from behind. Lucky is there and he's got me locked down in a full body hold.

"Let me go! Let me *go*, dammit!" I strain to get away and only manage to lift my legs up at the waist. Lucky holds strong, refusing to release me.

"No." He's grunting from the effort of holding on to me. "You need to calm down before you destroy your house."

"I don't care if I destroy my house." Twisting left and right doesn't earn my release, and neither does squeezing his arteries at the wrists. I'm going to tell Dev tomorrow how shitty his escape techniques are.

"You'll care later, trust me. Just calm down and we'll talk this through. This is not the end of the world, Toni. I'm not that big of an asshole."

It's him blaming himself that causes me to finally pause. My body just sags when I realize that he thinks I hate him. I don't hate him at all. I hate me.

Lucky drags me over to the couch that now has no pillows on it and we fall down onto it together. He grunts when his butt hits the heavy boards that make up the frame of the old settee.

"If I let you go, are you going to break something?" he asks right next to my ear.

"I might." I stick my chin out, being stubborn, even though I know I've lost the will to destroy my little world. I'm already regretting the vase. Thank goodness Lucky stopped me before I ruined that mirror. That was one of my grandmother's favorites.

"I'm not an asshole. I'll stand by you, no matter what."

I struggle to break free, but he's not letting me go.

"Why does it make you so angry when I say that?"

"Because. I don't think you're an asshole, and you don't need to stand by me. I can take care of myself."

Lucky slides me over and off his legs so that we're sitting side by side. He forces me to turn and look at him by twisting me toward him. Someone seeing us from the outside would think we were sitting on the couch embracing, when in actuality he's forcing me to look at the emotions written all over his face. They're too intense. I don't want to see what I think his heart is telling me. I don't deserve his kindness.

"You don't have to do everything alone," he says in a soft, kind voice. It's almost pleading in a way. "You have a family. You have me." He shakes me a little, and I can feel his biceps flexing against my arm and back.

"I don't have *you*, you. I have the team, and I have Thibault." I don't want Lucky pledging himself to me because he thinks he might have gotten me pregnant. That's not what we're doing here. This is not a game I am capable of playing and winning. I've already lost enough.

His voice is calmer than mine. "I know you're angry, and I know you're lashing out right now, so I'm going to let that slide."

I shake my head at him. "This is not me angry. This is me being honest. You should know the difference."

He shakes his head at me, joining the battle of wills. "Toni, when are you going to figure out that I *do* know you? I've known you since we were kids. You can't hide from me. You can't pretend you don't care when you do. I know you're scared, and I know you're in panic mode right now, but I don't think you need to be. This shit happens all the time, and people get through it fine."

I press my lips together to keep them from trembling. "We are not other people. We're different. I'm different."

He gives me a sad little smile. "I'll concede that you're special, but I won't agree that there's something wrong with you, which is what I think you're insinuating."

I've run out of energy to fight. I'm so tired now, all I want to do is go to bed. "Lucky, let me go."

"Why? What're you going to do?" He's studying my expression so intently I have to look away.

"I'm going to bed. I just need to get out of here and think."

"I'm coming with you."

I push him away, managing to free myself from his grasp. I stand and shove my hands into my front pockets. "No. You should stay, but stay down here. I'll be fine alone."

I back up a few steps and then turn to go, my feet crunching over the debris. I leave the room without looking behind me and mount the stairs to my bedroom. I make it all the way there before I start crying again. *Holy shit. What have I done now?*

CHAPTER TWELVE

For a long time, thoughts of my worst-case-scenario life swirl around my head, but I'm just getting to the point where I'm drifting off when a vision of Charlie comes into my mind. In my half-sleep state, I let him in.

Most of the time I manage to push memories or thoughts of him away, but I guess, with all that happened with Lucky and the anniversary of Charlie's death being here, it's just impossible for me tonight. The man I killed is standing in front of me with a trail of swirling smoke above his head, let loose from the cigarette that just left his mouth. Dark gray tendrils slip from between his lips as he smiles. It's not a happy expression.

"Look at you," he says. "Who would've thought? Little Antoinette Delacourte becoming a mama." He shakes his head. "Never thought I'd see the day. Maybe we'll have a little boy."

I feel like I'm going to vomit. I know this can't be real, that Charlie can't be here and he can't be the father of my hypothetical baby. He's dead because I killed him. None of what's happening is rational, but it feels completely real. It's like he's standing right here in my bedroom looking down at me in judgment, claiming my future for his own.

Is this what happens when you commit murder? Does the ghost of your victim come back and get to judge everything you do until you die? Control how your life plays out? As awful as it sounds, it also seems fair to me; I took his life and now he's taking mine.

I can't argue the logic of it, but still, I try to shake my head no at Charlie's ghost. I'm not having a baby. I'm not pregnant. It was just a little mistake, and God has already punished me enough.

"You should name him Charlie," the ghost says. More smoke leaks out from behind his teeth. I get the impression that the effect is not from that cigarette that's still between his fingers. It's as if there's a fire burning inside him. I'm sure any moment I'm going to see flames shooting out of his eye sockets.

I whimper in response. I want to cry out, *No!*, but the words won't come.

Charlie's face gets closer, looming over mine and getting bigger and bigger. "Will you call him Charlie? And when he's bad, will you shoot him in the heart? How many times will you shoot him, Bitch? Once? Twice? Five times?"

That's it. I can only take so much shit from a ghost. I reach out to hit him in the face, but he grabs me and holds me down. Charlie's ghost has never been able to do this before. Has the anniversary of his death made him stronger? I'm trapped! I scream, kicking and writhing, trying to get away. He's going to drag me down into hell with him, I know he is!

"Toni! Toni!" A voice is calling me from far away. It's Lucky. *Is he going after Lucky?*

"Lucky!" I scream. "He's here! He's here—run!"

My fist goes up and down hard as I throw a random punch, trying to free myself from the ghost of my mistakes.

"Oof . . . owww . . . dammit, that hurt . . ."

Something jabs me in the back of my neck. It feels like . . . *a chin?* I stop struggling, as I listen to someone experiencing great pain. *Is it Charlie?* For a brief moment, I feel as though I am the victor, that I've defeated the ghost who came to rob me of my life and my friend's life.

"You finally got me in the nads, just like you promised," says a strained voice from behind my back.

My brain finally comes back online, and I realize the voice I heard belongs to Lucky. He's behind me. *Behind me?*

My hand reaches out in front of me and touches sheets. I'm definitely in my bed. *Lucky is in my bed?*

I turn and look at him over my shoulder. The room is dark, but the curtains are open and the moon is full. In its glow, I see Lucky lying on the bed next to me. He's moaning.

"Damn, that was a good shot in the dark," he says between heavy breaths.

I turn over completely and look at him, reaching out to touch his head to make sure he's real. "What just happened?"

Lucky's breathing with difficulty. "You racked me with your fist."

Oh shit. "Do you want me to get some ice?"

"Might not be a bad idea," he groans.

I jump up from the bed and scramble out the door. I snag a bag of frozen okra from my freezer and grab a bottle of beer from the fridge. I've seen the guys go down in practice sessions at work enough times to know that sometimes they need a little bit of both to dull the pain.

I walk back into the room with both held out in front of me. "Here. Sorry about that."

Lucky reaches up with one hand, not moving from his spot on the bed. He puts the bag of vegetables right between his legs and holds it there with both hands, ignoring the bottle.

"I brought you a beer, too."

"I think I've had enough. I'm going to swear off alcohol for the time being, I think."

I put the beer on the nightstand and sit down on the edge of the bed, looking at him. "I told you to stay downstairs, dummy."

He looks up at me, his expression pained. "Which I was happy to do until you started yelling my name."

I frown at him. "You lie. You wish."

He tries to smile but doesn't quite pull it off. "I do wish, but I don't lie. Heard my name several times. I thought someone was up here killing you."

"It felt like somebody was."

Lucky tries to prop himself up on one arm. He looks at me, his voice not quite right yet. "You have nightmares about Charlie a lot?"

I narrow my eyes at him. "You knew it was Charlie? How?"

His smile is more genuine this time. "Well, it was either him or me, and I was kind of hoping it wasn't me."

I roll my eyes. "Shut up. I would never have a nightmare about you."

"Even if I knocked you up?"

I lean over and shove him out of the way, sending him onto his back.

He moans. "Aw, man, that hurt."

"You deserved it."

He's staring up at the ceiling, the bag of okra still gripped between his legs. "So, what if I knocked you up?" He tilts his head to look at me. "Would it be such a horrible, awful, terrible thing?"

Apparently tagging him in the testicles gives him brain damage. "Do you even have to ask that question?" It's so weird being here with Lucky like this. It seems like overnight we're slipping into some other type of relationship that I'm having a hard time defining. He's acting more like a boyfriend now than a brother. *Do*

I want that? Can I handle that? Am I completely deluding myself about how he feels? I don't feel qualified to answer any of my questions.

His hand comes up lazily and lands on my leg. His fingers travel up my thigh. "We'd make a good couple, you know."

I slap his hand away. "Shut up." Somehow, despite my horrible nightmare, suffered just minutes earlier, he's making a smile start to sneak onto my face. I refuse to let it show.

His hand comes back. "I'm serious. Everybody says so. I talk to Jenny about us a lot. She's good with advice. She says I should go for it and stop hiding from my feelings."

I lift his hand up and move it over to the okra. "Anyone who says that is a complete idiot, and you should stop listening to them." I knew it was Jenny getting into his head. May too, probably. Those chicks need to learn to mind their own business, and I'm going to tell them that the next time I see them.

Lucky play-frowns at me. "You are seriously damaging my ego right now. You know that, right?"

I snort. "Believe me, your ego is big enough to handle it."

Lucky frowns for real, going pensive. He reaches up and rubs his chin, wiggling it around a little bit. "Do you think I should grow a beard?"

"Why would you want to do that?"

He looks at me. "Jenny says I should grow a beard because I'm too good-looking. Maybe that's my problem. Maybe I'm too good-looking and that intimidates you."

I can't help it. I laugh. "Lucky, you forget; I've known you since you were, like, eleven years old. Remember those teeth you had?" I pretend to shiver in disgust. "Yikes."

He sticks his front teeth out at me. "Fixed themselves, didn't they? No braces, baby."

This is the Lucky I know, not the one sobbing over things he can't change. I'm more comfortable on what feels like solid ground.

"Maybe," I say, "but every time I look at you, all I see are those buck teeth."

"Seriously?" He sounds almost hurt.

I scoot back on my bed so I can lean on my pillows against the headboard. Lucky watches me go.

"Remember when we decided to make that clubhouse over on that bare lot where you were shooting your BB gun, the first day we met you?"

Lucky drags himself up to the headboard with me and lies on his back, staring at the ceiling. He's wearing a nostalgic expression that probably mirrors my own. "Yeah, I remember that. That was the coolest day of my life."

I laugh, but when I realize he's serious, I stop. "Really? Why?"

He looks at me. "Because the prettiest girl I ever laid eyes on came over to me and asked if she could try my gun. And when she couldn't hit the broad side of a barn with it, she asked me to show her how to shoot. And *then,* when I knocked all the cans off the wall, she told me I was pretty cool. Remember, I had those buck teeth, so any compliment was a big deal."

He probably expects me to shove him for saying that, but I don't bother. I'm ignoring his ridiculous assertions of having an infatuation with me since way back when. Talking to Jenny the overly romantic matchmaker has made him see his past in a way he never did before. I get it; it's nicer thinking of it that way than focusing on our real lives, on our parents and the reasons why we spent so much time not at home.

God, life was so easy when we were kids. We had no responsibilities, no parents hassling us or getting in our way—they were always happy to have us gone, too caught up in their own problems to deal with us—and no Charlie. I hadn't yet made any mistakes. Except maybe for that one big mistake I made not sticking with the buck-toothed nerd. He showed a lot of promise, even then.

He taps my leg with the back of his arm. "What are you thinking?"

"I was just thinking how life was so much easier back then, and how I wish I could start over."

"We can start over. You and me. Let's have a do-over."

I smile again, transported back to the memories of kickball. Same dirt lot, same group of friends. "Do-overs. Those were awesome. You could totally screw up and just yell *Do-over!* and if everybody agreed, you did it—erased the mistake and tried again." If we had only known the true power of the do-over back then and appreciated the fact that we couldn't carry it with us into the real world, we probably never would've grown up. "But we don't get do-overs as adults," I say. "When you do something, it's done, and then you have to live with the consequences." My words pull me back to the present. I look down at Lucky. "What are we going to do if I'm pregnant? Seriously."

He struggles to sit up until he's resting his back against the headboard right next to me. He takes my hand in his and laces our fingers together. We both stare straight ahead at the wall opposite us.

"It's going to be fine," he says. "You're not pregnant. But even if you were, we'd handle it. Just like we've handled everything else growing up together. Just like we handled Charlie, just like we handled Sunny. We're a team. We're going to be fine."

"We're not going to get any do-overs." Not for life and not for our relationship. What's done is done; we are who we are.

"No, no do-overs. But we don't need 'em. Moving forward won't be such a bad thing—I promise. Just wait and see. I'm almost never wrong."

I look over at him, tears shining in my eyes. "It's that *almost* that scares me."

CHAPTER THIRTEEN

One of the many things I love about my job is the fact that sometimes we get so busy, time flies and entire weeks can go by in the blink of an eye. I come in on a Monday and I work crazy hours until Friday, and then I'm relaxing in my living room on a Saturday morning with the newspaper—the entire week is a blur. Lucky and I may have a lot of things to talk about, but that's not going to happen anytime soon. Not with this job taking up all of our head space. He's been buried in computer work with Jenny. I heard through May that they've been pulling all-nighters, which is fine by me. I'm not really looking forward to our next conversation; it's bound to be awkward after all that oversharing we did.

A full week and a half has gone by since Lucky and I have had more than two minutes together. I'm in the back of the surveillance truck with May, and we're sitting a few blocks away from a location that is believed to host several members of the gang we're monitoring. We got this data from some of the tweets being shared between gangbangers. Jenny and Lucky are picking up on some of their code-words, apparently.

"Good," May says. "We're alone and there's nothing going on. Now we can finally talk about my wedding plans."

I'm hunched over the laptop computer screen, trying to figure out if I should focus our drone's camera in a little tighter on the backyard it's surveilling.

"Oh, goody," I say in a flat tone.

Most people would take my obvious lack of enthusiasm as a sign that they should change subjects, but not May.

"I was thinking we would keep it simple. Just the team and my mother, of course. Maybe a couple of other friends. What do you think? Do you think Ozzie would want to keep it small?"

I don't even look up at her. "I'm sure he's already told you what he wants. You should just listen to him."

"Yeah, but you know how men sometimes say one thing but mean another? I'm not sure I believe him."

"You should believe him." I look up at her. "He's going to want something really small. You should probably just elope." *Please, just elope.*

May shakes her head. "I know, right? That's what I was thinking."

I stop working. "I don't get it." I search her expression, looking for the joke that I assume is hidden in there somewhere, but all she does is shrug.

"He told me he wants to invite the police chief, and the chief's family, and a bunch of officers and commissioners." She rolls her eyes. "What am I supposed to do? The entire church is going to be lopsided."

"You can't be serious."

"But I am."

"He really said that? That he wants to invite all those people?"

She uses her first finger to draw a cross over her heart and then pokes that finger toward her left eye. "Cross my heart, hope to die, stick a needle in my eye. It's weird, right? Maybe I should just ignore it. Or maybe I should put my foot down and tell him no."

I want to agree with her, but my first loyalty will always be to Ozzie. Besides, it's his funeral, not mine. "He's paying for it, isn't he?"

"Well, yeah, but . . . I'd rather spend the money on a honeymoon than a wedding, wouldn't you?"

I go back to the computer, not in the mood to deal with this nonsense. "I couldn't say."

She keeps yammering on while I work on getting a better view with our camera. I hear her mention something about bridesmaids' dresses when something flickers on the screen.

I hold up a hand to stop her. "Shush."

She leans in close enough that I can smell her bubblegum-scented breath. "What do you see?"

"I'm not sure. It's somebody." We're looking for David Doucet's brother, Marc. He's rumored to be staying in this particular house, but we haven't caught any sign of him yet. He's younger than his brother, the guy otherwise known as May's attempted killer who's now in prison, and he's more interested in using technology and social media to work the business than the older generation was. He's smart and a threat to the entire city the way he's able to keep his business hidden from prying eyes. If we can at least confirm that he's here in this place, we can put some better surveillance in position and maybe hear something that can help the police department with their investigation. Hopefully it'll help Lucky and Jenny with what they're doing, too.

"Do you need me to do anything with the Parrot?" May asks.

"I don't think so." I use the arrow keys on the laptop to move the drone's eye. That's when I realize why I can't get the best picture. "Dammit."

"What's wrong?" May is leaning in so closely, she's blocking the whole screen.

I reach up and put my hand on the side of her head, pushing it gently to the left. "Do you mind?"

"Oh, sorry. What's wrong? I don't see anything."

"That's the problem. There's something on the lens. Did you clean it before you sent it up there?"

She turns to me and frowns. "Of course I cleaned it. I'm a photographer. A *professional* photographer." She goes back to looking at the screen. "You're right, though—there is something there. I think it's a bug's butt. Here . . . maybe this will fix it." She reaches up and hits the screen capture button several times, shooting off several pictures in a row. The bug that had planted its rear end on top of our lens disappears, frightened away by the movement beneath it.

May never ceases to surprise me. One minute she's talking about silly wedding plans and the next she's doing her new job like it's second nature to her. I try not to be jealous of that. I still suck at flying the damn drone and I've been practicing for more than a year.

May turns and smiles at me, all bright and cheery again. "See? You've got problems, I've got solutions."

"Good job." I've got to give credit where credit is due. I can definitely see better, and there's clearly someone coming out the front door. He looks to be about five foot ten, the same height as the guy we're looking for.

I point at the screen. "I think that's him. What do you think?"

May holds up a photograph that we received courtesy of the New Orleans Police Department, a booking shot taken maybe a year ago.

"It could be him. The jawline is good. His hair has changed a lot. Is that a new scar?"

I shake my head. "I can't see that. How are you seeing that?"

"It's right there." She points to the screen.

When I lean in and get really close, I see a hint of what she might be talking about. "Maybe."

"I'll get some better shots with the camera," May says.

I nod. "Good idea."

She goes into the very back end of the van and retrieves a camera and our biggest telephoto lens from the heavy, high-density plastic case that holds all the photographic and video equipment. Using the small window cut out of the blackout curtain separating the front of the van from the back, she slides the lens through so she can take photographs of the suspect, who's three blocks away.

"Yeah, it's definitely him," she says, shooting off a few frames. "I can see him clear as day. He's getting closer."

"What do you mean he's getting closer?" I look at the computer screen, and sure enough, he's walking in our direction.

"I mean what I said. He's walking this way." Her shutter is going like crazy, taking photo after photo. "He does have a new scar. It's really big. And fresh. Still red. Gross. I wonder who cut him. Whoever it was, he was no surgeon, I can tell you that much." She snorts at her own joke.

"How close is he?" He's walked out of the view of the Parrot, and I don't want to change its angle and risk having him hear the electronics moving around above his head. Our surveillance drone is attached to a power pole not far from where he is.

Her voice is incredibly calm. "I don't know. It's difficult to say from behind the camera."

I grit my teeth a little to keep my voice steady. "Can you line him up with a landmark and maybe give me an idea?"

"Uhhh . . . I think . . . he's about one block away now."

I grab her shoulder and pull her back, slapping the cover over the surveillance camera hole. My voice drops to a whisper. "Get back. He's probably figured out we're in here or he's at least curious. Just chill out for a little bit."

"Maybe he's going for a walk."

"Guys like him don't go for walks. Just shush."

My computer screen lights up the space. In the dim glow, I can see May's expression. She's finally registering the fact that this is not good for us.

"What are we going to do?" she asks in a normal tone of voice.

I slap my hand over her mouth and bug my eyes out at her, wishing I could scream, but whispering instead. "Would you be quiet, please?"

May nods her head and reaches up to take my hand off her mouth.

I let her, against my better judgment. I wish I could duct tape her trap closed until we're back at the warehouse.

Her next comment is whispered. "Are we going to try to drive away, or are we going to wait this out?"

"Just wait." I shake my head at her to discourage any further conversation.

I can hear my heart pounding in my ears. In several years of doing surveillance with Bourbon Street Boys, I've had a few run-ins with various neighborhood people who saw the truck and were curious enough to investigate, but I've never had an actual target approach me. Of course we've trained for the eventuality, but as we've all learned at one point or another in our careers, training can only approximate the real deal. There's always a lot more adrenaline pumping through the veins when a truly bad guy is walking up to your hiding spot.

Gravel and sand crunch under his feet. I'm silently praying that his footsteps are going to just keep on going by, but of course my bad luck holds, and they don't. He stops just next to the front seat area. At first there's nothing, but then there's a tapping on the glass.

"Hello? Anybody home?"

May grabs onto my wrist and squeezes for all she's worth. Six months ago that wouldn't have meant much because her grip was equal to that of a four-year-old's, but today, it means a lot. She's been doing a ton of weight training with Dev. I have to pry her hand off with my fingernails. At the same time, I'm shooting daggers at her with my eyes, telling her she'd better not dare answer him or whine about me forcing her hand off me.

Her head swings left and then right.

I know the fight-or-flight instinct when I see it, and she's ready to fly. I put my hands on either side of her face and stare into her eyes. Shaking my head very slowly, I say as softly as possible, "Don't . . . do . . . *anything.*"

May blinks a few times and then seems to get a grip on herself. She nods, her expression a little less panicky.

When I'm certain I can trust her to keep her damn trap shut, I let go of her face.

Another sound comes at the window, this time more insistent. "Knock, knock! I know you're in there!"

May opens her mouth, but I put my finger over the gaping hole in front of her teeth and shake my head. Speaking in a low volume, I say, "Let me handle this."

May has had a lot of training, but I still don't really trust her at crunch time. Maybe I never will. Ozzie would never forgive me if I let something happen to her while we were out on a job together. It's one of the reasons why I don't like having her on the team; when she's along, none of us can function autonomously or without worry. I always feel like I'm babysitting, because if she gets hurt, I'll get blamed. And what Ozzie thinks and cares about is important to me.

I stand, hunched over, moving to the back of the van. Our target is at the front, and I don't want him to see what we have inside, even though to him it won't look like much . . . just a big case and a computer on a desk. My plan is to jump out the back door and lock up before he has a chance to see anything. And then somehow I'm going to talk my way out of this shitstorm we've found ourselves in the middle of. I have no idea how, though. Hopefully, inspiration will strike.

I lean toward May so I can whisper in her ear. "I'm going out the back. Lock the door behind me."

May grabs me, shaking her head vigorously, but I push her away. If we don't answer this guy, he's going to start damaging the van, and I know Thibault would appreciate me avoiding that if possible. He's always bitching about keeping our unnecessary expenses down.

We've got our surveillance in place here now, and anything else we do for this case won't require that I be seen, since all of our surveillance is being done online and via bugs, so I'm not worried about blowing my cover. And I don't want to just take off and lay rubber behind because then the gang will know someone's watching and it'll ruin everything. No, this is my only option. I take a deep breath and make my move.

CHAPTER FOURTEEN

I go quickly, certain that if I delay, May will give me more trouble. I'm out the back door and shutting it behind me in less than five seconds. As soon as my feet hit the ground, I hear our target moving. I'm just pulling my hair out of its ponytail when Marc appears around the back bumper of the van.

"Well, well, well. What do we have here?" He looks me up and down like I'm a big, fat, juicy steak, and he's a really hungry paleo dieter. "Look what rolled into my neighborhood."

I lift my chin at him. "What's up?" I stick my hands into my front pockets, doing my best to look like a homegirl. My dark hair and olive skin allow me to blend into a lot of places. Obviously, he knows I'm not from his neighborhood, but New Orleans is a big place.

Marc looks at my van and then at me. "What're you doin' here on my street, chica? You spyin' on me?"

I smile and laugh a little. "Why would I want to do that? You somebody special, Hollywood?"

He shrugs, moving a little closer. "I don't know. Maybe I am. Maybe you're with the po-lice." Both of his hands go behind his back, where I'm certain he has a gun tucked into his waistband.

I left my weapon in the van, knowing he'd see it on me and take it as a threat. He needs to believe I'm not here to ask for trouble, and I need to get away before something stupid happens.

"Police?" I snort indelicately. "Please. I served my time. I ain't nobody's snitch."

His eyes narrow on me. "You served time? Where? When?"

I shrug. "Saint Gabe. Manslaughter. Couple years ago. I don't like to talk about it." I lift my chin at him again. "You live here?"

"Maybe. Maybe not. Who's asking?"

I open my mouth to answer, but I never get the words out. Suddenly there are three of us outside. May has decided to join us after stepping out of the driver's-side door and coming around to the back of the van.

My heart drops into my toes as she practically skips over, wearing the ridiculous black boots that she's convinced are great for fighting. That's what she said when she wore them the first day. She held them up at me and said, "Look, Toni! Now we both wear butt-kicking boots!" Hers have pink flowers embroidered on the sides.

I drop my gaze to the ground and shake my head, letting out a long sigh. Now we're in deep shit, and I have no idea what to do from here. I'm going to kill her when we're alone again. Hopefully she won't be dead already.

"Hey, guys! What's going on?" May puts her hand on my shoulder. "Did you ask him? About the reception hall?"

I look up at her with my jaw falling open. I have absolutely no clue where she's going with this.

May waves a hand in the space between the three of us. "Oh my god, my friend is so silly." She sticks her hand out at Marc. "My name is Allison. I like to tell people my name is Alice Inwonderland but it's not. It's Allison Guckenburger." She rolls her eyes. "I know. Crazy name, right? But the good news is I'm getting married, and I'm going to trade that name in for a brand-new one." She giggles, leaving her hand dangling in the air in front of the gangster who's probably trying to decide whether to shoot her now or wait to see what other ridiculous things she's going to say first.

Marc looks at me with a question in his eyes, but his hand comes out slowly and he takes the end of May's fingers to give them a little shake before letting go. Both of his arms fall to his sides, the weapon in his pants temporarily forgotten.

I don't find any relief in that, though, because I have a feeling the more he gets to know May, the happier he's going to be about the idea of shooting us. This is only a temporary reprieve. My mind is racing to generate ideas about how to extricate ourselves from this mess, but it's coming up empty.

I clear my throat before speaking. "Uhhh, *Allison* . . . I was just chatting with . . ." I stop myself just in time from saying his name, thank God, ". . . uh . . . this guy here, so maybe you could wait in the car . . ."

"Marc," he says, winking at me.

"Marc," I repeat. "I was chatting with Marc." My pulse is thumping hard in my neck. My fight-or-flight instinct is kicking, too. I use all my willpower to tamp it down, like I always do. No one looking at me would know I'm sweating this.

"I heard you guys," she says brightly, "and it didn't seem like you were getting to the point, so that's why I decided to get out and help you along." She gives me a giant smile before turning her attention to our target. "We're here scoping out the area for my wedding. And I don't mean to offend you when I say this, but can I just say that your neighborhood would be *amazing* for it. Ah-may-*zing*."

His face is screwed up as he tries to figure out what she's actually saying. "A wedding? For who?"

"For me, of course." She gives him another brilliant, ridiculous smile. "It's the newest thing, haven't you heard?" She looks around, breathing in deeply and letting out a long, satisfied sigh. "The urban wedding. Staged in the most raw of neighborhoods. It's amazing. The photographs I've seen would just blow your mind." She throws her arm out straight and moves it sideways, doing a slow, horizontal pan of the houses across the street. "Could you imagine? Tents on the front lawn. Old jalopies fixed up and painted gold." She stops and looks at Marc, her arm still raised. "You know those cars that go up and down with hydraulics? I'd want some of those. Maybe one that's purple and one that's blue, too, because those are my colors." She looks at me and nods. "Can you see it? It would be perfect." She goes back to Marc, putting her hands on her hips. "Do you have friends with those kinds of cars? Do you think they would let me rent them for the day?"

Marc shakes his head, looking her up and down. "Bitch, you crazy."

May looks offended. I can't tell if she's faking it or if she really feels that way. "Did you just call me the b-word?" For a second she seems frozen in time. Then she smiles and laughs, rushing over to throw her arms around Marc's shoulders. "That is so *perfect!* You are so in character. I would *love* for you to come to the wedding. I'm going to need your contact information." She releases him from her chokehold and pulls her cell phone out of her back pocket, standing poised and ready. "Give me your number. I'm totally inviting you to my wedding."

He points at her and looks at me. "Is she serious?"

All I can do is shrug. The only explanation for what's happening here is I've accidentally eaten a poisonous mushroom and fallen down into a giant, mystical rabbit hole. It explains everything, including Alice Inwonderland's cover name.

May waves in my general direction, her eyes never leaving her phone. "Don't worry about Gigi," she says, apparently referring to me. "She started out as just my neighborhood consultant, but we've become really good friends. She's totally coming to the wedding too." She looks at me and then Marc, winking. "You guys could maybe hook up. You know that's how the best relationships start . . . at other people's weddings." She turns her attention fully on Marc. "What was your phone number?"

It's like the guy's in a trance. He fires off some digits and May quickly types them into her phone.

"Perfect. Perfect, perfect, perfect. I am so going to invite you. Maybe I could call you if I have other questions? I need to rent several things and maybe you can help me source them."

He's smiling now. "Things like what?"

"Oh, I don't know. Where do you guys have your gatherings? Like your quinceañeras and stuff like that? I think I'd like to incorporate some of that stuff into my wedding, too. Make it more urban authentic."

He doesn't say anything, his expression slowly going stormy.

She smiles, but she's not looking quite as confident as she was a minute earlier. "Well, don't worry about it. You think on it, and I'll get back to you." She suddenly looks at her watch and acts overly dismayed. "Oh no! We're going to be late!"

"We are?" I'm afraid to ask what we're late for, but of course that's not going to stop Alice Inwonderland Guckenburger from telling the world.

"Yes! Of course we are. Remember? We're going to go get our mustaches waxed together."

Marc starts to snicker and backs away, his hand going up to his mouth.

I'm fuming, ready to wring her neck. I battle to keep my voice calm. "Oh, yeah. Our mustaches. How could I forget?" My smile is tighter than tight.

May looks up at Marc and gives him a little wave. "It was nice to meet you, Marc. I'll be talking to you soon. Come on, Gigi, let's go. We don't want you giving anyone the cactus treatment when you kiss him now, do we?" She pushes me toward the passenger side of the van and goes around to the driver's side herself.

I walk past Marc with my head down, my face flaming red. How did I lose control of that situation so quickly and so completely? And where and how does May come up with this crap?

I decide the answer as to why I lost control has to lie with Lucky. I'm distracted because of what happened between us almost two weeks ago, and, as a result, I've been thrown completely off my game. As to how May comes up with this crap? I have no theory on that other than the one suggesting she's a complete maniac who obviously has a lot of juice up in heaven; she must have ten guardian angels watching out for her to get away with the nonsense she does.

"See you around, Gigi," Marc says as I get into the van.

God, I hope not. "Maybe," I say out loud, affecting a casual air I definitely do not feel.

I wait until we're in the van and driving away before I grab a hunk of May's hair and yank it.

CHAPTER FIFTEEN

Ow! What'd you do that for?" May holds her head as she drives, scowling at me.

"Don't ask me that stupid question. You know very well why I did that. You could've gotten us both killed."

I have no idea how she's driving through the neighborhood streets so smoothly. She's normally not this cool after dealing with a stressful situation. If I were behind the wheel right now, we'd be laying rubber all over town getting away. I have enough adrenaline in me to power an elephant, and besides, nobody under the age of seventy drives slow around here; it looks suspicious. May can get away with it because anyone looking at her would know she doesn't belong here.

She's looking way too satisfied as she pulls out onto Tulane Avenue. "Are you kidding? I totally just handled that guy."

I snort. "You're lucky he didn't handle you. What was wrong with what I was doing? What made you feel like you had to intervene?"

"For your information, he was standing in the perfect position for me to look in the side mirror and see his backside. While you were *handling* things, he was reaching into his waistband pulling his gun out." She glares at me. "So you tell me what you think his next move was going to be. Huh? What do you think? You think he was just going to compare bullets with you?"

I feel a little sick to my stomach. "I saw his hands going back there. I knew he had a gun."

"Yeah, but did you know he was taking it out? And did you know that when somebody bothers to take their firearm out in public, they usually intend to use it?"

I have to grit my teeth to keep from yelling at her. "Yes, I've attended the same training you have."

"So then you know that when we see something like that about to happen, our job is to defuse the situation, which I did. So instead of pulling my hair out, you can say, 'Thank you very much, May,' and then I'll say, 'You're welcome, Toni.'" She has her nose up so high it's almost hitting the ceiling.

Guilt nags at my conscience. There's more than a little bit of truth to what she's saying, and we both know it. At this point, for me to continue denying it would be silly; but it really kills me to admit this out loud.

"Fine. You handled it. I was handling it, but you handled it better. Thanks for the backup."

"You're welcome. And thank you for rolling with my plan, even though I didn't share it with you in advance."

I nod. *As if I had a choice.*

"So, what do we do now?" May asks.

"We go back and tell everybody what happened. Put it in a report like usual."

May glances at me funny when we're at the next stoplight. "Are you sure you want to do that?"

The way she asks it gets my back up. "Why wouldn't I? I don't hide things from the team."

She shakes her head. "I wasn't suggesting that you do . . . I was just thinking that maybe . . ."

"Listen, I'm not mad at you. And I can take my lumps. If I did something wrong, if I created a training opportunity for the team, that's just the way it goes. I'm not perfect, and I'm not too proud to admit when I've got stuff to learn."

"Even when it's me? Even when I might be someone who could teach you something?"

I stare straight out the windshield because I don't want her to see the expression on my face. Honestly, it is hard for me to take lessons from May. She's green. She's one of the rookies on our team, and I've been working the streets for years now. But the fact is, sometimes her harebrained schemes work out better than the ones that I consider to be more rational. I guess she has the element of surprise attack down better than I do. I'm more subtle, but apparently subtlety doesn't always get the job done.

I sigh in defeat. "Yes. Even when it's you. I'm cool."

"Awesome. Because we have twenty minutes before we get back to the warehouse, and I really want to talk to you about something very important."

I look over at her, literally fearing the enthusiasm in her voice. "Oh, yeah? What is it?" I pray she's not going to tell me that she wants to hook me up with a one-on-one training session featuring her as my instructor. I'm afraid I won't be able hold it together if I hear that. I'm only human, after all.

"I was going to take you out to lunch and ask you this, but maybe it's more appropriate to do it in the van where we've had so much of our relationship develop and become special."

Every word out of her mouth brings me closer to the edge of panic. I'm more afraid of what she's going to say next than I was of Marc's gun.

"Ozzie and I would like to know if you would do us the honor of being one of my bridesmaids."

A groan escapes my lips as I imagine that actually happening. I attempt to cover it up with a different kind of verbal reaction. "Ohhhh. Boy. Wouldn't that be special." I wipe the sweat droplets off my upper lip with the back of my hand.

"I can't tell if you're being serious or if you're mocking me right now." She glances sideways at me.

"Oh, I'm being serious. It would be very special." I'm picturing myself in a dress that makes me look like some sort of rainbow-colored ice cream sundae explosion. It's not pretty. In fact, it's quite hideous. I stare out the side window, wishing the traffic lights would all turn green so we could get back to the port faster. *Come on, come on . . .*

"Excellent." She's smiling again; I can hear it in her voice. "I'm so excited. I already have the dresses picked out, and Jenny said yes too, of course, and since I would like to keep it kind of a small thing, it's just going to be you two. But don't worry . . . I'll have two flower girls and two ring bearers, so it won't exactly be a tiny wedding party."

"Fantastic." I'm not really listening anymore. She's going on and on about colors and locations and cakes and flowers and God knows what else, but all I can think about is how miserable I'm going to be.

I knew this was coming, that Ozzie would make an honest woman of May and that she'd settle for nothing less than a ring and a church and the whole shooting match, but I've been hoping it would be a while before that happened. Their relationship and what it's done to our team and to my friendship with Ozzie is still fresh. It's still raw. I'm not angry about it, but I wouldn't say I'm comfortable with it either.

I really wish I could fast-forward over this part of my life and get to the end part where I'm cool with everything. I'm being rushed into something I'm not ready for, but it's not exactly my life, is it?

May's voice leaks into my consciousness. "Are you listening to me?"

I look over at her. "Oh, yeah. I heard every word you said."

"Oh, yeah? What color are my flower arrangements going to be, then?"

My brain buzzes through all the words that may have filtered in. "Red?" It's a shot in the dark; I have no idea.

She rolls her eyes. "I knew you weren't paying attention. I said *pink*, Toni. *Pink* flowers. Please . . . red? Too bold. Red is for bold people like you. Pink is for softer people like me."

That makes me laugh. For the first time all day I feel a little bit of joy slipping into my heart. "You're not bold?"

She looks offended. "No, I'm not bold. I'm soft and demure."

I'm laughing so hard, I have to hold my stomach to keep it from exploding. I feel like I've done twenty sets of crunches.

"I don't see what's so funny."

We're pulling up to the warehouse door when I can finally speak normally again. "You're the girl who just basically attacked a gangbanger and forced him to give his phone number so that she could invite him to her 'urban wedding' in his 'hood." I shake my head. "If that shit ain't bold, I don't know what bold is."

She sniffs as she presses the button that will open the door. "I was just going with the moment."

I snort. "Yeah. Going with the moment in the boldest, baddest-ass way you possibly could have. There was nothing demure about that, let me tell you. If you're using pink flowers, they'd better be hot pink."

She's smiling as she pulls the van into the warehouse.

I look at her and can't help but smile too. "What are you so happy about?"

She throws the van into park and turns the ignition off, looking over at me with a goofy expression on her face. "The baddest-ass girl I know just called me badass." She grins harder. "Why wouldn't I be happy?"

CHAPTER SIXTEEN

I leave May to her photograph and video uploading in the cubicles and head upstairs, expecting to find Ozzie and Thibault. But when I get there, it's just Lucky sitting at the table with a cup of coffee in front of him. I hesitate in the doorway, wondering if I should turn around and leave. This is the first time I've seen him at work in a while and it's immediately awkward. A tiny slice of regret slides through me. We probably should have just left everything alone, but it's too late now.

"Hey there," he says, a smile lighting up his face.

I walk into the room, my heart speeding up a little. He's happy to see me, and I'm happy to see him too; I might as well admit it. A grin breaks out across my face, unbidden. "Hey there."

I sit down in the chair across from him, looking at my fingers as they fumble around together. I don't know what to do with my hands, when normally I don't give them a second thought. "What's up?" I ask, hoping he won't notice my nervousness.

"Not much. Just finished up a meeting with Jenny, and I was sitting here wondering what I'm supposed to do with the rest of my day."

"I just finished with May." I shake my head. "She's crazy."

Lucky stands, pushing his chair back with his legs. "Come on. You can tell me all about it over drinks."

It's on the tip of my tongue to say no, but instead I shrug. With my assignment done for the day, I don't really have anything better to do. I should probably write a report about what happened with Marc the gangbanger and Alice Inwonderland, but that can wait until later. It's not like I'm going to forget it.

I stand with Lucky, then lean over and grab his coffee cup to take it to the sink for him as he walks to the door.

When I join him there he smiles. "Thanks. You're a pal."

I slug him in the gut as I walk past and he bends at the waist, pretending to be injured. I can't stop smiling as I move through the sword room.

"My car or yours?" I ask.

"Are you kidding? My car, of course."

I turn around and walk backward so I can glower at him. "What's that supposed to mean? My car is nice."

"Yeah, but when we're in your car, you're always driving."

I stop at the door leading out to the warehouse. "What's *that* supposed to mean?" I narrow my eyes at him, trying to decide if he's messing with me or insulting me for real.

His eyebrows go up. "Oh, nothing. Forget I said anything." He slides past me, speeding up and practically running down the stairs.

I follow him, shaking my head. He doesn't know me very well if he thinks I'll chase him. He'll pay for his comments later, though. I'm an excellent driver, and everybody here knows it. Maybe I'll get behind the wheel of his vehicle and throw a few donuts in a parking lot somewhere so he can learn better than to mess with me. I smile, imagining the look on his face as the exterior of the car spins by our windows . . .

He's standing at the passenger door looking at me expectantly when I get down to his car. I stop in front of the grille, confused.

Does he want me to drive? After what he said, I find that doubtful. "What're you doing?"

He opens up the door. "What's it look like I'm doing?" He steps back, making room for me as he gestures to the interior.

I tilt my head at him. *Is this a joke?* "What's your game?"

He shrugs. "No game. Just being a gentleman."

I walk over, get into the car and buckle up. My ears are burning for some stupid reason. "Whatever floats your boat." Maybe I should be flattered by his gesture, but I'm not; I'm uneasy. I like our relationship the way it was. I don't want him changing anything. Why? Because first of all, everybody's going to notice if he starts acting funny around me, and then May and Jenny are going to get all up in my business with questions and advice and everything else. And second of all, I like the way we work together. Everything is casual, easy. *Why does he have to go and complicate things like this?*

He gets into the driver's seat, sliding in with a grace not many men possess. As he reverses out of the warehouse, he catches me looking at him and winks. "Anywhere special you want to go?"

I shift my gaze out the windshield. "Wherever. Pub is fine with me."

"The pub it is."

Lucky navigates the streets of the port and then those beyond. My mind races with different things we can talk about. *Work? Television shows? Movies?* Never before have I had to search for something to say to this guy, but now I'm second-guessing myself so much I can't even say a single word. I hiss out a sigh of annoyance.

"What's wrong?" he asks, turning to look at me for a moment.

"I hate how this is so awkward." I also hate that I just said that out loud.

But of course Lucky takes it all in stride, smiling like he always does. "It's not awkward. It's just different. When was the last time you and I were alone in a car together?"

I have to think about that for a few seconds. "I don't know. Other than that cab ride, it's been a long time, I guess."

"The cab ride doesn't count. It's been over a year. Remember last summer when we went to the state park for a company picnic?"

I smile at the memory. That was a great day. "Oh, yeah, I remember. Dev had just gotten that beast of a car and he asked us if we wanted to ride along with him, but none of us wanted to be stuck on the side of the road so we said no."

"Yeah, and that thing stunk, too. Damn, it was like a musky animal had made a den in it, remember?" He laughs.

I laugh along with him, enjoying our easy banter. The awkwardness slides away and I hardly even notice. "God, it was like something died in there."

"He had to hang all those Christmas tree air fresheners in there for weeks." He shakes his head slowly at the memory. "I don't think it still stinks, but some kind of miracle happened in there to get that smell out, I'll tell you what."

"You know how he finally got the stench out, right?" I can't believe Lucky didn't hear the story.

"No. Tell me."

"Coffee beans. He poured ground-up coffee beans all over the floor and seats, and two weeks later vacuumed them up."

"Really? I didn't know coffee beans had that kind of power."

I shrug, looking at my side window. "Well, you know . . . all those guys use coffee beans to hide the smell of their drugs from the sniffer dogs. Must mean something."

The car goes silent again, but this time it's not awkward. Neither of us says another word until we're pulling up to the pub. There's only one other car in the parking lot.

I look at my watch. "I guess we're here early."

"Fine with me. Only person I'm here to see is you." Lucky puts the car in park and shuts off the ignition.

My heart leaps at his words. It's like we're teenagers again, only this time we're flirting, fumbling around, trying not to say too much of what's in our heads. It feels good, but it also makes me nervous.

I open up my door quickly, afraid he's going to come around and open it for me again. I can only take so much of that gentleman crap before I start getting cranky. It makes me think he considers me helpless, and nothing could be further from the truth.

He follows me to the pub's front door without saying a word, but at the last minute, he leans in and grabs the handle, pulling it open for me. I just breeze through. If he wants to get my doors, fine. I'll let him. It's silly how it kind of makes me feel special. It's just a damn door.

As we enter the front room, Lucky raises his hand and signals Danny the bartender. He holds up two fingers and points them down at our heads. We take two stools at the far corner of the bar.

Danny comes over with two beers, but just as he's about to open one, Lucky holds up a finger. "Wait." He looks at me sideways and then smiles before turning his attention back to Danny. "Don't open those. We're on the wagon now, I forgot. Bring us two juices instead."

Danny lifts a brow at us. "Two juices? What kind of juice?"

Lucky strokes his beardless chin. "I don't know. I've never ordered juice in a bar before. What've you got?"

Danny rolls his eyes heavenward, giving the impression he's reading a menu up on his forehead. "Let's see, we have orange juice, cranberry juice, apple juice . . ."

"Two OJs." Lucky looks at me. "That okay with you?"

"I guess." I am decidedly unenthusiastic about this choice of beverage, but I know what he's getting at; if I'm pregnant I shouldn't be drinking. The whole idea just pisses me off all over again. This maybe-baby is already getting in my way.

Danny moves away and Lucky leans in closer. "Sorry about that. I wasn't thinking."

I roll my eyes. "At least you didn't tell Danny that I'm pregnant. I should count my blessings, I guess."

"Do you think he knows what's up?"

I shake my head. "I don't think anybody would suspect me of being pregnant ever. I'm sure we're okay."

Lucky frowns at me. "Why would you say that?"

I look at him to see if he's joking but he appears serious. "Because. It's obvious."

He turns more fully in my direction. "What's obvious? Spell it out for me, because I'm not getting where you're coming from."

I turn to face him so he can get a better view. "Look at me. I'm not mom material. I don't even *like* kids."

A flicker of something that looks like pain passes over Lucky's face before he's smiling again. "Are you kidding me? You look like you could pump out a whole litter of pups."

I snort and roll my eyes, turning back to the bar. "Ridiculous."

Lucky goes quiet for a little while, but then he nudges me again. "How come you don't like kids?"

I shake my head, looking down at the bar, sliding my fingernail along a scratch in the top of it as I speak. "It's not that I don't like them; I think it's more that they don't like me, and I'm cool with that."

"What? That's crazy. Kids like you. Dev's son likes you. Jenny's son loves you. Sammy thinks you're the most beautiful woman he's ever seen in his life. He told me just the other day he's going to marry you when he turns ten."

I laugh, my cheeks going a little warm. I have no idea why this embarrasses me; he's just a kid. "I think the little guy needs glasses."

Lucky mumbles his response under his breath. "No, there's definitely nothing wrong with his eyesight. Trust me on that."

I glance at Lucky, but he's not giving me any more information and I'm not going to dig for it. I shrug, going back to picking at the bar. "I just never saw myself as a mother. I'm too selfish."

He shakes his head but stares straight ahead. "I'm not buying it. I think you're just scared."

I snort. "Me? Scared of a baby? Please." But my heart does thump a couple times extra hard at the idea of holding one of the little buggers. I'd probably drop it and break it. Nobody should ever let me hold a baby. And this is exactly why I should never be pregnant. I would be the one mother in the history of the world not capable of holding her own child.

"We need to find out if you are or not," Lucky says out of the blue. "Because if you're not, we could order some beers and really get this party started."

I smile at that idea, liking it way more than orange juice. "Yeah. Let's get this party started. That sounds good to me." I could drown a few of my sorrows right now.

He spins around really fast on his stool and looks at me with his eyes wide open. "That's it!"

I look at him with suspicion. "What's it?"

"We need to get you a pregnancy test! We need to test your urine."

I screw my brows up at him. "You can't be serious."

He hops off his stool and holds his hand out. "Of course I'm serious. Let's go."

I stare at him, not sure what I should do from here.

He wiggles his hand, urging me to take it. "Come on. I'm serious. Let's go."

I look over at Danny, who's walking over holding two glasses filled with orange juice. "But our drinks . . ."

"Forget about 'em. We'll come back." He leans in and takes my hand, pulling me forcibly off the stool. "We'll be back in a little bit," he says to Danny. "Keep those on ice for us."

Danny pours the two orange juices out into the sink, rolling his eyes at us as we go by.

"Sorry," I say, forcing an expression of apology.

I'm not lying about being sorry. I would much rather be sitting at the bar drinking stupid orange juice than getting a pregnancy test. I don't want to fight Lucky about this here and have everyone at the bar watching us, but I'm not going to go do this with him. This is crazy. I'll break the news to him outside and he can just leave me here alone.

Lucky laces his fingers through mine, and I feel silly all of a sudden, like a schoolgirl, thrilled that her crush is acknowledging her feelings and returning them. I'm so absorbed in this ridiculous emotion that I don't even notice we're already at his car. He opens the door and gestures for me to go in, dropping my hand.

"Hurry," he says, "I want to get this over with."

I put my hand on top of the door and look at him over the window. "What's the big hurry? It's not going to change the result."

His smile is lopsided this time, not as certain as it normally is. "The curiosity is killing me. I just need to know."

I shake my head as I lower myself into the car. "Whatever." It's got to happen eventually, so I guess it might as well be now. But I'm no longer in the mood to chitchat or share details of my day. I buckle myself up and just stare out the front windshield.

The atmosphere in the car is tense once again as Lucky drives off. He probably doesn't even notice it, as intent as he is on getting to the drugstore, but I do. My skin is crawling with it. Thankfully, it's only two blocks to the nearest store, so we're there before I know it. He throws the door open and exits the vehicle.

"I'll be right back," he says, his face in the half-open window. "You don't have to do anything but pee."

I sit there in the parking lot, my head swimming with thoughts, most of them of the panicky variety. I can't believe we're doing this.

It's like we're boyfriend and girlfriend, and we're all excited about something because we have this big future plan together. But that's not my life, and that's not Lucky's life, either. We're just friends. Teammates. People who grew up together. He's not my boyfriend and I'm not his girlfriend. And if I am pregnant, it's going to be a nightmare. So why is he acting so excited? Maybe he's just looking forward to getting a negative result on the test so we can both have some drinks and then go home and get busy. I guess that's not such a horrible thing. I wouldn't mind another roll in the hay, so long as he's gloved up.

He's back to the car in a flash, and he tosses a white plastic bag in my lap as he gets in. It's full of boxes.

I open the bag. "What's in here?"

"I couldn't buy just pregnancy tests; that would have been too awkward." He pauses for a moment and looks at me, smiling. "I got some licorice, too. And some condoms."

I laugh. "That clerk must've thought you were nuts."

"He did look at me kind of funny. I got the impression he wanted to give me a lesson on the birds and the bees." He feigns an old man voice. "Son, I think you're confused about something . . . If you got one, you don't need the other . . ."

As worried as I am about the results of this test, I can't help but laugh at him. He's always been that guy for me—the one who could make me laugh even when I didn't want to.

"So, where should we do this thing?" I ask, looking around. We're traveling back in the direction we came from.

"These *things*, not this thing. Plural. I bought several, just to be sure."

I open the bag again and see that there are in fact three different boxes in there. I turn one over. Inside this particular box there are two test-sticks. I verify it's the same with the other boxes before speaking. "You have *six* tests in here."

"You can never be too sure."

"But you *can* have only so much pee in one bladder."

"Hmm . . . you may have a point there. We may have to down a few glasses of orange juice for my plan to work."

When he pulls into the parking lot, my smile slips; I feel something a little like panic crawl back into my heart. "Are you serious?"

He pulls into a space, puts the car in park, and turns the engine off. "What do you mean? Is that a trick question?"

I use the bag to gesture at the front of the pub. "Do you honestly want me to take a pregnancy test inside the pub?"

"Why not? It's private. There're separate stalls in the ladies' room, right?"

"Yes, but . . ."

"Plus we might need more orange juice, right?"

I shake my head, knowing arguing is futile. "Whatever. Let's just get it over with." I'm almost certain I'm not pregnant. What are the chances, right? We only did it one time without protection, and if the charts on the Internet are correct, I wasn't even very fertile then. Maybe only a little. *God, please let it have been only a little.*

"Come on, it'll be fun." He gets out of the car and comes around to my side.

Fun? He must be insane. My butt feels like it's glued to the seat. I can't move.

Lucky opens my door and leans in, holding out a hand. "Come on, I'll help you."

I slap his hand away. "No, sir, you are most definitely *not* helping me." I can just picture him in the stall next to me coaching me through peeing on a stick. I use the inside handle of the door to pull myself out of the car and stand. "I'm going in the bathroom by myself."

"Okay, whatever you say. You're the boss." He grins.

I stand there and stare at him, the bag held at my waist with both hands in front of me. "Don't piss me off, Lucky."

He leans in fast and gives me a kiss on the nose. "I wouldn't dream of it." He adjusts himself to walk at my side and puts his hand onto my lower back, urging me forward.

Rather than dig my heels in, which is my immediate reaction, I follow along. With every step I take, I feel like I'm walking toward my doom. I have never in my life been in this situation, but in all the stories I've heard of other people experiencing it, it was never like this. They were never being led into a bar by one of their best friends with a bag of pregnancy tests in hand. I'm starting to wonder if this is just another part of my punishment, justice for the mistakes I've made, for what I did to Charlie. The rightness of that hits me full force, like a sledgehammer in the chest. *It has to be.*

I resign myself to my fate, dropping my head as I walk into the pub and head for the bathroom, preparing myself mentally to face the music. If God is just and God is fair, I will be pregnant, because that would be the worst punishment I could possibly think of for myself.

CHAPTER SEVENTEEN

I cannot believe it. I thought I had resigned myself to this possibility and accepted my fate, but as I stare down at stick number four and see another faint pink plus sign in the window, I realize there's no way I could adequately prepare myself for something like this. I now know that God may be fair and he may be just, but he also has a wicked sense of humor.

I rest my forehead on the divider between the toilet I'm sitting on and the empty stall next to me. I am completely out of urine now, but it doesn't matter. Two more tests or four more tests or *ten* more tests aren't going to make any difference. I'm pregnant. What's done is done. According to the calendar, I could be as many as ten days along. There's no way for me to know for sure without a doctor getting involved. A fleeting thought floats through my mind. *It's not too late to do something about this.*

My heart stops beating and then spasms painfully. I may not go to church every week, but that doesn't mean I'm completely oblivious to the things preached there. And I learned how precious life is when I took Charlie's from him. I can't take another life away, I just can't. Maybe God is giving me a second chance and this is a test. Regardless, I don't really have a choice. This is how it has to be for me. Unless something crazy happens in the next eight and a half months, I am going to be a mother. I start crying and I can't stop.

There's a banging on the outer door that I barely register. I don't answer. I just drop the used test-sticks into the plastic bag at my feet and slowly stand, buttoning and zipping my pants as the tears continue to fall.

The door squeaks open loudly. "Are you okay in here?" It's Lucky, *goddamn him*.

"No, I am *not* okay."

The door opens farther. "Was it negative?"

Why on earth would I be so miserable if it were negative? If I didn't feel so shitty right now, I'd bust out of this bathroom and put him in a headlock just for being so stupid.

His voice is closer now, just outside the door of my stall. "Talk to me, babe. Tell me what's going on."

He's calling me *babe* again, and it's killing me. He's already acting weird. This is going to ruin everything between us. "I can't right now, Lucky. Go away." I put my hand on the door where his face might be but let my fingers slide away. I love him and I hate him. The feelings are hitting me with equal force. Have I always loved him? I think about it for a few long seconds and realize that I have. I've tried for ten years to love him like a brother, but it's not going to work anymore. Not that it ever did. Maybe that's why Charlie was always jealous of him. Maybe deep down, Charlie knew he wasn't the guy I really wanted.

"Are you going number two?" Lucky asks gently.

My jaw drops open and my hand clenches into a fist at my side. I'm half pissed and half delirious. A laugh escapes my throat before I can stop it. "No! Shut up!" And I thought today could not get any worse. My face is flaming red at the idea of Lucky catching me pooping in the ladies' bathroom.

I can hear the smile in the bastard's voice. "Listen, it's nothing to be embarrassed about. If you're building a log cabin in there, just say the word. I can come back."

He is so going to die. I race to get myself situated and the bag collected from the spot at my feet. "No, wait. I change my mind. Don't go anywhere. Stay right there so I can kick your ass." I turn around and kick the handle on the toilet to make it flush. Then I unlock the door and throw it open. I am so ready to hurt somebody right now.

Lucky is smiling and his arms are open wide. I have never seen him look as beautiful or as happy. "Come to Papa," he says.

There is so much hope there, so much kindness, and so much—dare I say—*love*, I can't deal. I feel like my head and my heart are both going to explode right here in the pub's bathroom. I take one step toward him and then I crumple, crying all the way down.

He moves lightning quick, gathering me in his arms and pulling me up against his chest. He holds me tightly while I sob in his arms.

"Shhh, shhh, it's going to be okay." He rubs and pats my back frantically, then his hand moves to my head where he does the same thing, turning my hair into a rat's nest of knots. "I'll take care of everything. You won't have to do anything but put your feet up and eat chocolate all day."

"This is not a joke," I cry out. "This is my *life*. My life is *over*."

Lucky forces me away from him so he can look me in the eye. "This is not just your life. This is my life too." He squeezes my shoulders hard. "This is *our* life."

My sobs lessen enough for me to speak. "Our *lives*."

He shakes his head at me. "No. Our *life*. Singular. This is you and me together as a team. This is not you alone or me alone with the two of us working on parallel paths. We're now merged into one, like it or not."

I glare at him, wiggling out of his grip. "Not."

He gets a cocky expression and shrugs. "Tough. You danced with the devil and now you're going to pay the price."

His words feel like a knife burying itself in my heart. Without thinking, I reach up and slap him hard across the face.

He doesn't move except to rest his hand on the cheek that's flaming red. His voice is very calm. "I have no idea why you just did that, but I'm going to let it go because you're pregnant. It's probably the hormones."

Angry tears drip from my eyes. "Don't you ever bring Charlie up to me again."

His expression goes from angry to confused. "Charlie? Who said anything about Charlie?"

"*You* did," I say bitterly, feeling betrayed. "That 'dance with the devil' bullshit."

He's still confused for a couple seconds and then his eyes widen. "That's not what I meant. I wasn't talking about Charlie; I was talking about my dick."

Now it's my turn to be confused. My gaze drops to his waist and the bulge beneath. "You call your dick the devil?"

His expression goes sheepish. "It was supposed to sound poetic. Dance with the devil. Sleep with me. Get it?"

In all the years I've been around him, I have never known Lucky to be so goofy. I start laughing and can't stop.

He sighs loudly. "It's really not that funny."

"Oh, yes it is," I gasp, and then fly into another fit of hysteria. I barely get my next words out. "Oh my god! Hilarious! I can't believe you call your dick the devil!"

"Shush!" he urges, trying not to smile. "I never called my dick the devil!"

The door opens all of a sudden and two girls come tumbling in. They stop short when they see us standing there. Lucky's last words are still ringing around the space.

I pause, gaining momentary control over my hysteria, but when I notice they're both staring at Lucky's crotch, I start laughing all over again.

"Excuse us. Sorry." Lucky grabs me by the shoulder and pulls me out of the bathroom. "We didn't mean to intrude on your private space."

I'm still laughing until his next words are offered to the two women as the door slowly swings shut. "She was really constipated so I had to come in and coach her through it."

Before I can react, he runs across the bar away from me. Instead of chasing after him, though, I walk over to the bar and sit down in my old spot. Throwing the stupid bag of pregnancy tests up on the bartop next to me, I breathe out a long sigh. I went into the bathroom as one person with one life, and exited as someone entirely different with a completely unknown and unforeseen life ahead of me. It's almost like the moment right after I killed Charlie: life changed in an instant, into something I never imagined for myself. *Unbelievable. Well done, God. You kicked my ass again.* I nod with respect. His power is undeniable.

Danny comes walking over with his eyebrows raised. "You ready for a beer yet?"

I shake my head. "No more alcohol for me. I'll take an orange juice on the rocks with a cherry, if you please." I feel like I've just done a whole handful of drugs. My heart has helium in it. I should be completely and totally destroyed by this news that has just been delivered in a bathroom stall at the pub I've been hanging out in for over ten years, but I'm not. Now that I've acknowledged the lack of control I have over my future, it's as if somebody has thrown open a door to a whole new world, and I'm on the threshold. I'm standing there trying to decide whether I should step through, and it's awful but invigorating at the same time.

And then Lucky is behind me and his shoulder is touching mine as he slides up onto the barstool next to me. I realize that we're both standing on that threshold, looking out across a vast expanse together. A mysterious world that I never dreamed I'd be a part of awaits. It feels a tiny bit better knowing I'm not alone.

"Make that two OJs," Lucky says.

Danny eyes us quizzically for a few seconds before moving off. I turn to look at Lucky at the same time as he turns to me.

"Do you mind if I sit here and have an OJ with you?" he asks.

"Could I stop you?"

He shrugs. "You could, but I really wish you wouldn't."

"I won't." I feel warm inside at the admission.

His smile is back this time, soft and slow, kind and sweet. He leans in and kisses me on the cheek. "You're one hot mama. Have I ever told you that?"

"No. But say that again in eight months, would you please? I have a feeling I'm going to need to hear it more then." I turn around and face forward as Lucky's arm slides across my back to rest at my waist.

"And every day until then," he promises.

CHAPTER EIGHTEEN

After Lucky drops me off at my house, I take my time getting ready for bed. Now that I know I'm pregnant, I'm imagining all kinds of crazy things, like I'm exhausted when I should have another four hours left in me. It's totally psychological, I know it is, but that knowledge doesn't help at all. I feel like I haven't slept in a full twenty-four hours.

I'm just laying my head down on the pillow a little over an hour later when my doorbell rings.

I go over to the bedroom across the hall and peer out the window with a view of my front lawn. The only thing I see is Lucky's car in the driveway.

I run out of the room and down the stairs. Shoving the small curtain in the side window of my front door aside, I catch a view of Lucky's back. He's headed to his car, and there are two suitcases on my front porch.

I turn off the alarm and open the door. "What the hell . . . ?"

Lucky comes up the front walk with two more suitcases under his arms. He's not breathing heavy, making me think they're empty.

"What are you doing?" I stand in the front entrance with my hand resting on my cocked hip.

He doesn't even look at me as he sets the two cases down. "What's it look like I'm doing?"

"It looks like you're bringing a bunch of empty suitcases over to my house. Did you suddenly run out of storage space?"

"These aren't empty." He looks up and flashes me a grin. "These are full, baby." He turns and goes back down my front steps, headed for his car again.

"Full of what?" Did he go out and buy baby clothes? We don't even know if it's a boy or a girl yet, and I read on the Internet that lots of pregnancies don't make it past the first three months anyway. This could be a complete false alarm.

"Full of my clothes and stuff. What else would they be full of?"

"Why are you bringing your clothes here?"

He shuffles up the stairs and drops the last two suitcases. Then he comes over and stands in front of me, putting his hands on my shoulders. He stares deep into my eyes as he speaks. "What's the matter? Do you already have pregnancy brain? Isn't it a little early for that?"

I knock his hands off my shoulders. "Shut up. Is that even a thing? What is that? Pregnancy brain . . ." I feel panicky again. I need my brain for work.

He reaches into the side pocket of a suitcase and pulls out a book. "I marked the page for you." He points to a dog-eared corner. "You should read this thing. You have no idea how much your body and your brain are going to change over the next nine months."

My panic increases as I take the book from him and look down at the title. "*What to Expect When You're Expecting.*" I look up at him. "Are you serious? You actually bought this?"

"Yeah. As soon as I dropped you off, I went to the bookstore. And then I started reading and I realized, you need me here." He huffs out a breath and continues. "I know it's not cool to just shove myself into your life, but hear me out . . ."

He pauses, maybe waiting for an argument to come from me, but I'm too stunned to find one. *He was reading pregnancy books in the store right after he left me?*

"Toni, you're an independent woman, and I respect that completely. I do. And I know you well enough to know that no matter how hard this pregnancy gets, you'll get through it. You'll handle it, and you won't ask for help, even when you need it."

"That's not . . ."

He holds up a hand, cutting off my disagreement. "Let me finish . . . As I was saying, you're very independent and you're used to doing things yourself. But, I think *this* time, it would be a mistake to try and do that."

"To be myself?"

"No, to do it all alone. This pregnancy will take over your whole body. And your head. You'll get sick and really tired, and you'll need help around here." He looks all around us. "Your place is huge. It's too much work for one person as it is, but a pregnant person? It's way too much. Impossible. The place will start falling down around your ears, and then a baby will arrive and it'll be hopeless."

I look at his suitcases, the book dangling in my hand. "So you left me here, went to the bookstore, skimmed a few books, and then you packed all your stuff?" *And he broke some kind of land speed record getting all this done in just over an hour.*

"Yes, I did. I started reading the book and I realized . . . It's not fair to you that you do all this work on your own. You need me here. I'm partly responsible for you being in this position."

That's when I realize that I'm not panicking nearly as much as he apparently is. I roll my eyes. "I'm pretty sure I can handle this myself and that my house is not going to fall down around my ears."

"Okay, maybe you can handle it alone, but you *shouldn't*." He picks up two suitcases, almost shoving me out of the way to get past and into the front hallway. "Just read the first chapter. You'll see what I mean."

I wander into the living room as I thumb through the pages. Different words jump out at me: *Fetus. Placenta. Pre-eclampsia. Mucus plug.* The pictures are horrible. I fall onto the couch, forgetting there are no cushions there. My butt hits a fabric-covered board and I moan, leaning sideways to rub my tailbone.

Lucky appears out of nowhere. "Are you okay? Are you having cramps?"

I look at him, scowling. "No, I'm not having cramps, fool. I fell on the couch."

He nods. "Yep. You're going to start losing your balance. It's totally normal, though, so don't worry."

"My balance?" I start skimming pages again. This shit is sounding scarier by the second. I thought all I had to worry about were stretch marks and a little weight gain.

"Don't worry, I bought a bunch of other books," he says from the front porch. "We'll study. We'll figure everything out, and I'll be totally prepared for the big day. No surprises."

I let the book drop to the couch at my side. "Don't you think you might be taking this a little too far?"

He brings in the last of his two cases and drops them at the foot of the stairs, shutting the door behind him. He locks it and sets my alarm code. "You're bringing a human being into the world." He joins me in the living room and sits on the table opposite me, our knees touching. "You thought working for Bourbon Street Boys was tough? Wrong. Forget it. Creating life and becoming a mother will be nothing compared to that. No, it'll be *everything* compared to that. We need to be prepared." He rubs his hands together like a mad scientist.

My ears feel hot. "You're starting to scare me."

"Good." He pats me on the knee and stands. "I'm going to go make you a steaming mug of herbal tea. No more caffeine for you anymore." He shouts from out in the hallway, "Cute PJs, by the way!"

I shake my head as the sound of his footsteps fades away. *What have I gotten myself into?*

CHAPTER NINETEEN

I sit there on the couch by myself for a little while as I listen to the sounds of Lucky preparing tea coming from the kitchen. I'm a little stunned by his drastic reaction. Sure, right now it looks as if we'll be bringing a human being into the world—I get that this is a big deal—but does he honestly think he needs to move in here? And does he really believe he can just do it without discussing it with me first?

Yeah . . . he's definitely panicking. I recognize that men do this when they're out of their depth; I've seen Thibault lose his shit on more than one occasion, usually when confronted with confusing female reactions to various things. There's a reason he's still single, and it isn't because he understands women.

I stand, knowing I need to handle this now and as gently as possible. Obviously, I'm going to have to channel some other woman's personality or something, because doing anything gently is not generally my style.

Walking into the kitchen, I'm struck by the warmth that fills me when I see Lucky standing at my counter getting mugs and sugar out of the cabinets. He already looks like he belongs here. Like he has a right to be here.

When that thought floats through my mind, I go a little bitter. I don't like people pushing me around and making decisions for me. Lucky doesn't have any more right to live with me than Dev does.

Guilt nags my brain. *Okay, so he might have just a little right to be involved in my life. But not this much.* I sigh at my waffling emotions. I thought it was just going to be the pregnancy thing that would be hard, but apparently, everything about it is going to give me fits, including my weird and undefined relationship with the baby's father.

Lucky has been in my life for a really long time, and it doesn't exactly feel wrong to have him here doing what he's doing. If I'm being honest with myself, I have to admit I've imagined what it would be like to share my living space with him. Of course, I always swatted those ideas away when I realized how horribly they'd mess up our situation with the team, but that doesn't mean they weren't there. I guess I'm going to find out what it would be like to live with Lucky, if only for one night. The idea thrills me way more than it should.

He looks at me over his shoulder, his expression serious. "You really shouldn't have any sugar."

I keep my response light, even though I want to tell him to shove his advice up where the sun don't shine. He's trying to be a good pregnancy partner, and I can't fault him for it. "That's fine; I don't like sugar in my tea anyway." I walk over to the table and sit down, taking my customary seat at the head of the table.

"I haven't had a chance to read much in the books yet, but I did see some things about diet in there." He pours steaming water from my kettle into two mugs. "You're supposed to limit your intake of sugar and caffeine, and you're not allowed to have any alcohol."

I sigh. "Don't worry, I get it. No more fun. My life is over." I roll my eyes to the ceiling and contemplate the stretch marks that will

WRONG QUESTION, RIGHT ANSWER

surely cover my body in the next nine months. *Awesome. Just what I wanted.*

He picks up the mugs and walks over to the table, putting one down in front of me before taking the spot next to me. He settles back into the chair and stares at me, tapping his finger on the handle of his mug. "Your life is not over. It's just starting." He smiles like it's no big deal, us sitting here talking about a baby growing in my belly.

I shake my head at him. "I love how you're so casual about all of this. I hope you realize it's not just my life that's going to completely change."

He leans in and puts his hand on my knee. "Trust me, I understand. I've been thinking about it ever since we were here in the kitchen last time."

My mind rewinds back to that moment when we were rolling around on the floor, just before we realized the colossal mistake we'd made. I nod absently. I cannot wrap my brain around how much my life has changed in such a short period of time. And nobody even really knows yet. I can't imagine what Thibault, Dev, and Ozzie are going to say. I can, however, imagine what May and Jenny are going to do: they're going to flip their wigs. I'm not looking forward to the crazy enthusiasm. Even the idea of it makes me queasy.

"What are you thinking right now?" Lucky asks me.

"I'm thinking about how this will affect the team."

Lucky nods before taking a sip of his tea, wincing at the heat. "Things are going to change, that's for sure. But it doesn't have to be bad."

"That's easy for you to say. Your life with the team isn't going to change at all." I sound bitter, I know I do, but who can blame me? "I don't want you saying anything to anybody about this."

He frowns at me. "What do you mean?"

145

"I mean I don't want you to say anything. This is my business, and I'm going to decide when the team is informed about the situation, not you."

I can tell by the way he sits up straighter and throws his shoulders back that he doesn't agree. "We'll see."

I shake my head, sitting up straight myself. "No, we won't see. This is my decision, not yours."

He cocks his head at me. "How do you figure? It's my child too."

I'm not going to play dirty and pretend like it could be anyone else's, but that doesn't mean he's going to start deciding what I do with my life. "We need to get something straight here, Lucky . . . Just because you failed to wear a condom, it doesn't mean that you suddenly get to make decisions for me about how I live my life."

Two bright red spots show up on his cheeks and his jaw muscle bounces a couple times as he works to control his anger. He speaks in a very calm voice. "I don't appreciate the way you're wording that, because I believe you're being unfair."

He has chosen his words very carefully, but I don't care. This is a conversation that we need to have right now, get it over with. I don't want him going into this thing under any illusions. I work to keep my tone civil.

"I'm sorry you don't like the way I am talking right now, but that doesn't change the facts. This is *my* body. And *my* work is *my* business. I will decide when, where, and how anyone on the team is informed about my condition, not you."

He takes a slow sip of his tea and waits almost a full minute before responding. The tension in the room is palpable. "I agree that it's your body hosting our child; however, the life inside it is as much my responsibility as it is yours, and I'm going to do whatever it takes to keep my child safe."

I narrow my eyes at him and my nostrils flare. He's begging for a fat lip. "Are you suggesting that I feel differently? That I would risk my child's safety?"

He shakes his head, his chin jutting out. "I'm not suggesting anything. But I think we both know that it's in your personality to take certain risks, and that you might not fully appreciate some of the risks you're taking until it's too late."

I'm trying so hard to stay cool right now, but my voice gives me away, going higher. "No, I don't agree to that. I know exactly what I'm capable of, and I know exactly what risk I'm taking every time I walk out the front door."

"Please don't get mad at me when I say this," he begs, leaning closer, "but sometimes, maybe a lot of times, you're impulsive and reckless, Toni. Just by getting behind the wheel you put yourself at risk. You have more speeding tickets than anyone on the team."

He's playing dirty now, and I'm not going to stand for any of that crap. "Screw you, Lucky." I stand up, my chair sliding out behind me with a loud screech. I point to the hallway. "Get out of my house."

He shakes his head slowly, looking up at me, his jaw set firm and his gaze unflinching. "I'm not going anywhere. You're stuck with me for at least the next nine months and probably longer."

I am so pissed at this alpha male bullshit, I don't know what to say. He's come in here and just railroaded me like he has the right to do it, like he hasn't known me forever and has forgotten what I do to guys who make me angry.

I breathe in and out deeply, trying to slow my respirations and calm myself down. He accused me of being reckless and crazy basically, so attacking him right now as a pregnant woman is probably not the best way to argue that he's wrong. When I can finally speak I'm proud that my voice comes out level and controlled.

"I appreciate that you think you're doing the right thing by moving in here, but I'm sorry; I'm not ready for that. I don't want you here. You need to take your bags back out to your car and go. I'll call you when I'm ready to talk to you again." I turn around to leave the kitchen, and his voice follows me out.

"We can talk about it more tomorrow, but I care about you and I really want to do my part. I need to!"

I pause in the middle of the hallway, trying to decide how to handle the situation. The decision is taken out of my hands when a knock comes at the front door and a key sounds in the lock.

I close my eyes and take another deep breath. *What the hell is this? God, haven't you punished me enough?*

The door opens and Thibault pokes his head in. "Hey, Sis. Glad I caught you awake."

I throw my hand up and let it drop down to slap my thigh. "Sure, come on in. Everyone else has."

Thibault steps into the front hallway, his eyebrows pulling together at the sight of all the suitcases in front of him. "Are you going somewhere?"

All I can do is shake my head. I'm too pissed to speak. A noise behind me tells me that Lucky has come from the kitchen to join us.

"Hey, man." Lucky stands just next to me, his hands shoved into his front pockets.

Thibault gives him a half smile. "Hey. What's up?" He looks at Lucky and then me and the suitcases. I can almost see the gears turning in his head.

I turn and glare at Lucky, trying to tell him with a look that he'd better not say anything to Thibault about the situation.

"I'm moving in," Lucky says.

It's taking every ounce of strength that I have not to slug him in the gut and knock all the wind out of him. Maybe he senses it, because he steps sideways and moves around me, walking over to greet Thibault with a handshake. "Your sister's going to need some help around here."

Thibault grips his friend's hand, but it's obvious he has no idea what's going on. "Help?" He shifts his gaze to me. "Are you remodeling or something?"

All I can do is shake my head. I'm so angry I don't trust myself to speak. But it doesn't matter, because Lucky's on a roll, the asshole. He doesn't look at me; all of his attention is focused on my brother.

"No, she's not remodeling. She's . . ." He stops, maybe finally realizing he's gone too far.

Better late than never.

"She's what?" Thibault asks. He turns his attention to me. "Are you sick?"

"No, I'm not sick. Not exactly. I'm pregnant."

The only audible sound now is the ticking of the wall clock my grandfather left me. And then the little door on the front of it opens and a tiny bluebird comes out and starts mocking me. *Cuckoo, cuckoo, cuckoo* . . . He says I'm cuckoo ten times, and I can't say as I disagree.

When the bird is done mocking me, Thibault responds. "Uhhh . . . I'm sorry . . . I think I heard you wrong. I could've sworn you said that you're pregnant." He glares at Lucky and then at me.

Before Lucky can say anything else, I throw both hands up like two stop signs. "Stop talking! We are *not* discussing this right now!" I glare at Lucky. "I told you to take your bags and get the hell out of my house, and I meant it." I point at his suitcases. "Start gathering your shit or I'm going to throw it out on the front lawn."

Thibault moves to stand between us, placing one hand on Lucky's shoulder and one on mine. My attempt to knock him away is futile; Thibault's grip is like iron.

"I don't know exactly what's going on here, but I think you guys need a referee." He pushes us both toward the kitchen. "Go on. Go sit down."

ELLE CASEY

Normally when my brother starts acting like my father used to I tell him to screw off, but this time there's a little piece of me that wants him to take over. I want him to stare Lucky in the eye and tell him to fuck off. I need somebody on my side, especially now when it feels like Lucky is standing opposite me, and Lucky's never been in that place before.

"You can say whatever you want, but I'm not going anywhere," Lucky proclaims as he heads to the kitchen.

Thibault says nothing and neither do I, and it makes me feel even more united with my brother than I did two seconds ago. It gives me confidence and fills me with hope. I am not going to be railroaded just because I'm pregnant. I am Toni the badass, according to my teammate May, and I am perfectly capable of doing all the things I've always done, and I don't need anyone's permission to do them. May's statement about me earlier today makes me proud of myself. I should probably thank her for having so much faith in my strength when it seems like no one else does.

Thibault takes another chair at the table, and I sit back down in front of my mug. The tea is cold, but I don't want it anyway. Lucky made it.

"So, is this true?" Thibault has turned his attention fully on me. "You're sure?"

I squirm under the attention. "Maybe. Yes. I guess."

His right eyebrow goes up. "It should be an easy question to answer. Are you or are you not pregnant?"

I grit my teeth a couple times to keep from growling at him. "Yes. Fine. I'm pregnant."

His expression softens. "Are you absolutely sure? Have you been tested?"

Lucky speaks up as my mouth opens to answer. "She did four different tests. It's for sure. She's pregnant."

I whip my head in his direction. "Do *not* speak for me. I am perfectly capable of answering my brother's questions without your help."

Lucky looks over at Thibault. "I'm here to be supportive, but she's not happy about it, obviously."

Thibault looks at Lucky, his expression as tough as I've ever seen it. "Maybe it's your approach that's the problem, bro."

Lucky is clearly surprised by the attitude. Joy surges through me.

"Toni knows I love her, man." He looks at me. "You know I do, Toni. You know I have your best interests at heart."

My heart feels like it's going to collapse in on itself. He used the L word. He probably doesn't even realize he said it, the idiot. "You don't decide what's best for me." I jab my thumb into my chest. "I decide."

Thibault holds up his hands like he's trying to slow us down. "Okay, I get that this is a seriously stressful situation, but I think we can work through this together without any bloodshed."

I'm not against shedding a little of Lucky's blood at this point.

Thibault folds his hands and rests them on the table. "Toni, everybody on the team knows that you're one hundred percent capable of taking care of yourself."

I nod. "Thank you." I sneer at Lucky. *Told you so, jerk.*

"However, I think anyone who knows anything about pregnancy and childbirth knows that it's much easier when you have a partner to help you through it."

I glare at my brother. *Traitor.* "I don't need anyone."

Thibault reaches over to take my hand, but I yank it away and rest my hands in my lap. He is not going to try to manipulate me by acting all nicey nice.

"Everybody needs somebody, and you're no exception, young lady."

My eyebrows go up. "You better be careful, *bro*. You don't get to call me 'young lady' and get away with it."

He smiles, the bastard. "Sorry. I was channeling Dad there."

"Bad move."

He nods. "Yeah. It just slipped out. Sorry."

I look at the two severely misguided men sitting in front of me and shake my head. "I don't know why you suddenly see this little girl who needs everybody's help sitting in front of you. Just because I'm pregnant, it doesn't change who I am. What's wrong with you guys?"

Lucky might be a tiny bit contrite. "I don't know. Logically I know you're as tough as ever." He shrugs. "I can't say why, but I'm definitely looking at you differently now. I guess I'm just a sexist pig or something." He looks down at the table with a confused expression on his face.

I slap my hand on the table. "Well, don't be that person! You've never been a sexist pig before, so don't start now. I'm still the same girl I was two weeks ago. Nothing has changed."

Thibault is shaking his head, his expression concerned.

I turn on him. "What? What's your problem?"

He's looking at me like he's one of our parents again. "You know that's not exactly true, Toni. Things *have* changed. You're pregnant, and you can't just disregard that fact. You have to deal with it."

It's not his words that have my back up so much as the tone he uses. "What's that supposed to mean?"

"It means that your duties at work are going to have to change." Thibault looks over at Lucky, and Lucky nods. They both look sad, but they're not nearly as sad as I am. I'm battling tears.

"Why? Nothing has to change as far as I'm concerned."

Thibault sits back and sighs. "You forget that I'm the one who handles the insurance for the group. I have to manage our risks to the extent possible. Sending you out into the field, into those neighborhoods where we go, is not an option right now. You'll have to work a lot more inside the warehouse. We need to lower your personal risk to as close to zero as we can."

Thibault's my brother, but he's also kind of my boss. If I fly off the handle now, he'll know that I can't handle my shit when stuff gets hard.

"I can see why you would think that, but you know that when I go out in the field it's pretty much no risk. We just go out, take a look at things, and come back and talk about it. That's it."

Thibault's brows go up. "I read May's report about what went down today. I wouldn't exactly call that a no-risk situation."

I want to explode, I'm so angry. "What report? I'm the one who was supposed to write the report, and I haven't submitted it yet."

"Actually, you were both supposed to submit a report together, but since you left work early, May did it herself. And I'm glad she did, because its contents are germane to this conversation."

Breathe in for five seconds, breathe out for six. In for five, out for six. It's the only way I can keep from jumping up and punching a hole in the wall.

Lucky leans in and puts his hand on my knee. "Babe, I can see you're upset, but I wish you would just listen to your brother for a minute."

I don't move a single millimeter. I just look at him, my expression dead. "I hear everything you're both saying. Trust me." Obviously, this pregnancy has turned them both into cavemen, but I've got news for them: I ain't no cavewoman.

He's almost pleading now. "I know you hear the words, but I'm not sure you appreciate where they're coming from. We just care about you so much, and we worry that in an effort to prove yourself, you'll take too much risk and end up getting hurt. You could hurt the baby."

Tears rush to my eyes, and I battle to keep them from falling down my cheeks. "Are you saying that I'm the type of mother who would intentionally hurt her child?" I guess I can't blame him for thinking that; I am a murderer after all. But it still hurts.

He grips my knee hard. "No, I would never say that. And I would never think it, either. You're misunderstanding me."

"Toni, come on, you know he didn't mean it that way." Thibault sounds disappointed in me, which feels like a knife to the gut. "Stop turning this into a pity party."

I stand slowly, unable to deal with these idiots anymore. "It's late. And as you've pointed out many times already, I'm pregnant, and I guess that means I'm more tired than I would normally be. So I'm going to go upstairs and leave you cavemen down here to make your plans and dream your dreams about how you're going to start running my life for me. But . . ." I look at each of them in turn, ". . . you need to keep something very clear in your heads: this is *my* life and *my* body and I'm going to do whatever the hell I want with it. And if you try to control me or if you try to tell me how I'm going to live, you're going to be very sorry."

I spin on my heel and leave the room, slowly mounting the steps as my heart cracks into a bunch of small pieces. I'm so mad at them at this point, I'd be willing to walk away from Bourbon Street Boys altogether. It's killing me.

Whenever the vague idea of being pregnant entered my mind before, I imagined it being pretty crappy, but I never thought it would be this awful. Two of the four men in my life, guys who I respect more than anything in the world, have essentially turned on me. They're treating me like an idiot, like a possession. Like they don't know me at all. I feel so alone. Where have all the men who respected me gone?

Then I remember: I don't just have Thibault and Lucky at my back. They're not the only ones who respect who I am and what I'm all about. The thought brings instant relief and a plan. I'm going to wake up tomorrow morning first thing and go talk to Ozzie about this. Ozzie will fix it. Ozzie will know what to do. I know I can count on him.

I go into my room and collapse on the bed, falling instantly into a fitful sleep. I'm not one bit surprised when the ghost of Charlie arrives to haunt me once more. This time I don't fight it; I let him come. What's one more man trying to destroy who I am? The darkness that represents the love I used to have for the man I killed surrounds me and I listen once again as Charlie lists all the reasons why I shouldn't be allowed to be a mother.

CHAPTER TWENTY

I go to work, my goal for the day to sit down with Ozzie and talk to him about the problems I'm having with Lucky and Thibault. I'm confident he'll back me up. He knows that my being pregnant doesn't change anything about my abilities. He's told me many times how much he values my contribution to the team, and I know he doesn't want to put me behind a desk when I could be useful elsewhere.

Unfortunately, I quickly learn that Ozzie's goal for the day is to schmooze the chief of police. First, he's gone all morning in meetings at the police station, and then I hear through May that he's at lunch with the chief and a couple detectives who we work with frequently.

I'm tapping my pen on a legal pad over and over as I search through hours of videotape, frustrated that I'm getting nowhere with my personal life.

"What's up with you?" May leans back in her squeaky chair from the cubicle next to me, headphone wires dangling from her ears. I'm doing a search of our video recordings and she's doing the same with the sound files. We traded chores for the day to keep things interesting.

I don't bother looking at her for more than two seconds before turning my attention back to the video. "Nothing."

She pulls her headphones out of her ears and swings one of the earbuds at me, hitting me in the arm with it. "Liar, liar, pants on fire."

I pause the video and sigh loudly, hoping she'll take the hint. "Trying to work here."

"You've been working for three hours straight. Take a break. You know what they say—all work and no play makes Toni a dull girl."

I turn to look at her and find her smiling like a lunatic. "Don't you get tired of being goofy all the time?"

"Don't you get tired of being grouchy all the time?"

My frown jumps back into place. "I'm not grouchy. I'm . . ." I almost let it slip that I'm stressed. *Holy hell.* That's all I need to do—feed her fire with more gossip fuel.

She rolls her chair closer to mine. "What's that? What's going on? You can tell me. I promise, I won't tell a soul."

"Except for your sister and Ozzie, of course."

She shrugs. "That's a given. But I figure nobody minds if those two know what I know."

She's probably right about that. Neither of them would ever use one of my secrets against me. But that doesn't mean I want to share with anyone right now. "I'm fine. I just want to talk to Ozzie about something."

"Oh, is that why you keep asking where he is?"

I roll my eyes. "Why else would I be asking where he is?"

May shrugs. "I don't know."

The tone of her voice makes me suspicious. I look more closely at her expression and see worry there. "How many times do I have to tell you . . . I have no interest whatsoever in your boyfriend."

She winks at me. "Fiancé. He's my fiancé now. But anyway, I know you're not interested in him."

157

It's on the tip of my tongue to ask her what her deal is, because there's clearly something going on in that crazy head of hers, but I really don't want to open up a conversation about my boss with his fiancée. Lord only knows what private information she'd share with me that I'd never be able to scrub from my brain.

I go back to my video and press the play button so I can watch more frames of a front door that hardly ever opens. We saw Marc come out of that house the other day, but there's been no sign of him since.

"Can I ask what you want to talk to Ozzie about? Is it personal?"

I shake my head. "No, you cannot ask."

"Okay, then, I'm going to assume it's personal. So, what could Toni want to speak to Ozzie about that is so personal she doesn't want to share it with me?"

I refuse to rise to the bait, but her next statement catches me by surprise.

"You could talk to him tonight at the pizza party."

I hit the pause button on my video again and turn to face her. "What pizza party?"

She rolls her eyes at me and shakes her head. "Don't you read my emails? I sent you the information yesterday."

I tend to save her emails for one mass reading when I have the strength reserves handy to keep my patience. She sends more of them than anyone else on the team by far, and half of them are useless babble as far as I'm concerned.

I switch over to the email system and log in my personal details, bringing up eight emails that I've not yet read. I scan them for mention of a pizza party and find it. "Sorry," I say distractedly. "I've been busy."

May mumbles under her breath. "Busy filtering me out."

I scan the information in the message. Apparently, there's a pizza party tonight at Jenny's house and the entire team is invited.

I chew my lip as I consider my options. Lucky stayed in my brother's cottage last night, saving me from throwing a total bitch fit at him in the morning. If I had seen him sitting in my kitchen after I woke up from all those Charlie-nightmares, I would've lost my temper for sure. Thankfully, Thibault knows me well enough to realize that Lucky was better off with him than me.

I need to talk to Ozzie before they do. I don't want them poisoning his mind with the idea of viewing me as a helpless fool. I also want to get his advice on what I should do about Lucky. Ozzie knows both of us better than anyone, even better than Thibault does, and I trust his judgment more than my own. I have a habit of dealing with things in the harshest way possible, but this situation demands a little more finesse than that. Even I can see that.

"Where is Ozzie going after his lunch with the chief?" I ask.

May is busy with her earphones in her ear so I have to lean over and pluck one out. She looks at me all innocence, trying to cover up the fact that I've hurt her feelings by ignoring her emails.

I battle the urge to growl at her. "I just read your emails. Sorry about waiting. If it makes you feel any better, I didn't read anybody else's emails either."

She smiles a little. "Actually, it does make me feel better." Her smile drops off. "Does that make me a bad person?"

"Did you hear my question? Where is Ozzie going after his lunch?"

She shrugs. "I have no idea. But he told me he'd see me at the party, so I have to assume that means he won't be here before then, because he knew I was going to be stuck in the cubicles from hell all afternoon."

I look at the frozen video on my screen, tapping my pen as it all comes together for me: if I want to talk to Ozzie, I'm stuck with the pizza party, because this is not a conversation I want to have over the phone. Unfortunately, pizza parties could be my least favorite thing in the entire world, especially when they include the whole team and everyone's family; it's just too much noise and chaos for me. But if this is where I'm going to find Ozzie, then this is where I need to be.

"I guess I'll see you at the pizza party, then."

"Yay! I'm so happy. I'll email Jenny right now and tell her you're coming."

"I'm sure she doesn't care."

"Well, you are wrong about that, Little Miss Grouchy Pants. Jenny and I both love it when you come to our events."

I go back to watching my video, completely unconvinced about the truth of that statement. *Wouldn't it be nice, though, to have a group of people looking forward to me showing up?*

I don't know where that thought just came from, but it's seriously unsettling. *Yikes.* Never in my life have I wanted to belong to anything other than the Bourbon Street Boys team. My fingers tremble as they hover over the keyboard. I'm afraid this pregnancy is already giving me brain damage.

CHAPTER TWENTY-ONE

I'm standing on Jenny's front porch and I can hear the noise coming from inside her house with the door still closed. I deliberately waited until I knew the party would be in full swing before showing up, hoping that Ozzie would be happy to talk to me out back because it would be a welcome break from all the chaos.

I pause at the front door, my fingers resting on the handle for just a few moments. Butterflies slam dance in my stomach as I imagine myself telling Ozzie about my situation. Up until now, it's been just a concept: I'm going to talk to Ozzie and get his advice. But now, moments away from the actual event, I'm picturing myself looking up at my friend and advisor and saying I'm pregnant, and I'm getting sick over the thought of his possible reaction. *Maybe I should just turn around and run away.* It's a tempting thought, but I know I can't follow through on it.

I have to tell the man I respect more than anyone else in the world that I lack the control it takes to pause in the heat of the moment and tell a guy to put a condom on. The humiliation runs deep. But there's nothing to do about it now; what's done is done and I just need to face up to it. I press on the handle's button and let myself in. The door swings open and the noise hits me like a heavy woolen blanket, scratchy and suffocating.

"Toni! You made it!" May comes running over on tiptoe, a slice of pizza in one hand and a glass of wine in the other. "I'm so happy to see you." She envelopes me in a hug made with her elbows.

I glance first to my left, and find myself looking into a glass of wine dipping precariously toward my head, and then to my right, where a slice of pizza is about to jab me in the eye. I stiffen and wait for the one-sided love-fest to be over.

She backs away and looks at me, smiling.

"You have pepperoni in your teeth." I blink at her, waiting for her to react.

"Really? Where?" She smiles harder.

Jenny comes over and nudges her sister to the side. "Hi, Toni. Good to see you. It's been a while." She pulls me into a hug, this one without wine or food joining in.

I reach one hand around her ribs and pat her on the back. "Thanks for inviting me."

May is busy sucking pizza out of her teeth as Jenny leans back and smiles at me. "I hear you want to talk to Ozzie. He's out back with Lucky and Thibault. Can I get you a glass of wine or a beer?"

I press my lips together and shake my head. Every horrible thought I can possibly come up with is rushing through my brain all at once. *What are they doing out there? Are they talking about me? Are they making a plan to keep me out of the business? Are they kicking me off the team? Are they going to lock me up in my house and make me drink non-caffeinated beverages and eat fresh fruits and vegetables until I'm ready to explode?* I'm anxious to get back there with Ozzie, but I don't want Jenny or her sister to know it.

I shrug. "I'll just have some water if that's okay."

Jenny gives me a funny look. "Water? Okaaay. Water it is." She turns away and walks to the kitchen, grabbing her sister's sleeve as she goes. May looks like she's trying to decide whether to follow her sister or to continue to interrogate me, but when Jenny calls out to her, the conflict ends. May turns on her heel and walks down the hall behind her sister, taking another bite of her pizza as she goes.

I look to my left once the two of them are farther down the hallway and see Dev sitting on the floor with a whole pile of kids. Sammy is in his lap and his son's wheelchair is next to Sammy. Sammy is resting his hand on Jacob's foot while Dev's son is leaning over to walk an action figure over the top of Sammy's head. Sammy is smiling at the offense.

Crazy kids. I have the strangest urge to reach down and rest my hand on my lower stomach, but I resist. This pregnancy might not even last. One of the books that Lucky left in my house says that over thirty percent of first-time pregnancies end in early miscarriage. Maybe my mistake will fix itself without any help from me. I suddenly feel like crying.

"Hey, Toni," Dev says, looking at me funny.

All the kids look up at his comment and catch me in the hall-way. My heart constricts at all those innocent eyes staring me down. I feel like they can see right through me, into my soul. I fear they'll find blackness there, and I don't want it to rub off on them. It reminds me what a horrible mother I'm going to be. *Maybe I should think about adoption.*

"Miss Toni," exclaims Sammy. "You came to the pizza party." He jumps up from Dev's lap and runs over to me with his hand out.

I've met the kid, like, a hundred times already, but he always greets me with a handshake. If my baby turns out like him, maybe it won't be so bad.

I bend over and hold my hand out, taking his little fingers in mine. "Hello, Sammy. How've you been?"

"I've been really good. Did you notice anything different about me?" He sways a little on his feet with his hands on his butt, looking especially cute.

I rest my hands on my thighs, still bent over, examining him closely. "Did you grow a new freckle on your nose?" I point at his face. "I think I see a new one there."

He shakes his head. "No. That's not it. Try again."

I take a moment to examine him for real this time, but the kid looks exactly the same to me. I don't get these games that they play. I shrug. "Sorry, bud, but I don't see anything different about you."

Sammy nods. "Very good, Miss Toni. You are *very* observant. But the difference you will see in me is not with your *eyes*." He's talking so funny, I almost missed it. But then I realize Sammy's giving me the biggest hint he possibly can without actually giving away his secret. All the other kids are completely silent, waiting with bated breath to see if I'll figure it out.

I don't know why a warm glow spreads through me when I look into his eyes and wink. "Maybe I hear something a little different about you . . . ?"

Sammy jumps up and down, clapping his hands, reminding me eerily of his Auntie May. "You got it! You got it! I've been going to speech thhhherapy."

"I noticed. You talk differently now."

He puts his little hands on his hips and nods once. "Yes, I do. Thank you for noticing. It's very hard work, but Miss Tansey tells me that if I keep trying and if I'm nice to myself and don't get too mad when I mess up, I'm going to go far."

I stand up straighter and nod, patting him on the head. "I'm sure she's right."

I glance over and catch Dev giving me a thumbs-up. His son mimics the gesture. I wave to them and continue down the hall. "I have to go talk to Ozzie. I'll see you guys later."

The entire room responds in a loud chorus. "See you later, Miss Toni!"

I have to rub my chest by my heart to ease the cramp out of it. I am so conflicted right now. I don't like kids and they don't like me, but these little guys aren't so bad. *Is it possible my kid won't be so bad? Is it possible he won't hate me?* I don't even want to think about it.

Taking things in steps feels like a good idea. I think I just need to do everything one step at a time, one day at a time. Kind of like handling alcoholism. The analogy doesn't seem so far off to me. After everything happened with Charlie, I realized that I'm addicted to darkness, but having a child is the opposite of that. I never would've chosen this for myself, but it has been chosen for me, or it has been chosen as a result of my irresponsibility and lack of forethought. Either way, I know that there's no room in my life for both darkness and light. One of them is going to have to win out, and I pray it will be the latter; but if my history holds, it will be the former.

What will that mean for my child? The inevitable answer pops into my head, making me want to cry. But maybe it wouldn't be so awful if my child grew up in a single-parent home with Lucky in charge. Maybe they'd both be better off without me. The whole idea makes me sadder than sad. When I walk out onto the porch and the three men standing there immediately stop talking, the feeling only grows.

CHAPTER TWENTY-TWO

Thibault, Ozzie, and Lucky move apart as I approach. I feel as though I've broken up a very private conversation, and it pisses me off. Lucky is not one of my bosses; there is no reason for him to be in on a private conversation with Ozzie and Thibault without me present, unless of course they're talking about me and they don't want me to know what they're saying.

I walk up and fill the space they've left for me, nodding at Thibault and Ozzie, but ignoring Lucky. I can't even look at him right now. I don't trust my emotions not to run away on me.

"Hey," Ozzie says.

"Hey." I glance at Thibault and he nods at me.

"What's up?" Ozzie's expression shows only curiosity. It gives me hope that these guys haven't been standing here talking about me.

"Can I talk to you for a sec? Privately?"

Ozzie shrugs. "Sure." He looks at the guys. "Could you give us a minute?"

Thibault says, "Sure."

Lucky shakes his head. "I'd like to stay." He folds his arms over his chest.

I turn on him. "You're not invited to the conversation."

He opens his mouth to say something, but Ozzie steps in, his hand up almost in Lucky's face. "I don't want to hear it. Toni has asked for a private meeting and she's gonna get it."

For a moment there's a blaze of defiance in Lucky's eyes, but then he looks away and backs off. "I'll be inside."

Thibault moves toward the back door and pushes Lucky on the shoulder, keeping him in front of him. Lucky jerks his back away, his anger showing in his body language.

I watch him go with a scowl. How dare he think he can decide who I talk to and what I say? He is totally off the range, and I'm definitely going to make sure Ozzie knows that I don't appreciate it.

I wait until they're inside the house with the door shut before I turn back to my boss. "Well. So. How'd you like that drama?"

Ozzie sticks his thumbs in the corners of his front pockets. His chest and biceps bulge out at me as he throws his shoulders back. I'm used to it. He's always been big, and he never skips a workout. It makes me feel safe to know that this guy has my back and my best interests at heart.

"Something is going on, I take it."

I look up at him. "You noticed?" I try to laugh, but it comes out sounding kind of crazy. I give up on finding humor in the situation and go back to bare honesty. "Lucky is driving me nuts and I just need it to stop."

Ozzie frowns and tilts his head in confusion. "I think I missed something."

Okay, so the guys definitely did not tell Ozzie about my pregnancy. *Points for them.* I feel only a tiny bit guilty that I was accusing them of it in my mind.

I'm trying to think of the best way to word the situation, wondering if it's possible to let Ozzie know that Lucky is bothering me without also revealing that I'm pregnant, but I'm immediately uncomfortable with that idea. It feels dishonest to me, so I drop the thought two seconds after it pops into my head.

I stare at the deck and open my mouth to speak, hoping the right words will fall out since no grand plan is making its presence known to my brain. "Well, there's kind of a lot of shit going on right now, and I get why Lucky's upset with me, but I'm not okay with it at the same time." I pause, looking up at Ozzie with an apologetic expression. "I'm not being very clear, am I?"

Ozzie shakes his head. "Nope."

He's not going to give me any rope. I suppose that's fair. We're both adults here; I should be able to communicate like one. I take a deep breath in and out so I can start over, making sure I keep eye contact as I speak this time.

"Something happened between Lucky and me a really long time ago, and a few weeks ago, we all met at the pub on a Friday night. Do you remember?"

Ozzie merely nods.

"So, we kind of repeated the mistake we made when we were fifteen, only this time we went a lot further with it and we were supposed to act like adults about it, but we didn't."

"Are you dancing around the subject because you think I can't handle it or because you're embarrassed?"

I know it's his personal hallmark to go right for the jugular, but it's really inconvenient for me right now.

"All right, fine. I'll just be straight with you."

He gives me a slight smile. "That would be nice."

I can't look at him when I speak. I fear his judgment too much. I stare at the wood deck we're standing on. "Back when we were fifteen years old, we went to a dance together with Thibault, and Lucky and I kind of hooked up. We didn't go all the way, but whatever . . . it's not important. Anyway, that night at the pub on

Friday, we hooked up again, and he followed me home. I was really drunk, as you know, and we were both acting really stupid, and one thing led to another, and . . ."

"You slept together."

I jerk my eyes up at him. "You know?"

He chuckles. "No, I don't know. But isn't it obvious?" He shrugs, as if he's apologizing for reading me so easily.

I shake my head, hissing out a sigh of frustration. "I know. I'm sorry. This has really messed me up."

"I don't really see what the problem is. So you slept together? Big deal. Move on."

I give him a smile that holds no humor. "Wouldn't that be nice?" My sad smile starts to melt away, and I feel stupid tears rising up in my eyes. "Unfortunately, we were both drunk and we're both terrible communicators, so we ended up having sex without using protection."

Ozzie's face goes completely blank. His hands fall out of his pockets and his arms hang at his sides, making him look like a giant gorilla.

My insides shrivel up and start to spasm. The judgment coming off him in waves is literally making me queasy.

"What exactly are you telling me?" he asks, his voice devoid of emotion.

I open my mouth to answer him, but then I realize that there's something more urgent than words that wants to leave my mouth. I run over to the edge of the deck and lean over a planter, vomiting on the flowers it contains.

I can't see Ozzie but I can hear him. He turns, his boots sliding on the deck under him.

"I guess that answers my question," he says. He sounds tired.

I spit the sour taste from my mouth and toss my hair over my shoulder, wiping my lips and chin with the back of my hand.

ELLE CASEY

Luckily, I haven't eaten anything all day, so there really isn't much to worry about with the clean-up. *Sorry, plants.*

Holy crap, how embarrassing. I answer questions by vomiting? What's wrong with me? I turn around to face him. "Yeah. So . . . I'm pregnant."

His face is morphing through so many different expressions it's impossible to tell what he's thinking.

"Would you say something, please?" I plead.

He lifts a hand and runs his fingers through his hair, scrubbing his head when he's done. His face is tipped downward toward the deck as he massages his neck, so I can't read his expression. But then he lifts his eyes to mine and gives me a sad smile. "Congratulations?"

His words are like a knife right through my heart. The floodgates open and the tears come flowing out unchecked.

"Wrong answer," I choke out before turning around to walk back into the house.

He's faster than I am. He grabs my wrist and pulls me back. The force he uses is strong enough that it sends me flying into his chest. He wraps his strong arms around me and squeezes tight, kissing me on the top of the head like a father might do to his daughter. "You're not going anywhere."

I struggle to be free. "Let me go, Ozzie. I don't want to be here."

"Too bad. This is where you are and this is where you're going to stay until I say so."

I don't like his choice of words. It triggers something in me. I start screaming and struggling, punching him on the back so he'll let me go.

He immediately thrusts me away from him, but keeps a strong grip on my shoulders. He bends over and looks into my eyes, his face only inches away. "*Stop.* Stop it *right* now."

I freeze, knowing in that moment how a deer standing in front of a set of headlights feels. I'm afraid, but I don't know what of. *Is it Ozzie or myself?* I'm too messed up in the head to be sure.

He's glaring at me. "You need to get ahold of your emotions right now."

I speak through trembling lips, my voice nearly a growl. "Don't tell me what I have to do. You don't own me."

His expression softens as does his grip on me. "I know that. You know that I know that." He shakes his head and hisses out a long breath. "Toni, you've gotta talk to me." He lets me go and we stand there, facing off against each other. "You know that I'm here for you, but I can't do anything to help if you won't calm down and talk to me."

I can't stop my stupid chin from quivering or my lips from trembling, and the tears don't want to quit either. This has got to be the pregnancy taking over my body again, because the normal non-pregnant Toni would never be such a wimp. I hate being pregnant; it's official now.

"I came here to talk to you, but apparently I can't."

He sounds hurt. "Why not?"

"I don't know!" I look left and right, the desire to run filling every inch of me. "I don't know what's going on in my life anymore! Everything is changing and I hate it!"

He reaches up and strokes my upper arms, his touch much more gentle this time. "I get it. I get that this is scary for you. Hell, it's scary for me." He gives me a goofy smile and chuckles. "But we're going to be okay. You're going to be great." He leans in a little. "So tell me . . . what's going on with Lucky?"

I throw my arms up, dislodging his hands. "I don't know! He found out that I was pregnant and moved in." I seriously want to kick something, but the only thing available is Ozzie's shins and he doesn't deserve that.

Ozzie frowns. "Moved in? To your house?"

"Yes!" My eyes are practically bugging out of my head. "He just showed up with all his shit and demanded to be let in. He said he's moving in, but I am *not* okay with that."

Ozzie nods. "I get that. I wouldn't be okay with it either."

"Thank you!" I let out a long, shaky breath, finally feeling some peace seeping into my bones. "That's what I said. I mean, this is not the Middle Ages. A man can't decide for me how to live my life or who my roommate is going to be."

Ozzie continues to nod. "I get it. You're absolutely right. You want me to talk to him?"

I am about to say yes, but I stop myself. Do I really need Ozzie fighting my battles for me? I bite my lip.

"If you don't want me to, just say so. But if you want me to, I will." Ozzie puts his hands up like he's surrendering. "I'm here to help you out, that's it."

"This pregnancy is totally messing with my brain. I can't even think straight anymore."

Ozzie moves in slowly and hugs me again. This time he's not here to control me, he's here to console me, and I can live with that. "I hear that happens to pregnant ladies. Just do me a favor, okay?"

I look up at him, resting my chin on his chest. "What?"

"Be gentle with yourself. I've never known anyone who is harder on herself than you are. Right now I think you're going to need to have a little extra patience with everyone, including you."

I look away, seeing through the back door that May is headed in our direction from the kitchen. I step away, putting distance between Ozzie and me. All that crazy girl needs is a hint that there's something going on between us and she'll be a thorn in my side I can't dislodge. I already have enough of those.

"I'll try," I say, not sure I mean it.

The door opens and May steps out, full of her customary cheer. "You guys ready for some pizza? It's getting cold."

Ozzie holds up a hand. "We'll be there in a second. We just need to chat for one more minute."

May hesitates, looking uncertain. I don't think she was expecting that answer. "Okay. I'll see you guys inside. With the cold pizza." She slowly backs away and shuts the door behind her, but she stares at us for a few seconds through the window before leaving.

I smile up at her boyfriend. "She thinks I've got the hots for you."

He smiles and shakes his head. "I know. I tell her all the time I have no interest in you, but she doesn't want to hear it."

"I think she likes drama."

Ozzie gives me a teasing look. "When she finds out your little secret, it'll feed all her drama needs for the next year, so maybe I should thank you for taking the heat off me."

I roll my eyes and turn toward the door. "Don't remind me. I'm planning to hold off telling her until I'm out of the hospital."

Ozzie laughs. "I'm not sure that's going to work. She's one of the most observant women I've ever met." He gets to the door ahead of me and opens it.

I look up at him and frown. "Please don't start getting my doors for me too."

"Too?"

I walk through the door. "Lucky is treating me like I'm made of glass."

Ozzie steps in but stops me with a hand on my shoulder, keeping me from going farther into the kitchen. I turn around and look up.

"Don't be too hard on Lucky. He really cares about you. I'm sure he's just trying to do the right thing, and you can't blame him for that."

"He needs lessons on how to deal with women."

Ozzie shakes his head. "Those lessons won't work with you, Toni."

"What's that supposed to mean?"

Ozzie drapes his arm over my shoulder as he walks with me through the kitchen. "You're not like any other woman. You're an original, but he knows that. You came to me for advice and this is it: Give Lucky a chance. I think he could make you happy."

A warm sensation fills me as we arrive in the family room. Maybe it's hope I'm feeling, I don't know. I'm not ready to examine it too closely right now. His arm drops away and May comes over with a slice of pizza and a smile for each of us. I try to return the emotion, but the moment the fumes from the sausage float up into my nose, I know there's no hope for me.

I shove the plate back in her face and turn around, running for the bathroom. I make it just in time to barf up my guts into the toilet. When I'm done dry-heaving and wishing I were dead, I stand and look in the mirror. Both Jenny and May are like statues in the entrance of the bathroom with their eyes bugging out at me.

I close my eyes and sigh. "Oh, Jesus Christ."

CHAPTER TWENTY-THREE

Jenny and May step into the bathroom and lock the door behind them. I flush the toilet, refusing to look at them.

"Okay, what's going on?" May asks.

"Shush, let her talk." Jenny is trying to reason with her sister, but I know better. She's just as curious as May is and she'll probably keep me prisoner in here until I spill my guts.

I don't turn around, fearing they'll use their gossipy wiles to trick me into telling all. "There's nothing wrong. I have a stomach bug. I don't think that sausage was a good idea for me."

"I saw you at work today, and you were fine," May says.

I pull off some toilet paper and use it to wipe my mouth before turning around. Trying to act casual, I shrug. "It just started. I threw up in the backyard, too. I'm sure it's just a twenty-four-hour thing, but you probably don't want to get too close to me." I hold out my hand, hoping they'll back away.

Unfortunately, neither of them takes my very obvious threat into account. They both lean in closer.

I bend my spine as far backward as it'll go. "Seriously, you guys . . . I'm totally contagious."

Jenny narrows her eyes at me and then at my chest. "Your boobs are bigger. *And* you're vomiting." She smiles all sly-like. "I'm pretty sure what you have is not contagious."

I look down at my chest. I did notice that my bra was a little tighter today, but I wrote that off as a laundry mishap. I have those more often than I'd like to admit. I look up at the two of them, trying to channel as much confidence into my voice as I possibly can. "It's a different bra. It's a push-up. With extra padding."

May reaches over lightning quick and pokes the bottom of my left boob. "Ha! Liar, liar, pants on fire, *again*. That is *so* not a push-up bra." She looks at her sister and nods. They share a quick high-five before turning their attention back to me.

I grab the offended body part and glare at her. "What the hell, man . . . Don't touch my boob!"

May shrugs. "Hey, I know a push-up bra when I see one. I'm a photographer, you know. A *professional* photographer."

I can't help it; I mimic her voice, emphasizing the way it comes into my ear as the most annoying whine I have ever heard. "I'm a *professional* photographer."

Jenny and May share a meaningful look. Then they nod again.

Jenny turns to face me first. "You're extra moody, aren't you?" She puts her finger on her lower lip and rolls her eyes to the ceiling. "Let's see . . . Nauseated? Boobs getting bigger? Especially emotional? And all the males around her acting like idiots? What does this add up to?" She pauses and looks at her sister.

May nods and then looks at me, her face twisted up in a triumphant smile. "Pregnant."

They both stare at me, and they wait. And they wait. And they wait some more.

I stick my chin out. "You guys are crazy."

May matches my expression. "We may be crazy but we aren't pregnant." Her voice slips a little on the last word.

Jenny turns to look at her sister and puts her hand on May's shoulder. "What's the matter, babe? Are you sad?"

May shakes her head vigorously. "No. I'm fine."

Jenny folds her arms and stares her sister down. "Now whose pants are on fire?"

May pushes her sister's shoulder gently. "Shut up."

I sense my opportunity and jump on it. "Is something wrong with you and Ozzie?"

May's eyes open wide, perhaps with fear. "Why would you say that?"

I shrug, maybe overdoing the drama a little bit, but almost deliriously happy to have the heat off me. "Oh, I don't know. We were just talking out back . . ." I leave her to draw her own conclusions, and it doesn't take her more than a couple seconds to jump to the wrong ones.

"Did he say something to you?" She grabs my forearm and squeezes.

I shrug. "Not much. But you should probably talk to him."

May turns to look at Jenny. "I told you there was something going on." She scrambles to unlock the door and takes off from the bathroom, leaving me with just one busybody to contend with. We watch May disappear into the darkness of the unlit hallway. Then Jenny turns to me and nods slowly.

"Respect."

"What?" I'm feigning an innocence I definitely do not feel. I seriously want to do a victory dance right now.

"That was one of the most amazing redirects I have ever seen in my life. Good for you. But you do realize, I hope, that this will now increase our curiosity tenfold."

I walk around her to the doorway, wishing I weren't sweating so much. "There's nothing to be curious about."

I leave to the sound of Jenny responding in a singsong voice. "Liar, liar, pants on fire, underwear's hanging from a telephone wire . . ."

I slip out the front door before she leaves the bathroom and without anyone else at the party seeing. Since the pizza's making me sick and I've had my chat with Ozzie, there's no reason for me to stay. The relief that fills me as I leave that noisy place is almost palpable.

I'm halfway to my car when I hear the door opening and shutting behind me. Turning around, I see Lucky silhouetted in the porch light. *Great. So much for a clean getaway.*

"Where are you going?" he asks, his hands shoved into the front pockets of his jeans. The muscles in his arms bulge, making my heart quicken. *Traitor heart . . . when will you learn?*

"Home." I reach my door and unlock it, opening it so I can get inside and take off before he gets it into his head to follow me.

"Do you want me to bring you some pizza?"

Talk about clueless. I get into my car and then lean out of the window to shout my answer. "No! I don't want you to bring me anything, and I don't want you at my house!" I reverse out of the driveway, leaving tire tracks in the street when I peel out for home.

I fume all the way back, expecting to see Lucky's car in my rearview mirror the entire way. He has no idea the piece of my mind he will suffer if I so much as catch a glimpse of him anywhere near me. But I arrive home safe and sound and all alone. At the top of my front porch steps, I pause, listening for the sound of his engine, but it never comes.

I lie in bed that night surrounded by complete silence. It's what I thought I wanted, but now I find myself sad that Lucky didn't insist on being here with me. Up is down and down is up. Nothing is making sense anymore. Ozzie's advice comes back to me: *Give Lucky a chance.* I hate that I got so mad at him earlier when all he was doing was offering to bring me dinner.

I rest my hand on my lower belly and talk to the individual who has apparently taken over my brain and is not doing a very good job of it.

"You and I need to work as a team, little baby person. I don't think I can take nine months of this confusion." I feel nothing in response, so I fall asleep in a slight panic, worried that I'm going to give birth to a child who wants nothing to do with me.

CHAPTER TWENTY-FOUR

After the nearly sleepless night I had, I'm thrilled to be going into work, even though it means I'll probably be sitting directly across the table from Lucky. My feelings about his pushy behavior have softened a little, but I'm still not ready to discuss the situation with him. I know we'll find a solution eventually, but there's no need to rush into things, especially when my emotions are still so raw. Thankfully, Ozzie was cool about everything; it's making it easier for me to be forgiving of pushy men.

When I get upstairs to the meeting area, Ozzie is already talking. A quick check of my watch tells me I'm two minutes late. I rush over to take the only empty seat, which just so happens to be right next to Lucky. I glance at him and give him a perfunctory nod before turning my attention to Ozzie. I focus on calming my racing heart. Sitting next to Lucky never used to be a problem, but I can see it is now. *Has he always been this sexy?* I think my pregnancy is sending my hormone levels on the fritz.

"So far, so good on the review of the surveillance tapes and recordings." Ozzie checks his notes before continuing. "We have a list of possible code-words that Jenny and Lucky pulled from some social media accounts of suspected gang members that we need to match up to the surveillance and the dispatch logs I got from Detective Adams, to see if we can connect any dots." The boss looks over at me. "Toni, I need you to continue with what you were doing and try to get it finished up today. Then take this list of codes and the logs, and note where they showed up on Facebook and Twitter. See if any activity happening around the same times gives us any clues as to what those codes might mean."

He looks at his girlfriend next. "May, I want you to go out with Thibault and set up some more surveillance at a new location we discovered after we got some intel from the detectives working on the case."

My ears start to burn at this little development. May has never gone out with Thibault, just the two of them. If Thibault's mission is to work surveillance, I'm the one who rides shotgun, not her.

I lift a finger, letting Ozzie know that I want to say something, but he just shakes his head at me and continues, shifting his focus to my right.

"Lucky, where are you and Jenny with the social media hacks? Is this all we can expect or is there more?"

Lucky clears his throat, but I don't look at him. I stare at Ozzie, hoping to catch his eye. I could just be paranoid, but it almost seems like he's avoiding looking at me.

"Jenny's hooked into five different accounts now, I think? I'll have to double-check her last email to me on that. I think we have a couple more to access, but we can get in and get transcripts put together really quick if you need us to."

Ozzie nods. "Yes. Do that and get them over to Toni. Good job. Keep it up. Let me know what's going on as it evolves. I have another meeting with the chief in a couple days, so it would be great to have more information for him."

"You got it."

I lift my finger again but Ozzie turns his attention to Thibault. "You have everything you need for the job today?"

Maybe it's my imagination again, but I think Thibault sends a worried glance in my direction before he answers. "Yeah, we're all set."

"Okay, that's it then." Ozzie claps his hands together once. "Short meeting. If everyone could make sure to get your reports in on time so I can collect everything for the chief, that would be appreciated." Ozzie finally looks at me, and I take his expression for a scolding.

Yeah, okay . . . so I didn't do my report before Miss Perfect May did it for me. Whatever.

I'm fuming inside. I feel like I've been completely disregarded, and I'm pretty sure I know why, too. I wait until everyone filters out of the room, including Lucky, before I stand. Ozzie has turned and is headed back into his private quarters, but I stop him with a word. It comes out sharper than I meant for it to.

"Ozzie."

He pauses and turns partway. "Yeah?"

"Can I talk to you for a minute?" I open and close my fists at my sides, trying to get a handle on my temper.

He lets out a long sigh and turns completely to face me. "Sure. What's up?"

I stand in front of the table, hoping I don't look as aggressive as I feel. Ozzie does not respond well to threats.

"I was just wondering why you've put me at a desk when I should be out in the field with Thibault."

Ozzie's eyebrows go up into his hairline. I've never questioned his decisions concerning the business before, and maybe I shouldn't be doing it now, but it's not like he can sweep this shit under the rug. I deserve an explanation.

"Are you sure you want to have this conversation?"

My heart starts beating way too fast. *No, actually I'm not sure I want to have this conversation now, but I've already started it.* And I'm not one to walk away from something I've started without finishing it.

"Yes, I'm sure. I told you before, I don't want people treating me differently just because I'm pregnant."

"What makes you think anyone is treating you differently?"

"Because. Like I said, I should be out in the truck with Thibault. May doesn't belong out there."

It's only a flash, but I see his jaw muscle twitch. That's when I know I've pushed him too far. His biceps flex a couple times, sealing my fate. "I don't really think that's your call, do you?"

I glance at the floor for a second before staring at his shoulder as I respond. "Probably not. But that doesn't change the fact that it's true."

"I think you need to take a closer look at the people around you and stop focusing so much on what you see in the mirror."

My jaw drops open, but I don't know what to say to that. *Is he calling me self-centered?*

"I know you have a lot going on and a bunch on your mind, so I'm going to let your comments about your teammate May slide. I'm also going to let the fact that you think you know better than me what's good for my team slide. But just a little friendly reminder in case you've forgotten: I'm the boss here, and I decide who works where. That hasn't changed, even if your situation has." He turns partway to the door before sending his parting shot over the bow. "Now do me a favor . . . go get your work done, and before you leave for the day, make sure you draft a report and put it on the table." And with that he leaves me standing in the middle of the room feeling like a complete asshole.

"Great," I mumble to myself. "Well done, Toni. Way to make an enemy out of the only person in the world who ever supports you."

I walk toward the door with my tail between my legs and my heart full of regret. Ozzie was completely right; I was out of line, and I knew it two seconds after opening my mouth, but I just had to keep going. I had to keep digging my grave deeper, as usual. *When am I ever going to learn?*

Just as I'm reaching my hand out, the door opens and smacks me in the knuckles. "Ow. Dammit!" I put my injured finger against my mouth with a hiss of pain.

Dev sticks his head around the door. "Oops. Sorry. Did I get ya?"

I shake my hand out. "Yeah, but it wasn't your fault. I should've heard you coming." Normally you can hear Dev from several yards away because each footstep sounds like a giant beast clomping over the earth. The fact that he's seven feet tall makes it really hard for him to operate in stealth mode, even when he's walking on carpet.

He brings the rest of his lanky frame around the door and smiles. "Hey, you haven't had a workout in a while. You got time for a session?"

I shake my head. "No, I'm on surveillance review all day, and I've been told I need to submit my report before I leave."

There must've been something funny in my tone, because Dev looks at me more carefully. "Are you in trouble or something?"

I shrug. "Maybe. I guess I didn't turn in my report fast enough last time I was on the desk."

Dev nods. "May said something to me about that. But I wouldn't let it bother you. We all take a little bit of time off here and there when we need it." He glances down at my stomach.

I stare at him until he starts to sweat, getting angrier by the second.

"What?" He looks left and right. "Is there something on my face?" He touches his cheeks and nose gingerly.

I shake my head at him. "No. I'm just wondering why you're looking at me funny."

He backs up a step, his heel hitting the open door, making him trip a little. He rights himself and then smiles at me way too hard. "What? Me? I'm not looking at you funny. I would never do that. I like my body in one piece too much." His gaze drops to my stomach again.

I point at his face. "There! You did it again. Jenny said something to you, didn't she?" I am so pissed right now. She probably went running over to Dev with my big news before I was even out the door of her house last night. *Bitch.*

He puts his hands up in front of him like he's surrendering to somebody threatening to shoot him in the chest. He's lucky I don't have a gun.

"What? Hey, don't put me in the middle of that stuff. I don't know what you're talking about." He literally has to fight not to look at my belly again; the entire internal struggle plays out on his stupid face.

I hiss out an annoyed breath as I shake my head. "Those two can't keep a damn thing to themselves. Not one single thing."

Dev lets all of his air out and his shoulders sag, his arms hanging down at his sides like two giant pendulums. "I wasn't supposed to say anything. I swore on my grave I wouldn't. Please don't tattle on me. Jenny will kill me."

I shove him out of my way as I walk through the door. "Don't worry about it." I stride across the room, on a mission to do some damage to somebody or something. Someone has to pay for my pain. I know it's not Dev's fault that he's hooked up with a blabbermouth.

"I'm not going to say a word!" he yells at my back. "And I would really appreciate it if you would keep our little secret!"

I don't say anything, not trusting myself to be kind.

"Seriously, Toni! You can count on me! I won't tell anyone you're pregnant! Not a soul! Not that it's really a secret anymore!"

I pause for a minute with my thumb hovering over the keypad to the next door. I can't believe he's actually making a joke about this. Like it isn't my entire completely messed-up life that he's talking about.

I press the PIN code and open the door when the lock disengages. Stepping through, I stare down onto the first floor of the warehouse. May and Thibault are loading up the van with the photography and video equipment. May's about to go do the job that I should be doing, Dev is behind me making fun of my messed-up life, and my boss and mentor is punishing me, forcing me to work behind a desk just because I'm pregnant. Ozzie, the one guy I thought I could count on, is pretending everything is completely normal, like he's not stabbing me in the back. I don't know who he thinks he's fooling, but it's not me.

I run down the steps, almost falling in my hurry to get to the bottom. I stride over to my car and get inside, slamming the door shut. Thibault is looking at me strangely and May is waving goodbye as she frowns. I ignore both of them, pulling out of the warehouse with screeching tires. I don't give a single shit that I just left rubber behind. Screw this place. I'm not working at a stupid desk when I should be out in the field.

I take off out of the port with no destination in mind, but I'm not really surprised when twenty minutes later I find myself at the place where it all started, the place that used to be an empty lot where a beautiful man stood as a boy shooting cans off a barrel with his BB gun.

There's a parking lot here now. I eye a spot in the farthest corner and slide my car into it, putting the vehicle in park and turning off the ignition. I rest my arms on my steering wheel and drop my head to the center, letting the tears come.

I used to have a plan. I used to know exactly who I was and what I was all about. Now I have no idea what I'm going to do with the rest of my life. Hell, I don't even know what I'm going to do for the next minute of it. So I just cry. And I cry, and cry, and cry . . .

CHAPTER TWENTY-FIVE

I've been reduced to hiccups. All the tears I'm capable of manufacturing have fallen onto my steering wheel. A tapping on the glass at my left ear wakes me out of my stupor. I twist my head slightly to the left so I can see who's there. The gorgeous face of Chance "Lucky" Larieux is staring back at me. He frowns, as if commiserating with me.

"Go away," I say with my tear-soaked, raspy voice.

"Not going to do that. Open up." Sand and gravel crunch under his feet. When I turn to look again, he's gone. But then there's a noise on my right. Lucky is standing at the front passenger window.

He points to the corner of the door, gesturing to a spot where the lock would be if this car had been manufactured in a prior decade. "Let me in. I just want to talk."

I sit back in my seat and stare at the ceiling, exhausted by nearly a half hour of crying. Hunting by touch, I find and use the automatic button by my left hand to give him access. Seconds later, he's sitting in the seat next to me, staring at me with so much concern in his eyes it almost makes me start to cry again.

"Babe . . . why are you so sad?"

My lips tremble as I battle not to cry any more. "I can't believe you're asking me that."

He gives me a sad smile. "Probably the dumbest question I've ever asked, huh?" He puts his finger up to his temple and pulls an imaginary trigger.

I nod. I don't feel like smiling, but his mea culpa does make me feel a little better.

"I knew I would find you here." He leans forward a bit so he can look out my side window at the parking lot. "Remember this place? I spent so much time here."

"So did I." I sigh. "I really wanted to use your BB gun."

He smiles at me, this time not looking nearly as melancholy. "I was so happy I had that thing. I would've worn it in a holster if I could have, but it was too long. Believe me, though, I tried."

"Why?"

"Because. Every time I had it with me, this gorgeous girl showed up asking me if she could borrow it." He shrugs. "It was like a chick magnet for the only chick I ever wanted to talk to."

I shake my head at him. "So pitiful." It's amazing to me, hearing that when we were kids, he was into me. I never guessed, never even saw a single sign of it. It makes me wonder if he's making it up now in an attempt to make me feel better.

He shrugs one shoulder. "Whatever works."

We stare at each other until I can't handle it anymore. I drop my gaze to his leg. "You didn't have to come out here."

His voice is gentle. "I know I didn't have to, but I wanted to."

I shift my gaze to look out the front windshield, not knowing what to say. I feel so lost.

"I know you don't really want to talk to me or even see me right now, but I just had to make sure you were okay. I know you're pissed about what happened at the meeting."

I can barely summon the energy to shrug my shoulders. "Nothing happened. It's just business."

"Bullshit. It's not just business, and we both know it. You got stuck on desk duty because you're pregnant, and that's not cool."

I look at him, surprised at his reaction. "But you're the guy who thinks I need some kind of nursemaid living in my house with me. I would've thought you'd be happy about Ozzie's decision."

Lucky shakes his head and leans over, taking my hand and holding it between his. "You've got it all wrong, Toni. I'm not there to be anybody's nursemaid. I'm there to be a partner with you in this thing. I don't think it's fair that you have to do everything yourself. I'm the one who got you pregnant, so I should be shouldering half the load." He lets go of my hand and sits back against the door. "I was wrong to go all caveman and force myself on you. I was just . . . I don't know . . . feeling overwhelmed after reading that stuff in those books." There's an apology in his eyes. "I'm worried, but that's not an excuse. We all have to stop acting crazy about this situation and just let you be you. Ozzie was out of line, and I'm going to say something about it." His jaw bounces out as anger settles in.

I shake my head. "Don't. I already said something to him, and it didn't go over well. I don't want him to be pissed at you too."

Lucky's eyebrows go up. "What'd you say?"

I shrug. "Pretty much what you just said. I also might've mentioned that May shouldn't be the one going out in the field because she doesn't belong there."

Lucky winces. "Ouch. I'll bet he didn't like that."

I laugh sadly. "Nope. Not at all. He called me out for questioning his authority."

"Well, whatever. He'll get over it. But you should be allowed to go out into the field just like you used to."

"You're not worried about me messing up because I'm pregnant?"

He shakes his head, looking right at me. "I know you're just as capable as a pregnant person as you are being a non-pregnant person. But I'd be lying if I said I wasn't worried about your safety."

"Why now if you weren't worried about it before?"

"Who says I wasn't worried before?"

"Because you never said anything."

"Doesn't mean I wasn't worried." He stares at me and I stare back. The temperature in the car rises.

"I really wish you'd let me move in with you. I promise I won't step on your toes." He looks so hopeful, it's almost painful.

"I think I just need my space." My words are meant as an apology, but he takes it as caving in.

He sits up straighter, leaning toward me a little. "I promise I'll give you space. All that you need. I'll sleep in a different room, I'll eat my meals at a different time . . . You'll hardly even know I'm there."

I can't hold back a smile. "What would be the point of you being there if you're going to be a ghost?"

He smiles. "Hey, if you want me to come sleep with you, I'm in. I'm just trying to make you happy. Whatever it takes."

My face goes warm hearing all of his thoughtful, kind words. He's trying so hard. To keep denying him would be bitchy. Part of me doesn't care, but the other part of me, the one that made a baby with him, does a little.

I sigh in defeat. "I guess we could try it. Maybe for a little while."

"Let's call it a trial period," he suggests. "I'll take the room down the hall, and you won't even know I'm there unless you want to."

"I'm not going to get all dressed up and put on makeup just because you're there," I say. He doesn't know this about me, but I can be seriously ugly when I don't put my mind to looking otherwise.

"So what? I've seen you without makeup a hundred times."

"But you've never seen me at my worst."

He blows out a breath. "You don't care about me because of how I look; why should I be any different?"

"Maybe I do care about how you look." I'm teasing him now, but I'm surprised to see his face fall. He doesn't say anything, so I nudge him in the arm. "I'm kidding."

He shakes his head, looking cocky again. "That's it. I'm growing a beard."

I laugh. "You'd better not. You'll be totally ugly and then I'd have to kick you out of my house."

"Good. I'll find out if you really do like me for who I am or if it's just my pretty face you're after. I don't want to be any chick's arm candy."

I hiss out a laugh. "You are so crazy."

I look out my side window, and the parking lot disappears. In its place is a dirt lot, and there's a barrel in the corner with cans lined up on it. I can still hear Lucky's young voice coming from the spot just next to me. "Watch this one," he says, smiling at me with those buck teeth of his. "I'll nail it right in the center."

"Bet you can't," I dare. I love watching him focus, his eyes squinting and the trigger under his finger. He's so serious when he shoots. When he's not shooting, though, he's either smiling or laughing. I like the juxtaposition of one personality against the other. It's like there are two people inside him, making him a total mystery.

All this time I thought he was trying to practice being a sharpshooter when he was probably just trying to impress me. I picture him wearing the gun in a homemade holster and it makes me go all warm inside again.

"What're you thinking right now?" the grown-up Lucky asks me. The parking lot comes back into focus.

"I was just thinking how much easier life was when we were kids."

"I bet you never thought you'd be making a baby with that guy holding the BB gun." His voice is soft, almost vulnerable.

"Nope. I didn't think I'd ever be making a baby with anybody."

"I'm glad it was me."

"Me too." It almost kills me to admit that, but it's true. I didn't want to do this, but if I were going to do it with anybody, Lucky would be the one I'd choose.

He takes my hand and holds it. The only sound in the car now is my heartbeat. I wonder if he can hear it too.

"We're going to be okay," he says. "No matter what."

"Not if you grow that beard," I say, looking at him and holding my breath as I wait for his response.

He pokes me in the side and makes me laugh. Then he pokes me more and I have to work at fending him off. He succeeds in dragging my attention away from my imagined dirt lot as we start wrestling. I get a few good jabs into his ribs before he captures my hands in his and pulls me up against him.

Our faces are just inches apart, and I can smell old coffee on his breath.

"What's the matter?" he asks, frowning at me. "Is it my breath?"

"No. Yes. Maybe."

He grins. "Aww, you just tried to be nice to me, didn't you?"

I attempt to pull my hands out of his grip. "No." It's silly how he can make my heart beat faster so easily.

"Yes, you did." He leans in. "Give me a kiss."

"Shut up. No." I'm acting like I want him to go away, but I'm not giving it much effort. Even with his stinky coffee breath, I find him pretty much irresistible.

"Come on. Just one. I'll close my eyes." He does just that, his lids going down as his eyebrows arch up and his lips pucker.

I can't resist. I lean in and lick his cheek before thrusting him away from me.

He opens one eye, letting my hands slide away from his. "Wow. That was a good one. Lots of tongue. Just how I like it."

"You are so sick." I turn the key in my ignition and shift the car into reverse.

"Hey, you have to let me out." He puts his hand on the door.

"Just one thing, first." I reverse out of the parking space at high speed and then slam the car into gear.

"Oh, shit," he says, buckling his seatbelt and bracing himself against the door and the dashboard.

"Hang on, hot stuff!" I shout as I throw my car into a righteous donut, sending tires squealing and rubber burning. The outside scenery spins past our windows as I simultaneously brake and accelerate, swinging the wheel around so we'll burn a perfectly arced three-sixty.

"Ahhhhhhh, you crazy . . . woman!"

Lucky screams like a girl and I laugh like a maniac.

The sound of law enforcement sirens is what finally stops me, but not before I've left some serious tracks on the asphalt.

"Hit it!" Lucky yells, pointing at the street.

"Yes, sir!" I yell, coming out of a turn with the car heading toward the exit. We slowly make our way out onto the road, going the speed limit. We're just calmly turning right at the first stoplight when a cruiser comes around the far corner, headed for the scene of the crime.

I hold out my hand for a high-five and Lucky doesn't disappoint; our palms meet with a loud crack. We roll down the avenue, both of us grinning like fools.

"Please don't ever do that again," he says, coughing after like he's dying of bronchitis.

"Just had to do it once more, get it out of my system."

"You ready to be a boring pregnant lady now?" he asks.

I shrug. "Might as well. I am pregnant, after all."

"Yeah, but you could never be boring."

I look over at him, wondering if he's regretting that about me. "I could try."

His expression is pained. "Please don't."

I can't stop grinning, all the way back to the parking lot so Lucky can retrieve his car and follow me back to the warehouse.

CHAPTER TWENTY-SIX

Lucky leaves me to finish my desk duty alone. I'm glad he's giving me space. That moment we shared was a really big deal, and I could use some mindless surveillance data-crunching to get my mind off it. It's not that I didn't like it, but it's more emotion than I generally deal with on a regular day.

Soon enough, I lose myself in the process. Frame after frame of video goes by, and I take notes of anything that I deem significant. Most of the day feels like a waste of time, but near the end of the video feed, after the sun has gone down and the infrared function comes on, the activity picks up at the target house and I gather some usable information. Matching it up with the data Jenny found and what I'm seeing in the police department's dispatch logs, it's starting to paint a picture of their operation. It's pretty slick, if I do say so myself.

Now I can confirm with relative confidence that every time someone in their group tweets that there's a full moon, someone or several someones leave the house where we saw Marc and drives off within five minutes. When they tweet that the wolves are howling, there's some sort of gathering happening on enemy turf. And when their messages say the hunter's got game, Marc's group has done some damage to their enemy, either a drive-by or a mugging or something. The only problem is that I haven't been able to identify Marc in all of it. I can't be sure he's calling any of the shots.

Regardless, all of the social media messages line up with what we've recorded and the dispatch logs we received from the detective in charge of the case. With this information, it's possible the cops can catch them in the act and make some arrests. Maybe they won't get Marc himself, but they can put a big dent in his operation, and that's great news. Even though Ozzie gave me a serious dressing-down today, I'm glad I won't disappoint him with my report. We're getting closer to shutting this whole thing down, and it was me who put it all together. I'm almost glad I didn't go out with Thibault today.

As I'm signing off the computer, the telephone on the cubicle desk rings. I stare at it for a few seconds trying to figure out what's going on. Nobody ever uses these phones.

I lean over and pick up the handset. "This is Toni."

"Toni! Hey, it's me!"

She doesn't have to say anything else. I would recognize May's enthusiasm anywhere.

"Are you done yet?"

"Just finishing up." *Is she checking up on me? Does she think that she's Ozzie's right-hand girl now, in charge of what I do?*

"Okay, cool. When you're done, could you come upstairs?"

I take a few seconds to calm myself down before answering. "Ozzie already told me I need to bring the report upstairs and put it on the table. I don't need a reminder."

"Uhhh . . . okay." She sounds confused.

Now I feel bad. Maybe she wasn't bossing me around. "I'll be up in a few minutes. Just let me type the report up."

"Okay. Bye."

She's hurt. *Dammit.* I sign back onto the computer. Truth is, I actually forgot that Ozzie wanted me to put the report up on the table. Usually he's okay with me doing the work from home and emailing it, but I don't want to push any more of his buttons tonight. I'm not sure if he knows that I took off after he told me to get to work, but if he did see me go, I don't need to give him any more reason to be angry with me.

Using our standard template, I quickly type up the report, filling in the notes section with all of the timestamps that show significant activity. I share my thoughts on what I saw and then finish it off with a summary of the amount of time and the days that I reviewed.

"That should make him happy." I sign off the computer for the second time today and stand. Stopping on my way out of the cubicle area, I grab a copy of my report off the printer. I only made one, but I'm sure that'll be fine. If Ozzie wants someone else to see it, he'll share it himself; there's a copy of the file on the network accessible to anyone on the team.

As I'm walking past the workout area headed to the stairs, a voice comes out of the darkness to my left. "Hey, Toni! Think fast!"

I've heard those words shouted out in this warehouse a couple hundred times by now, so it doesn't take me by surprise. I spin around with my hand up, getting into position just in time to catch a singlestick flying through the air at me. It smacks the palm of my hand and carries a sting. I drop my papers and shift the weapon to my other hand.

"Bring it on, punk," I say, bending my knees and getting into fighting position.

Out of the shadows comes the giant Dev, and he's carrying his own singlestick weapon.

He has no idea how ready I am for this. I'd been trying to come up with ways I could work off all this anxiety, and my opportunity has magically presented itself. *Yeah, buddy.* I swing my stick around awkwardly, acting like I've forgotten all my training. I've seen May bring Dev to his knees enough times to know his weak spot. *Make him underestimate me. That is how I'll win.*

I barely register the sound that's coming from behind me, I'm so intent on bringing Dev down, but after it repeats itself twice, the voice finally breaks through my kill-mode and stops our sparring before it even really begins.

"What do you think you're doing?" Thibault demands.

Dev straightens and drops his arm down, his weapon hanging by his thigh. "What's it look like we're doing? We're sparring."

"Ozzie wants you upstairs. Pronto."

Dev is too busy looking up at my brother to pay me any attention, so I take advantage of the situation. "Think fast!" I throw the singlestick at him.

Unfortunately, Dev isn't nearly as quick on the draw when the stick is coming at him as he is when he's sending it off. The heavy end catches him in the nads, and he immediately doubles over in pain.

"Awww . . . damn . . . Right in the jewels."

"Oh, shit, I'm so sorry." I can't help it; I start laughing. The look on his face is classic dude-in-pain.

He drops his stick and then waves his hand feebly at me. "Don't worry about me. Just go on about your business. I'll be fine."

"You need some ice?" Thibault yells down at him.

Dev hobbles away with his hands between his legs. "Nope . . ." he groans out, disappearing into the shadows. "Just going to save the trouble and have them surgically removed this time, I think."

I grab my scattered papers and mount the stairs with a huge smile on my face. It wasn't pretty, but I won that challenge. I'm sure Dev'll be lying in wait for me again, but at least this time the points were all on my side.

I get to the top of the stairs to find Thibault shaking his head at me.

"What?"

"You play dirty."

"He's the one who came after me. Rules say we can defend ourselves however we need to." I walk past him, ignoring his judgment. He should know me well enough by now to realize that I always play to win; dirty or clean, whatever it takes.

"Did you get your report done?"

His words grate on my last nerve. "Yes." I hold the papers above my head as I walk through the room and head toward the kitchen area. "Right here."

Thibault follows behind me wordlessly. Thank goodness, because if he dares say anything else to me about my work, I don't know what I'll do to him. I am so not in the mood to take any more shit from anyone today. Who knows what May is going to say to me when I get in here, but if she even *thinks* about telling me how I should be doing my reports or spending my time, we are going to have some words. And Ozzie had better not back her up, or I'm outta here. I've been on this team a lot longer than she has, and everyone knows I'm a hell of a lot more qualified to do the work than she is. She and Ozzie had better respect that.

I enter the room and immediately feel like I'm interrupting something. Ozzie and May are embracing near the stove. When they see me, though, they break apart.

"Toni, you're here!" May comes over and hugs me, not bothering to find out if I want to return the affection first, as usual. She's acting like she hasn't seen me in months.

When she's done she pulls away but she keeps her hands on my arms. "You look so pretty. You're seriously glowing."

I roll my eyes. "Give me a break." I sidestep and walk around her, intent on putting my report on the table so I can get out of here. I need to go home and get into the bathtub or something. Anything but hang out and intrude on their little love-fest.

"I've got your report right here." I put it down on the table, pausing when I see that there are two gifts there. They're beautifully wrapped with bows and everything. Each one has a little card attached to it, but I can't read what either of them says.

I turn around to look at Ozzie. "Did I forget somebody's birthday or baptism or something?" I'm suddenly worried. *Is the pregnancy already messing with my memory?* The book I was reading last night said that happens. 'Pregnancy brain' they called it, just like Lucky said.

He just shakes his head at me, his expression neutral.

May walks up to me and grabs one of the gifts, holding it out at me. "It's for you! Open it up."

I look down at it, confused. "For me? It's not my birthday for another couple months."

She giggles. "It's not for your birthday, silly. Just open it."

My hands lift slowly with no conscious thought coming from my brain. It's either I take the gift or have it shaken in my face for the next five minutes. I think May is prepared to shove it up my nose if necessary.

I use my finger to push the card over and see the writing, reading it aloud when it comes into focus. "For my partner in crime. Congrats. Keep being kickass. Love, M." I look up at May and then Ozzie. "I don't get it."

May huffs out a sigh of frustration. "It's from me, of course. Just open it. You'll see."

I tear the paper, never one of those people who saves the stuff for another gift. Under the flowers and bows is a cardboard box.

May starts clapping her hands and dancing in place. "Open it, open it. You're going to love it so much. I know you are."

I pry the tape apart and lift the flaps of the box. Wrapped in some nondescript paper is something heavy and black. Even when I pull it from the outer layer, I'm still not sure what I'm looking at. It's only when May grabs it out of my hands, turns it over, and points it at me with a maniacal grin on her face that I finally get it.

"You bought me a Taser?"

"Yes! I bought you a Taser! Isn't that so cool?" She shifts over so she can stand next to me, holding the Taser out toward Ozzie. "Now you can fight people from afar. You don't have to get right up in their faces or kick 'em with your boots, which might get awkward as you get bigger. You can just shoot them from up to fifteen feet away."

She points the gun at her fiancé and pretends she's releasing the electrified barbs at him. "Pew! Pew! Zap! Crackle! Pop!"

Ozzie puts his hands up to his heart and pretends to fall backward a little bit. Then he stands up straight and goes back to being his regular, serious self.

I don't know what to say. She actually bought me a weapon? How did she know I like weapons so much?

She turns around and puts the Taser back in my hand, grabbing the box for me. "There are several cartridges in here too, so you're all ready to lock and load." She pulls them out and throws the empty box onto the table, holding the cartridges out in front of me. "Here, take them. They're yours."

I'm so stunned by the fact that she even gave me a gift I don't know what to say.

Her face starts to fall. "Don't you like it?" She looks over her shoulder at Ozzie and then back at me. "You totally hate it, don't you?"

I swear to God I can see tears shining in her eyes. I panic, grabbing her arm. "No! I love it. Seriously. It's cool."

"Are you sure? I was just thinking that if you're pregnant, it's probably dangerous for you to do hand-to-hand combat, but if you have a Taser, you can still kick ass and take names like you always do, just from a distance."

For some silly reason I get choked up. It feels like there's a giant lump in my throat, and it aches. I reach up and pat her on the shoulder until I can finally speak again.

"It's cool. I love it. I'll keep it in my bag forever."

May's cheer seems to be restored. She leans to the side and picks up the second box from the table. This one is covered in gray and black striped paper.

"This one is from Ozzie," she says. "He bought it all by himself. He didn't even tell me he was doing it." She turns around and gives him a silly smile.

I carefully put the Taser and the cartridges down on the table and take the package from May. I can't even look at Ozzie right now, my heart is thumping so hard in my chest. I was really rude to him earlier today and he hasn't said a word about it. And now I find out that he went out and bought me a gift when I was thinking about how much I hated him and hated how he was acting?

"I don't know what he got you. He won't tell me anything." She looks over at him and pouts.

I slowly rip the paper away and pull out a long, thin box. It looks like he's given me some sort of fancy pen. *Is this another giant hint that I'm going to be working at a desk for the next nine months?* I slide the inner box out of its sleeve and then open the hinged box.

Lying in a bed of dark blue velvet is a silver spoon. I stare at it for the longest time, trying to figure out what the hell he's giving me a spoon for.

May's voice goes all goofy. "Awww. He bought a silver spoon for your baby. You know what that means?"

I look up and shake my head at her.

203

"It means that he's going to make sure that your baby always has the best of everything. That your baby deserves a silver spoon. Baby's first silver spoon." She looks over at Ozzie. "That was totally awesome, honey. You're so sweet." She runs over to her fiancé and throws herself into his arms.

He envelops her in a hug but looks up at me. "Congratulations," he says. "I'm happy for you." He detaches himself from May and she lets him go. He walks over and stands in front of me.

I look up at him, the silver spoon in my hands. I speak softly because I don't want May to hear what I'm saying. "I'm sorry I was such a bitch earlier."

He shakes his head. "Not another word about that. We're fine. We're good. Just don't think you're going anywhere, because I'm not going to let you. You're part of the team forever. 'Til death do us part."

I can't say a word because I don't trust myself not to bawl like a baby. I just put my arms around him and give him a hug, so happy he doesn't hate me or want me to go find a job somewhere else.

"You can keep working in the field like you always have, for as long as you want. I'm going to let you decide what you can and can't do."

I nod. "Thanks. It wasn't so bad today." I'm telling him the truth, not trying to suck up. It wasn't crazy and it wasn't fun, but it also wasn't dangerous. "I found a lot of great stuff. It's all right there in the report. You should probably read it and contact the chief."

He nods. "Good job."

Relief floods me. Lucky was right. I can't keep living my life like it hasn't changed. It's not just me I have to worry about; there's a little somebody inside me now who I need to be worried about too. I can't do stupid shit like I used to do.

I let go of Ozzie and back up, gathering my gifts from the table and shoving them into my bag. "Thanks, guys. Really. I mean it. You didn't have to do this. It was real nice, though."

Thibault is standing in the doorway. "I feel like an asshole," he says. "I didn't get you anything."

I smile at him as I walk by. "Don't worry about it. You can pay me back in babysitting."

He scoffs, but then I hear his voice coming from behind me, a hint of worry there. "Are you serious? Are you sure I'm qualified?"

I launch my parting shot as I go through the next door. "You're just as qualified as I am." *And that's going to have to be good enough.*

CHAPTER TWENTY-SEVEN

I am now eight weeks pregnant and Lucky has convinced me that I need to go see a doctor. I fought it for as long as I could, but after reading more of those books he bought me, I realized he's right. I need to have some professional eyes on this baby, because I have no idea what I'm doing. Thankfully the New Orleans Police Department made some good arrests based on the information we gathered in our reports last night, so we have a couple days of breathing room while they conduct interrogations and try to gather more data for our team.

Lucky's driving, still convinced I take too many risks when I'm behind the wheel. I don't care enough to argue with him about it. It could be because he was right about one thing: I do have more speeding tickets than anyone else on the team. But in my own defense, I've always been a cop magnet. Buying a mini-van might solve that problem, but I'll be damned if I'm going to do that. My baby's going to be riding around in style, just like I am.

We arrive at the doctor's office ten minutes ahead of schedule because Lucky insists on leaving way too early. He parks the car and turns off the engine, but he doesn't take off his seatbelt.

He looks over at me and gives me a nervous smile. "Are you ready for this?"

"As ready as I'm ever going to be." I take off my seatbelt and put my hand on the door, but Lucky's hand on my wrist stops me. I look down at his touch and then up at him. "What's up?"

"I just wanted to tell you that I really appreciate you letting me stay at your place."

I shrug. "It's not like I even know you're there." I'm trying not to be bitter about that. He told me that he was going to stay out of my way when I agreed to let him move in, but he's stayed way too true to his word. I have literally only seen him twice in the past few weeks. He's working crazy hours, he goes to the gym to work out, and he shops for our groceries. I don't ask where else he hangs out, but it's not at my place.

"I told you that I wouldn't bother you. I just want to be there in case you need me."

The next words fly out of my mouth before I can stop them. "How will you know if I need you if you're never there?"

He focuses really hard on my eyes, maybe trying to read my mind. "Are you saying you want me around more often?"

I shrug, looking out the front window. "I'm not saying anything. I was just making a comment." Admitting to him that I might actually want him around is way more difficult than it should be, probably, but I have a problem showing weakness, and that's what this feels like.

I can hear the smile in his voice. "I can be around more often if you want. If you need someone to rub your feet or your back . . ."

I pull my wrist out of his hand and open the door. "Shut up." I know he's just joking with me. I cannot even imagine him sitting there at my feet rubbing them. I don't think he's ever even seen my toes before.

Lucky shuts his door and meets me on the sidewalk. His hand moves to the small of my back as we walk up to the front door together. Women walking by us do a double-take and stare. Even with the stupid beard he's started to grow, he's still too good-looking.

He opens the door for me, and I roll my eyes at him glaring when I'm done.

"What's wrong?" He strokes his chin. "You don't like my beard?"

"Of course I love your beard. Who *doesn't* love giant tufts of pubic hair on a man's face?" I leave him standing there in the entrance, thrilled that I got the last word in about his stupid attempt at making himself ugly. As if he could ever be anything other than gorgeous.

I walk up to the front desk and give them my name, and I'm asked to sit down, fill out some forms, and be patient.

"Of course," I say as I take a seat and pick up a magazine, handing Lucky the papers.

Lucky sits next to me. "Of course what?" He starts filling out the forms. He knows way more about me than I realized.

"Of course I have to be patient. It's not like you can say you have an appointment at ten o'clock and have the doctor actually see you at ten o'clock. No, that would make too much sense. That would be too easy. Ten means eleven, probably."

Lucky looks around the room and drops his voice. "I think it would be some kind of miracle for a doctor to stay on schedule with the kind of stuff they deal with every day."

I laugh to myself as I page through the magazine. He's probably right. There's nothing like a good old-fashioned pregnancy to get a woman panicking. I'm normally pretty cool about stuff, but even I worry about the weird things I'm reading about in the books. I don't even want to think about the childbirth part of things. I've pretty much just been blocking that out of my mind entirely.

I hear my name being called five minutes later and look up to find a girl wearing a set of pink scrubs smiling at me and gesturing for me to enter the inner sanctum. I get up and Lucky follows.

I talk to him under my breath. "You sure you want to do this?"

"Yep. Absolutely."

We follow the girl into an examination room that has a big machine in the corner. The lights are very dim.

"Go ahead and take everything off from the waist down and then lie on the table. You can put that paper over you." She smiles once more and then disappears. I look at the closed door, at Lucky, and finally at the table. "Is she serious?"

Lucky rubs his hands together and smiles. His teeth practically glow in the dark. "Now, this is what I'm talking about. X-rated doctor visits."

I hiss out a breath of annoyance. "Shut up. If you keep acting like you're twelve, I'm going to kick you out."

He immediately stops doing his imitation of a fifth grader. "Fine. You want mature? I can be mature." He folds his arms. "Take your clothes off and get up on the table, woman. I haven't got all day."

I try not to smile as I put my bag on a chair and start disrobing. I'm not worried about Lucky seeing me. First of all, I wore my best underwear, and second of all, it's not like he hasn't seen it all anyway. At least I don't have a baby bump yet. I'll still be sexy for another month or two before I lose it all.

Lucky starts to whistle like a guy strolling casually down the street might. I turn around and find him with his back to me as he stares at the ceiling. It makes me smile to think that he's giving me privacy or that he's embarrassed to be caught staring. For some crazy reason it makes me want to get naked with him. I quickly shove the thought away. Being naked with him has already gotten me into enough trouble.

I'm up on the table with a disposable paper draped over me when a girl walks in. "Hello," she says. "I'm Amanda and I'm going to do a quick ultrasound on you."

I'm a little confused as to why I'm having this procedure done when I haven't even met a doctor yet, but what do I know? I'm just a patient. "Okay."

She checks the folder in her hand. "You're Antoinette Delacourte, right?"

"Toni. Just call me Toni."

"Great," she says. "Go ahead and lie back. I see that you're eight weeks pregnant according to the information form that you filled out for us, so I'm going to have to use a different kind of ultrasound wand than you may have heard about in order to take a look at your uterus."

It sounds ominous, whatever this thing is, so I sit up. "What's that mean?"

She holds up what looks like a big dildo. "I'm going to insert this into your vagina so that we can look up into your uterus basically through the angle of your cervix."

My jaw drops open. "Uhhh, no, you're not."

Her brows furrow. "Excuse me?"

I shake my head and look at her matter-of-factly. "Nope. You are not putting that anywhere in me."

Lucky steps over and puts his hand on my shoulder, pushing me back. "Don't listen to her. She's just nervous." He looks down at me. "Babe, all the girls do this. Just relax."

I fix him with a glare. "That's easy for you to say. You're not getting your hoo-hah probed by a giant dildo."

The girl barks out a laugh before she controls herself. "I'm sorry. That was unprofessional."

Lucky and I both look at her and say the exact same thing at the same time: "Don't worry about it."

Lucky leans down and stares at me, his nose just inches from mine. "Babe, would you please just do this? For me?"

I sigh. "You're not going to be able to use that on me every time you want me to do something I don't feel like doing."

"Why not?"

"Because. It'll lose its power and then you won't have it when you need it. Besides, if that beard gets any longer, I'm going to start carrying my Taser in a holster."

His voice goes really soft. "But I really want to see our baby."

I can't think of a single thing he could've said that would have influenced me more than that. I let out a long sigh of defeat. "Fine. Go ahead and probe me with the damn dildo."

I can tell the girl is trying not to laugh again. Her voice comes out all wobbly. "Okay . . . I'm going to put some gel on the, *a-hem*, probe, and then I'm going to insert it very slowly. I promise to make it as comfortable as possible."

Lucky's grin gets bigger.

"Do not say a word, Lucky. I swear to God . . ." I am so ready to grab his throat.

He shakes his head and battles to keep a serious look on his face. At the same time, the girl starts putting her probe in. I have to look at the ceiling and avoid Lucky's eyes. I cannot believe I'm doing this with him standing right next to me. Talk about embarrassing.

I hear some noise and some buttons clicking, so I look over at her machine. At first there's just darkness on the screen and then what looks like static, but eventually we see some circles and other things moving around. Every time she moves the angle of her probe it changes the weird things on the screen.

"What are we looking at?" Lucky asks. He's holding onto my hand but leaning toward the machine, squinting his eyes.

"Well, I'm just checking on her cervix first, making sure everything looks good . . . and it does." There's a long period of silence before she speaks again. "And now we're going to go ahead and take a look at the uterus and see what's inside."

"Maybe it'll be nothing," I say, almost hoping I'm right. But there is a small piece of me that hopes there's a baby in there. I guess I've kind of gotten used to the idea.

"Well . . . I definitely see *something*." She says this with the weirdest tone to her voice.

I lift my head up and stare at her. "What's going on?"

She looks at me and she's grinning. "There's nothing going on except for the fact that I have a little bit of a surprise for you."

"We already know I'm pregnant."

She winks at me. "But did you know you are pregnant with *twins*?"

"*What?*"

Lucky leans so far over me toward the screen that all I can see now is the back of his head. "*What* did you say?" He sounds like he's ready to slap the girl.

She clicks a bunch of buttons on her machine and wiggles the probe around some more. "I'll go ahead and take some pictures for you so you can bring them home and show your families."

"But wait a minute . . ." Lucky says, "I thought I heard you say that there were *two* babies in there. That's what twins means, right?"

I'm forgiving him that stupid question, because he's echoing what's in my head. Twins means two, right? Or is that some crazy medical term that means something totally different? *Please let it be that!*

"I'm going to go ahead and let the doctor discuss this with you. I've probably already said too much. But don't worry—everything looks great."

My heart is going nuts, as if it wants to beat itself right out of my chest. I swear it's like I'm sitting in a movie theater watching somebody else's life fall apart in front of my eyes.

"This is not happening." I'm talking to the ceiling.

Lucky's face appears above mine. "I'm sure it's just a blip on the machine," he says. The expression on his face tells me he's not really so sure of that.

I shake my head, still staring at the ceiling, ignoring Lucky's face there. "This is not happening. This is not my life. This is somebody else's life."

I'm so locked in my daze that I don't even pay attention to the fact that the tech is gone from the room and I'm getting dressed. Somehow I'm going through the motions like a robot, but none of it is really sinking in. Lucky has to help me zip my pants. I'm too busy trying to figure out what the hell's going on to focus on the mechanics of it.

"Come on," he says. "Let's go find this doctor."

I follow him out the door, holding his hand. For once I'm glad he's there and I have someone to hang on to.

"If you'll follow me, I'll take you to the doctor's office," says a young girl, meeting up with us in the hallway. This is not the technician who probed me and took pictures of my insides, printing them in black and white on shiny paper. Lucky is holding one of the prints she made, but I can't look at it. It makes it all too real, to see an image like that.

Lucky pulls me along and we walk into an office whose walls are covered in plaques. Shelves behind the desk are piled high with books. A man stands to say hello and he's a couple inches shorter than I am, which is not something I see in a grown man very often.

I hold out my hand. "Toni. I'm Toni." *The girl who's forgotten how to talk, apparently.*

He shakes my hand. "I'm Doctor Ramandi." He turns his attention to Lucky. "And this is . . . ?" He shakes Lucky's hand.

"I'm the baby daddy. You can call me Lucky." He nods his head and smiles, guiding me into a chair before he takes his own next to me.

The doctor sits with his hands folded on the desk in front of him. He smiles at both of us before beginning. "Congratulations. I hear you are pregnant with twins."

I shake my head. "I think you'd better check the tape. I'm pretty sure that's a mistake."

He holds up a paper and wiggles it at me. "I already have. I definitely see two embryos implanted in your uterine lining and everything looks great. They're about the size I would expect them to be at eight weeks."

I shake my head, refusing to believe this is true. One baby is bad enough but two? My world is crumbling down around my ears.

"What are the chances she'll be able to maintain a twin pregnancy?" Lucky asks.

I look over at him like he's crazy. *What the hell? Did he go to medical school and I somehow missed that?*

"Well, she's a healthy young woman, she doesn't drink, and she doesn't smoke, so I suspect she has a pretty good chance. It is true that sometimes with twin pregnancies one of the embryos will disappear, but we'll keep an eye on it, and if anything like that happens, of course you know we will be here to answer whatever questions you have. But let's go ahead and assume that they're both healthy and they're both going to continue on to full gestation, and make plans to deal with that. How does that sound?"

"Sounds good to me." Lucky looks at me. "What do you think, babe? Is it a good idea?"

I shrug. "Okay." I'm on autopilot. None of this is truly sinking in. I feel like I'm going to wake up in an hour and realize I had a horrible dream about a double pregnancy. The only thing missing right now is Charlie walking in saying that he's going to be my doula.

The doctor yammers on and on about nutrition, vitamins, and weight gain, and Lucky responds with what seem like normal

WRONG QUESTION, RIGHT ANSWER

questions. But I've got nothing to say, and I'm really not listening very closely to anything the two of them are discussing. All I can think about is my life with two children in it. Does that qualify as a pack of kids? A herd? A flock? It should. It sounds like way too many. How is this happening to me? I'm starting to think that God has abandoned me to the hands of the Devil. This definitely seems like a game a devil would enjoy playing with someone's life.

Lucky stands and brings me to my feet with a gentle tug on my hand. "Thanks, Doctor. Really appreciate all the information that you gave us."

The little guy holds his hand out and shakes Lucky's. "It's my pleasure. You have our number, so if anything comes up, give the office a call and one of my nurse practitioners or a midwife will get back to you. We'll want to see you again in another month just for a regular checkup, and if you guys want to know the sex of your babies, you can do that around eighteen to twenty weeks' gestation. Go ahead and make the appointment for another ultrasound today for that. Sound good?" He smiles at both of us.

I nod numbly, unable to converse with another human being right now. My brain just won't work.

"Great. See you later, Doc." Lucky pulls me out of the room and down the hall to the front desk. He even digs in my purse and fishes out my insurance card to take care of the administrative part of my visit. When I try to give him money for the co-pay he refuses and pulls cash out of his wallet instead.

I don't have the energy to deal with that right now, but we're definitely going to have to have a conversation about it. I don't want to be beholden to him down the line because he helped me out financially. I'll let him do his part by paying for diapers.

We go out to the car and Lucky opens my door for me. When I settle into the seat, he actually leans over and puts my seatbelt on for me. I look up at him, gazing with confusion into his beautiful eyes. "What are you doing?"

He kisses me on the forehead. "Taking care of my babies' mama." Then he leans into the car farther and looks at me so closely, it makes my eyes cross. "That's babies *plural*. We've got two." He reaches down and gently pokes my belly two times. "One and two. Romulus and Remus." He pulls his hand away and starts grinning at me like a fool.

My ears ring as I realize what all of this means. I'm having twins with Lucky. *Lucky!* I can't decide whether to laugh, cry, or scream. I settle for arguing. "We are not naming our children Romulus and Remus."

He shrugs. "Okay, fine. We'll name them Yin and Yang."

I try really hard not to smile, but it doesn't work so well. "No. Not gonna happen."

He shuts the door and keeps talking as he walks around the front of the car. "Okay, how about Cain and Abel?"

I have to laugh at that. "Knowing my luck, that's probably what they're going to end up like."

Lucky gets into the car and grabs my hand, kissing the back of it. "Don't say that. They have me as a daddy, which means they're going to be lucky. They're going to be angels. We'll name them Milli and Vanilli."

I roll my eyes at him and sigh. "If you try to name my children Milli and Vanilli, I will shoot you."

He laughs. "There's my Toni. I thought I'd lost you for a few minutes back there." He starts the car and revs the engine.

I pull my hand away from his and stare out the front windshield. "Nope. I'm still here, unfortunately."

He pulls out of the parking lot and pats me on the leg. "Don't worry, babe, I'm still here, too. You haven't scared me away yet."

I sigh, trying not to be sad about what feels like a budding romance between me and the perfect guy—a romance that will surely crash and burn in a fiery, painful inferno. "Just give me time. I'm sure I'll manage."

"Never gonna happen."

He sounds so sure of himself. I wish I had the confidence he has in me and the two of us together, because I have no idea how I'm going to raise two babies on my own.

CHAPTER TWENTY-EIGHT

Maybe it's because we never made an official announcement of the actual pregnancy, but I'm really, really nervous going into work today. Lucky and I are sharing a ride, something we don't normally do. I have a strong need to keep him closer. I'm feeling overwhelmed, and I haven't even had a single baby yet.

"My mind is still blown," he says. "I had two cups of coffee hoping it would give me clarity, but I'm still not there." He looks over at me in the passenger seat, a watery smile letting me know he's definitely off kilter, just like I am.

"I know how you feel, trust me." I look out the windshield at the scenery passing us by. I've gone this way to work so many times I've lost count, but today it's an entirely different trip. Today I'm driving past all of these trees and these houses and these businesses as a mother of twins. *Yep. Mind blown.*

"What do you think everyone is going to say?" Lucky asks me.

"I think they're probably just going to pray for us."

"That's good. We could probably use some prayers about now."

"I don't think there're enough prayers in this city to get us all the help we're going to need."

Lucky reaches over and squeezes my thigh. "Don't be so negative. It's going to be fun."

I look at him like he's lost his mind, which he clearly has. "You must be a glutton for punishment."

He shrugs. "We'll be fine. We're a team, remember?" He winks at me.

I shove his hand off my leg. I'm not angry, but I am a little frustrated that he's being so clueless right now. "I think you'd better read some of those books you bought."

"I have. I also saw another one online that I think I should get."

"Oh, really?" I look at him, seeing him in profile. His beard seems longer and bushier already, in just one day. Pretty soon he's going to look like a mountain man. Unfortunately, it's not accomplishing his goal of getting uglier. Somehow, he manages to make pubic hair on a man's face attractive.

"Yeah. It's a book about organization. I think that's going to be the key for us. If we could just keep everything organized . . ."

I laugh. "Yeah, right. Because all those books you already bought talk about how babies just fall right in line with their parents' plans."

His beard moves around as he chews on his lip. "You might have a point there. I do remember somebody telling me that having to organize more than one kid is like trying to herd cats."

"That was Jenny. She's said that many times, and all her kids are way past the baby stage. She never had twins." The more I talk, the more panicked I start to feel. I need to change the subject. "Doing anything special this weekend?"

He shakes his head while frowning. "Nope. Just hanging out."

I'm trying to act casual while digging for information. I hope I can pull it off. "You know, you don't have to hang out at my place all the time if you don't want to. I mean, if you want to go out or whatever, you can. You don't have to feel like you're tied to me just because you got me pregnant."

His expression goes dark. "Thanks."

I try to read his mind but it's like he's pulled a shutter down between us. "What's wrong? Did that piss you off?"

He shrugs. "Nope."

I reach over and bang him on the upper arm with the back of my hand. "Yes, it did. I know that look on your face."

He reaches up and strokes his beard. "You can't even see my face anymore. I'm in stealth mode."

"No, you're not. You're in ugly-face mode." I laugh at my joke. *As if.*

He grins, making the tufts of hair on his face move up with his smile. "You know it, baby. I'm just waiting for someone to call me Sasquatch."

"That's never going to happen."

"Oh yeah, it will." He pulls on the bottom of his beard. "Just wait until this baby is down to my chest."

"Whatever you say." I'm picturing Lucky holding his two babies, one in each arm. That means there'll be four tiny hands reaching up to grab ahold of that beard and pull it. I'm pretty sure the facial hair is going to come off not very long after the babies are born, but we'll see. Maybe he's a stronger man than I imagine.

"I was thinking I would cook you dinner, actually," he says.

I raise an eyebrow at him. "Why? You don't like my food?" We've shared a few meals since he moved in. Nothing fancy, basically just warmed-up canned, frozen, and boxed things . . . My specialty.

He glances at me with a pained expression. "It's not that I don't like charcoal, per se, but I was just thinking maybe you'd like to sample some of my cuisine for a change."

I whack him on the arm, only harder this time. "Charcoal? What are you talking about?"

He's smiling way too hard. "You're the only person I know who can actually burn black the entire square surface of a piece of bread." He leans over toward me and stretches his lips back, exposing all of his teeth. "Do I have any of that charcoal in my teeth?"

I shove him away and look out the side window so he won't see me smiling. "Shut up. There was no charcoal on that toast."

"You mean there was no *toast* on that toast. It was pure black." He holds up a finger. "The good news is, though, if anyone tries to poison me it won't work now."

I look over at him, confused. "Oh, yeah? Why's that?"

"Because . . . I have enough charcoal in my system to absorb any toxins I ingest."

I cross my arms over my chest and stare out the front window. I didn't burn the toast that badly. "You better get an official food taster for your meals from now on. You don't know what I might slip in there."

He shrugs. "Doesn't scare me." He pats and rubs his stomach. "Like I said . . . I'm all charcoaled up."

The interior of the car goes silent for a while until I catch him ogling me at a stoplight. "What're you looking at?"

"Your boobs," he says, sounding mesmerized. "They're huge."

I pull my arms away from my chest and place them at my sides, resisting the urge to plaster my hands over my chest. "Why are you looking at them?" My face is hot and I'm sweating.

"Why wouldn't I? You have the nicest rack of anybody I've ever seen."

"Rack? Could you be any ruder?" I'm trying really hard not to smile.

He taps his thumbs on the steering wheel to the beat of the music. "I call it like I see it."

All I can say is, he's lucky he's so cute and the father of my babies. They're the only things keeping me from slugging him in the gut. My face stays warm for the next several blocks as I imagine him ogling me and liking what he sees. I resist the urge to toss my hair over my shoulder.

We pull into the port and up to the warehouse. The engine purrs as we wait for the big door to slide open.

"So what's the plan?" he asks me.

"Plan for what?"

He gives me a funny look. "For telling people about the twins, of course. How can you be so casual about this?"

I shrug. "What differences does it make? I'm still pregnant. It's not like it's going to be that big a shock to everybody."

He hisses as he shakes his head. "I think you underestimate your co-workers."

I try to ignore the twinge in my chest. I don't even know what the emotion is that I'm experiencing. *Am I worried? Scared?* It's not like me to be timid about anything. "I don't have a plan. If you want to tell everybody you can."

He smiles. "Okay, I will."

His enthusiasm worries me. "When are you going to do it?"

He pulls into the warehouse and puts the car in park. "I don't know. I'm going to let inspiration strike, I think."

He shuts the engine off and we get out of the car. Dev and Ozzie are standing at the edge of the workout area watching their girlfriends do some sort of push-up competition on the floor in front of them. Thibault is standing at the bottom of the stairs clapping slowly, encouraging their progress. I get out of the car and walk around to the front of it, joining the crowd. Lucky comes over and drapes his arm over my shoulders. Then he clears his throat loudly.

"Everyone . . . can I have your attention, please?"

I look up at him, stunned at his volume and confused for a moment as to what he's doing.

"I just want you all to know that my girl Toni is pregnant with twins!" A huge, beaming smile breaks out across his face.

My jaw drops for the second time today. I'm staring up at him, speechless. He called me his girl in front of the team, *and* he told our big secret like he's proud of it. *Is he insane? Did he mean it?*

May screams first and then Jenny joins in. They act like they just saw the Beatles walk through the door. The two of them have fallen into a tumble on top of each other and they're scrambling to get up.

"Did he say twins?" This is from Jenny. She's on her feet and jogging over toward me.

May comes speeding up from behind her, shoving her out of the way. "Me first." She runs toward me like she's going to tackle me.

I hold my hands up to fend her off, but it doesn't stop her. She grabs me in a hug and lifts me off my feet. She's covered in sweat and stinks like iron.

"Congratulations! That is so cool!" she squeals.

Jenny joins us, pulling us both into a hug of her own, while May continues to yell in my ear. "Twins! I can't believe it! Lucky's luck is rubbing off on you!"

Jenny pulls away and looks me in the eye, our noses almost touching. "You are totally not getting any sleep for the next two years."

Now May is looking at me, grinning with a sparkle in her eye. "Jenny and I can each have a baby to play with. This is so cool."

I wrinkle my nose, feeling queasy all of a sudden. "You guys stink. Get off me."

The two sisters high-five each other and let me go. Then May grabs me again, squealing nonsense into my hair. I can't understand a single word coming out of her mouth. I really want to shove her away from me, but that would be mean, and I don't want to burst her bubble. Apparently, my twin pregnancy is the best thing since sliced bread.

Jenny's looking down to my waist. "I think you're already showing. It makes sense that you have twins in there. That's how you found out so soon."

May lets me go and stares at my belly. "Oh, my god. Adorable baby bump. Hollywood-worthy. I can't even believe it." She looks at me. "I'll bet that's why you've been so sick. You've got twice the hormones coursing through your veins."

I feel myself blanch a little at that. I don't like the idea of twice the hormones anywhere, let alone in my veins.

Lucky comes up and puts his arm around me, pulling me a little away from them. "Let's give her some space, girls. We don't want her barfing on anybody."

I jab him in the ribs with my elbow, but he ignores me, pulling me closer to kiss me on the side of my head. Then he lets me go and walks over to accept congratulations from the guys. I stand alone, stunned at how crazy this scene is. And I'm smack-dab in the middle of it.

Ozzie catches my eye and nods at me. It fills me with warmth to know that he's not angry about it. I don't know why I expected him to be, though I suppose this means I'm definitely on a desk for the rest of my pregnancy. Even I know better than to risk my health now. I guess my body's going to be doing double duty with these babies, so I might as well get used to the idea of sitting my butt in a chair.

"It's a little early in the day, but why don't we go upstairs and have a celebratory drink?" Thibault suggests.

May raises her hand up high and everybody looks at her. "I've got fresh-squeezed orange juice," she says brightly.

Ozzie grabs her in a hug and kisses her right on the mouth in front of everybody. "Good job, babe." He looks at all of us.

"Come on, let's go upstairs. We can have a drink while we talk about the day ahead."

Everybody waits for me to go up the stairs first. I know it's completely stupid, but it makes me feel special, like I'm some kind of royalty in this place. It's the first time since I found out I was pregnant that I've felt maybe it won't be completely horrible.

CHAPTER TWENTY-NINE

Desk duty really isn't as awful as I expected it to be. For the past several weeks, May has been with me more often than not, and she's gradually lost some of her crazy enthusiasm and settled into an almost normal personality. In fact, today, she's especially calm. It makes me suspicious. Almost paranoid.

I should probably leave well enough alone, but a conflict-free life has never really been the track I've run on. "What's wrong with you?" I'm leaning on the arm of my chair, looking over at her as she stares at her video. I know she can hear me, but there's no change in her expression. "Hello? Is anybody in there?"

She shakes her head. "Nothing's going on. I'm fine."

I watch her for a while longer, pretty sure I see unshed tears shining in her eyes. I take one of my earbuds and swing it out at her, causing it to land on her arm.

She shrugs it off.

That's when I know there's something really going on and that it's probably nothing minor. *Do I want to get involved?* No. That's an easy question to answer. *Should I get involved?* That's the harder question. I hem and haw over it silently for a little while, knowing that once I open this can of worms, the situation's going to squiggle and squirm and probably get slimy. *Oh well.*

"Something's wrong. What's up? Maybe I can help you."

May shakes her head. "No, you definitely cannot help me."

I actually find that a little offensive, but I try really hard not to lose my temper because I am in helper-mode right now.

"Maybe I could. You should try me."

May shakes her head. "No. I just need to figure this out on my own."

"Ah-ha! So, there is something wrong . . ."

May looks at me, a hint of mutiny in her eyes along with some tears. "You wouldn't understand."

My voice softens without my meaning for it to. "You should try me. I'm actually a pretty understanding person when I put my mind to it." I have no idea where that statement came from. These baby hormones are seriously messing me up.

She shakes her head, an actual tear falling from her eye. "Not this time. You're too good-looking."

She's mad because she thinks I'm pretty? This makes no sense whatsoever.

"I don't think you need to worry about that," I say. "I'm about to get really fat and probably blotchy and pimply too." I've been reading my pregnancy books.

"It doesn't matter how pimply or blotchy you get; your babies are going to be gorgeous. How could they not be with you and Lucky as the parents?"

I smile, knowing this can't be the reason for her distress, but distracted by her mention of Lucky. "I know, right? He thinks he can grow a stupid beard and he's suddenly going to be ugly." I shake my head. "Men."

I glance over at May, expecting to see her mollified, but all she does is act angrier.

"What? What'd I say? What's the big deal about Lucky's beard?"

May slams her hand down on the cubicle desk. "It has nothing to do with Lucky's beard!"

I lift my eyebrows way up, waiting for her to calm down.

The look on my face must trigger something in her, because she lets out a big, long stream of air and slumps down in her seat.

I take a couple moments to settle my voice and try again. "Honestly, May, you're my wingman back here in no-man's-land. You can't keep secrets from me because it'll drive me crazy all day long and then I won't get my work done and Ozzie'll yell at me again."

She tilts her head at me. "Since when do you care about people keeping secrets from you? Usually you want people *not* to share anything with you."

I shrug. She isn't wrong about that. "I don't know. I'm blaming it on the babies."

She nods. "They can seriously twist your brain." The funny way she says it has my ears perking up.

"Do you have something you want to tell me?" I ask.

Her head shakes so vigorously I know she's full of crap.

"You *do* have something you want to tell me."

"No."

I sit up straighter and fix her with my mean stare. "Time for you to 'fess up. What's going on? I know it involves me."

She looks confused for a second but then she shakes her head again. "No. Not directly, it doesn't."

I stand. "If you and Lucky have been talking about me behind my back . . ."

She jumps to her feet and waves her hands at me. "No. No, no, no. It's nothing like that at all. I haven't even said anything to Lucky or anyone else about this." She slaps her hand over her mouth and looks around.

I narrow my eyes at her. "So, there's something really bothering you that involves how good-looking Lucky is and you haven't told Ozzie . . ." My mind is spinning, trying to come up with answers to the question floating between us.

"Do you have a crush on Lucky?"

She reaches up and grabs two fistfuls of her hair and pulls while she growls. "Rrrrr, no! Why would I have a crush on Lucky?"

I shrug. "Because he's hot as hell?"

She lets go of her hair and lets her arms fall down to her sides. "He *is* hot as hell. And that's the problem."

I reach out and pat her on the shoulder. "Ah, I see. Unrequited love. It sucks. Don't worry, it'll pass. I used to have a crush on Lucky when I was a kid, but I was able to ignore it for, like, ten years, so I'm sure you'll be able to do the same."

I'm actually not convinced she has a crush on Lucky, but I know saying this might be enough to bust the top off her little can of secrets so she'll unload on me. I'm almost enjoying this.

She shrugs me off. "I told you, I don't have any feelings for Lucky. He's a nice guy, but I don't want to go to bed with him."

"But do you want to have a baby with him?" I'm afraid I'm getting close to the actual truth of the situation.

She screams at me really loudly this time. "No! Why would I want to do that when I'm already pregnant?!"

The room goes suddenly silent and her eyes bug out of her head. I'm pretty sure mine are bugging out too.

She slaps first one hand and then the other over her mouth and shakes her head. Tears stream out of her eyes.

I step closer to her and take her wrists, pulling her hands away from her mouth. "Did you just say you're pregnant?" I'm speaking softer now, because I'm pretty sure she doesn't want the entire warehouse to know her situation, even though she just screeched it out like a war eagle.

She nods.

I reach up and wipe the tears off her face as best I can. It's not easy because they keep coming. "Does Ozzie know?"

She shakes her head no.

"Is there any particular reason why you're not telling him?" I can't imagine Ozzie being anything but thrilled to hear this news.

She nods but doesn't explain further.

I shake her gently. "You're really not going to make me guess, are you? You're slobbering tears all over the place. I'm going to need a towel soon. Just tell me."

She drops her chin to her chest. "I don't want to say it out loud. It's already bad enough that it's in my head."

I push her down into her seat and then roll my chair right in front of hers and sit in it. We're knee to knee, and I've got both her hands in mine. I really don't know what I'm doing; I'm just imagining what Jenny would do if she were here in my place. According to Lucky, she's good at giving advice and listening to people.

"Tell me everything." My throat almost seizes up at that statement. I really don't want her to spill her guts, but I know that Jenny would.

She stares off into space for a little while before looking at me. "I'm worried that my baby is going to be ugly."

I bark out a laugh before I realize she's serious. "What? I don't think I understand."

She pulls her hands out of mine and gestures at my face. "Look at you! You're gorgeous, and Lucky is like an angel. You're about to give birth to the two most beautiful babies who ever walked the earth, and then I'm going to come along behind you with this plain old baby and nobody's going to want to tell me the truth about him, but they're all going to feel sorry for me, and then Ozzie won't love me anymore because I gave him what looks like an ugly child compared to yours but might actually be a fairly cute one."

I have to turn sideways in my chair and pretend like I'm cough-ing to hide my laughter. *She cannot possibly be serious, can she?* She's being completely ridiculous. Hell, if she can love that ugly-ass Chihuahua mutt she's got, she can love anything. His ears are like shovels planted into his skull, his head's the size of a baseball and twice as big as it should be, and his eyes always look like they're in danger of popping right out onto the floor. May's love is deaf, dumb, and blind.

With that thought, I remember a couple paragraphs from my pregnancy book telling me how emotional women can get when they're pregnant, and how unreasonable some people might consider them to be. The lightbulb goes on: she's got pregnancy brain. And if this happens to me, I'm going to want a lot of under-standing people around, so I have to be that person for her. I imagine myself as Jenny again; she's one of the most understanding people I know.

I turn back toward her. "May, listen to me. Right now you have a lot of pregnancy hormones in your system that are causing you to hallucinate. Badly. So what you need to do is listen to me, because I'm not being crazy like you are." I wait for her to nod her accep-tance before continuing. "First of all, there is no way that any baby made by you could be ugly." I gesture at her head, hoping to find inspiration there. "You have gorgeous, thick hair. It's not frizzy, it's not thin, it's not any of those things that girls hate. So if you have a girl or a boy, you're cool with the hair."

She wipes a tear from under her eye. "I do have pretty thick hair. You're right about that."

I bump her knee with my fist. "See? And your face . . . Your face is awesome. You've got a really nice complexion and no scars." I lean in closer and point to my temple where Charlie hit me with a fork once. "You see that? A scar. My face isn't nearly as pretty as you think it is. You just need to look closer."

She uses the heel of her hand to push my forehead away from her. "Be quiet. You know you're gorgeous, and your babies aren't going to inherit your scars."

Thank God for small favors. I point at her chin. "Look at your jawline, though. Perfectly feminine. You could have been one of those chicks with a really manly jaw, but you're not. You look like a girly girl. Like . . . a fairy princess or something." I pulled that right out of my butt, so I cringe, waiting for her to scowl and yell at me.

A shy smile comes out and starts to glow from her face. "A fairy princess? No one has ever called me a fairy princess before. And you never lie, Toni. You would never say anything just to make somebody feel better."

I nod enthusiastically. "You're right. If you were ugly, I'd just tell you. Boom. You're a dog. But I wouldn't say that to you because it's not true." It may or may not be entirely correct to say that I always tell the bold-faced truth, but I don't need to share that insight with her. I don't need to tell her that these babies growing inside me have turned my innards to butter and that I'm finding it really hard to be harsh with people anymore.

"But even though I might look a little bit like a fairy princess and Ozzie's gorgeous, it doesn't mean our babies are going to be as cute as yours."

I frown at her. "Are you crazy? When your baby comes out, it's going to be the most beautiful creature you've ever seen. Ozzie too. There's no way he'd look at my kids and compare them to his own kid and find his own kid lacking."

She looks like she's not sure whether she should believe me or not.

I plow ahead, knowing I've got her on the ropes. "Seriously. Besides, my pregnancy book says that there's some kind of hormone or something that triggers when a father sees his own face on the baby. It makes them think that the baby is super cute even when it's not. That's why Mother Nature made it so babies look like the father when they're born. It's all about survival."

She narrows her eyes at me. "Really? Are you telling the truth?"

I hold out my arms. "As you said . . . I don't say nice things just to make people feel better. You can trust me." This time I am telling the truth. And I know for a fact that if May looks down at her baby and there's any hint of Ozzie on that baby's face, she's going to think the kid can walk on the moon without a spacesuit.

"I need to get the title of that book from you." She wipes the rest of her tears away and sniffs loudly.

"Sure, no problem. I've got a whole bunch. I've already read most of them so you can just take 'em."

She smiles at me. "I never took you for a girl who would do research when she found out she was pregnant."

"I'm not." I smile. "Lucky bought them for me. He's in serious research mode right now. He's starting a whole library. Right now he's reading about toddlers."

"Awww . . . that's so cute." Her regular May-smile is back on her face, which brings me a huge sense of relief. I can only imagine what Ozzie would do to me if she walked away frowning. I'd get blamed for sure.

May rolls her chair back over to her cubicle and acts like she's going to pick up where she left off with her work. I sit there and stare at her until she looks over at me.

"What?" she asks.

"You're not going to just sit there, are you?"

"I have to finish my work."

"But you haven't even told Ozzie you're pregnant yet." Maybe she has a grand plan she's failed to share with me.

May shrugs, looking at her computer screen. "I have to pick the right moment. We weren't really expecting this. I was supposed to be planning a wedding, not a birth."

I lower my voice. "Does Jenny know?"

May looks over at me, the air surrounding her thick with guilt. "No. She's going to kill me."

"Why? Won't she be happy?"

May sighs and turns her chair to face me again. "It's really complicated. We're doing all this wedding planning, and we have all the dresses picked out; but if I know Ozzie, he's not going to want to wait to get married. He's going to want to get married quicker so the baby can be born after the ceremony." She rolls her eyes. "He's a little old-fashioned."

I snort. "Not that old-fashioned." I point at her stomach.

She rubs her belly and smiles. "Okay, so he's not that old-fashioned. But anyway, I know him; he's going to want to get married right away."

I shrug. "So? Do it. Everyone can move their schedules. Not a problem."

She sighs. "Obviously, you've never planned a wedding. My sister has a caterer on board, a florist, dresses to be fitted . . . It's going to be a nightmare."

I refuse to buy into that garbage. "No. It's going to be easy. We change the venue to Jenny's backyard, we all go to the store and buy dresses off the rack, and any restaurant in the area can whip together a little reception party with just a few days' notice. You don't need to get all froufrou with it."

She pouts. "But I was kind of hoping for a *little* bit of froufrou."

"Fine. Don't you have to make those little favors or whatever you were talking about the other day? Those can be really froufrou."

She grins. "So you *were* listening."

I shrug. "A little bit filters in here and there."

She stares off into space again, nodding her head slowly as her eyes narrow in concentration. "Maybe we could pull this off."

"Not without help. You'd better go tell your fiancé you're pregnant so the rest of us can find out and then we can start doing what needs to be done." I stand up and spin her chair around to face out of the cubicle area. I try to tip the chair and dump her out of it, but it barely budges, merely leaning a bit.

She jumps up and turns around, glowering at me. "Be careful! I'm pregnant!"

I smile and point. "Go. Go tell your man he knocked you up."

May turns to go, but three steps into her journey she stops. She spins around and comes running back to me, throwing her arms around me and squeezing for all she's worth. "Thank you so much, Toni. I had no idea you were so good at giving advice."

Her hair is covering my face and I'm all stiffened up, waiting for the affection to be over. "Sure. Anytime." I cringe at my words, hoping she won't take me up on the promise they contain. I actually suck in the advice department on a normal day, but this time it wasn't so bad.

I pat May on the back and then push her away from me. "Go. I can't stand knowing a secret that Ozzie doesn't know."

She pulls back and looks at me, smiling. "You're probably his best friend. Did you know that?" She tilts her head at me.

I feel the light of joy beaming through my heart. "No, not really."

She nods. "Trust me. I know things." She gives me a little wave with her fingers and turns around to go, her thick, beautiful hair flying out behind her in its ponytail.

I smile watching her go and then laugh. That girl is so crazy. But I must admit, when she's back here in the cubicle room with me, it does seem a lot brighter than when I'm alone.

CHAPTER THIRTY

I arrive home to the smell of garlic cooking in the kitchen. I inhale cautiously, hoping my stomach isn't going to rebel. Now that I'm in my sixteenth week of pregnancy, it seems that my queasiness has pretty much disappeared. Only the odd smell, like cigarette smoke or broccoli, puts me on edge.

When I get to the kitchen, I find Lucky at the stove, stirring something in a sauté pan. This is almost normal for us now. He's a way better cook than I am, and he's usually home first. His being at the stove gives me time to settle in and wind down from the work-day before we eat. I like sitting with him as the sun goes down; it's relaxing. I never saw myself as a person enjoying that kind of thing, but here I am, doing just that.

"Smells good." I drop my bag in a chair and go over to stand next to him.

He keeps his eyes on the pan, but his free hand comes up and wraps around my neck, pulling me closer so he can kiss me on the head. I love it when he does that; it makes me feel almost like his girlfriend, even though we haven't yet had any discussions about where we stand. I'm not pushing for it, either. I like where we are now; it's comfortable for both of us, I think.

His beard fluffs against my face, tickling my skin as he turns his head back to the food and lets me go. "I thought you might like a little linguine with clam sauce tonight, since you don't seem to be as sensitive as before to the smells."

"How did you know that's my favorite?" I'm smiling up at him, maybe a little bit amazed that this man knows me so well. We've been living together for a while now, but he still pulls surprises out of nowhere sometimes.

"Every time we've ever gone out to an Italian restaurant, that's what you order." He looks at me and winks. "I like it too, so this one's easy."

He's been cooking ever since my charcoaled toast disaster, and I haven't had one single complaint since. He doesn't even need to defrost things to put dinner on the table.

"Can I do anything to help?"

"You can set the table."

I hum a random tune under my breath as I gather utensils and napkins, placing them alongside the dishes on the table. I hesitate at the cabinet that holds the glasses. "Do you want wine tonight?"

He shakes his head. "Nope. I'm on the wagon, remember?"

"You don't have to stop drinking just because of me."

He slides the sauté pan off the fire and puts it over on an unlit burner. He turns and looks at me as he leans against the counter. "I know I don't have to, but I want to."

I shrug and pull out two water glasses, filling them at the sink before bringing them to the table. I can feel him staring at my back. I take a seat and look at him. "What's up?"

"Nothing. I was just taking a little look. I can see your belly now, you know."

I look down and rub my tummy. There's a decent-sized bump there now, I have to admit. I thought I would hate it, but I don't. "I've really started noticing it. My jeans are getting tight."

"We're going to be able to find out the sex of the babies in a couple weeks. Do you want to do that?"

I shrug. "Sometimes I think I do, and other times I think not. What about you?"

I try to read his expression as he speaks because I know a lot of times he says what he thinks I want him to say and not what he really feels. I want to be sure I'm hearing the actual truth from him when he answers this question. I've slowly come to terms with the fact that even though this is my body and I'm growing these babies, they're just as much his as they are mine, and he needs to make decisions with me. It's a fifty-fifty deal.

"At first I was thinking I would like for it to be a surprise, but then I was thinking it would be kind of nice to know so we could buy a couple things," he says.

"That's what I was thinking, too. But we could always just buy neutral things to get us started and then get more stuff later."

Lucky turns around and goes about putting a pot of water on to boil. "Did you read the book that talks about scheduling? I'm worried that we aren't going to have any free time to shop after the babies are born."

"I did read that. But I also read that other book that was saying how we shouldn't let our lives change too much. We should still go out and do stuff and just bring the babies with us. Or get a babysitter sometimes." As soon as the words are out of my mouth, I worry that I've overstepped, that he'll look at me funny and ask me why I think he'll be here doing stuff with me after the babies are born. I say "we" too much for someone who hasn't defined whether there actually is a "we" going on here.

"Yeah." He nods, giving me no indication that what I said was too presumptuous. "I read that too. It seems like there's so much information out there, it's almost getting hard to sort through."

I nod because I know exactly what he's talking about. At this point I feel like I'm suffering information overload. "The only thing I'm looking at now is that book that has the weekly update on what's happening with the babies and their development."

"That's probably a good idea. You can read me this week's information tonight after dinner."

Normally after we eat in the evening, he goes up to his room or he leaves the house entirely to go back to work or hang out with Thibault, keeping his promise to stay out of my hair and not put pressure on our situation. It's starting to wear on me, though. I find myself growing more attached to him as the weeks go by.

Last night as I lay in bed alone staring at the ceiling, I decided that I want more of his attention than he's giving me now, but there's no way for me to express that desire without sounding weak, and I hate losing my strength even for a second. This pregnancy already makes me feel somewhat outside of myself. I'm tired a lot, and my memory pretty much sucks these days. I've started putting Post-It notes all over the place to remind me of appointments and other things I'm supposed to remember.

Needless to say, the idea of us being together after dinner makes me really happy. "Maybe we could play cards or something," I suggest. "After we read the book or whatever."

He nods. "Yeah, that would be great." It's impossible to tell if he's being serious or if he's just being nice. "Or we could play a board game," he says, looking over his shoulder. "I'm a pretty mean Scrabble player."

I can't help but smile. I'm pretty sure he's being serious. He sounds enthusiastic enough. "Fine. Scrabble it is."

A few months ago, if someone had told me I was going to stay inside and enjoy playing a Scrabble game with a guy, I would've laughed at that person, or I might've even slugged him in the arm.

But now the idea thrills me. That, more than anything, shows me how much this pregnancy has changed me.

Would Lucky and I have gotten to this point together without the babies there to push things along? Probably not. Knowing me, I would have shoved him away and things would have gone back to the way they were. That idea makes me sad now.

I told Lucky before that I didn't want him here, and he promised to stop acting like a caveman, but I'm comfortable with us starting a new ritual. It feels right to have him around more. Instead of him going his way and me going mine, we can go the same way together for a change. Sometimes I get the feeling that he's thinking the same thing, but he never says it out loud. I can't really blame him, though; I did threaten him over it before.

"You know, you don't have to try so hard to stay out of my way anymore." I can't believe I said that out loud, but the instant the words are out there, I'm glad I did. Unfortunately, my stomach ties itself in knots as I wait for his response. It's slow in coming.

He dumps pasta into boiling water and sets a pot lid halfway over the top of the bubbling liquid. He crumples the box that the noodles came in and puts it in the recycle bin before he comes over and sits down across from me.

"Are you sure about that?" he asks. His voice is soft and gentle.

I shrug, flustered. "It's not a big deal."

"It *is* a big deal. You're not used to having somebody in your personal space. I don't think you realize how different it will be from your normal routine."

I shrug, trying to act cool and casual when I'm anything but. "I lived with Thibault and my family for a hell of a lot of years before I was alone. I'm pretty sure I can handle it."

Lucky smiles. "It's been really hard staying away from you, I have to admit."

"Really?" I smile like a fool. I can't believe how much this means to me. *Am I in love with Lucky, or what?* The answer surprises me when it pops into my head: *I think I am.*

My ears start burning at the thought, and I'm sure they're turning dark red. I look at the wall, the ceiling and the floor—anywhere but at him.

"Yes," he says. "Very hard. I hope this doesn't mean anything bad about me, but every time I see you and that little bump you're carrying around, I just want to get you naked."

My face joins my ears and heats up until it feels like it's on fire. I'm not normally a prude or embarrassed about my body, but the idea that he wants to see me naked while pregnant sends me for a loop. *Do I want him to see me naked?* Yes. I definitely do.

Now I can look at Lucky when I talk to him. "I don't think there's anything wrong with you. If there is, it's something wrong with me too." My emotions shift to something hotter. I so want to have sex with him right now.

His expression darkens and he looks ten times sexier all of a sudden. "What are you saying?"

I draw invisible circles on the table with my fingertip because I can't look him in the eye again. "I don't know. Maybe that it's hard living with you and not *being* with you." I shrug. It's not easy for me to reveal my innermost thoughts to anyone, even the guy who planted two babies in me.

"Maybe we could try sleeping together."

His suggestion hangs in the air between us. *Is this what I want? Is this the next logical step in our lives together or is it a mistake? The beginning of a real relationship or the ending of everything?* There's no way for me to know the answer to my questions unless I take a risk and try it. Trying has never really been hard for me in the past, but this feels like a really big deal.

"We could do a trial basis thing," I say.

Lucky gives me a tentative smile. "Sure we could. We did the trial basis deal for me to live here and it worked out okay, right?"

I nod, feeling hopeful. "Yep. Turned out just fine."

Lucky stands. "You ready for some dinner?"

"Sure." I'm trying to roll with the quick change in topics. One second we're talking about sex and sleeping together, moving on to what seems to be an actual relationship, and then the next second he's talking about linguine. "Are the noodles ready already?"

"I got the quick-cooking kind so they should be ready very soon. I'll go check." He walks over to the stove, moving around like he knows what he's doing.

For the first time in my life, I don't feel completely unlucky. Maybe all of Lucky's good fortune is rubbing off on me.

An image of Charlie intrudes on my thoughts. It's a very effective reminder that no matter how much I hang out with a guy named Lucky, there's always my past right there behind me reminding me that I have a tendency to screw things up.

I'm so conflicted. I want to believe that everything that happened with Lucky isn't bad luck, that forgetting to use protection, that me getting pregnant with twins, that all of this is somehow his good luck intervening in my life. But it seems too good to be true. Something bad is going to happen.

I feel a little panicky when I realize that the most horrible thing that could ever happen to me now would be something involving my children. I feel a flutter down there and rub my hand over it. *Great. Now I've got gas.*

That's one thing Lucky has not yet seen with me. He's been sleeping in his room and I've been sleeping in mine, and I've been able to hide the fact that these babies are giving me serious intestinal problems. I feel the blood leaving my face as I realize that this is a secret I'm going to have difficulty keeping if we're sharing a bed together. *Oh, God.*

Lucky turns around and looks at me for a few seconds. "What's wrong?"

I shake my head to get it out of the weird place it was in. "Nothing. I was just thinking . . . about us sleeping together."

He gives me a sly smile. "You were, huh? Got any special requests?"

I can't help but laugh at him. "No." Now that my mind has hosted visions of Charlie and thoughts about my digestive problems, all that hot and bothered stuff has given way to the practicalities of my life. By the time I make it to bed at night, I'm so tired, I feel like a zombie; I'm asleep before my head hits the pillow. If Lucky's going to be sleeping with me, we're going to have to be responsible and realistic about this whole thing. I don't want to lead him on, because that'll only lead to disappointment. The last thing I want to do is disappoint Lucky.

"And don't think you're getting sex out of the deal," I say, trying to sound firm. "I need to get my sleep. When I said we'd sleep together, I meant *sleep*."

He gives me a mysterious look. "We'll see."

It's impossible for me not to smile at that. A big part of me is hoping he'll push the issue tonight. Maybe I don't need to be *that* responsible. Maybe I don't need *that* much sleep.

I have a hard time focusing on the little bits of conversation and the taste of the food. Lucky and I are going to sleep together tonight, and although I told him I don't plan on having sex with him, my body knows otherwise. I'm ultrasensitive, and everything is tingling in anticipation.

Everything.

CHAPTER THIRTY-ONE

I wasn't able to eat a whole lot of the dinner. All I could think about was sleeping with Lucky later. But there's still one outstanding issue to deal with before that can happen . . .

"Are you ready?" He gazes across the table at me with his gorgeous blue eyes, the promise of excitement ahead.

"Hell, yeah, I'm ready. Ready to kick your ass." I reach inside the drawstring bag and pull out seven letter tiles, lining them up on the plastic holder in front of me. "You're going down, clown."

Lucky laughs and selects his own tiles, shaking his head and smiling as he sets them up. "They don't call me Lucky for nothin', babe. It's you that's goin' down like a clown."

What ensues is the most rousing game of Scrabble I've ever participated in. Lucky alternately begs for mercy, prods me into taking risks I shouldn't, cries in defeat, and yells in triumph. I'm not sure he wins with actual spelling skill, but there's no doubt he comes out ahead in points. I'm pretty sure it was his strategy to mess with my mind all along. He kept touching me gently, winking at me, complimenting me . . . An hour later, I'm a puddle of mush and he's 100 points ahead when the last tile is laid on the board.

He leans back in his chair, lacing his fingers together and placing them behind his head. "I told you I'm good at Scrabble."

"You cheated." I sweep all the tiles together and dump them into the bag, folding the board up and putting it in the box. The game still looks brand-new, but I have a feeling over the next few months we're going to wear it out. This is the most fun I've ever had staying in.

"I'm going to make some tea," Lucky says. "Would you like some?"

"No, thanks." I want to go upstairs, brush my teeth, and shave my legs before I get into bed with him. It's not that I expect something to happen, but if it does, I want to be prepared. Like May said to Marc . . . no guy wants to get the cactus treatment when he snuggles up close.

While Lucky busies himself with the kettle in the kitchen, I race upstairs, headed right for my bathroom. I haven't been this nervous or excited about a guy in as long as I can remember. It's almost like we're going out on a date, but it's in the house, and he's my roommate and the father of my twin babies. Heck, maybe he'll be my boyfriend one day.

This is so not like me to be worrying about a man's status in my life. I'm going to blame it on the babies throwing my hormones out of whack.

Of course, because I'm in a hurry, I cut myself shaving. I hiss with the pain. *Dammit, I knew I shouldn't have used a new blade.*

A knock comes at the door. "You okay in there?"

"Yes. I just cut myself shaving."

There's a pause before he answers. "Do you always shave before you go to bed?"

"Yes." I hold my breath, wondering if he's buying my lie.

"Okay. I'll be in bed waiting for you."

My heart races. *Is he going to be naked?* I can't remember what he looks like without his clothes on. I think I was too busy rolling around getting sweaty with him to pay much attention. I know he's got awesome pecs and a serious set of abs, but the rest of him . . . I have no idea. I just know that we fit together like two pieces of a very complicated puzzle.

I brush my hair out, amazed at how long it's getting. The prenatal vitamins I've been taking are making everything grow, I guess. I brush and floss my teeth and then brush a second time, following it up with a heavy-duty dose of mouthwash that I gargle for twice as long as it says to, leaving my gums stinging.

From a drawer in the attached walk-in closet, I pull out my sexiest nightgown. It's dark red and silky, with black lace around the edges of the bodice. Hopefully it won't stay on me for very long, because it's not the most comfortable thing to sleep in. Plus, I definitely want to do this sex thing. Screw just sleeping together. If we're going to live together, we might as well enjoy some of the added benefits, right?

I slide the nightgown over my body and let it fall into place. The hem ends just below my butt. It's loose enough that Lucky won't see my belly, which I consider a bonus. No need to remind him that there are two babies floating around in there. *Talk about a turn-off.*

I lean in close to the mirror, checking for flaws. May says I'm really pretty, but I don't see it. My face looks average to me. I swear I'm starting to get wrinkles around my mouth. May would say it's because I frown too much. I stick my tongue out at my reflection. *I think I frown just enough, thank you very much.*

When I'm finally satisfied that everything is as good as it's going to get, I walk through the bathroom door and into the bedroom. I let out the deep breath that I took in and stare at my bed.

Sprawled out on the left side of it is Lucky. He's on his back, his eyes are closed, and his mouth is gaping open. A snore comes from somewhere deep in his sinus cavity.

I walk closer, taking in the details. He's removed his shirt and unbuttoned his pants but left them on. He doesn't have a lot of chest hair, but what he does have meets in a line in the middle of his pecs and goes down the center of his belly and disappears into the top of his Calvin Kleins. He looks positively edible. My pulse quickens as I imagine him with his pants off.

I war within myself. Should I wake him up and get this party started or just stand here and gawk for a little while longer? He's got to be tired with all the hours he's working. He wasn't up here for longer than ten minutes, max. There's a cup of tea on the nightstand next to the bed and it's still half full.

I walk around the bed and lie down next to him carefully and slowly, trying not to jiggle him too much. He's close enough now that I can feel the warmth coming off his body. I can smell him, too. Lucky has a scent I could never describe adequately, but I know what it reminds me of: all the times I've looked at him and smiled, all the times he's come up to me and put his arms around me, all the hours, days, weeks, months, and years we've spent together, first as friends and now as lovers and partners in child rearing. He smells like home.

He moves a little in his sleep and then cracks open an eye. "Hey," he says tiredly.

I smile. "Hey, sleepyhead." I reach up and push his nose. "You snore."

He frowns, his voice sleepy and sexy. "No, I don't. That was you."

I giggle, loving his sense of humor and the intimate way he's sharing it. "That would be pretty difficult, since I was standing on two feet when it happened."

"Lies and rumors. Rumors and lies. I've never snored in my life." He rolls over, putting his back to me, and lets out a big, long snore, this time fake.

I snuggle up behind him, spooning him and burying my face in the back of his neck. I know it's bold, but it feels right, like I should be here doing this with him. I inhale a deep breath of Lucky, smiling as it hits the pleasure spot in my brain. I'm so glad I opened my big mouth and told him how I felt about him not disappearing every night.

"I could get used to this," he mumbles into the pillow.

"Good. Me too." I mean it. I like this peace that I'm finding between us. We're completely alone and nothing can intrude. I feel safe and warm. Maybe even loved. Respected at the very least. I haven't found this place very often in my life.

"Do you want to fool around?" he mumbles.

I smile, my teeth grazing his skin. "Maybe."

He lifts my arm off his waist and turns around so that we're face to face. "I think you're going to have to make the first move."

"Why? You chicken?"

He nods very earnestly. "I've never had sex with a pregnant lady before."

"Me neither."

He barks a laugh right into my face.

I reach up and pretend to wipe something off my eyelid. "Thanks for that."

He takes my hand in his and kisses the backs of my fingers. "I really like you. A lot."

I try hard not to smile but I know I'm failing. He didn't say he loves me, but I like this better. It feels safer. Liking each other is a great place to start. "I like you a lot too."

"I want to take your clothes off now."

"Don't let me stop you."

The soft material of my nightgown tickles my skin as he slowly lifts it up. I wiggle around to help him get it off, and soon it's going over my head and being thrown across the room. It sails through the air as if caught by a breeze before falling gently to the floor.

He looks down at my completely naked body. "My god, woman. You are a work of art."

I shove him on the shoulder gently. "Shut up. You're so goofy." I can feel my face burning at his compliment.

"No, I'm serious. Deadly serious." He slides his hand down my arm to my waist and then to the front of me, stopping at my belly. His finger circles my navel and then moves down to the triangle of hair below.

I have to force myself to remain still, even though his touch is sending pleasant sparks of electricity through me.

"I don't want to hurt you," he says.

"There is nothing you could do that would hurt me, except . . ." I stop myself before I mess things up with too many words and too much information.

"Except what?"

I shake my head. "Never mind. I wasn't going to say anything."

His hand comes up and rests on the side of my cheek. He stares into my eyes. "Just tell me what you were going to say. I promise I won't judge."

I think for a few moments about whether I want to say anything. My first instinct is to make something up, to lie. But I'm a mom now; I need to do the right thing and tell him what I was thinking. What's the worst that could happen? He could leave me, and I'd be alone, which is what I've been most of my life, so I can handle it.

"I was just going to say that the only way you could hurt me would be to leave me. But if you need to leave me, I get it. I don't ever want you to stay because you feel obligated."

His smile looks almost sad. "Why do you think I'd want to leave you?"

I shrug. "I don't know. People leave people. It happens." The ache in my heart is heavy. I don't say the words that are really there: that I don't think I'm a person worthy of hanging around with for long. Not for a guy like Lucky, anyway.

"I've been around you for more than half our lives. What makes you think I'd want to leave you now? We're part of a team. We're making a family together." He looks like he wants to say more, but he stops.

For some reason his words and his hesitation afterward make me want to cry. I work really hard at keeping that emotion buried. "But sometimes shit happens. I get that."

"You should know me better than this, Toni. I don't disappear when things get tough. I stick. I've learned my lesson."

His last statement throws me off. "Your lesson?"

"Yeah. With my sister. I wasn't there for her when she needed me, and look what happened."

"You're not blaming yourself for what she did, I hope."

"No, not exactly. I've talked to Jenny quite a bit about it, and she's helped me see a lot of things more clearly. So did you when we talked about it a while back. But the fact is, my sister needed to talk to somebody, and I wasn't there. And maybe she wouldn't have talked to me anyway, but if I'd been around more, if I had prioritized our relationship a little bit more, maybe I could have taken her to someone who she could have talked to. At least helped her find some peace."

"There's no way you can know that now. There's no point in beating yourself up about it."

"But what if I'm a terrible father? I was a terrible brother. It's not a big stretch to think I might suck at it. My father was no prince, that's for sure."

"Are you kidding me? That's nuts. You were a great brother. Remember? I was there. You brought your sister everywhere until she was old enough to decide she wasn't interested. And who cares about your dad or what he did or didn't do? You're going to be a great father. You're kind, considerate, funny, patient . . . You can't let things that happened to you in the past that you had no control over determine who you'll be in the future."

He strokes my arm. "I could say the same to you about Charlie, you know."

My blood instantly goes cold. "What's he got to do with anything?" I pull away a little bit and the space between us turns almost frigid.

"Nothing. I'm just saying . . . that you're a lot like me. You blame yourself for things that aren't your fault."

I snort in disgust. I don't really know who the emotion is for, though—him or me. "I killed Charlie. There's no way to sugarcoat that. I'm going to pay for that mistake for the rest of my life."

"But he hurt you. He hurt you badly. All you did was protect yourself."

"One bullet was for protection. The other four . . . not so much."

"No, I don't buy it. I know you think the judge believed that and you've convinced yourself of it too, but it's not true. It doesn't matter how much training you've had, Toni." He moves some hair off my forehead and continues. "You know that when you're in a situation like that, where stress levels are maxed out, you don't have the presence of mind to say, 'Oh, one bullet is all I need. There you go. Bang.' All you know is you've got a threat coming at you and you need to end that threat. You need to put a stop to it."

"I wish it were that simple."

"It *is* that simple. Look at all of the police shootings we've had in the city over the past five years. I've read the reports—have you?" He waits for me to shake my head no before continuing. "In every single case, the police officers, arguably the most well-trained individuals in the use of firearms under stress, used more than one bullet to subdue their suspects."

"Because they were shooting from far away, probably. They weren't sure they hit the suspect, so they had to keep going." I can't look Lucky in the eye anymore so I stare at his chin. "Charlie was shot from practically point-blank range."

"No, that's not true. In several of the cases that I read, the officers were within five feet of the suspects. No one ever uses just one bullet. There's too much adrenaline flowing and too much at stake."

Why was he reading those reports? I don't remember anything like that being part of a case we've worked on. *Did he do it for me?* A little piece of me really wants to believe what he's saying, but I know what he's doing; he's just trying to make me feel better about the horrible thing that I did.

"I don't want to talk about this anymore." And I'm not in the mood to do what we were *going* to do, either. The warmth hasn't returned to the space between us. Now I just feel empty of emotion. *So much for shaved legs.*

He runs his hand up and down my arm and then pulls me into him, hugging me close. "I'm sorry I brought this stuff up. Talk about a mood killer."

I pull away and roll over, turning my back to him. I hate feeling vulnerable, but that's exactly where I find myself right now. "Could you just . . . hold me tonight?"

"Of course," he says, moving closer. "I'd love to."

Memories of Charlie intermingle with thoughts of Lucky, our past and the future we might have. I'm obviously deeply scarred from my last relationship and the way I handled it. I feel like I can't move forward until I fix what's in the past, but I also know it's impossible to undo what I've done. Spin, spin, spin, round and round my thoughts whirl . . . If only there was a way to fix things . . .

WRONG QUESTION, RIGHT ANSWER

A lightbulb goes on in my brain, and the clarity it brings is immediate. It hits me like a bolt of lightning, right in the center of my brain. I know what my problem is now and why everything in my life feels so doomed and bound to be awful, no matter what I do to try to fix it. This thing with Charlie is like an open wound for a reason. I can't believe I didn't figure this out sooner. *This* is why I felt the need to drunk-dial a guy who tried to kidnap a friend of mine to get to me. Even drunk off my ass, I knew what my heart needs. It needs *closure*.

I can't undo the things I've done, and I'll never not regret those things or not feel terribly guilty for what I did to Charlie, but maybe if I could find a way to put some things behind me, I could move on with Lucky and the babies with light in my world and not all this overwhelming darkness that threatens to take over all the time.

The sparkle of hope that lights up my heart is like a drug I want to overdose on. My mind goes into overdrive as I think of my options. *How do I find closure for taking the life of a man who claimed to love me?* It doesn't take me long to reach the conclusion that there really is only one way to get this done: if I could just get someone who loves Charlie to forgive me, someone who was important to him, I could start to forgive myself. And therein lies the path to closure, the elusive elixir that I'm convinced will make healing possible.

I run down a mental list of his relatives and fixate on the most logical one. *Of course.* It's so obvious now. My hand slides down to my belly, and a tiny little poke comes from inside me. I smile as I realize one of my babies is talking to me.

This is good. This is right. It's crazy and nuts, yes, but it's the only way I know of to make things right for my future. And I've never shied away from crazy and nuts before. I can do this. Besides, I have more than just myself to think of now; I have the babies and maybe Lucky, too, if he wants to stick around and move our relationship on to the next level. I owe them this effort. My whole body goes warm at the idea of starting over with an almost clean slate.

"Lucky?"

"Yeah."

"One of the babies is kicking."

His hand slides around and rests on my belly. I place my fingers over his, trying to predict the next spot where a kick will appear. It's there again. A little flutter.

"Did you feel that?" I ask.

"Oh my god. I think I did. It felt like a little bubble."

"Well, it's either gas or a baby."

"That is so cool," he whispers against my neck. "You're a mommy."

"Yep. And you're a daddy."

I feel certain of what I need to do now. I need to talk to Charlie's mother. I need to apologize for what I did to her son, to her family, and to her. She was there in the courtroom when I was convicted. She has it in her mind to hate me until she takes her very last breath, but maybe if I talk to her, mother to mother, she'll find something in her heart that will allow her to at least hear my apology. That could be enough.

Hope makes my heart soar.

CHAPTER THIRTY-TWO

I'm happy with the way things are progressing at home with Lucky and at work with all of my teammates. I never thought I would enjoy a routine, but this one feels comfortable. Each night, Lucky and I have dinner together and then either play cards or a board game, and then we go upstairs to my room together. So far, it's been only PG-rated cuddling going on in the bed, but I have other plans for us.

He's been letting me call the shots, and normally I wouldn't shy away from having sex at the drop of a hat, but I find my attitude about things like that changing. I still like sex, of course, but it means more to me now. I've been waiting to figure out what Lucky and I actually are to one another before complicating it with a more intimate relationship. Lucky's not just some guy I met at a bar or an old childhood flame looking for a roll in the hay; he's the father of my children and the guy I live with, the guy I play board games with and tease about having a crazy-ass beard that doesn't even come close to making him ugly. The next time we have sex, it's going to be very different than the last time; we're going to be making love. I'm not sure I've ever done that before. Not even with Charlie.

"Will you go shopping with me this afternoon?"

May's question startles me out of my reverie. She's looking over at me from the neighboring cubicle. The two of us joke now that we're the cubical crew . . . cube crew for short. Ozzie has given us the power to decide for ourselves whether we want to go out into the field or stay in to do the tamer stuff, and we've both volunteered for cubicle duty. Morning sickness aside, it just seems safer and smarter. Whenever I think about working in the field with May, I picture Marc the gangbanger reaching into his waistband for his weapon; then it's an easy decision to stay on the cube crew. With all the arrests that have come from our work, there's not a whole lot left to sift through, but we keep at it, hoping one last piece of the puzzle will present itself; Marc Doucet is still at large, and while we've been able to track his movements via his telephone to some degree, thanks to the quick thinking of Alice Inwonderland Guckenberger, he still hasn't implicated himself in any actual crimes.

I shake my head. "No, thanks." I can't think of a better way to torture myself. Clothes shopping with May? Nope. Motherhood hasn't changed me that much.

"But you have to," she whines. "We're finishing up the wedding plans and I need your input."

"I already masterminded the plan to get your wedding back on track by moving it forward and finding you that caterer. I think I've done my duty."

She frowns at me. "Don't make me put you in another headlock."

I have to smile at that. She did take me down once, but I doubt she could do it again. I'm ready for her now, plus I'm no longer encumbered by nausea.

I point at her as I click a button on my keyboard, rewinding the current recording a bit. "Listen here, Bo Peep . . . you even try to put me in a headlock, and I'll have you so tangled up in your headphone wires, you'll have to call in a posse to rescue your sorry butt."

She leans in close and whispers loudly, "If you do that, I'll tattle on you. I'll tell them you did it and overexerted yourself at the same time. Lucky will scold you big time."

"You'd better not." I'm trying to stay serious, but it's impossible. Somehow, whenever I chat with May, I end up feeling like I'm ten years old again. I think I was a lot less bitter back then, too, because I'm finding her more funny than annoying these days. Damn hormones . . . they're making me soft. After these babies are born, I'm signing up for double workouts with Dev.

"Please?" she pleads. "I'll buy your babies matching booties."

It's so stupid, but her silly little bribes always manage to get me. Who cares about booties? Apparently, I do. "Fine. I'll go shopping with you, but I'm not going for more than an hour."

"No problem. I can power-shop. The question is . . . can you?" She wiggles her eyebrows up and down at me.

I snort. "Please. I can power through anything, including one of your silly shopping trips."

"Better wear your running shoes," she says under her breath, putting her headphones on and clicking keys on her computer.

CHAPTER THIRTY-THREE

When May said power-shop, she wasn't kidding. Jenny is her wingman and I'm the slacker trailing behind, whining about my feet. She was right; I should have worn running shoes, but I stuck with my work boots, which have heels that are doing a great job of killing me. We've only been here for forty-five minutes, but I swear to God, we've already visited half the stores in the mall and covered about five miles in the process.

"Come on, you have to keep up. We still have another four shops to go into before our time is up." May snaps her fingers over her head at me.

"Can we stop for a drink or something?" My tongue feels like it could stick to the roof of my mouth with little effort.

Jenny answers me when something shiny in a shop window catches May's attention. "You can have some water; that's it. Everything else in this entire mall is either caffeinated or full of sugar."

I roll my eyes, making a mental note never to shop with either of these two again. They're hardcore and of the opinion that every single piece of fabric in the entire place must be touched and evaluated before we can move on to the next. I don't say anything else, deciding that drawing attention to myself is a bad idea. I need them to focus on their mission and get this over with.

Twenty minutes later, we're finishing up at the last store, the place where we're supposed to pick out our bridesmaids dresses. Jenny holds up a black cocktail number.

"This one is gorgeous," she says, shaking it at me.

I roll my eyes. "Sure, if you don't mind my potbelly hanging out on the front of it." The thing is skintight.

Jenny fake-frowns at me as she moves the dress away. She puts her hand on my belly and rubs it. "How dare you. This is not a potbelly. This is a baby belly."

I look down, a little shocked that she's actually touching my stomach. It feels weird to have another woman put her hands there without any warning, but at the same time, it's not entirely unpleasant. The babies are in there, after all, and she's practically an aunt to them.

Her eyes open wide. "Was that a kick I just felt?"

I smile. "Yep. Baby's telling you to get your hands off the merchandise."

Jenny jerks her hand back. "Oh my god. I'm so sorry. That is *so* rude of me."

I shake my head, feeling bad that I embarrassed her. "No, don't worry about it. It's no big deal, really."

May joins us. "Did you guys find a dress?"

I grab the hanger out of Jenny's hand and hold the gown up in front of me. "Yep. Looks great, right?" This is my ticket out of here.

"But you have to try it on," Jenny says.

I look at my watch. "Don't have time. I'll try it on at home. If it doesn't fit, I'll bring it back and get another size."

May points her finger at me. "You'd better do it right away. We're running out of time. The wedding is next week."

I nod. "I know, I know. Remember? I'm a bridesmaid. I'm central to this entire production."

May surprises me with a hug. Then Jenny joins in and makes it a group thing. I sigh, letting the dress dangle off to the side.

"In a week you're going to be my sister!" May squeals.

I frown over her shoulder. "How's that?"

Both girls pull away and grin at me. I never thought they looked that much alike before, but seeing them side by side with both of them wearing those silly smiles on their faces, I can see it now. It makes me wonder if my babies are going to look exactly alike or if they'll be fraternal twins.

Jenny answers my question. "You're practically a sister to Ozzie, so that makes you practically May's sister-in-law when she's married, which will make you my practically-sister-in-law."

"I'm not sure your family chart will hold up under scrutiny." I'm quoting words I've heard my brother use when he's talking about evidence. *Will it hold up under scrutiny?* is always the question he's asking when we hand in our reports.

May waves her hand in the air, effectively dismissing my negative comments. "It doesn't matter what the law says; it only matters what the heart says." She places her hand on my shoulder and stares at me. "You will be my sister in less than one week, so you'd better get used to it. I advise you to just embrace this and not fight it."

I laugh. "Trust me, I know you well enough to know that it's pointless to fight you on anything you get stuck in your head."

She drops her hand from my shoulder and smiles. "See? You get me. I knew we would come to an understanding eventually." She turns her attention to her real sister. "Are we all set with the bachelorette party?"

"What bachelorette party?" I ask.

"Lunch at my house the day before," Jenny says. "No big parties for this fiancée." She jabs her thumb in May's direction. "She's pregnant, so we're not allowed to have too much fun, unlike the men."

"The men?" I ask. This is all news to me.

"Yeah. The guys are going to some bar tonight. I thought you knew," May answers.

I shrug. "Lucky didn't tell me anything about it." There's no reason for him to do that, really; we haven't laid claim to one another, even though we've spent every night of the last three weeks together at the house.

I have to work at not being annoyed. I switch my focus back to May's shindig at Jenny's. "You can still have a stripper if you're pregnant, you know."

The two sisters open their mouths but nothing comes out.

"I was just joking. Relax." *Kind of joking.*

Jenny puts her finger on her chin and looks up at the ceiling, her eyes sparkling with mischief. "I don't know . . . Maybe we could do it."

"Don't you *dare*." May has lowered her voice to a whisper and she's looking around as if making sure no one has heard her.

I can't resist; I raise my voice so I can be heard across the entire store. "I think a stripper is a great idea, May! Great suggestion! Do you want the same Village People group that we used for your birthday party?!"

May comes at me like a slap-o-matic, her hands waving in front of her in a blur as she reaches out to make contact with my body. I hold my forearms up to fend her off, laughing so hard it makes my stomach ache. This feels way better than worrying about Lucky hooking up with some random girl at a bar during a bachelor party while I'm at home being pregnant.

"I didn't say that!" she yells, looking over her shoulder at the salesgirls, who are staring at us. "I don't like strippers!"

Jenny is laughing right along with me. The two of us duck and run to the cash register. May decides not to follow us, going out of the store and into the mall. Jenny and I stand at the counter grinning like fools, both of us out of breath.

She holds up a hand and I give her a high-five.

"Good one," she says.

"Yeah, I thought so." My veins feel like they're pumped full of happy drugs. I guess shopping with May and Jenny can actually be fun. *Huh. Imagine that.*

I'm tempted to text Lucky and ask him what his plans are for tonight, but I resist. It's his life to do with what he wants, and if he wants to go party, he should go party. I'll just go to bed early.

CHAPTER THIRTY-FOUR

I'm sound asleep in my bed when a banging coming from downstairs wakes me up. Then there's a bunch of weird beeping as Lucky tries to turn off the alarm. He texted me as I was leaving the mall to say that he'd be out late at the bachelor party, so I wasn't expecting to see him until the sun was up, but it's pitch black out and a glance at the alarm clock tells me it's three in the morning. My ears perk up when I hear more beeps than I should.

Oh shit. He got the code wrong. I run out of my room, but not before the alarm starts going off. As I race down the stairs, I hear cussing mixing with the siren, and I can smell the booze on him before I get to the bottom step.

I stride over and push him out of the way so I can punch in the correct code and shut the alarm off. It stops squealing in our ears, but now I have to get to the telephone in the kitchen so I can talk to the dispatcher whose job it is to check on activated alarms. It rings within thirty seconds and I'm there waiting. I pick up the handset and give the operator my secret code so she won't send the cops over.

After thanking the operator for her diligence, I slam the headset back down against its cradle and turn around to glare at Lucky.

He's right behind me, running his hands through his hair. It's standing up all over the place and, along with his rumpled clothes and crazy beard, makes him look like he just spent the night in a gutter. He should look ugly to me, but he doesn't. He's just as hot as ever, but he woke me from a sound sleep after partying it up with the other members of our team, so I'm not feeling very charitable.

I fold my arms over my chest and glare at him.

"Hey, babe." He gives me a sheepish grin.

"I was sleeping."

"I know. I tried to be quiet." His words are slurred.

I don't remember ever seeing him this drunk before. He starts to lose some of his attractiveness when I realize who he reminds me of: *Charlie*.

I shove past him to go upstairs, but he grabs my wrist and pulls me to him.

I yank my hand from his grasp and back up a step. "Don't." My voice comes out sharp with an edge of fear to it. My heart is fluttering in my chest and adrenaline is flowing into my veins. I'm having some kind of flashback. All I can think about right now is Charlie and what he used to do to me.

It was always the beginning of any bad moments between us, when he would go out and get drunk and then come home and try to interact with me. Nobody has perfect control when they've had that much booze, I don't care who they are. Lucky is no different.

Lucky frowns, reaching weakly for me. "Come on, babe. Don't be like that."

I'm furious. How dare he come home to me like this. He knows Charlie used to do that and that it never ended well.

I slap his hand away and glare at him as he sways on his feet. "Be like what? Be like a pregnant person who doesn't appreciate being woken up in the middle of the night by a drunk asshole?"

He pulls his furry chin into his chest, almost stumbling with the effort. "Wow. That's harsh. What'd I do to you?"

I shake my head at him, realizing that this conversation is completely pointless. He's too drunk to even know what he's saying or doing. He probably won't remember any of it in the morning.

"Never mind. I'm going to bed. You can sleep in the other room."

He is so not getting anywhere near me with that stinking booze-breath of his. And he's drunk enough that he'll probably try to touch me, and then I'd have to break one of his bones. It's not worth taking the chance.

I attempt to walk past him, but he grabs me again. When I try to wrench myself out of his grip, he holds on tighter.

I pause my efforts to escape in an attempt to get a handle on my emotions. Really bad things could happen right now if I'm not careful. I take a deep breath in and out before turning to look at him. My wrist remains trapped between us.

"Lucky . . . you need to let me go. You're drunk and you're acting stupid, and I don't have a lot of patience for that tonight."

His voice softens. "But I need to talk to you about something. It's super important."

I sigh really loudly at him so he'll know how annoying I find him. "Fine. What is it? Hurry up, because it's late and I have to go to work in the morning."

"Work?" He's frowning in confusion. "It's the weekend."

I shake my head, realizing I almost revealed my secret. I plan to do a little more recon on Charlie's mother tomorrow. I've been driving around her neighborhood off and on over the past three weeks when I've had time alone after work, making sure she's there, seeing who she spends time with in the evening, getting to know her routines. Last time I heard, she was single, but it's been a while. So far I haven't seen anything to tell me different, but I need to be sure. I have no desire to spill my guts to a crowd. This has to be just between us.

"I meant shopping. I have to go shopping for the wedding." That little lie will guarantee me a solo trip. Lucky is no more into these wedding plans than I am.

"Oh. Well, okay. I'll probably be sleeping and then suffering a major hangover." He smiles and hiccups, putting the back of his hand up to his mouth and wiping his lips.

I raise an eyebrow at him. "You had something you wanted to tell me?"

"Yeah." Now he's animated again, his eyes sparkling. He leans toward me and takes my other hand in his. We're standing face to face and there isn't enough space between us. His breath is like high-octane, pure alcohol stink coming at me in waves.

My instinct is to fight him off and get away, but I don't. *Settle down . . . this isn't Charlie; it's Lucky. He's not going to hurt you.*

His words come out all jumbled together. "I was thinking tonight, when I was out. About stuff. About us. And I was seeing all these girls dancing around and the guys joking around and stuff . . . but I really wasn't having any fun."

I shake my head at him. "I find that really hard to believe. This is the booze talking."

He steps a little closer, giving me a clear view of his bloodshot eyes. "No, I swear. I used to like that stuff, but now that I've been here with you, and the peas are coming . . ."

"Peas?"

He glances down at my belly. "Peas in the pod. Two of 'em." He looks up and grins at me before continuing. "I just don't like the same things that I used to like. They make me mad, actually." He shakes his head and looks confused, as if he doesn't understand himself.

I shrug, realizing what he's trying to say, even though he's drunk as a skunk and probably talking out of his ass. "I know what you mean. I used to be right there with you guys, but now I just want to stay in and beat your ass at board games." I give him a sad smile. "I guess this is the beginning of my new, lame life."

He squeezes my hands and looks at me so earnestly it almost makes me sad. "See? That's what I mean. We're both moving in the same direction. We both want the same things. But you don't win at those board games—you lose, but that's okay. I still love you. And we're having a family together. You know what that means?"

Forget the fact that he just used the L word on me again; I can write that off as a natural side effect of too much alcohol. I fear something worse is about to happen. I shake my head at him, worried about where he's going with this. I should shut him up, but I don't. Something inside of me wants to see where this is going to end.

"No," I say. "Why don't you tell me what it all means, Mister Drunk Philosopher?"

He grins, spreading his alcohol-induced happiness all over me. "It means we love each other and we should get married. We should totally do it, just like Ozzie and May." He lowers himself unsteadily onto one knee as he looks up at me, swaying to the side a bit before he rights himself.

My heart seizes up in fear and frustration. Before he can gather himself enough to speak, I make my move; I have to act fast to keep him from destroying everything. I lean over and shove him on both shoulders, knocking him down.

He falls onto his side in the hallway, his head banging the wall. "Hey! What're you doing?" he slurs out. "I was going to propose to you."

I walk by him and kick him in the ribs as I go. "Don't you *dare*."

I am so pissed right now, I'm almost to the point where I could shoot him, and that's never a good place for me to be. I run up the stairs to my bedroom and slam the door behind me, locking it to be sure he can't follow. I knew he was drunk, but I didn't know he was *that* drunk. *Holy shit.*

I pace the floor of my room, wondering what I should do next. Angry tears fall and I swipe them away. He's wasted, and obviously stupid, so I'm afraid to leave him alone. But I don't want to see him either.

This whole situation makes me feel cheap, like a girl not worthy of a normal life, of real, unadulterated, pure love. Every bad thought I have about myself is confirmed because Lucky thought it was a good idea to get wasted and then declare his love for me. Am I really the kind of girl who gets proposed to only after a night of drunken, strip-club debauchery? Apparently, I am. I haven't felt this low around Lucky ever.

I walk over and snatch my phone up off the nightstand, sending out a text to Thibault.

Me: Lucky is being a drunk ass. Come get him.

I wait until I get a response, relieved when my brother texts back saying that he's on his way over from the cottage to collect the idiot who had the audacity to propose while he was breathing alcohol stink all over me.

A knock comes at my door along with some heavy breathing. "Toni. Babe. I need to talk to you."

I shout so he can hear me through the door. "Go away! I don't want to hear anything you have to say right now! You're an idiot!"

"Why are you so mad? I was gonna say something nice." He runs his fingers down the door, making a scratching sound.

"Why am I mad? Don't be stupid, Lucky. You know better. You don't say anything like that to me when you're drunk, you understand? If you want to talk nice to me, if you want to make plans with me about our future together, you do it when you're sober."

The sound of his clothing dragging down the door comes through to my room. I can tell he's leaning on the door for support. It's possible he's sitting in the hallway and drooling on my door.

"I'm sorry. I wanted to say it sober, but I didn't have the guts."

I lift my chin and rest my hand on my belly. "Then you don't have the guts to be with me either. Thibault's coming to get you. I don't want you sleeping here tonight."

I start crying and my weakness only makes me more furious. How dare he be such a chickenshit? It makes me worry that he's not up to the job of being a father, let alone a partner.

This crap isn't just about us; it's about his sister, too. Lucky's like me in that he hasn't moved on. He doesn't have closure yet, and he's weighed down by the guilt. The difference between him and me, though, is that he's feeling terrible over something that wasn't even close to being his fault. She was a sad girl for a really long time, and there was nothing anyone could've said to change that. We all tried, many times. Even Lucky tried, but he's conveniently forgetting that so he can blame himself.

Maybe I should be more forgiving of his attitude, but I can't right now. This is my life, and I need to get it straightened out. The urgency of the situation strikes me like a fist in my gut. I have a wedding to go to in a few days, and then I'm going to be too far along in this pregnancy to do anything about Charlie. It won't be safe or smart to execute my plan so obviously pregnant; as it is, I can barely cover it up with a big shirt. This is my last chance to put things right.

Maybe if I can get this closure for myself, my bad luck will stop rubbing off on the father of my children and he'll get his shit straight, too. My fear that happiness will only come to us if I can find a way to show Charlie's mother how sorry I am has grown tenfold. *Time is running out. I have to get this done.*

CHAPTER THIRTY-FIVE

All of my research and recon has panned out. I know where Charlie's mother Eunice is living, I know what time she gets home from her job, and I know that she's alone most of the time. Sunday night she was tucked in front of her television with a TV dinner by six o'clock. It'd be pretty convenient if she eats at that time every night; this way, I can catch her before Lucky's finished making our dinner. I assume we'll go back to our normal routine starting Monday night.

I don't see him all weekend or before I leave for work Monday, but he knows I don't hate him. I brushed off his texts asking me to hang out and talk over the weekend, but I left him a note on the counter this morning that said, *I'm not mad anymore. Let's talk after work.*

Lucky wants to apologize to me, but I'm not ready to hear it or discuss his seriously misguided proposal yet. I need time to get the specter of Charlie out of the house and out of my head. When Lucky came home drunk, it brought back a lot of bad memories, but I'm okay now. I have a plan and it's going to fix everything. Until that happens, I feel like I'll never be able to move on with my life and accept anything good Lucky might be offering.

A long weekend of slacking off and thinking about how far Lucky and I have come together has convinced me that he deserves a break. Everyone is allowed to make mistakes in a relationship, especially one as complicated as ours. Hell, we don't even know what our relationship is. Lord knows I'm not perfect, and I'm bound to screw a bunch of stuff up. I'm going to want his forgiveness when that happens.

I spend part of Sunday at the mall, returning the dress that didn't fit. Jenny was a little too enthusiastic the other day about my figure and apparently didn't notice how big my belly is getting, even though she had her hand all over it. I suppose I should take it as a compliment, but all I'm doing now is mourning the loss of my waistline. It used to dip in on both sides, but this morning in the mirror I noticed that it goes straight down from my armpits to my hips. And the baby-pooch in front of me seems to be getting bigger by the day.

A blog written by a mother of twins keeps me busy reading for several hours on Sunday. It puts me in the loop about a lot of things I should be expecting, one of which is the rapid growth of my waistline. Most women are barely showing in their first pregnancy at twenty-four weeks, but I look like I'm a couple months away from giving birth, when I actually have four left.

While shopping, I help myself to a few pairs of jeans that have an elastic pouch in the front instead of a zipper and button. I've been keeping my regular jeans closed with a rubber band for several weeks now, but it's starting to get uncomfortable. I breathe a sigh of relief when I slide my new preggo-jeans on Monday morning.

I'm up early for work, but instead of going directly to the port, I head over to the cemetery to pay a visit to Charlie's grave. So many things are going to happen to me this week, but it seems like none of them will have any meaning until I do this one thing first.

WRONG QUESTION, RIGHT ANSWER

I haven't been to his resting place in a long time, but it seems appropriate, since I'm going to be seeing his mother tonight, and soon I'll be watching my life change into something it never could have been with him in it. I have the sense that I'm finally ready to say a real goodbye to him.

I sit down next to his headstone and pluck little blades of grass, building up the courage I need to say the things that have finally become clear in my mind. A slight breeze blows strands of hair over my face as I talk. "Hey, Charlie. Hope you're okay. I'm sure you are." I always assumed Charlie went to heaven. Even though he was a shit to me sometimes—okay, maybe a lot of times—he wasn't all bad. We shared some good times. I wouldn't have stayed with him for five years if that weren't the case. He never stooped so low as to kill anyone, unlike me.

I pluck more blades of grass. "I don't know if you bother checking on my life, but it's gotten pretty crazy." I pause, considering the fact that I'm talking to a ghost who probably wants to haunt my sorry ass. I wait to see if I feel anything or sense his presence. Nothing comes, other than some jostling from the babies. They seem to like it when I talk, so I continue.

"I'm pregnant with twins. You're probably not too shocked to know that Lucky is the father. I know you were always jealous of him and you used to accuse me of having an affair with him, but you were always wrong about that. I never did anything with him until you were gone. Long gone." I sigh, feeling like I'm sitting in a confessional. It's not the worst feeling I've had.

"Since I'm being honest, I should probably admit that I've had feelings for Lucky for a long time. Since before you and me." My smile is sad when I think about how things worked out. Maybe I shouldn't have walked away from Lucky all those years ago, but it's too late to change that now. "He's the reason I went with you. I had to get him and that kiss we shared out of my head, and you were

ELLE CASEY

the answer. You were the only thing strong enough to snuff that out.
I guess you were too good at it." I sigh. "I'm sorry I used you that
way, Charlie. It wasn't fair at all."

My mind struggles with what to say next. I believe that people
who've passed on can watch over us and communicate sometimes,
but I don't know if he's listening to me. Why would he? I'm the
reason he's here in the ground.

"I have a plan, Charlie. I'm going to go visit your mother." Just
saying the words aloud makes my heart race with both anticipation and fear. "I know she never really liked me when you were
alive, and after what I did, she hates me, but I feel like I really need
to do it anyway." A flash of memory hits me: the night I called
Rowdy from the bar. "I could apologize to one of your brothers, but
it wouldn't be the same. I'm going to be a mom soon, and I think I
get it now. You were a part of her, and I took that away. I stole you
from her like a thief. No matter what you did to me, that fact still
stands. Our abusive relationship has no bearing on what I did to
her." I'm angry at myself that it took me so long to figure this out.
Self-defense or not, it makes no difference to Eunice; her son is dead
and I'm the one who took his life. I need to apologize for that.

"If I can look her in the eye and tell her I'm sorry, get her to see
how much I regret what I did and that I understand where her pain
is coming from, I feel like maybe I could finally think about finding some peace in my life. I know she won't forgive me—I mean,
how could she, right?—but maybe it will help her to know that
I get it and that I wish I could take it all back." I smile sadly. "Or
maybe it'll just piss her off. I don't know. But I can't know unless
I try. And if she spits in my eye and tells me to go to hell, I'll walk
away. I promise I will. I won't do anything physical against her, even
if she says what's on her mind or slaps me across the face."

I lay my hand on my belly. I haven't even seen these babies yet,
but I could almost imagine what it would be like if someone were

274

to take one of them from me with violence. I'd kill them, plain and simple. Hopefully, Charlie's mother has more forgiveness in her than I do. She was always going to church, and she sure forgave her own husband enough of his violence over the years. Maybe she won't decide to take an eye for an eye.

Movement catches my attention, so I look up. Across the cemetery there's a group of people gathering around an open grave. Their body language is stiff, their heads tipped down. Most of them are wearing black. A few of the older women in attendance have fancy hats with veils.

I didn't go to Charlie's funeral; I was in the county jail. But I can imagine what it was like. He had a lot of friends and family. Most of them are now in jail themselves. I read in the news that his mother was there and that she threw herself on his coffin, screaming his name. When I asked my brother for details, he refused to give them to me. He told me I had to walk away and let it go.

Sorry, Thibault. Can't do it.

I get up from my spot on the ground and place the handful of grass I picked on Charlie's headstone. I stay there until the wind has blown away the last blade. "I'm so, so sorry for what I did to you, Charlie. You didn't deserve to die. There were a hundred other better ways I could have handled our disaster of a relationship, but I failed. I snapped, and I'll never not feel terrible about that. But I'm going to try to do something for your mom. I want her to know how sorry I am. She deserves to hear that from me, at least. Maybe it'll make a difference to her."

I walk away, headed for work. I'm going to execute my plan tonight, after I leave the port and before I head home to make up with Lucky. For the first time in too many years, I feel like I'm on the cusp of moving forward instead of falling backward or running in place.

CHAPTER THIRTY-SIX

May comes in late, looking almost green when she sits down in the cubicle next to me. I pause the recording I'm listening to and look over at her.

"You look like crap."

She unwraps a lollipop and sticks it in her mouth, dropping her purse on the ground next to her chair. "Thanks. I actually feel like doo-doo warmed over, so that's perfect."

"And a lollipop is going to help that?"

She nods, pulling it out and holding it up in front of me. "These are ginger lollies. Jenny bought me a huge bag of them. She said they'll help with the morning sickness."

"Ginger ale helped me, so I guess that makes sense."

May nods her head and sticks her lollipop back in her mouth as she boots up her computer. "I can't keep anything down, and I have no appetite either. Everything smells gross."

"Yep. Been there, done that."

May looks over at me. "When is it going to end? The nausea."

"Very soon. How far along are you now?"

"Sixteen weeks."

I shrug. "Any day now, you'll be fine. At least that's what my books say."

May goes back to her computer. "I guess I should just thank my lucky stars I'm not having twins."

I don't have anything to say to that. She's right. She is lucky.

"I'm sorry. I shouldn't have said that." May leans over and puts her hand on my arm. Her lollipop dangles out of the corner of her mouth like a cigarette. "That was insensitive. I'm a jerk."

I shake my head, putting my headphones back on. "It's not a big deal. I totally get it. Believe me."

May waves at me, telling me to take my headphones off. I remove one ear cover.

"What's up with Lucky? Jenny hasn't been able to reach him all weekend."

I shrug, my attention back on my computer screen, even though there's really nothing to look at. All I'm dealing with today are sound files. "He came home drunk after the bachelor party, and I told him to go sleep at Thibault's. I haven't seen him since."

"Hooo, drama. Is he still in trouble?"

I shake my head. Maybe if I didn't have a plan in place to move forward with my life, this crazy stuff with Lucky being drunk and stupid would bother me more, but right now, it's taking the back seat in my carload of worries. "No. We're going to talk about it tonight. It'll be fine." I'm not going to tell her about his botched proposal. Although the gossip it might generate could be a good cure for her morning sickness, I'm not willing to sacrifice my privacy to ease her pain.

"I'm going to text Jenny and tell her that she can reach Lucky through Thibault," May says.

"Fine with me."

I speed through the voice files and throw together the report in record time. We're super close to nailing Marc Doucet. I just identified a conversation that I'm pretty sure was him recruiting a gangbanger from a rival group to deal with someone they've code-named Wolfman. I stand up at five o'clock, putting my headphones down on the desk with a thump. My report is on the server and an alert has been put in Ozzie's inbox so he'll know to check it out.

May looks up at me. "Are you done already?"

I turn off my computer and throw my bag over my shoulder. "Yep. I'll see you tomorrow."

"Don't forget the bachelorette party tomorrow."

"Wouldn't miss it for the world!" That's not exactly true, but oh well. The sentiment is close enough. I know May and Jenny are excited about it, and it won't be completely horrible. They can be really funny when they get on a roll.

I'm headed out of the cubicle area when May shouts out behind me, "Where are you going?"

"Home! See you later." I hurry off, not wanting to encourage any further questions by making myself available. The less May knows about my plans the better.

CHAPTER THIRTY-SEVEN

My mind races as I drive over to Eunice's house. *What's going to happen? Will she slap me? Will she just tell me to leave?* It doesn't matter; I just want Eunice to know how sorry I am for what I did to her.

Charlie's mother doesn't live in a very good neighborhood, but I spent a lot of my youth around here, so it doesn't bother me. Groups of boys and men stand on the corners of the main streets, some of them holding paper bags around beer cans. They get a cheap thrill out of being able to drink in public right under the local cops' noses. So long as they don't reveal the can under the bag, they can't legally be stopped and searched. People around these places often feel like they're at the mercy of law enforcement, so they get their jollies where they can.

I tap the steering wheel with my thumbs to the beat of the song playing on the radio, running through various scenarios in my mind. I'm still trying to guess how Eunice will react to seeing me at her front door. I can't imagine what I would do if my child's killer showed up at my house years later apologizing. I'm trying to stay positive, but I worry that Eunice will be like me, incapable of accepting an apology.

My cell phone rings next to me and I glance down at the screen. Lucky's calling. I don't want to answer, because he'll ask where I am and I'll have to lie. I don't want to lie to Lucky ever. Besides, we still need to resolve the issue of his drunken proposal, and that's not going to happen over the phone. He can wait.

I'm just a few blocks away now and I'm starting to sweat. It's especially humid tonight, which isn't helping. The babies are kicking up a storm, having a little boxing match inside me. A beep comes from my phone as I rub my belly. I look down at it expecting to see the indicator telling me a voicemail is waiting for me, but instead there's a text there. As I pull up to a stop sign, I grab the phone and hold it up in front of me.

Lucky: Where r u? We need to talk. I'm sorry.

Dammit. I was hoping to avoid this. I could ignore the text, but I don't want him to call out a posse and come find me. They could easily track my phone; we all have the app loaded onto our cells for safety reasons. I quickly type out a response before I leave the stop sign.

Me: I'm stopping at the store. Be home soon. We'll talk then.

I feel positively ill. Facing the mother of the man I killed could never be easy. This is the hardest thing I've ever done in my life, but Eunice deserves this. I owe it to her.

When I reach the edge of Eunice's neighborhood, my heart rate picks up. I'm not exactly panicking, but I wouldn't say I'm cool either. The concept of talking to Eunice and apologizing sounded great when I played it out in my head, but now that I'm just a few driveways away from her front door, it's all getting bigger and scarier in my mind. I'm almost ready to turn around and race the hell out of there when I see a car approaching from the other direction, which then pulls into her driveway.

It's her. Eunice is home, and I've timed my arrival perfectly, or so it seems. I speed up before any of my doubts work to dissuade me, and roll up to the curb in front of her house.

She pauses as she walks up her front porch steps and squints at my car over her shoulder. This is not the same vehicle I was driving when I knew Charlie, so she doesn't know it's me yet.

I turn off the engine and undo my seatbelt, taking a couple deep breaths before throwing the door open. Seeing her standing there reminds me strongly of Charlie . . . more than I imagined it would. Charlie will never be truly gone for me, but for Eunice, he always will be. And that's why I'm here.

I get out of the car and smooth down my pants, resisting the urge to pull up the elastic pouch over the babies. I wore a big shirt today so she wouldn't see that I'm pregnant. The last thing I want to do is rub the idea of a baby in her face. She's already been hurt enough by me.

As I walk across her lawn, I see recognition blooming in her eyes. First her lids widen and then they narrow. She turns to face me more fully, her purse sliding off her shoulder down to the crook of her elbow. She's wearing purple polyester pants and an orange, purple, and black top.

I stop ten feet away, ankle-deep in her thick, loamy-smelling crabgrass lawn.

"What're *you* doing here?" she asks, her voice sounding frog-like from all the cigarette smoke she's inhaled over the years.

It's a fair question. I don't take offense at her tone of disgust. At least I know now how she'll react to seeing me. *Not well.*

"I came by to talk to you."

She sneers at me. "I ain't got nothing to say to you."

I take another tentative step forward. "I know you don't, and I don't expect you to say anything to me. I was just hoping that you'd hear me out, that's all."

She cocks her hip and jabs a finger out at me. "You got a lot of nerve, hussy, comin' here to my house after what you did."

I nod. "I know. I know this is bold and probably really stupid, but I had to do it."

"Why?"

I can't look at her face anymore. The pure unadulterated hate in her expression is making me feel like something is shriveling up inside me. The babies flip around like they're doing gymnastics. I focus on her shoulder as I speak.

"I've felt terrible about what I did for a long time, but I realized that I never did the right thing after; I never apologized directly to you. I should've done that before now, and I'm really sorry I waited. I'm sorry for everything . . . for taking Charlie from you and for not understanding what that meant to you as his mother."

"Charlie's dead because you killed him," she nearly growls. "You can't change that fact, no matter what you say."

"I know. I wish I could undo what I did, but I can't. But I'm sorry, regardless. I wanted you to know that. And I wanted you to know that I get it. I know why you can't forgive me. I took a piece of you away, and that wasn't fair to you or to Charlie or to the rest of the family, either."

"Well, you're right about one thing: you can't change anything. And you're sayin' you're sorry now?" She spits on the ground. "Get outta here before I make you sorry you ever lived."

I look up at her, surprised by the tone in her voice and how eerily familiar it is. Charlie talked to me this way sometimes, right before he punched me in the face. A trickle of fear leaks into my heart.

"I just came by to apologize, Eunice. I'm sorry I upset you; that was not my intention. I'll go now." I take a step back.

She closes the distance between us to just five feet. "Oh, you're sorry about that too, are you? Sorry?" She takes another step. "Let me tell you how much your sorries are worth to me." She pauses before continuing with a snarl in her voice. "Nothing. Less than nothing. I'd like to take that sorry and smash you in the teeth with it."

The hatred rolling off her in waves is so strong I have to step back away from it. I hold up my hands in surrender. "I don't want any trouble from you, Eunice. I just came to apologize, and now I'm going to leave."

She shakes her head, pressing her already thin lips together until they disappear. Her double chin waggles on her neck as spittle gathers in the corners of her mouth. She reaches into her purse and pulls something out.

"Nah, you ain't leaving yet. I got a little something special for you right here in my purse." She mumbles her last words. "Sorry, my ass . . ."

My heart flips over and spasms painfully when I imagine she's getting ready to point a gun at me. But when her hand emerges from her bag, all I see is a short black stick.

She shakes her fist once and the bar extends itself.

Oh shit. My brain short-circuits. She's got an extendable steel baton in her hand, and she looks like she's going to enjoy using it. This wasn't part of my plan. This wasn't supposed to happen. I'm in so much trouble. I swore to Charlie's ghost and myself that I wouldn't hurt this woman. I came to apologize and that's it. I can't fight back.

My jaw drops open as I realize I'm about to get my ass kicked by a double-chinned granny. In all of my training sessions with Dev and the other guys, I was fighting off a man. Never once was

ELLE CASEY

I presented with a senior citizen as an opponent, nor a situation where I had to hold back. A crazy part of my brain is telling me that she's the mother of the man I killed and I pretty much owe her my life in exchange for the one I took. It keeps my feet rooted to the ground when they should probably be pumping like hell, sprinting me into the next county.

She raises the stick above her head at the same time that she drops her purse on the ground. "I've been dreaming about this day for years. I'm gonna give you a little taste of what you gave my boy. You thought you felt sorry before? Just wait. You ain't seen nothin' yet."

She shortens the distance between us a lot faster than I would've expected her to. One second she's four feet away and the next, she's on me.

I used to be more agile before I had two babies in me. I try to duck, but I'm not fast enough. The steel stick comes around swiftly and whacks me in the side of the head.

I scream and bend over from the pain, my hand flying up to my ear. My head feels like there's a giant bell ringing inside it. Something warm and sticky oozes through my fingers. *Blood.* I've never been afraid of bleeding before, but I am now. I share this blood with my children; I can't afford to lose any of it.

I try to run away and get back to my car, desperate to reach safety, but she whacks me in the middle of the spine with her heavy baton before I can take more than two steps. I arch over backward as the pain rockets through me, and I stumble, falling to the ground.

I'm stunned, my mind whirling as I try to figure out what I'm going to do to save the situation and myself. I can't fight back. It wouldn't be right. I promised Charlie I wasn't here to do any harm. And besides, I took this woman's son from her. Is it wrong to let her take something from me? I don't know the answer to these questions and my body is wracked with pain.

Suddenly Dev is in my head, yelling, '*Block, block, block!*'

I twist onto my side and hold my forearms up over me, kicking out with my legs feebly, hoping I'll catch her in the shin and maybe slow her down. As more blows rain down on me, Dev's voice is drowned out by another's.

Not the babies, Lucky's saying. *Don't let her hurt our babies.*

I can't block her blows and protect them too, so there's only one thing for me to do: I curl up into a ball as tightly as I can to protect my unborn children, praying it'll all be over soon.

She pauses and then yells at me, her voice coming out as a screech. "What's that . . . ? Are you pregnant? You *bitch*! My son never got to have any babies! I ain't never gonna get no grandbabies from Charlie because of you!"

I'm in a desperate panic now, thinking the Devil let her read my mind. She knows. She's going to try to kill the peas in the pod, Milli and Vanilli . . . take them from me like I took Charlie from her.

I try to look up at her so I can block the next blows, but there's blood in my eyes and it stings, blinding me. I scream as loud as I can, hoping somebody will hear me and come to my children's rescue. My legs are numb and don't seem to want to work, making me fear she's bruised my spine.

This is not generally the type of neighborhood where Good Samaritans hang out, but after five or six more whacks with the baton, most of them to my ribs and arm, I hear voices and then somebody yelling.

"Quit, Eunice, quit!" It's a man, but I don't know who he is.

"I'm-a kill this bitch," she yells as another crack comes, this time against my skull.

I'm woozy, sliding in and out of consciousness. I feel euphoric, though, over the fact that despite the decent shots she's laid on my body, she hasn't gotten a single hit in on my abdomen yet and there are witnesses here now. There's hope my babies will survive this.

I don't trust Eunice is done trying to hit my belly, even with witnesses standing around, so I stay in the fetal position and pray that the scuffling noises I hear around my head are my rescuers getting her away from me.

Onion breath hits me in the face. "Are you okay? What's going on? Why's she hitting you like that?"

I try to answer, but my jaw doesn't seem to want to work. All I can mumble out is a single, unintelligible syllable. "Uhhhhnn . . ."

Someone's shouting over my head. "Go check her car. See if she has a phone or somethin'. Somebody we can call."

"I think you better jus' dial nine-one-one," says a female voice.

Eunice is screaming. I can't quite make out what she's saying . . . something about a murdering bitch. *Oh. That's me she's talking about.* I hope her neighbors don't take up the stick and finish the job for her. I'm too worried about the babies to think about getting up. I continue to huddle in on myself, waiting for the sounds of sirens to signal my rescue. They sure do take a long time to come.

Through the haze of pain I'm suffering and during a very long ambulance ride, I think about my friends and family. Lucky's going to be so upset. Ozzie's going to be very disappointed. Thibault's going to be pissed. May and Jenny will never understand.

Hell, nobody's going to understand, because what I've done defies reason. But I get why I thought it was good before, and regardless how it ended, I'm not going to back away from that. Sometimes a person just has to stand up and do what she thinks is right and live with the consequences.

CHAPTER THIRTY-EIGHT

I'm on some sort of mild painkiller that's not doing much for me. The nurse told me there's a concern of narcotics traveling across the placental barrier and feeding the babies things they shouldn't be eating, so I'm stuck with something about as strong as Tylenol.

I look at the clock, begging it to slow down. My phone rests on my hospital bed next to my hand. There are about ten text messages there, all of them from the team. Everyone wants to see me, but I've been holding them off, telling them the doctor doesn't want me to have company yet. Now that the mission-accomplished euphoria has faded, I find myself embarrassed over what I've done. I can't face them and the recriminations and scoldings they're sure to lay on me. I took a risk with the babies I shouldn't have. I should have discussed it with Lucky before I went to Eunice's house and given him a chance to talk me out of it.

The sound of people shouting comes from the hallway. For a moment I panic, thinking that Eunice has followed me here and she's come to finish the job. But then the door bursts open and Lucky's standing there. A male nurse has him by the front of his shirt and is trying to yank him out of the room.

"Get off me! I need to see her! Those are my children she's carrying!" He struggles against the wall, pushing with all of his strength to get past the big guy.

I sit up, wincing at the discomfort it brings me. My entire body aches. "It's okay. Let him in." I have to hold my ribs as barbs of pain lance through my chest.

The nurse loosens his hold on Lucky but shakes him once, hard, before letting him go. "You need to *listen* to us when we tell you to wait." He shoves Lucky away and looks over at me, smoothing down his scrubs. "Talk to him about how to act in a hospital. We don't have time for this kind of behavior in here."

I nod. "I will. I'm sorry. It's my fault."

Lucky frowns at me. He straightens his leather jacket and walks over, stopping at the foot of my bed with his hands balled into fists at his sides. "When are you going to stop blaming yourself for other people's behavior?"

I look at him, confused about his attitude. It's not what I expected. "When are you going to stop acting like that?"

"Acting like what?"

I pause, wondering what I was getting at. "I don't know. I'm totally confused now." I reach up and touch my forehead gingerly, quickly learning there are bruises there. "I'm sorry. I'm on painkillers right now but they're not really working."

Lucky leans in closer, his fists opening as he rests his hands on the bed's footboard. "Is that okay for the babies?"

I shrug. "No worse than getting my ass kicked, I guess."

His expression softens and he walks over to rest a butt cheek on the mattress next to me. "Babe, what were you thinking going over there?"

Tears come to my eyes, much as I would like them to stay away. "I don't know. I guess I was thinking that if I could apologize and get her to see that I mean it, that I really regret what I did, I could figure out how to move on." I look up at him, my lips and chin trembling. My entire face is having a seizure. "For the babies. For us."

He shakes his head, his own chin shaking with emotion now, too. Taking my hand, he lifts it so he can kiss my fingers. "You don't need her forgiveness to move on, babe. You just need to forgive yourself."

"I know." My voice hitches. "But it's really hard. I killed him. I can't take that back." The tears will not stop streaming down my face.

Lucky nods, swallowing a few times and battling emotion before he responds. "Yes, you did do that, and it was a regrettable thing for sure. But Charlie wasn't even close to innocent or blameless, and everyone but you can see that."

"It doesn't matter. There's no excuse."

He sighs, shaking his head at me. "You have it so bad."

"I have what so bad?" I use the back of my hand to wipe tears away, careful not to disturb my IV.

"I forget what it's called. It's when the victim blames herself for the abuse. You do it all the time."

Now he's making me mad. "No, I don't."

"Yes, you do. I was out there causing trouble with the nurse and you blamed yourself."

"Of course I did. I was ignoring your texts. I was telling them to keep you away from me, and your babies are in here. I get it. I would've done the same thing you did."

He points a finger at me. "Exactly. That's what I'm saying. You allow other people to react with violence in a situation where they should be reacting with violence but you don't allow it for yourself."

"It's one thing to blame myself for somebody getting cranky with a nurse. It's another thing when you're talking about killing someone."

He sighs. "There's nothing I can say that's going to make you understand, is there?"

I shake my head. "Sorry, but no. I don't think so. Plenty of other people have already tried, believe me."

Lucky puts his hands on either side of me and leans in closely, staring into my eyes. "Can you do me just one favor?"

I nod. "I think I can. Maybe. What is it?"

"Could you *try* to forgive yourself?"

"I've tried, but I can't."

Lucky looks at my belly and reaches down to rub it through my hospital gown. "Can you try to do it for the peas?"

"Do you mean Milli and Vanilli?"

Lucky's eyes brighten as he looks up at me. "Really? Can we call them Milli and Vanilli?"

I laugh, resting my hand on his arm. "Only when they're in utero. After they're born, no way in hell."

Lucky holds out a hand. "Deal."

I shake his hand, letting him pull my fingers up to kiss them again.

I let out a long breath before speaking the words that are in my mind and my heart. "I'm going to try to figure out this forgiveness thing, but only if you will too. We both need to find a way to live with the tragedies in our past so we can move on to our future."

He stares at me for a long time before nodding. "I can do that. For you and the babies. Milli and Vanilli."

I grin, feeling for the first time that it might actually be possible to learn to live with my mistakes. I might never be able to completely forgive myself, but with Lucky's support, who knows?

"What are we going to do now?" he asks, his voice and expression lighter.

"I don't know what *you're* going to do, but I need to go face the music."

"What do you mean, face the music?"

"I have to talk to May about her wedding and the bachelorette party I won't be attending."

Lucky cringes. "Yeah . . . you're not going to make a very pretty bridesmaid."

"Is it bad? I've been afraid to look in the mirror."

His smile is pained. "Let's just say that you may have to invest in a little bit of makeup."

"How mad are they? Jenny and May, I mean . . ."

Lucky's expression doesn't change. "I'm not exactly sure."

"You're lying."

He sighs and looks down at our hands laced together. "Everybody's worried, of course. And they're all a little bit confused as to why you would go see Charlie's mother." He looks up at me. "But I get it. I do."

Maybe it shouldn't matter, but it makes a difference that he feels that way. He gives me the sense that I'm not alone in this waking nightmare I've been living for years.

"Thanks for saying that. Even if you don't mean it."

"No, I mean it. I'm serious. You know, you and I are not so different."

"What do you mean?"

"We both have a huge load of regret we carry from our past that we wish we could fix with a do-over, but we can't. So we just have to learn how to move forward with it."

"I don't think what you did is anything close to what I did, though."

"I think, on the cosmic balance sheet, it's difficult to say whether one thing is worse than the other. Yes, you killed Charlie. But he was coming after you to kill you. If he hadn't succeeded in doing it that day, he would have on another. The violence was getting really bad between you two, and you know it. And I didn't shoot a gun at my sister, but maybe my negligence or failure to notice what was going on and do something about it was just as bad." He shrugs. "I've tortured myself over it long enough. You showed me that. It's you who made me see the truth. I think you've tortured yourself over Charlie long enough, too. It's time we both try to put our regrets in the past where they belong and move forward."

"I would really like to be able to do that." I squeeze his hand hard, my desperation coming through in my grip. Even though it makes my arms and shoulders ache and the bruises pulse, I hang on. I feel like he's keeping me from drowning.

"Scootch over," he says.

I do my best to make a space for him on the narrow mattress.

He lies down next to me, placing his hand gently on my belly. "Nobody said that life was going to be easy, but I think together we can make it more peaceful."

"I think so too." I feel like I'm going to throw up when I say that, but it's only because the emotions are so huge and so alien to me. I've never felt comfortable depending on somebody else, so it's a big sacrifice for me to even allow the idea that Lucky is going to be a part of my life and a part of the decisions that I make.

"I was a real asshole that night I came home drunk."

My mouth trembles as I fight to keep from crying again. It feels so good to hear him say this. Charlie never apologized to me for the things he did.

"Yeah, you were."

"I shouldn't have put you through that. It was careless and unkind."

"Yes."

"You were right to not let me back in the house after. I needed to think about what I'd done to you and to us and to decide what I wanted from our situation."

"And did you decide?"

"Yes. I did." He holds my hand and strokes the back of it with his thumb. "I want us to be together. Like a real couple."

I smile, relieved and overjoyed. A little scared, too. It's a big commitment. "Was that hard for you to say?"

He kisses my fingers. "No. I thought it was going to be. That's why I got drunk that night. I wanted to say all these things to you and express how I was feeling, but I wasn't sure I could do it sober. It was stupid of me. You were right when you said I have to be a strong man to deserve you. I can be that man, Toni, if you'll let me."

"You really hurt my feelings." I have to fight the tears away. My heart is burning. "It made me feel like I wasn't worth the effort of doing it the right way."

"God, that's horrible," he says, his voice trembling. "I'm so sorry. Please let me make it up to you? Please? I promise I'll do it right this time. I don't think that way about you at all."

The burning in my heart cools to a soothing warmth. I'm done punishing him over a stupid mistake I could have easily made myself. I'm not always the bravest person in the world, either. "What do you have in mind?"

"Let me surprise you."

I squeeze his hand. "Okay. I look forward to it."

He leans in and gives me a gentle kiss on the cheek. "You won't regret letting me into your life, I promise."

"I know I won't."

The babies move under his hand as he strokes my belly gently. "Go to sleep, Milli and Vanilli. Your mama needs her rest."

Minutes later, I close my eyes and drift off. I don't know if it's the drugs or Lucky's presence, but no nightmares of Charlie come to visit me that night in the hospital.

CHAPTER THIRTY-NINE

I'm able to put off seeing any more visitors until I'm home, but then I'm anxious to get the face-to-face meetings over with. I have some apologizing to do.

Talking to Charlie's mom that way was a harebrained idea; I know that now. Unfortunately, when it comes to my life, clarity often exists only in hindsight. But I have Lucky now, and I feel confident that with the two of us together, we'll be able to make better decisions. This is an especially good thing, because these babies are acting like they're going to bust through my belly any day, even though they have a lot of growing to do between now and their due date.

As I sit on the couch waiting for Ozzie to arrive, I see a little bulge pushing up from inside me. I poke at it with my finger, wondering if Milli or Vanilli can feel me in there. I tap out some Morse code on the baby's heel. *I love you.* The idea that we can communicate makes me smile.

The door opens and shuts, and then Ozzie's heavy footfalls come into the foyer.

"I'm in here." I brace myself to get up off the couch but then give up when I realize it's going to be too much effort and too painful. My body aches all over. Eunice did a great job of kicking my ass. Because I was so intent on protecting the babies, I ended up with a split scalp, a broken cheekbone, two cracked ribs, and a bruised vertebra. Several other areas of my body host multiple bruises, but at least there's nothing broken there. I'm only allowed to take Tylenol, but I'm happy to have it. I'm thrilled to be alive. If Eunice had had her way, I'd be in the ground right now.

"Hey," Ozzie says, advancing into the room.

"Hey."

He sits in a chair next to the couch and leans forward, resting his elbows on his knees and clasping his hands in front of him.

"Do you want something to drink?"

He shakes his head. "No, I'm fine. I'm not going to stay long. I know you need your rest."

I lean back on the couch. "Stay as long as you like. Lucky is busy waiting on me hand and foot, so I don't really have to move anywhere. I've been sleeping half the day."

Ozzie nods. "He's a good guy."

My voice softens just thinking about him. "I know."

"Do you?"

Ozzie doesn't have to say anything else. I know what he's asking.

"I do. I know he's good for me, and I'm done looking for trouble." I rub my ribs. "I'm too old for this shit."

His smile is sad. "I wish I could believe that."

I lean forward, desperate for him to understand, ignoring the pain in my side. "I mean it, Oz." I put my hand on his and squeeze. "Trust me. I've had a lot of time to think about it, and I've got a lot of bruises to remind me of my bad decision-making skills. And I've got Lucky now. We've been talking a lot. We're going to help each other. Support each other. Commit to our family and each other."

"What does that mean, exactly?"

I shrug, feeling a little silly talking about this with Ozzie, but glad to be saying it out loud to him at the same time. "We haven't exactly defined it. I mean, he proposed, but he was being an ass at the time, so I told him to forget it."

Ozzie gives me a half smile. "Did you call for a do-over?"

I grin back, memories of our younger days flashing through my mind. "Yeah. We both called a do-over. He says he's going to surprise me, and I'm cool with that."

Ozzie nods, looking more hopeful. "That's good. You guys need one another. I don't want either one of you to screw this up."

I shake my head. "We won't. Because it's not just us now: we have the babies to think about. I think it helps both of us to have something beyond ourselves to worry over."

He nods. "I get it."

I give him a weak smile. "How's everything going with May?"

He doesn't look very happy. "Okay, I guess. She's a little pissed at you."

I cringe. "I know. She has every right to be. Now she's only got one bridesmaid."

His eyebrows go up. "Oh, no. She has two bridesmaids. She expects you to be there."

I point at my face. "Have you seen this?"

He shrugs. "Better buy some makeup. I'm serious. If you don't show, she's going to be off-the-charts unhappy."

I nod, accepting my fate. "Fine. I'll be there."

He sighs heavily and leans back in his seat, resting his elbows on the arms of the chair. "I'm sorry. I tried to talk some sense into her, but she's just kind of out of her head right now. She has bridezilla-itis really bad."

I find myself giggling as I imagine her making everyone crazy. Apparently, there is one side-benefit to getting one's ass kicked by a double-chinned granny. "She's pregnant. Go easy on her."

"I know, but it's not just that. She really cares about you. She was so worried that you were going to die. She wouldn't believe anybody when they said you're going to be fine. I had to give her a sedative."

I laugh, but there's not a whole lot of mirth to it. "I'm so sorry. I can only imagine what you've been going through."

He dips his head back and stares at the ceiling as he scrubs his scalp. "I love that girl so much."

"I know you do. You guys are meant for each other. I promise I won't screw this up. I'll be at the wedding."

Ozzie tilts his head up to look at me. "I'm sorry I was hard on you the other day at work. You didn't deserve that. I was just worried about you. You caught me on a bad day. This case has been driving the chief nuts, and shit rolls downhill right into my lap."

"I get it. Really. Don't apologize. It's weird."

He smiles, and this time it's genuine. "See you on Thursday?" The wedding was delayed for a day in deference to my cracked ribs. I would have preferred longer, but something with the florist made that impossible.

He nods. "See you Thursday." He stands and looks toward the kitchen before turning back to me, his right hand splayed on his chest. "Can I get you anything before I go?"

I point at the doorway as Lucky comes in carrying a tray. "Nope. I think I'm all set."

"Hot tea, homemade cookies, toast, and jam from the farmers' market," Lucky says, walking carefully so he doesn't dump the items on the silver tray.

I smile at my guy. He winks at me and places the food and drinks on the table.

"You want to stay for some tea, man?" Lucky asks Ozzie.

Ozzie answers from the front doorway. "A tea party? No, thanks. I don't want to have to hand in my man-card."

I grab Lucky's hand and pull him down onto the couch with me, trying to cover up the wince of pain that follows. "Don't listen to him. You're so manly you have two man-cards in your wallet."

"You know it, babe. Got your twin-making super-sperm right here." He leans in and kisses my lips and then my belly, and I let myself drown in the happiness. The front door opens and shuts as Ozzie lets himself out.

CHAPTER FORTY

May's big day is here. I've applied half a bottle of foundation to my face, and I'm pretty happy with how it turned out. The swelling by my cheek is still bad, but the weird blue and green marks around my left eye are almost completely hidden. My hair covers the stitches in my scalp.

Unfortunately, the dress I'm supposed to wear is mostly sleeveless, but I find a black sweater in the back of my closet that's lightweight enough to manage the hot weather. I slide it on, covering the bruises on my arms. Dark hose do a pretty decent job of masking the marks on my legs. When I stand in front of the full-length mirror, I smile. I look almost normal.

Lucky walks up behind me, cinching his tie.

"Damn." I stare at his reflection. "Could you be any more gorgeous?"

"You like?" He smiles, holding his arms out. His beard has been brushed and shaped into a point under his chin.

I ignore the beard part. "Definitely. When my ribs are better, we're totally having sex."

He leans closer, talking earnestly. "We could do it right now. I'd be very gentle."

I push him away with a finger and laugh. "Go away. I have cracked ribs." It's still hard to take a deep breath, but I have them wrapped so tightly in bandages, it gives them the support they need. The bandages and my Tylenol are going to carry me through the night.

Now I just have to survive the tongue-lashing I'm sure to get from May and Jenny, and I'll be golden. I don't expect Eunice to show up at my door looking for another helping of my ass, so I'm good there. She got in some decent licks, but she only did it because I came to her being a dumbass, serving myself up on a silver platter. I definitely won't be doing that ever again.

I still haven't seen Jenny or May. Every time they've come over I've been asleep, and Lucky is a tough caregiver. He won't let anybody disturb my sleep. Whenever they tried to argue, he brought out the big guns, otherwise known as Milli and Vanilli. He's not too proud to use our children as weapons, but I'm thankful for it. I've been sleeping about eighteen hours a day, and I'm pretty sure my body has needed it.

Jenny's backyard is in full bloom. It looks like an entire truck-load of extra flowers has been brought in. There's an arbor set up in a far corner and chairs are lined up in front of it with an aisle down the middle. The seats are already filled with people and classical music is playing from a speaker, adding a nice ambience to the whole place. I'm standing in the dining area inside the house looking out through the window when I feel a tap on my shoulder.

"Hey," Jenny says when I turn around. She holds her arms out and takes me in a gentle hug. "How are you feeling?"

I shrug when she releases me from the embrace. "As good as you might expect. Happy to be here."

Jenny tilts her head. "Are you?"

I nod. "I definitely am." I'm not blowing smoke up her skirt, either. After my brush with Eunice and her baton, I realized how lucky I am to have these people in my life. So I got stuck with a couple of chicks who like to talk and goof around a lot? It sure beats having a woman beat you to death with a nightstick. To be fair, I didn't mind the shopping that much either, and May is one half of the cube-crew team.

Jenny grins. "Good. May was worried that she was forcing you into this."

I laugh. "Well, she kind of was, but I got over it." I hold out my arm so she can see my sweater. "Sorry I had to wear this, but my bruises are really ugly."

Jenny reaches over to the back of a nearby chair and pulls a black wrap off it. "Not to worry. I brought something too. I knew you'd have to cover up."

She wraps it around her arms and winks, checking behind her before turning back to me. "Do you want to go upstairs and see May now?"

"I would like to, but stairs are really hard for me. Every one of them jiggles my ribs."

"Oh, that's right. I forgot. Let me go get her." She rushes off, her high heels clicking on the kitchen floor and then down the hallway.

I stand at the window for another five minutes, growing more nervous by the second. Maybe May doesn't want to come down to see me. Maybe she's still angry. I wouldn't blame her. I pretty much managed to ruin the most special day of her life single-handedly. The old Toni may not have cared, but the Toni I am now does very much.

May's voice comes from behind me, interrupting my pity party. I turn around to greet her. It's silly, but my eyes well up with tears seeing her in her pretty white dress.

I can't believe I gave her and Ozzie such a hard time before. They really are perfect for each other. Her silliness is such a great contrast to his serious attitude. She helps him relax, bringing humor and levity into his life. Just like Lucky is doing for me.

"I'm really sorry that I screwed everything up," I say. "I'm an asshole for doing that."

May doesn't say anything. She stops a few feet away and folds her hands in front of her.

"You look really beautiful." I gesture at the dress. "It's perfect. Really perfect. Like one of those magazines you're always reading."

May looks down at herself and then gives me a serene smile. "Thank you."

I breathe out a sigh of annoyance. I'm not mad at her; I'm mad at myself. "Seriously. I'm so sorry. This day should be all about smiles and happiness, but instead, you've had to worry about your bridesmaid getting busted up and ruining the whole thing. If you want me to go, I'll go. You won't hurt my feelings at all."

May looks at the ground for a long time and I'm almost moving to leave, but then she looks up at me, her eyes bright with unshed tears. "I don't want you to go. But I do want you to understand that I care about you, and I really don't want you doing anything else that's going to put you or your babies at risk. It's very stressful for me, and it's very stressful for Ozzie. And I don't like it when Ozzie gets stressed out."

"I understand. I don't like it when he gets stressed out either. And I don't like it when you're not smiling at me. It makes me actually pretty sick to my stomach if you want to know the truth."

A very tiny smile starts to appear. "I thought you said I was too hyper. You said I smile too much."

"When I say things like that, you just need to ignore me. I have this grouchy default attitude that I fall back on, but it's not how I want to be. Not anymore."

She nods. "Lucky is a good influence on you."

"Yes, he is. I love him."

She almost glares at me. "Does he know that?"

"Yes. Probably."

"Have you told him?"

I'm squirming in my dress under her scrutiny. "Not exactly."

"What's that mean—*not exactly*?"

I have to answer her, as uncomfortable as the conversation makes me. She's been a good friend to me and this is what friends do; they talk about shit that makes people like me want to cry with confusion.

My face is burning with embarrassment. "It means that this is the first time I've acknowledged it out loud."

"Why?" She takes a step toward me, her voice filled with pity or sadness, maybe.

I shrug. "I haven't allowed it. I don't know why. Maybe because it didn't feel right to let myself fall in love with someone so good." I have to stare at the ground rather than at her or risk crying.

Her smile grows bigger. "You should tell him. Here, at my wedding. Now."

Getting a grip on my runaway emotions in response to her sudden enthusiasm for my certain humiliation is surprisingly easy. Knowing May, she's expecting me to announce my devotion to Lucky over a bullhorn across the backyard or something equally loud and obvious.

"Sure, we can do that. Maybe later, though," I say. "Right now we need to focus on you and Ozzie."

She claps her hands together twice before stopping herself. "I know, isn't it great?" She leans in closer and lowers her voice. "I have such an exciting surprise for him. One of my good friends who's an awesome photographer is here to take pictures. And I booked us a cruise for our honeymoon. He has no idea!"

"He's definitely going to be surprised." I laugh inside at the expression I can already picture on his face. Ozzie hates cruises.

But hell, what do I know? Maybe May will change his mind about that like she's changed his mind about a lot of things. Maybe he'll love it. He probably won't even notice he's on the water because he'll be too busy staring at May the entire time. She's going to look adorable in a bathing suit with that baby bump of hers. It's just starting to show, but I'm afraid to say that to her, worried that she won't want to know that at her wedding.

"It's almost time," I say. "Are you ready?"

She reaches behind her and pulls a small bouquet of flowers out of a long white box on the table. "These are for you."

I take them from her and turn them over, admiring all the colors. "They're beautiful. What's your bouquet look like?"

She pulls a larger version of what I'm holding out of the box. "These are mine. Jenny helped me pick."

"Gorgeous. Jenny did a really good job."

May nods, wiping a tear from her eye. "She did. She's the best sister in the world." She puts her hand on my arm and squeezes it gently. "And now you're my other sister. And I know you're crazy and impetuous and sometimes foolhardy, but I love you anyway."

I can barely get the words out between my tears. "I love you too, May." I expected to feel pain at admitting that because love has often brought me that sensation, but I don't. I feel . . . lighter.

She throws her arms around me and squeezes, and I gasp from the pain, but when she tries to let go I don't allow it. "I'm so glad you joined the team," I say.

"I am too," she says. "Now stop crying before you ruin my makeup."

She pulls away and I smile, trying to wipe the tears away. "Ruining my makeup would be worse, trust me."

Her smile falters. She points at my face. "Oh my god. You need to go fix that. Right now!"

"Where's Jenny?" I ask as I move around her giant dress, trying not to trip on the train. The thing is a mile long, it seems.

"She's in the living room. Go find her and fix your makeup, stat. I've got a wedding to start and I can't have one of my brides-maids looking like she ran into a bus with her face."

I walk as fast as I can with my bum ribs to the living room and show Jenny my disaster. She wastes no time getting me fixed up. She's patting the last of the powder on my cheek when she bends down and looks me in the eyes. "All done. Are we ready to do this?"

I nod. "We're ready."

CHAPTER FORTY-ONE

The music is playing and I'm waiting at the end of the aisle with Jenny. When the regular music switches over to the Wedding March, Jenny urges the four little kids to move into position. According to May, ring bearers and flower girls are supposed to be at the end of the wedding party's procession, but neither she nor her sister believed they could be trusted to execute their roles properly without supervision, so here we are, letting them go first.

Sammy pushes Jacob's wheelchair down the aisle as Jacob holds a pillow with rings attached to it in his hands. Both boys wear sober expressions, concentrating on their very important jobs. Jenny is beaming.

The girls come next, happily throwing flower petals all over the place, not limiting their spread to the aisle itself but also sprinkling plenty on the guests sitting nearby. I put my bouquet up to my face to hide my smile. Lucky and Ozzie are looking down at their folded hands, battling laughter. It looks like flower bombs are going off and the guests are taking on shrapnel.

Jenny is next. She follows sedately, pausing from time to time to brush petals off guests' heads and shoulders. I consider this a good call on her part, because May would probably panic if she knew her nieces were attacking guests with her flowers. The little girls are currently in a wrestling match over their baskets; the older one seems to be winning. Jenny arrives at the temporary altar under the flowered arbor just in time to referee.

I'm just looking over my shoulder at the back door of the house, expecting May to walk through the opening behind me, when something weird catches my eye. A wedding guest standing with the catering staff off to the side steps out from behind the group to become visible. I shouldn't recognize him because he's definitely not a cop or family, but I do.

My heart leaps up into my throat when I look at the guy more closely and see the scar on his cheek. *Holy shit, it's Marc Doucet!* I glance left and right, my mind racing. *Why is he here?* No one invited him, that's for damn sure. *Are there members of his gang with him?*

Scanning, scanning, scanning . . . I'm looking all around, as casually as I can, and everything seems in order, but I wouldn't put it past him to take out his anger at having his operation shut down on this wedding party.

There's no time to think about the risk or the danger I'm putting myself in. I have to handle this situation before everything blows up.

"I'm just going to go check on the bride," I say loudly, walking as quickly as I can into the house. I know I'm causing a stir by not going down the aisle as expected, but I'm hoping everyone will write it off as a bridesmaid helping a nervous bridezilla.

As soon as I cross the threshold, I throw my bouquet to the side and rush over to Thibault and May.

She's frowning at me. "Why'd you throw your flowers on the ground like that? The petals are breaking . . ."

"Shush, we don't have any time." I turn to Thibault. "Doucet is here."

He looks at me like I've lost my very last marble. "What?"

I point out to the yard, getting more desperate by the second. "He's here!" I'm whispering as loudly as I can. "He's out there! With the caterers, dressed in a suit."

"No, he's not," May says. "I didn't invite him or anything. I was only joking about that." She pauses as she bites her lip. Then her expression changes drastically to one of worry. "I maaaay have accidentally butt-dialed him once, though." She cringes as Thibault and I both turn our full attention on her.

"What did you do?" he asks, his voice dangerously low.

She huffs out a breath and drops her voice to a loud whisper. "I'm sorry! I didn't think anything happened, so I just hung up and forgot about it." She looks over her shoulder at the backyard. "Are you sure he's here? Maybe it's someone who just looks like him."

I grab her hand and shake it, causing a few flower petals in her bouquet to loosen and fall. "May, listen to me! He's here! And he can't possibly be showing up just to try to catch your garter at the reception."

Thibault takes me by the wrist and pulls me over to the window. "Show me."

I point through a pane of glass while I rest my free hand on my aching ribs. "There. Black suit. Red tie." Thankfully Doucet's attention is on the wedding guests and not the house.

I look at Thibault and watch as recognition dawns. "Who else is here?" he asks.

I shake my head. "Could be anyone. Caterers? I have no idea. He's the only one I recognize from our surveillance photos and video, though. He could be flying solo. Most of his guys are in jail right now."

"Who's he after?" Thibault asks. He might be thinking out loud, but I answer anyway.

"May. It's gotta be May. Maybe the chief, too."

We both look at the gray-haired man sitting in the front row. Knowing Marc, he'd be happy to take down the five people sitting next to the chief of police, too, in his bid for revenge.

Thibault's expression hardens. "We need to take him out."

"Yes, I agree. How?"

Thibault looks at me, his jaw pulsing. "You feel like doing a little bit of acting?"

I grin, glad to be involved in ending this bullshit. "Hell, yeah."

"What're you guys doing?" May asks, coming up behind us. Her voice is trembling. "Is he really here?"

I nod.

"How did he know about my wedding? How did he find Jenny's house?"

My mind is going a thousand miles an hour. May has butt-dialed me several times, leaving me inane recordings of conversations that go on for ten minutes or more. "Maybe you left him a voicemail when you butt-dialed him. All you've been talking about for weeks is the wedding. You called me eight times yesterday about it."

Thibault interrupts. "Doesn't matter right now; we'll figure that out later. Right now we need to get this taken care of without risking the lives of the guests." Thibault pulls his phone from his pocket and taps out a text to the team.

We watch through the window as every single one of them ignores it.

"Send it over and over until they answer," I say.

Thibault re-sends the message five times before everyone on the team takes a look at it. They lift their heads and nod in our direction.

Good to go.

"I need to get out there," I say. "The guests are getting restless. It's going to make Marc nervous if we delay any longer."

Thibault nods. "You're right. So what's the plan?"

It comes to me so clearly it's as if I'm watching a movie play out in my head. As far as I can see, this plan is the only way to shut Marc down and avoid any collateral damage. I'm also holding out hope that the wedding will still happen and I won't have to wear this dress twice.

I speak quickly. "Here's what we need to do . . ."

CHAPTER FORTY-TWO

I wait until Thibault has sent out another text to the team before walking over to the door and picking up my discarded flowers on the way. I try to put them back in order, yanking out a few that are too far gone.

"What do I do?" May asks, breathing heavily down my neck from behind.

I turn and point at Jenny's hallway. "Get your piece, hide it in your flowers, and shoot his ass if he gets too close."

"My piece? I left my piece at work!" She looks around desperately. "I don't have my piece!"

I point at my bag. "My Taser's in there. Get it. It's fully loaded." Not that a Taser is going to help her at this point, but I need her to stay calm and not freak out. Having a weapon will make her feel more secure.

She runs over to retrieve the weapon, getting buried in her veil on the way, and I steady myself on the threshold. I can't concern myself with her; I have to worry about the plan and making sure I get my part right. I take a deep breath in and out, smoothing my dress over my baby bump. *Prepare and execute. Come on, Milli and Vanilli. It's up to us now.*

"You got this," Thibault says, kissing me on the cheek.

"You know it."

"Don't get hurt," he growls.

"I'll do my best."

I take a step out into the sun and make my way down the aisle, acting like I don't have a care in the world.

The sun is gorgeous, warm as it filters through leaves of a great oak that shades most of the guests. The scent of roses floats past me, riding a light breeze that teases small hairs away from my sweaty forehead. All movement drops into slow motion as I make my way down the aisle to the sounds of the Wedding March.

The man I love more than anything in the world is ahead of me, standing at the end of the aisle next to Dev and Ozzie. I wish I had some way to tell him how I feel right now, but I don't. All I've got is a dress, a handful of flowers, and a shitty plan. *God help me.*

Guests line the walkway marked by a pink runner on either side of me, sitting in white folding chairs decorated with bows. The catering staff and at least one murderer are standing in a group next to some bushes, off to the side in Jenny's backyard.

My teammates are all on alert, ready for anything. Thibault is walking from the front door to Jenny's side yard as quickly and as quietly as he can, headed to a spot directly behind Marc Doucet. His job is to take this criminal down while the rest of our team protects the guests and looks out for accomplices who may have wiggled their way into the celebration.

Hands are resting lightly on guns in holsters covered by jackets. Any obvious movements on our part could make bad guys' fingers go to triggers and pull, so we need to avoid that if at all possible. We know how these gangbangers operate. As long as we keep them thinking their plan is still in motion, we have a chance of stopping it before it starts.

When I'm halfway down the aisle, I stop, putting my hand to my belly. "Oh!" I yell out with exaggerated volume, trying to look surprised.

Several guests turn to look at me, frowning in confusion.

I drop my ratty bouquet and clutch my belly with both hands, slouching as best I can in my stupid dress. "Oh, my god. I think I just had a contraction!"

The people closest to me stand.

I hold out my hand. "No, sit, sit, sit, I'll be fine." When the man nearest me holds out his hands toward me, I glare and growl at him. "*Sit*, I said!"

His wife pulls him back and he takes his seat reluctantly.

I try to grin through the pain of aching ribs as I whisper, "Sorry. Just playing a part here." I take another step and then stop, bending over again and gasping. I speak as loudly as I can without being too obvious. "Ow! What the heck! I think I'm in labor!"

Hopefully, Marc Doucet doesn't know a hell of a lot about pregnancies, since I don't look like someone nine months along. I risk a glance in his direction and see him standing there with no expression on his face. He's stone-cold serious as his hand moves slowly into his jacket. Time slows.

Thibault's too far away. He's just made it to the gate separating the side yard from the backyard. I can see him through the chain link. He'll never make it in time.

I bend over again, yelling louder. "Oh, boy! That was a big one! Watch out!"

Lucky takes a step toward me.

I hold out my hand to stop him. He needs to stay out of the line of fire. I can't let him get hurt.

Marc starts pulling his hand slowly from his jacket. I see the butt of a gun coming with it.

"Oh, hey, Marc!" a high voice yells out from behind me. "You came! Oh my god, you are so crazy!"

What the . . . ?

I turn with my jaw dropped open to watch May streaking out from the house with her dress's train gathered up in one arm and her bouquet in the other. "How did you know the address? I forgot to call you!"

Everyone . . . and I mean *everyone* . . . in the entire place just stares at her. Even Marc. My feet are rooted to the ground, but even if they weren't, I wouldn't be able to stop this train wreck from coming down the rails. Thibault is still too far away to intervene and Ozzie doesn't have wings. It's all up to May now.

She stops about ten feet away, when his hand comes out of his jacket with a pistol in it. She tilts her head to the side. "What are you doing, Marc—trying to ruin my wedding?"

I see everything happening at once like it's part of a film I'm watching from a movie theater seat:

Thibault pulls his piece out of his holster and throws the gate open.

Ozzie leaps away from the arbor and starts running toward May.

Lucky runs toward me, his hands out as he hopes to block anything from reaching me.

Marc puts his finger on the trigger of his gun and turns the muzzle to point it at someone sitting in the crowd of guests.

And May raises her bouquet up at Marc and yells, "I change my mind! I don't want an urban wedding after all!"

Two barbs from the Taser hidden in her bouquet come flying out from the flowers and embed themselves in Marc's chest. His gun angles up and then falls from his limp hand as his body seizes several times and he arches over backward toward the ground.

May walks toward him, and, with each step, she pulls the trigger again and again, sending several jolts of electricity down the wires. "Take *that*, you horrible, awful wedding crasher!"

CHAPTER FORTY-THREE

May appears in the doorway of the house leading into the back-yard, hanging onto Thibault's arm. Across from where Jenny, the kids, and I are standing at the arbor awaits May's husband-to-be and his two groomsmen, Dev and Lucky. Lucky winks at me, making my cheeks go warm. I don't have a bouquet anymore and neither does May, but we don't need them because we're badass bitches and we make our own rules.

May has never looked so pretty. Her sister fixed her hair and makeup, both made damp by an excess of tears, and the dress is perfect, both elegant and sweet at the same time, much like the girl wearing it. May 'The Electrician' Wexler—a name she's been calling herself for the past hour—is finally ready to walk down the aisle, now that the man responsible for upsetting the bride has been arrested and two cups of chamomile tea have made their way into her bloodstream.

Ozzie looks like a gentle giant standing under the heavily flow-ered arbor. He doesn't seem nervous, but I know him pretty well. Under that chest of steel beats a heart that feels everything, absorbs every emotion from the people around him and yet somehow manages to remain wide open and available to those he loves. A lot of women have come and gone from his life, but only one has stuck. May. I wasn't sure about her in the beginning, but I'm sure about her now. She's the one for Ozzie. The only one. Who else would have the lady balls to stop a murderer cold in the middle of her wedding by tazing the shit out of him? Only May. She's an original, that's for sure. Ozzie deserves nothing less.

I move my gaze back to Lucky. He's definitely the one for me. I used to try to fool myself into thinking it was Charlie, but I was so, so wrong about that. I almost convinced myself it was true, too—blinded by his attitude, by the danger he brought with him that I craved. I was trying to outrun my past, the trouble I suffered in my youth, but it was always right there next to me, riding shotgun. Charlie was the last thing I needed, but I couldn't see that then. Like Lucky said, I was the girl who always blamed myself for what others did to me. There was no way I was in a position to choose a healthy relationship for myself. That's probably why I never noticed Lucky crushing on me. But I'm not that girl anymore. I refuse to be.

May reaches the arbor and Thibault hands her over to Ozzie, stepping to his friend's side to act as best man; he's pulling double duty today. The vows begin, but I don't hear any of it. I'm too busy staring at my boyfriend. He stares back and smiles. That silly beard only makes him sexier. I didn't like it before, but it's grown on me. He could probably shave his head bald and I'd find it sexy. I think this is what love does to you: it makes you blind by opening your eyes.

Rings are exchanged and the happy couple kisses, sealing the deal. I cheer along with everyone else, bracing myself against the pain it causes my ribs. Inside, I'm pain free, though, celebrating their love with them. I could not be happier for my boss and my co-worker—my friend and fellow cube-crew member, May 'The Electrician' Wexler.

The reception starts as soon as we're down the aisle. The caterer opens up twenty chafing pans at the buffet across the lawn, and the champagne is poured. I stand in a far corner with a glass of fresh-squeezed orange juice in hand.

"You having fun?" Lucky asks me, drinking a glass of juice at my side.

"Yep. Getting tired, though. My ribs will not stop aching and my head is throbbing."

"You want me to take you inside?" His hand is on my lower back as he readies himself to guide me across the lawn.

I shake my head. "Not yet. I want to watch them dance some more."

I'm talking about all of the members of our team. They're ridiculous. I'm bummed that I'm on the injured list. I wish I could cut a rug out on the dance floor like they are right now. They're making fools of themselves, something I've never wanted to do before, but I find myself jealous of it tonight. I'm ready to let my hair down and not care what anybody thinks of me. I should have done this back in junior high when Lucky asked me to dance. It took me ten years to find the right path, and now I'm too injured to take it. Thankfully, this is only a temporary problem. Lucky and I will be dancing soon enough.

"I've been thinking," Lucky says after we spend a few moments watching our co-workers do some form of swing dance I've never seen before.

"Oh, yeah? About what?"

"About this shindig." He waves his glass of juice around the backyard.

"Pretty nice, eh? Jenny's good at last-minute plans. The Wexler girls don't even let a would-be murderer ruin things."

"Yeah." He pauses before continuing. "Maybe she could plan our wedding."

My heart skips a beat or two when I realize what he's hinting at. "Maybe. You'd have to ask me first, though. And of course I'd have to say yes . . ."

He chuckles. "You're not going to make this easy on me, are you?"

I shrug, still facing the dancers but not really seeing what they're doing anymore. "Nope."

"Fair enough." He puts his hand on my arm and turns me toward him. "Dance with me." He pauses to take our glasses and set them down on a small nearby table before turning back to take me in his arms.

We both look down at my belly and laugh. "Easier said than done," I say regretfully. It feels like I'm getting bigger by the hour.

He puts his hands on the sides of my belly and starts to sway. I go with the motion as I stare into his beautiful eyes. The sounds of the party fade and I can only hear him now.

"Toni, do you think you could be happy with a guy like me for the rest of your life?"

My heart feels like it's going to explode. I love him so much, but I'm afraid to jinx what we have by letting him know. "You've been there all along, haven't you?"

He shakes his head. "You have to say it, babe. You can't keep running away from the hard stuff."

I give him a teasing punch on the arm. "You calling me a coward?"

He pulls me in closer and leans toward me, kissing me softly on the mouth. "Chicken licken, bawk, bawk, bawk . . ." He's smiling as he rests his lips on mine.

I grab him around the back of the neck and pull him in for a deeper kiss, reminding him who he's messing with for a few moments before letting him go. "Fine—you want me to say it? Yes. I could be happy with you forever." My ears are ringing with the admission. I can't believe I just said that to Lucky . . . the kid with the BB gun, the buck teeth, and the glasses who I've been running away from for way too long.

He pulls back and stares into my eyes, his joking expression gone. "You did it."

"Did what?" I feel silly now. I try to pull away, but he won't let me.

"You let me in." Tears well up in his eyes.

Normally I'd cuff him again for being so ridiculous, but I realize what this means to him and to me. To *us*. I nod, crying right along with him. "Yep. Now you know my big secret. I'm just a big wimp underneath it all."

He draws me gently into a hug. "You're my little wimp. I love you so much."

I rub his back, my spirit soaring at his words. "You did it."

He leans back to look at me. "Did what?"

"Let me in."

He nods and we stare into each other's eyes for the longest time. And then a sound breaks into our little bubble. It's May, and she's using a bullhorn.

"Hey! Toni and Lucky! Did you guys tell each other you're in love with each other yet or what?"

I slowly shake my head at her as we watch Ozzie pull the bullhorn out of her hand and spank her lightly on the butt.

"She is so going to regret that," I say, making a mental note to seek revenge after her honeymoon.

Lucky drapes his arm over my shoulder. "She means well. She offered to plan our wedding, you know."

I drop my head into my hand. "Oh, dear God, spare me." I can already picture it: me in a dress so big I can't fit through the door, fifteen bridesmaids, and a crew of ten kids carrying flowers and rings.

Lucky laughs and squeezes me tight. "Don't worry, babe. I got you."

CHAPTER FORTY-FOUR

When my labor comes, everything's all orchestrated and planned out. Lucky is wearing scrubs and he's sitting on a stool near my head, and a green surgical curtain blocks my view of my belly. One of our babies—Milli or Vanilli, we're not sure which—was being stubborn and refusing to turn around and head out of the warm home he or she has been enjoying for the past almost nine months, so the doctor ordered a C-section. I'm shaking with nerves and whatever medications they have me jacked up with.

"Excited?" Lucky asks me, a piece of his beard not covered by his mask tickling my face as he leans in closely.

"Very. And nervous. I don't want to die."

He frowns at me. "You're not going to die. Don't be ridiculous."

"You're going to be just fine," the anesthesiologist says through her mask. "I'll be watching you like a hawk." She looks up at the monitors over my head that are attached by wires to my chest, my arms and about five other places, it seems.

I ignore her in favor of staring at my babies' father. "I want to get married," I blurt out.

I'm guessing his grin is huge. He's wearing a surgical mask, and all I can see are his eyes, but they pretty much disappear into his cheeks.

"Now?"

I nod, holding his hand with a grip of iron. "Yes. Right now."

He laughs. "We can't do it *now*, silly. You're about to have two babies." He glances over his left shoulder, looking over the curtain. "I think they're getting started."

He turns his attention back to me. "Hold that thought, babe. I promise, I'm not going anywhere. Let's get Milli and Vanilli outta there, and then we'll call Jenny. She can make all the plans."

I nod, breathing in and out as evenly as I can to calm myself. Jenny will do it. She handles everything like a pro. She'll tell May no big dresses or big hair.

"Just relax," the anesthesiologist says. "Everything's going to be fine. Tell me if you feel nauseated or dizzy."

"Ready to get started?" the obstetrician asks. He peers at me over the curtain, his dark brown eyes twinkling in the surgical suite's lighting.

I nod. "Yes. Ready as I'll ever be."

"Okay!" He disappears behind the curtain again and I feel pressure down below. My whole body is really warm, but I'm still shaking.

"Things are going to move pretty fast," he says, jerking my body a little with whatever he's doing. "Here we go . . ."

Nurses rush over and another doctor leans in. "Baby A is coming out . . ." my doctor says.

We didn't opt to find out the sex of the babies, so all I can do is yell the name we've been using for Baby A. "Milli!" I yell.

There's a faint cry of an infant and then some laughter. "Milli is a boy!"

ELLE CASEY

I start crying right along with my baby. "Milli is a boy, Lucky—did you hear that?"

Lucky's crying too. And then he stands, looking over the curtain. "Oh my god, he's gorgeous." Lucky looks back at me, laughing and crying at the same time.

The doctor holds the baby toward me so I can see him. I catch a glimpse of a tiny red body and a scrunched-up face before he disappears. He's handed off to a nurse, who takes him over to a bassinet. I watch as best I can, wishing the anesthesiologist would move out of the way. She's blocking my view with her fat doctor head.

"And Baby B . . ." A second baby is lifted from me and starts crying right away too. "Is a girl!"

"Vanilli!" Lucky and I yell together. Then we laugh and cry, too. Our life is so crazy right now.

She's lifted over the curtain so I can take a look at her before she's handed off to another nurse. She looks like a tiny prizefighter, her hands in miniature fists, bloody goo on her body, and her eyes swollen shut. I've never been prouder. *My little fighter!*

Lucky sits down and strokes my cheek with his gloved hand. "You are so beautiful, babe. You did such a good job baking those peas."

"You can butter me up all you want, but you're not naming our daughter Vanilli."

He laughs and leans down to kiss me. Everything falls away in that moment but him, his lips on mine, his tongue, the smell of his soap. I love every bit of it.

"Love you," he says when he pulls away.

"Love you, too." I'm crying again. It's starting to wipe me out, being this emotional.

He looks over the drape and cringes. "They're putting you back together. Mind if I go take a closer look at the peas?"

I nod, wanting a moment to get my head straight before I see them myself. When Lucky's hanging over me, it's hard to concentrate, I love him so fiercely. "Sure. Go ahead. I'll be right here."

He kisses me quickly on the forehead and stands, joining the nurses, who've put the two bassinets together. Everyone is *oohing* and *aahing* over the babies, exclaiming over their weights. Both of them are over seven pounds, which is something special with twins, or so I read in one of my books.

My body jiggles a little as the doctors work to sew me up. My mind drifts into a haze and I find myself thinking about Charlie. For the first time I can imagine him not looking angry. The face I see in my mind now is the one I always liked. Charlie wasn't always a mean drunk; sometimes he was happy and generous and full of love for life.

I'm so sorry I took this from you, Charlie. So sorry. I've been trying to figure out how to get my life straight ever since that night I shot you. I've had a really hard time with everything, and now I know why. All this time, I've been asking the wrong question. I shouldn't be asking why I did what I did or who's to blame for it or why I can't go back and change things. Why does anything happen the way it does? A thousand actions and decisions of a thousand people come together in a single moment and there's an outcome. Change any one of those variables and the outcome changes, too. Control is merely an illusion. I really don't know that there is a right question anymore, but I know what the right answer is. Love is the answer. Love is why I'm here, it's why I keep struggling, it's why I need to move on from the mistakes I've made and look forward to an imperfect but fulfilling future. If I'd truly loved you or loved myself, things would have gone differently, I'm convinced of that. It was a lack of love that made everything so dark and wrong and destructive between us. Charlie, I forgive you for what you did to me and to us, and I forgive myself, too, for what I did to you and to me. Wherever you are, you're good now, I know that. You're no longer weighed down by the imperfections of our human perceptions and egos and all that garbage. You're surrounded by God's love now, and it gives me great joy to know that you've found that peace.

A light fills me from the inside out, making me feel like I must be glowing. I look around me, but everyone is acting normal, like they don't see it. But both of my babies immediately stop crying. They sense it. Just like me, they feel the perfect love that fills this room.

Lucky turns around with an astonished expression on his face. "What just happened?" he asks, laughing.

I mouth the words to him from across the room. *I love you.*

His whole face trembles as he realizes what I've said. Tears slip past his defenses and he nods. *Love you too*, he mouths at me.

"Bring me those babies," I say, trying to sound demanding.

Everyone laughs, and ten seconds later, I have two tiny babies, one who resembles a pink burrito and one who resembles a blue burrito, looking down at me from the arms of my husband-to-be.

ABOUT THE AUTHOR

Elle Casey, a former attorney and teacher, is a *New York Times* and *USA Today* bestselling American author who lives in France with her husband, three kids, and a number of furry friends. She has written books in several genres and publishes an average of one full-length novel per month.